JIM MARTIN

DARK NIGHTS ON SHADOW LAKE

Dark Nights on Shadow Lake

Author correspondence: nightmare_alley@cox.net

Jacket design by Jim Martin

ISBN: 978-0-692-87960-3

ACKNOWLEDGEMENTS

Special thanks to David Fell and the staff of the Phoenix Café for providing the oft needed early morning caffeine to keep my imagination fueled.

For all the readers who supported my first effort. This book would not have been possible without you.

DARK NIGHTS ON SHADOW LAKE

ALSO BY JIM MARTIN

A Madman's Song

DARK NIGHTS ON SHADOW LAKE

DEAD THINGS

"Wrap yourself in the pristine beauty of Crystal Falls. Where good times await, and adventure is all around you!"

– *Crystal Falls brochure, 1977*

1

AUGUST 20, 1978 – 7:40 PM

Dead in the water is what she was.

Rusty sat in the driver's seat for several long seconds before giving it one last go.

"Come on, baby. You can do this," he mumbled, giving the ignition key a twist.

The entire bus shuddered as the starter cranked repeatedly, its once powerful bursts sounding long and labored with the waning charge of the battery. Prior to this moment, Rusty had avoided stomping on the gas for fear of flooding the engine, but now his foot worked the pedal like a jackhammer.

He clenched his teeth together and snarled. "Come on!"

His face was cherry red, veins bulged across his forehead, and the little bits of hair that remained atop his dome stood in disheveled tufts, giving him the appearance of a mad scientist.

With a loud screech, the starter seized and ground to a halt.

"Son of a bitch!" the old man growled, beating the steering wheel with his fists.

"Maybe it's just out of gas," a voice behind the driver's seat said.

Rusty looked up at the oversized rearview mirror and focused his gaze on the young boy behind him. The kid's

God-given name was Simon, but the thick-rimmed glasses he wore had earned him a new moniker: Four Eyes.

Rusty had nicknames for all the children he shuttled around, both on his regular school route and on the charter events such as this one—retrieving the little shits from Crystal Falls Camp in the remote hills of Shadow Lake and returning them to the city.

"A dirty job, but someone's gotta do it," he'd once commented to his drinking buddies at the local tavern. Like Rusty, none of them were parents, and most shared his general disdain for the pint-sized pissants. All, that is, except for the bartender, Joe. The jury was still out on him.

"You were a kid at one time, too. We all were," he'd remarked.

"Yeah, but I wasn't anything like these hoodlums today. I knew how to act," Rusty had replied.

"Maybe so. But, like it or not, they're our country's future."

"God help us all, Joe. Better pour me a double."

Looking up at Simon now, Rusty wanted to give the boy a good smack. He was on the clock, however, and the job dictated that you had to try and be nice to the little bastards.

"There's plenty of gas, kid. Filled her up before I drove out here. You got any other bright ideas?"

Simon shrugged, averting his gaze and turning to look out the window.

Rusty picked up the handset from the CB radio bolted beneath the instrument panel, stretching the coiled cord until the microphone was positioned near his mouth. "This is twenty-nine. Sally, you out there?"

He released the talk button and waited for a response. There was only static.

"Twenty-nine calling for assistance. Anybody listening?"

"I don't think they can hear you," Simon chimed in.

Rusty shot the boy an impatient glare before returning his focus back to the radio.

"Sally, I'm getting nothing but static up here. If you can hear me, we are stranded on Old Falls Road, south of Black

Water Pass, about three miles from camp. Any help would be appreciated, over."

The old CB crackled a few times before emitting a wavering squeal. It was the same sort of wobbly sound Rusty would get from the radio in his '67 Impala each time he'd turn the dial to move between stations. For one brief second, he thought Sally's voice was about to break through, but then the white noise of static returned. With obvious frustration, Rusty returned the mic to its holder and slouched back in his seat.

What now?

The way he saw it, there were only two options: walk the few miles back to camp and use the phone to call the station, or stay holed up in the bus and hope to hell some concerned parent would head up this way for a looky-loo whenever their little Tommy or Janie hadn't returned home in a timely manner. Neither option was appealing, but the potential pitfall of having to spend the better part of the night with a bus full of fifth-graders made the latter choice the more unbearable of the two.

"What is that, Mr. Morgan?" It was Todd, the one Rusty referred to as Goldilocks because of the boy's long wavy hair.

That was another thing. Why did dudes these days want to go around looking like chicks? It was a mystery which still eluded Rusty. He hadn't understood the trend when it had started in the sixties with the hippies and the counter culture movement (a sign of rebellion against the societal norms it had been said, albeit, a stupid one in his opinion), but a decade later, he really didn't get it. After all, what would a nine-year old boy be rallying against? His idiot parents, perhaps?

Rusty stood up and looked in the direction Todd was pointing. Roughly two hundred yards due north of the bus, a flickering light moved through the woods.

"What is it?" Todd asked again.

"I don't know. A kerosene lantern, maybe? Probably just a hiker or a fisherman," Rusty replied.

"What if it's the lost lady of the lake?" shouted a tubby kid near the back of the bus.

There was a brief silence amongst the children as this newly proposed theory settled upon their young brains. One or two of the older kids snickered in disbelief, but most were wide-eyed and shocked. Even Simon's eyes appeared much larger than usual beneath his Coke bottle lenses. When one of the girls began to cry, the portly kid at the back ribbed his buddy next to him and they both smiled a satisfied grin.

"That's enough!" Rusty shouted. "You start that crap on my bus and some old lady will be the least of your worries. You hear me?"

"I'm scared," another girl howled. Her name was Brenda, or Brandy, or something of the sort. Rusty knew her only as one of the twins. Her brother, Brian, sat at her side. He slipped an arm around his sister and did his best to console her.

"Don't you worry, little lady. You'll be home before you know it," Rusty said.

That was a lie, of course, but it seemed to temper the situation for now. The girl wiped her eyes, rested her head on her brother's shoulder, and said no more.

The driver scanned the woods for the light. It was still out there, though more distant than it had been only a minute ago. He needed to find the person behind the lamp before they got away. The sun was already dipping below the horizon and, once night fell, Rusty knew it would be blacker than black up on this mountain. He didn't exactly relish the idea of having to make his way back to the camp with nothing but a small flashlight to guide him.

"Listen up," he said, turning to address the children. "I'm going to find the person ahead and see if they can give me a hand. In the meantime, I need you to sit tight until I get back. Do not get off this bus for any reason."

There were several nods and a chorus of '*okays*' in response.

Rusty retrieved a flashlight from the glove box and tucked it firmly into the pocket of his pants. He directed Simon to close the doors behind him, stepped down out of the bus, and headed in the direction of the light.

This was certainly not how he had envisioned the evening. He hated weekend charters. His original plan had been to kick back in his recliner with a TV dinner and a cold beer to watch *All in the Family.* That show killed him. And that Archie fella . . . now there was a guy he could relate to. Rusty wondered how Archie would handle being stuck in the sticks with a broken-down bus and a gaggle of snot-nosed children. Just the thought of it made him chuckle. Probably the *only* laugh he would get tonight.

From the west, the remnants of a dying sunset filtered through the trees, casting a warm amber glow across the narrow roadway. While it was still enough to see by for the time being, the surroundings were growing dimmer by the minute. It was no matter, for the mysterious light lay directly ahead, just beyond the tree line.

Strange. Has that thing gotten closer, or have I been so lost in thought that I walked this far already?

The lantern, if that's what it was, was moving at a methodical pace, as though the person carrying it were searching for something rather than taking a casual stroll through the woods. To reach the source of the beacon, Rusty would have to scale a small embankment, the thought of which had him grumbling under his breath. He enjoyed physical activity about as much as he did children, and while the temperature was a moderately cool 74 degrees and dropping, Rusty was already perspiring heavily from his brief trek. He stopped at the edge of the road, cupped his hands around his mouth, and yelled in the direction of the lantern. "Hello in there! Can you hear me?"

The light went out.

"I didn't mean to startle you. My bus won't start. I was hoping you might be able to help me out."

There was no reply.

For the first time since leaving the bus, Rusty noticed the unusual stillness in the air. Nothing moved. There were no birds calling, insects buzzing, nor any twigs or leaves snapping under the weight of forest animals skittering about.

Nothing.

Rusty wasn't the type who spooked easily, but even he found the sensation to be an unsettling one. Between the eerie silence and the impending darkness looming on the horizon, he thought it a good time to leave. It was then that the calm broke.

A frigid gust began to blow from the tree line outward, causing the hairs on the man's arms to stand at attention. It sounded as though there was a voice carried in the wind as well. It was only a whisper, really, but it had seemed to call out the man's name.

Another noise broke the air: a sharp *clack!* Like a jet, it zipped away, moving through the woods and along the path in the direction of the bus. In the next instant, a myriad of screams erupted in the distance.

Rusty ran down the road as fast as his worn-out knees would allow. By the time he reached the bus, the screams—and the strange clacking noise—had ceased. The tall yellow doors stood wide open, creating a feeling of unease in the driver. He bounded up the steps, turning to stone once he reached the top.

The bus was empty.

This can't be happening. Where are they?

The old man's mind reeled. He walked up and down the aisle, looking behind every seat. There were suitcases, backpacks, crayons, a Raggedy Ann doll . . . but not a trace of any of the children.

Think, Rusty. Think!

Those noises, whatever they were, likely gave the kids a fright. But why would they have left the safety of the bus? And why wouldn't they have run in the same direction he himself had gone? None of it made any sense.

Rusty climbed out of the bus and walked a wide circle around the vehicle, looking in every direction.

Where could they have gone? What if something bad has happened to them? What will I tell my boss? No, forget about that asshole. How do I tell the parents? Oh, dear God!

Exasperated, he bent over, clutching his spent knees and hanging his head low.

I think I'm going to be sick.

A faint giggle broke from beyond the trees.

What was this? Some childish prank? Well, he wasn't laughing. And neither would those kids be once he caught them. No, sir, he'd show them.

More laughter now, followed by the pitter-patter of feet moving away.

"Run, run, as fast as you can," a voice cooed.

Rusty walked into the woods at a brisk pace, cursing. He stopped and listened, then ran in the direction of the footsteps. About twenty yards in, he stumbled over a rock, pitching forward and catching his left hand on a jagged branch.

Hissing in pain, Rusty surveyed the long gash across his palm. It wasn't deep, but it bled like a stuck hog. He wrapped the wound with a handkerchief from his shirt pocket, balling his hand into a fist to stop the bleeding.

Laughter echoed through the trees again, first to the left of him, and then to the right. Rusty pulled himself up and dug the flashlight out of his pocket. The light was scarce here in the thick of the forest and he didn't want to risk another spill. Focusing the beam of light on the ground near his feet, he pressed onward.

A voice echoed from somewhere ahead, taunting from the cover of darkness. "Run, run, as fast as you can. You can't catch us, mean bus driver man."

The words were spoken in a slow and deliberate manner. Instead of sounding whimsical, like children playing a game, they resonated in a perverse and threatening tone.

Rage boiled inside of Rusty. "You kids get your asses back here, right now!" he screamed.

But the children did not stop. They only ran faster, and deeper, into the woods.

Perspiration poured from the old man's body, dotting his shirt with dark, wet splotches. His heart hammered, his side ached, and there was fire in his left hand, yet sheer anger propelled him forward.

Several minutes later, Rusty emerged from the trees into a clearing. The packed dirt floor of the forest gave way to solid rock, forming a steep bluff overlooking the lake. Straight ahead, standing at the end of the precipice, were the twins. They stood side by side, their hands entwined and their feet perched on the edge.

"What are you doing?" Rusty hollered.

His question went unanswered. The pair stood with their backs to him, looking out over the water as if they hadn't heard a thing. The boy shuffled one foot forward, collapsing a small piece of ground and sending bits of rock tumbling down the cliff.

Alarmed, Rusty cried out again, "Get back from there before you get yourselves killed!"

The girl turned her head and met his gaze. There was something not quite right about the way she looked at him, something cold in her stare that he'd never seen in any child before. It was something almost . . . wicked.

Stretching out his bandaged hand, Rusty silently beckoned the girl away from the edge. Her mouth twisted upwards in a sinister grin and she turned away. Without further hesitation, the twins simultaneously tipped forward and tumbled out of sight.

The old man cried out in horror. He rushed to the lip of the rock wall; afraid of what he would see when he got there. What he found was a sheer drop of fifty feet to the water below, but not a sign of the twins. The surface of the lake appeared as a shimmery pane of tinted glass, with no ripples or wake whatsoever. But where else could they have gone if not in the water?

Rusty cut his eyes back and forth across the lake in a desperate search for the children. He didn't have to look for long. The girl's face appeared first, her lifeless features slowly perforating the water with a wet plop. The boy emerged seconds later in much the same manner, his mouth hanging open and the bridge of his nose slightly askew.

But that wasn't all. There were more faces.

One by one they floated upwards, bobbing on the surface of the water. A few belonged to other children from the bus, but most were older—men, women, and teenagers who were bloated and puffed like marshmallows, their skin frigid and blue. Some peered back with soulless, inanimate eyes; others with deep crimson sockets where eyes had once resided.

Rusty covered his mouth in utter dismay, his hands trembling profusely. "Dear, God. What ha—"

An abrupt blow to the back sent him toppling over the cliff's edge and into the murky depths of the lake. Momentarily disoriented, Rusty sank downwards, hearing only the dull alien sounds of an underwater world and the hollow gurgle of air escaping his lungs.

As he came to and began to ascend, a hand reached up from out of the depths and latched onto his left ankle. The cold chill of its grip was like razors against his skin.

Another arm shot out from the right and seized him by the wrist.

Sheer terror gripped the man as the faces of the dead—the same ones he had seen just moments ago—swam towards him. They spawned from every direction, gliding through the water with an effortless ease.

Rusty kicked and flailed, churning the water into a thick white froth as he frantically fought for his life. More bodies collided with his own; hands and arms clawing and pulling, teeth gnashing and biting. He felt himself being pulled further down, all the while being slowly ripped to pieces. A massive flood of air erupted from his lungs as he opened his mouth in one final muffled scream.

Seconds later, billowy plumes of blood rippled beneath the water, spreading across the surface like a vast red storm cloud. At that same instant, somewhere high atop the rocky ridge, a child laughed.

2

PRESENT DAY

The road spooled out for miles, carving a serpentine corridor through the lush, tree-lined hillsides. Pines and evergreens stretched hundreds of feet in the air, drinking in the mid-dawn sun and perfuming the air with their sweet fragrance. Overhead, thin ribbons of clouds moved idly across the sky, making the most of a lazy May morning.

Amy held her hand out the passenger side window of the yellow Jeep Wrangler, feeling the cool air glide between her fingers and watching as the landscape rolled by in an abstract mural of green. She wore a forlorn expression, her mouth turned down in a sullen pout. Wind-blown strands of auburn hair masked a pair of hazel eyes which were damp and joyless. Though she tried hard not to think about the past week, the long ride from Portland to Shadow Lake had given her mind ample time to reflect on the oppressive memories.

"Ames? Hello? Earth to Amy. You still with us?"

The sound of John's voice snapped Amy out of her trance and she turned to face him in the driver's seat. He sighed when he saw her dour condition. "You've been thinking about Scott again, haven't you?"

Amy smiled weakly and gave a feeble nod.

John reached over and brushed the hair from her face, tucking it away behind her left ear. "You okay? Maybe this trip wasn't such a good idea."

His deep brown eyes, set like raisins between thick brows and plump cheeks, radiated with warmth. He was a hefty sort, but not fat in the traditional sense. Standing 6' 1", he was stout and solid, his weight evenly distributed across a thick frame which possessed just a hint of pudginess. His face was boyish and clean-shaven, with dimples that appeared each time he smiled. Coupled with his gentle nature and dogged sense of humor, John was a teddy bear in every sense of the word.

"No, it's fine. *I'm* fine," Amy replied.

John gave her a sidelong glance. "I've known you since you were five years old. Certainly, long enough to know that you are *not* fine. And why would you be? You and Scott dated for over three years. A breakup like that is going to be rough."

The mere mention of her ex-boyfriend's name sent another crushing wave of agony through Amy. She felt the bitter sting of fresh tears near the corners of her eyes. "Yes," she agreed, quickly brushing back the moisture from her lids.

It had been twenty days now since Scott ended their relationship. He'd said with the two of them starting college in separate states soon, a long-distance relationship wasn't what either of them needed. He hadn't asked her opinion on the subject, and when she'd tried to give it, it was clear he wasn't interested in hearing anything she had to say. His mind was made up.

Amy was crushed. Though Scott hadn't been her first boyfriend, he was the only one she had ever fallen in love with. She'd lost her virginity to him, dreamed of a life beyond high school by his side, and believed—blindly, it now seemed—that he'd loved her in return. Now she found herself crying at the drop of a hat. At the onset of the trip, she had even asked John to change to radio over to hard rock (something she normally couldn't stand) because too many songs on the Top 40 station reminded her of Scott and their time together.

"I'm really sorry, Ames," John said, his soft eyes affirming the sympathy he held for his friend. "You know I hate seeing you this way. If I could change things—"

"I know you would. Because you're cool like that." Amy reached over and gave John's arm a playful punch. He smiled, dimples forming small craters in his roly-poly cheeks.

"This is real sweet and all, but does anyone know how much longer we have in this tin can? I'm going to need to find the shitter real soon."

"Nice, Dagger," John said, addressing the person in the back-passenger seat.

Dylan was the man's birth name, but ever since being suspended in the sixth grade for having a pocketknife in his locker (with which he'd threatened to use on Bobby Dugan after the boy had tried to kiss Dylan's then girlfriend during gym class) he had been called Dagger.

John liked the new name better. To him, Dylan conjured up images of a cardigan-wearing, Ivy League prep boy with his hair neatly parted to the side, whereas Dagger was the antithesis of that; befitting of the Converse-sporting, muscled up, rough and tumble football player that his friend was.

"Why do you have to be so crude?" That was Beth, a thin, waif of a girl with strawberry-blonde hair and Dagger's on-again off-again girlfriend since the previous summer. She was also a staunch vegetarian who was quick to advocate her position to anyone who'd listen. Notable, because she had famously first broken up with Dagger after he'd consumed a steak during one of their early dates. Though it had taken some time, both had put the incident behind them and agreed to disagree. The other breakups had come about simply because Dagger was Dagger—the type who gave all other guys a bad name.

Regardless, the two always ended up back together. John figured the girl was either truly in love, or simply a glutton for punishment. She sat now, smacking on a piece of gum—the same pink wad that had started out in Dagger's mouth. John had seen it passed back and forth between the couple as they'd made out in the backseat. Currently, it was Beth's turn to chew.

"No disrespect to Amy and her problems, but when you've got to hit the head some things need to be put on hold. You know what I mean?" Dagger asked.

"I get it," Beth replied. "But can't you see she's upset? Why don't you at least try to show some compassion?"

"It's alright," Amy interjected. "I've known Dagger as long as I have John. If he were to act any differently, I'd be a little concerned."

"See, babe? She gets me. Why don't you?" Dylan grinned.

Beth sat back in the seat and rolled her eyes. "Even so, I'm sorry, Amy. I may have only known you for a year, but it's clear to me that Scott is making a big mistake. If he can't see that, then he's a loser. I say, screw him!"

"I'm pretty sure she already has," Dagger laughed. Beth smacked him across the chest, which only made him laugh all the harder.

"Ass!" She scooted across the seat, pressing against the door and putting distance between herself and her uncouth boyfriend.

John returned his focus to the road and shook his head. Based on the overall climate in the backseat, he doubted his friend would be getting his gum back anytime soon. The thought made him chuckle.

Dagger had some good qualities, but empathy and tact were not on the list. Had they not been close with the guy since childhood, John was uncertain as to whether he and Amy would have found much common ground with the man later in life. Nevertheless, the bonds formed during those impressionable early years had made them all friends, and one thing Dagger *did* have going for him was that he possessed a fierce loyalty to those he was tight with. For that very reason, John was certain Amy would take no offense at the remark made by their rag-tag buddy and would let it roll off.

Dagger was all too aware of this as well, but knew an apology was in order if he wished to get out of the doghouse with Beth.

"Sorry, Amy. I didn't mean to be a jerk. Are we cool?"

"Yeah," Amy nodded. "We're cool."

Dagger glanced over at Beth, trying to gauge her mood. After several seconds, he decided her expression was ambiguous, so he palmed his hands together behind his head and leaned back in his seat. *Oh, well. She'll bounce back soon enough.*

"Alright, Casanova," John said, peering up at Dagger in the rearview mirror. "I'll pull over at the next stop so you can do your business."

"Casanova? What the hell is that?"

Beth broke her silence. "Casanova? It's not a *what.* It's a person."

Dagger shrugged. "Are you all like . . . Facebook friends or something?"

Beth shot her boyfriend an incredulous look. "Are you kidding me? You've never heard of Casanova? He lived in eighteenth century Europe, or somewhere thereabouts, and is widely regarded as *the* greatest lover of all time."

"Oh, I get it," Dagger replied. "John went from playing Dr. Phil to being his usual funny self. Okay, if that's how you want to play things, I'm down, mister Johnny-One-Time."

John groaned. "Not that again. I hate when you call me that."

Beth sat up straight, her interest piqued. "I guess I haven't heard this story."

"Should I fill her in, Johnny?" Dagger jested.

John glanced over at Amy with a look of defeat on his face. She wrinkled her nose. "You sort of opened the door on this one."

"Yeah, I guess I did, didn't I?" He sighed and then twirled his hand in the air, gesturing for his friend to continue.

Dagger clapped his hands together with glee and a devilish glint filled his eyes. It was clear he relished the opportunity to rag on his pal.

"Two years ago, John had the hots for this girl, Cindy. Now, I wouldn't say she was a knockout, although I guess she was cute in her own sort of way. But ol' Johnny over here thought she hung the moon. Anyway, my parents were out of town one weekend and I threw a big party—"

"Did Cindy come?" Beth interrupted.

"Yes . . . and no, if you catch my drift," Dagger laughed. "But I'm getting to that."

John groaned again. "Just shoot me now." He looked over at Amy, who was doing all she could to hold her composure. She was smiling, though, probably for the first time since they had left Portland. If he had to swallow his pride so that Amy could enjoy herself, then John figured it was well worth it.

"Cindy *was* there," Dagger continued, "and virgin boy Johnny was walking around with a hard-on all night. I told him he was going to have to man up and make a move, so he could take care of that thing, otherwise I was going to put him to use by turning him into the community coat rack."

Beth cupped her hands over her mouth and laughed.

"It took over an hour just to get him to go talk to her. I was exhausted by the time he finally said hello. But, I guess she must have liked him, too, because she didn't run away. Long story short, they got liquored up and spent some time together in the closet during a well-timed game of *Truth or Dare*. Awhile later, Johnny comes out beaming like he's just seen the good Lord and tells me he got to second base. I was proud of him, so I offered him the use of my bedroom. Thought he might be able to land on third, right? Turns out, this guy ends up scoring a homerun!"

"Oooh, you stud, you!" Beth exclaimed. "I'm guessing something else happened? I mean, since they call you Johnny-One-Time and all."

"Yeah," Dagger replied. "Cousin Red didn't show up on time and Cindy freaked. It was a false alarm, but she basically turned into a nun afterwards. Poor Johnny hasn't played ball ever since."

Beth turned out her bottom lip and made a long face. "Aww, that sucks. I'm sorry."

Dagger started laughing. "But wait! I haven't told you my favorite part. You see, just when things were heating up, Cindy asked Johnny, '*How do you like it?*' And do you know what Romeo here says to her?"

"No. What?"

"With pickles and onions," Dagger replied, slapping a knee and cackling. "Can you believe that? Pickles and onions! Talk about a mood killer."

"Oh, you didn't?" Beth quizzed.

"Yes, I'm afraid so," John grimaced.

"It's a wonder he ever scored at all," Dagger added.

"Help me out here, Ames," John said. "How bad was it, really?"

Amy pursed her lips together, attempting to stifle her own laughter. "Umm, on a scale of one to ten, I'd probably put it at a solid eight."

"And you dare point your sarcasm at me with that Casanova remark, when here you are, the Ronald McDonald of the bedroom," Dagger roared.

Amy and Beth followed suit, carrying on until they were both red in the face. Even John had to laugh.

"I've got the best friends," he said to Beth. "In case you couldn't tell already."

"I'm sorry," Amy said between bursts of giggling. "I love you dearly, J. But that was funny."

John dipped forward in a mock bow. "It's good to see you laughing again."

Amy met his gaze, a familiar spark shimmering in her eye. She mouthed the words *thank you.*

A few miles further up the mountain, John motioned out the window as the Jeep coasted around a bend in the road. "Look there," he remarked, pointing towards a service station ahead. "Now, I may not be an expert when it comes to love, but I *do* understand the power of chocolate therapy. Whadda ya say?"

Amy beamed.

"I'd say chocolate trumps pickles and onions any day, my friend. You might just understand women better than you think you do." She reached over and gave John's hand a squeeze. "Let's go!"

3

The service station was old.

It was one of those Mom-and-Pops; the type bordering on extinction now that there was a corporate-owned mega store residing on nearly every street corner in America.

Resembling a small house, the clapboard structure—once white in color—had been rendered a dingy gray by the steady progression of time. A beat-up wood framed door rested on tired rusty hinges and served as the entrance to the store. It was flanked by two large windows with traces of weathered green paint around the trim.

Clustered around the windows, a bevy of tin signs in various stages of deterioration were pinned to the siding. There were endorsements for Meadow Fair ice cream bars, which touted their product as being *'Sweet, creamy, and all together dreamy,'* and Sunbeam, featuring a young girl with blond locks and a gingham dress biting into a fresh slice of blue ribbon bread. Soda ads were the most prominent, however, with Coca-Cola, Hires Root Beer, and Orange Crush all on display.

A couple of wooden benches sat against the building, one on each side of the door, facing two decades-old mechanical gas pumps. The sides of the pumps, with their rounded corners and smooth edges, were red in color. An access door on the front of the unit was painted a contrasting white and sported a long chrome handle to one side, making the overall appearance of the apparatus more akin to an ice box from the past rather than the all-digital machines of today.

Along the front façade of the building, painted in the same green hue as the window trim, were the words:

EASLEY'S ROADSIDE SERVICE
GAS - BEER - LIVE BAIT

John brought the Jeep to a stop alongside one of the pumps. The place reminded him of an antiquated country store near his grandparents' rural home. The Outpost, it was called. He'd visited the place many times while growing up and had always found it interesting that the locals never paid upfront for their purchases, keeping a running tab instead, which they would pay off monthly. He wondered if the people around here did the same.

The group climbed out of the vehicle and made their way inside the store. The spring-loaded screen door snapped shut behind them with an emphatic slam, startling the girls. They clutched each other and laughed, while the boys looked on in amusement.

"Gotta watch that thing. She'll get you," said the man behind the counter.

Middle-aged, with a speckle of silver running through thick dark hair, he had one of those instantly likeable faces—the type that exuded goodwill and kindness. Wearing a yellow button up shirt and khaki pants held up by suspenders, the man possessed a slight paunch, the by-product of enjoying too many beers out on the bench with his regulars. "Anything I can help you find today?" he asked.

"Just a bathroom," Dagger replied.

The clerk pointed towards a hallway at the rear of the store. "Straight back and on your right." He then turned and addressed the remaining three with a gracious smile. "And what may I get for you this morning?"

"Something sweet," Amy answered.

"Well, of course," said the clerk, as if he had known all along what Amy would say. "There are donuts and coffee up front here, should you still be in the mood for a little breakfast. The aisle directly behind you is where you'll find the candy, and back near the drink coolers is a freezer full of novelty ice cream bars."

Amy thanked the man and set about browsing the candy selection with Beth close at her heels.

John stepped to the register, where he fished several bills out of his wallet and slid them across the counter. "I'll take thirty on the first pump. And whatever the ladies pick out."

He turned to leave when Amy called after him. "Hey! Aren't you getting anything?"

"I'm good." He paused for a moment and then turned on his heels. "On second thought, would you grab me a bottle of water?"

"Just water? You want any chips? Or candy?"

John placed a hand over his belly and feigned a look of insult. "Are you out of your mind, woman? And wreck this extraordinary physique?"

"What was I thinking? Please, sir, can you ever forgive me?" Amy asked, with an equal measure of dramatic flair.

John laughed and stepped outside, the screen door clapping shut in his wake.

Leave it to him to make her feel better. Amy could always count on John to bring a smile to her face no matter how down she got. The pain of the breakup was still present, but here in the company of her friends, it now seemed to hurt a little less.

She thought about what Beth had said in the car earlier. *Screw him* was exactly what Amy was thinking about Scott at this moment, and not in the carnal sense of the phrase.

This was the last outing she and her friends would take before they went their separate ways to attend college. She had looked forward to this trip for a long time, so far be it from her to let Scott ruin everything now. After all, he would be nothing but a distant remembrance soon enough. Her friends on the other hand, had been—and always would be—there for her. She owed it to them to make this final trip a memorable one. With that in mind, Amy made a silent pact, affirming that Scott wasn't worth the tears and vowing to enjoy herself over the next few days.

With a renewed tenacity and her emotions back in check, Amy set about finding the right candy for further elevating her mood. In the end, she settled on a package of Reese's peanut butter cups. She also snagged a Kit-Kat and a Hershey bar for good measure, just in case further chocolate therapy was needed later.

After grabbing a bottle of water for John and a Diet Coke for herself (the irony of which was not lost on Amy, given the amount of candy she held), she went to check on Beth, who had wandered off to another aisle. She found her friend reading the label on a package of snack cakes.

"Look at this," Beth chided. "...contains partially hydrogenated fats and/or animal shortening. It also has TBHQ. That shit is used in varnish! I can't eat this crap."

She tossed the cakes back on the shelf. "I suppose I'll have to stick to my Twizzlers."

"Oh, because those are *so* much better for you," Amy laughed.

"Not one bit," Beth mused. "But at least they are vegetarian friendly . . . and varnish free."

"Touché, mon amie. You ready to go?"

The girls walked their goods to the counter where the clerk went to work ringing up the sale and bagging the items.

"It's quiet here. You ever get lonely working by yourself?" Beth inquired.

"Oh, it picks up as the summer wears on. Mabel brings fresh donuts twice a day from her shop in town, and there are several retirees that come by just to hang out. I think they like being able to get out of the house, you know? And I've always got my trusty friend, Boo, here to keep me company." The man motioned to the floor behind him.

Beth and Amy raised up on their toes to peer over the counter. A cushioned dog bed sat on the ground and was occupied by a black Labrador retriever. The old hound was stretched out wide, basking in the cool breeze from a box fan whirring softly nearby.

At the sight, both girls gushed. Boo glanced their direction, lifting a brow and thumping his tail. It was clear, however, that he had no intention of leaving the cozy confines of his bed.

"He's a bit stiff in the hindquarters these days, so he doesn't run around much. I can tell that he likes you, though. He's always had a soft spot for the ladies. In his younger days, he was a real charmer."

"Aww," Beth chirped. "He's still a charmer. Aren't you, Boo?"

The dog signaled his agreement with a few more thumps of his tail.

After collecting their change, the girls gathered up the items they'd purchased and made their way outside, where Beth immediately went to work opening her package of Twizzlers. That was when Amy first noticed the man.

Adjacent to the store, on the western end of the lot, stood an auto service garage which looked to be as old as the building it neighbored. The bay door was open, and sitting out front was a classic Mustang with its hood raised.

Standing next to the engine compartment, smiling back at Amy, was a young man who appeared to be in his early twenties. He wore a tattered pair of jeans and a black t-shirt with the iconic lips and tongue logo made famous by the Rolling Stones. He bore a passing resemblance to the clerk inside of Easley's, though much younger and sturdier. He had a rugged handsomeness about him, with his chiseled jaw, tousled dark hair, and slightly bronzed skin. For a moment, Amy found herself captivated by the man.

"My, what do we have here?" Beth had a rope of licorice stuck between her teeth and her gaze focused squarely on the boy next door. "Amy, I think he likes you, dear. You should go say hello."

"I'm not sure that's a good idea," Amy replied. She could feel a nervous heat in her cheeks and knew she was blushing.

"Why not? He's cute. And you're single now, so what's it gonna hurt?"

"I just—"

"Just what?" Beth asked, after a long pause.

"I mean, yes, he's attractive. But it's not like I will ever see him again after today. So, what's the point?"

"The point is, he's hot. And he seems to think you are, too. For Pete's sake, Amy, it's not like you have to bear his children. I just think it would be good for your ego. You know, to help you realize you're an attractive and desirable woman despite how that dumbass Scott made you feel."

Before Amy could protest further, Beth grabbed her by the arm and pulled her in the direction of the young mechanic. She considered breaking away and running for the Jeep, but how would that look? Besides, a part of her did want to talk to the guy. Once again, Beth had been right. That girl was on a roll.

"Hi. My name is Beth. This here is Amy. She's recently back on the market."

At the remark, Amy wanted to crawl under a rock. She shot her friend a cold stare, which was promptly dismissed.

"Hello," the man said, still smiling. He wiped his hands on a work rag before extending his right towards Amy. "Very pleased to meet you. I'm Eric."

"Hi. Do you work here?" she blurted out.

Amy thought it a stupid question the moment she asked it. She prayed to God that she wasn't beet-red in the face.

"I used to, but not so much anymore. I can't seem to stay away from the place though."

"The guy inside, is he your dad?" Beth asked.

"No, but we're related. This store has been in my family since the 1930's. The garage here, she was added in the early '50's."

"I like your car," Amy spoke up. "Mustang, right? This one is a classic, but it looks brand new."

Eric lit up. "Impressive. You know cars?"

"Not really. But I can always recognize a Mustang when I see one."

"Fair enough," Eric replied. "Well, this one is a '69 Boss 429 painted in Raven Black. It's got a scooped hood, Goodyear Polyglas tires, Top Loader close ratio four-speed manual, and a 375 horse, semi-Hemi combustion engine that will do zero to sixty in 6.8 seconds."

The man may as well have been speaking Portuguese, as Amy understood very little of what he had just said. She simply nodded and tried to go with the flow. "What are you doing to it?"

"She's riding a little rough. I'm just giving the carburetor a little tweak. Someday I'd like to replace it, along with the cams and the intake. Maybe coax a little more out of her."

"And that would . . . make it go faster?" Amy asked, sounding uncertain.

Eric laughed. "Yes, that's right. She'll be faster."

Over at the pumps, John watched the interplay between Amy and the mechanic with a morbid curiosity, aware of an all too familiar emotion rising from within. It was always the same—that burgeoning ache in his chest which, if left to its own devices, threatened to suffocate him. It had always been this way. Whenever Amy would get a new boyfriend, or show any interest in a guy, it would feel like a punch in the gut to John.

Was it jealousy? Of that he was never sure. He didn't like to think of himself as the jealous type and had certainly never done anything to spite Amy, nor made any attempts at sabotaging her relationships. On the contrary, he had always been glad for her. Maybe not right at first, but he always came around. It would have been petty and selfish not to. She depended on him, confided in him, and regardless of whom she chose to love, he only wanted to see her happy.

Admittedly, he had never expressed his own feelings for her, but that was another matter altogether, and one which he had struggled with for several years now.

"Suck it up, man," he muttered to himself. "She's smiling. That's all that matters."

John looked away from Amy and turned his attention to the task at hand. He placed the filling nozzle back in the slot on the side of the pump and capped the gas tank on the Jeep.

The door to the store opened just then and out stepped Dagger. One hand held a large grocery sack with a family-sized bag of chips sticking out of the top. He clutched a 2-liter bottle of soda in the other. "Ready to roll!" he shouted.

"Dude. Is that all for you?" John asked.

"Hell yeah, it is. I don't know what kind of food is going to be at this camp you're taking us to. Besides, you never know when you might get the munchies in the middle of the night." He reached the Jeep and tossed the snacks in the backseat. "Where are the girls?"

"Over there." John pointed in the direction of the garage. "You think Beth is buying you a new car?"

"Damn, I wish," Dagger replied, scoping out the Mustang. "Ladies," he called out. "You coming with us?"

Amy turned around and held up a finger to indicate she would be another moment.

"Looks like your friends are waiting," Eric said. "It was nice talking to you. If you don't mind my asking, where are you headed?"

"We're actually staying at a camp near here. Crystal Falls, I believe it's called."

Eric's countenance fell. The muscles in his neck tightened and his expression became strained. "Don't go," he belted out in a grave tone.

The sudden change in the young man's mood was jarring, leaving both girls taken aback. They looked at one another in stunned silence, confirming that each had indeed heard the same thing. Amy was the first to speak up. "I'm sorry, but wha—"

“The camp, stay away from it.”

"What do you mean? Why?”

"Is it rat infested or something?" Beth joined in.

Eric shook his head and appeared visibly distressed. "Yes. I mean, no. It's not rat infested. At least, I don't think it is. But there *is* something wrong with the place. There’s something wrong with this entire town."

He was pacing now. The wrench he held in his right hand began to twitch back and forth in a nervous dance. "Listen, I know this is going to sound crazy, but this place is cursed. Bad things happen around here. People disappear, never to be found, and people die."

At that, Beth's eyes bugged and she began to inch backwards. "Uh, okay . . . I . . . I think we should probably get going."

Eric held up his hands in an apologetic plea. "I'm sorry. I didn't mean to frighten you. It's just that I've seen too many things happen to good people. There's not enough time for me to explain, and you'd probably just think me a nut job if I tried, but I implore you, I beg of you, to leave here. Stay east on Black Water Pass for another twelve miles until you pass the sign for Newfield County. The town of Mary’s Bend isn't far beyond. There’s another camp. You can't miss the place. It's much nicer, and you'll be safe there."

Amy was dumbfounded. Was this guy for real? While she could have brushed him off as some quack who liked to get his kicks by toying with tourists, she detected a very real fear in the man’s eyes which gave her pause.

Across the way, Dagger banged on the side of the Jeep. "If you two take any longer I'm going to have to visit the bathroom again."

"We're coming!" Beth shouted back.

"Alright," Amy said softly. "I’m not quite sure what to make of all this just yet, but I'll tell the guys what you said. Maybe they’ll agree to check out the other camp."

Eric ran a hand through his hair and let out a heavy sigh. “Okay,” he nodded. “And listen, I know this all sounds really out there, but it’s important that you make them understand.”

“You can count on it,” Beth declared. Right now, she was willing to say just about anything to get away from the man. With an insistent tug, she nearly pulled Amy over while attempting to make a hasty retreat. Once they were out of earshot, Beth delivered a solid punch to her friend’s shoulder. "That dude is straight-up creepy as hell. What were you thinking?"

"Me?" Amy protested. "If I remember correctly, it was you who dragged me over to talk to him."

"I know. But you told that lunatic where we were staying. What if he shows up in the middle of the night with a chainsaw or something?"

"You've seen too many movies. And anyway, I don't think you'll see him again."

"How can you be certain?"

"Why would he tell us to leave town if he wanted to kill us?"

Beth opened her mouth to speak, but then went silent. She was going to need more time to ponder the question before she could offer up a convincing argument.

"Besides, I feel sorry for him," Amy went on. "He's definitely afraid of something. Whatever it is, I think he means well by trying to protect us."

She turned and glanced back at Eric. Though he still wore a tortured expression, he lifted a hand in a gesture of goodbye, managing a slight smile in the process. Amy returned the wave and offered a cautious grin of her own.

"He trying to sell you those wheels?" Dagger asked Beth, once she’d reached the Jeep.

"Not hardly," she replied.

"Good. Because if he knows what he’s sitting on, you couldn't afford it, anyhow. It’s worth a mint. Do you have any idea what that is?

"Of course, I do. It’s a ’69 Mustang Boss 429 edition. Top loader close ratio four-speed manual, scooped hood, original

Raven Black paint, and a 375 horse, semi-Hemi combustion engine that will do zero to sixty in just under seven seconds," Beth replied, repeating almost verbatim what the mechanic had just spouted. "How did I do?"

Dagger was speechless. He never knew his girlfriend had such an intimate knowledge of cars. His mouth hung open for a few seconds before he could continue. "I think I love you," he said with a whimper.

In all actuality, Beth knew zilch about cars, but she wasn't about to inform Dagger of that just yet. She was enjoying the look on her boyfriend's face too much. "Of course you do, babe," she replied, giving him a pat on the chest before climbing into the backseat.

Near the garage, the young mechanic watched with a harried stare as the group drove away from the station. Would they heed his warning? As much as he wanted to believe they would, he knew all too well that history was like a dog chasing its own tail. No one ever listened. Why would they?

Shadow Lake was a majestic spot; a seemingly tranquil place steeped in natural beauty. Who could fathom that it masked something much darker? That it was home to such abject evil? Or that the worst terrors imaginable lurked just beneath the clear waters, nested deep within the emerald forests, and resided in the very bones of the town itself?

Eric knew the truth, however, having learned long ago that deception oftentimes comes wrapped in the prettiest of packages. Although he prayed the outcome might be different this time around, he feared Amy and her friends were already just as lost as he was. They just didn't know it yet.

In a sudden fit, Eric gave the wrench a shake and chucked it into the garage, where it clattered against a metal oil drum. He fell back against the Mustang and slumped to the ground in a tempest of emotion. His lungs birthed a terrible cry, one of both embittered rage and raw agony. The wail echoed through the surrounding forest, sending flocks of roosting birds soaring into the air in a maelstrom of flight.

"Dear, God, when will it stop?" the young man beseeched.

When the heavens did not answer, he buried his face in his hands and wept.

4

"He's a wacko!"

Dagger popped a chip in his mouth and mashed it between his teeth. The resulting sound was like that of car tires crunching over gravel. "Dude is just messing with you."

"No, I don't think so." Amy's resolve was firm. "He has reason to believe this place is dangerous. Maybe we should listen to him."

"I think *he's* dangerous," Beth said from the backseat. She had set aside her Twizzlers and now worked an emery board around one of her fingernails with the precision of a chisel-wielding sculptor. "There was major creep vibe coming off him."

Amy turned around in disbelief. "Says the girl who was just discussing how hot the guy was not more than ten minutes ago."

Beth stopped filing and met Amy's gaze. "Hey, there's no rule that says serial killers can't be sexy."

"Oh, now there's a calendar for you," John cracked.

Dagger let go with a hearty laugh and moved forward to offer his friend a high-five.

"I'm serious, guys," Amy lamented. "Aren't any of you the least bit concerned? Am I the only one who thinks there might be some truth in what he was saying?"

"I don't know, Ames," John replied. "It's just a bit strange. I mean, you said he seemed fine until you mentioned the camp, and then, not only does he tell you *it's* dangerous, but goes on to say this whole town is cursed. If that were true, don't you think that guy back at the store would have mentioned something?"

"Right," Dagger mumbled through a mouthful of food. He held up a finger to pause the conversation and swallowed before continuing. "Old boy should be turning tail if people were disappearing and getting popped. I think that mechanic was just trying to get in your pants."

"What?" Amy balked. "You can't be serious! What kind of approach is that?"

"You know, guy trumps up some spooky story to get you all frightened, then shows up later acting like he just saved you from certain death. You swoon and ... *boom*! Your panties fall right off."

Amy grabbed her head as if a migraine were pummeling her brain. "Do you hear yourself? If you honestly believe that, then you're living in a fantasyland. Who would use something like that as a pick-up?"

"I would," Dagger replied straightaway. He tossed another chip into his mouth and wiggled his eyebrows.

John had to chuckle, both at the sheer absurdity of the answer and because he knew his friend might have been half serious.

"That guy better not show up again." Beth said, shaking her emery board at Amy in a scolding manner. "You never should have told him where we were staying."

Amy fell into a defeated posture. It was clear that she wasn't being taken seriously. Rather than exhibiting any concern for what might await them at their destination, the primary focus in the backseat centered on whether Eric was a hunky homicidal maniac, or just some svelte chap whose means of swag was using the illusion of murder as an aphrodisiac.

Sensing her frustration, John stepped up with his own—and somewhat more plausible—theory. "I doubt the guy is out to get anyone. I mean, look at this place. It's hardly a hub for violent crime. If it were, we would know it, right? That's not to say he doesn't have an agenda, though."

"What's that?" Amy asked.

"Well, he said his family owned the store, right? And it wasn't until you mentioned the camp that he became concerned and tried to sway you from staying there."

"That's right."

"So, maybe his family owns the place over in Mary's Bend as well."

"Yes!" Dagger cried. "It's all a ploy to send business his direction and keep the money coming in to buy those expensive cars."

"Exactly!" John proclaimed.

"Right on, Johnny boy," Dagger grinned, tapping a finger against his noggin. "You've got real smarts. And so does that mechanic with a plan like that. I should have known any guy who loves the Stones couldn't be all bad."

"Wait! Now he's okay because he likes the Stones? Are you implying that a real killer would have lousy taste in music?" Beth asked.

"I'm just saying. Look at the classic rock era. People back then weren't going all postal; shooting up schools and shit. You know why? Because they had cool cars and badass music. Nowadays, dudes are rolling around in a Prius and being subjected to Justin Bieber on the radio. They're getting their balls chopped off and don't even realize it. That's enough to make anyone crazy."

Amy let out a dispiriting moan. "Please tell me you aren't planning on majoring in psychology."

"Nope. Gynecology. Why?"

"Oh hell," John snorted in amusement. "I'm not sure what's worse, having a Dagger in your head, or a Dagger poking around between your legs."

A bout of laughter ensued, and while Amy joined in the fun, it was obvious to John that her attempt was a half-hearted one.

"This stuff about the camp is really bothering you, isn't it?"

Amy's voice was wrought with anxiety. "The way Eric looked . . . I don't know. Something about his eyes and the way he tensed up. He seemed afraid. If he was lying, then he's one hell of an actor. How much do you really know about this place?"

"Not a lot," John shrugged. "I passed through here a few times with my parents when I was younger, but we never stayed. Mom and I wanted to, but dad always said, '*Once you've seen one mountain or tree, you've seen them all.*' He wasn't much of a nature guy.

"Anyway, when the idea came for this trip, I was anxious to get online and find some resorts. At first, nothing stood out. Then, a few days later, when I got back on the travel site to make my final choice, there was Crystal Falls. I'm not sure how I'd missed it before, but as soon as I opened the link, I *knew* this was the place. I mean, wait until you see it, Ames. It's gorgeous!"

"I don't doubt it's beautiful, but are you aware of any bad things happening around Shadow Lake?"

"To be honest, I was never much of a history guy. My grades the last few years will bear that out," John grinned. "So, no, I haven't delved into the town's past. But, like I said before, if it were high crime, we'd have heard something in the news. The only thing I ever recall seeing were some sporadic reports of hikers who turned up missing. I would imagine that sort of thing happens in any remote location where people go off trail. They get lost. Remember that couple that disappeared near Astoria last year? They never found them, either. I hardly think that makes the place dangerous."

"He's right, Amy," Dagger added. "People who have no clue what the hell they're doing wander off into the woods like it's fuckin' Central Park. Kind of like those idiots who go to a drive through animal park and roll their window down to get a better picture of the lion. It's no wonder they end up with bad juju. Besides, if we skip out on this camp, Johnny's going to lose his deposit."

Amy regarded John with a quizzical expression. "Is that true?"

John tipped his head a fraction to the left and right in a non-committal sort of nod.

That was enough for Amy. "How much?" she inquired.

"First night. But don't you worry. If you don't feel safe there, we'll go somewhere else."

"No," Amy exhaled. "I don't want you to do that. I'm probably just being stupid."

"You're not stupid," John admonished. "Listen, I'll make you a deal. We'll check out Crystal Falls and see what it's like. If for any reason it seems sketchy, then we're out. No questions. I could care less about the deposit."

Amy sat in silence for a long moment. While not wholly convinced there was nothing to worry about, she was persuaded by John's assurances that she could leave if things didn't feel right. "Okay, deal," she finally spoke up.

"Awesome!" John gripped the wheel and pressed down a little harder on the gas pedal, speeding the group towards the foothills of Shadow Lake and the camp at Crystal Falls.

"It's going to be amazing, Ames. Just you wait and see."

....

Four miles south on Old Falls Road, just beyond the bridge over Cooper Canyon, the street began to taper, descending downwards in a series of switchbacks before coming to an end at the bottom of a valley.

It was there the camp was situated, lying in the bosom of the basin and surrounded by mountains to the south and west. On the eastern edge of the lowlands, chunks of late morning sunlight shimmered over the calm waters of a bay. The curved, finger-shaped cove stretched several miles out on the horizon, where it narrowed slightly, passing between a quarter-mile jagged cut in the tall rock and forming an inlet into the wide expanses of Shadow Lake.

It was one of the most beautiful sights Amy had ever seen. No matter which direction she turned, the composition was a magnificent spectacle. It was as if she had stepped into a grand photograph; one of those sublime slices of nature which graced the likes of calendars and screen-savers the world over. So taken was she with what she saw around her, that all the uneasy notions she'd formed about the place since leaving the service station melted away in an instant.

How could a place such as this hold any menace whatsoever?

Maybe the guys had been right. The only threats which existed here were those common in nature—predatory animals, exposure to the elements, and endless wilderness, the breadth of which one could easily become lost in without a compass or some form of navigation. All presented challenges and perils which many big city dwellers might be ill equipped to deal with.

John turned at the end of the road and parked the Jeep in front of a large log cabin near the mouth of the valley. Above the entrance, hanging by a pair of small chains, the word OFFICE was carved into a plank of cedar wood.

As the group exited the vehicle, John sucked in a long, deep breath, closing his eyes as he exhaled. The outside air was warm and woodsy, smelling of sweet pine and crisp ozone.

"You smell that?" he asked, to no one in particular.

"It's clean . . . and nice," Amy answered.

"Doesn't get much better."

Within the dim confines of the office, however, the environment stood in stark contrast to that of the outside world. The climate inside was frigid and stale, possessing a slight lingering sour note which was thinly veiled by cheap air freshener.

Goosebumps sprung up across John's naked calves and he considered that whoever resided within must have hailed from the Arctic.

Beth must have felt the same. Rubbing her arms for warmth, she crossed the lobby to the check-in counter where

Dagger stood, nuzzling into him to absorb some of his residual body heat.

The decor of the lodge was sparse. A few mounted elk heads adorned the walls and a pair of padded wingback chairs flanked a small table in the center of the lobby. Fanned out on the table, a handful of camp brochures were spotlighted by an outdated lamp fixture which looked to be a kitschy survivor of 1970's interior design.

Behind the counter, a small tube television glowed in the back corner. Onscreen, a gaggle of women chatted about current events in an animated fashion.

Sitting a few feet away from the set, an elderly woman occupied a well-worn rocking chair. Her features were pinched and haggard, with sharp protruding cheekbones exaggerating a pair of dark sunken eyes. Folds of loose skin hung in a tired fashion from around her jaw, while a thin set of lips, drawn tight beneath a slender sliver of a nose, gave the woman an almost skeletal appearance. She wore a pair of white cotton pajamas with pink rose print, and her long silver hair spilled loosely over the back of the chair.

A vintage doll, porcelain-skinned and adorned in a threadbare prairie style gown, was splayed across the woman's lap. Its cheeks were plump and ruddy, the sullen mouth framed in an aberrant shade of red. Delicate, hand painted lines formed a small set of brows that framed a pair of glass eyes capable of rolling up and down to emulate the appearance of wakefulness or sleep. The chestnut colored hair, an unkempt mass of frayed ringlets and bristled fluff, clung to the top of the head in irregular chunks, interweaving the dark nap between bits of exposed fleshy scalp.

The woman sat in silence, cradling the doll in one arm; transfixed on the television set in front of her.

John reached for the service bell on the desk and gave it a quick tap. It resonated with a striking *ding!*

The lady remained motionless, without as much as a blink.

"C'mon, man," Dagger said, reaching for the bell and sliding it closer. "Ol' gal is probably half deaf. You've got to put some muscle behind it." He proceeded to hammer the ringer several times with a closed fist, as if he were pounding on a bar top for another round of drinks. "Hello? Ma'am?"

The old woman continued to gawk at the television with a hollow, vacant stare, the rickety chair creaking beneath her. She lifted a shaky hand and began to stroke the knotted patchwork of hair atop the doll's head. "Hush, hush, Eleanora," she coddled. "It's alright. Sleep now. Mommy's got you."

Dagger threw his arms up in desperation. "What the hell?" he muttered.

Pins of anxiety began to prick at Amy's stomach again. She shot John an uncomfortable look.

He knew what was to blame for her troubled gaze, but before he could say anything, a door opened near the back of the office, and a middle-aged man stepped through it.

The newcomer appeared weather-beaten, with deep lines carving a roadmap across his rectangular face. Ash-brown hair was swept back, a few errant strands hanging across a wide forehead, and he sported a silver-tipped goatee which was neatly trimmed. A navy flannel was worn over a pair of indigo jeans and mid-hiker boots, contrasting with the light bluish-gray tint of the eyes. He had the unmistakable appearance of an outdoorsman who, with such a penetrating set of baby blues, might be capable of looking directly into a person's soul.

"Hello!" he exclaimed, grinning as wide as a televangelist. "My name is Robert. Welcome to Shadow Lake. My apologies, I hope you weren't waiting long."

"Only a minute or two," John replied.

"Oh, good! I was just putting the finishing touches on your cabins and hurried down here as soon as I noticed your car parked outside."

The man began to shuffle through papers strewn about the desk. "Now, let's see. Where is your reservation?"

"Hey, man. Is she like . . . okay and all?" Dagger asked, pointing towards the woman in the chair.

"What's that?" Robert asked. He looked up with some confusion and, once he realized who the boy was talking about, gave a dismissive wave of his hand.

"Catherine? Oh, yes, yes. She's fine."

He then went back to work, poring through stacks of disorganization.

Dagger looked at the rest of the gang and shrugged. He gestured toward the old lady again, made a loop around his temple with his index finger, and mouthed the word, *crazy*.

Beth frowned. Dagger ducked away in expectation of a swat that never came.

"She's really got him trained," John remarked to Amy. The two of them laughed.

The busy innkeeper was too distracted to notice any of it.

"Ah, here it is," he said a moment later. "Three cabins, two nights. If you're ready, I can take you to them."

John looked over at Amy. "Are you good?"

Though Amy still had some misgivings about the woman, she thought her too old and feeble to pose any real threat. And the man, she decided, reminded her of Mr. Forrester, her favorite teacher back at Lincoln High. This bred a warm sense of familiarity in the young woman which helped to alleviate the gnawing in her gut. Feeling more comfortable about the camp overall, she gave John a nod.

"Okay, then. I guess we're ready to go."

Robert retrieved three sets of keys from under the desk and led the group outside, pulling the door shut behind him with a solid *thunk*.

The room went still again, save for the faint babbling from the television. With no other sounds, and nothing stirring, the seconds rolled by in a laconic march. After about a minute had passed, a sharp creak pierced the tranquility of the room. The decrepit chair began to pitch back and forth in a slow, steady rhythm.

Peering down at the doll in her arms, Catherine twisted an index finger through one of the frazzled ringlets of hair. In a low, breathy tone, she said, "Shush, now, Eleanora. They won't bother you any longer. Mommy will see to that."

With the *cree-craw* sound of the rocking chair keeping time, the old woman gazed out the window and began to sing. Her voice sounded strangled and craggy, but the words were clear:

"The wheels on the bus go round and round . . . round and round."

5

Just a short walk from the office, half a dozen quaint log cabins lay nestled under a canopy of spruce trees. Arranged in a crescent moon pattern near the westernmost edge of the forest, the cottages—which had once served as quarters for camp counselors—were both rustic and cozy. Each had its own covered patio and wooden porch swing, providing an ideal spot for relaxing with a good book or enjoying a cold beverage on a tepid summer evening. From this vantage point, one also had a front row seat for the twilight show—that glorious time of day when the last rays of golden sun would slant over the mountaintops and adorn the surface of the lake in a resplendent gown of orange and yellow sapphire.

Inside, parallel to the window overlooking the porch, an antique brass bed rested against the wall and was blanketed with a handstitched quilt. Farmhouse style nightstands stained in warm walnut flanked each side of the headboard, standing in contrast to the honey colored logs which comprised the walls.

Opposite the foot of the bed, on the adjacent wall nearest the bathroom, was an extra-wide dresser matching the style of the nightstands. To the left of the dresser, the small bathroom held the usual: a simple vanity and sink, a framed mirror, and a basic white toilet. A little less basic, however, was the old claw foot tub in the far corner of the space. A shower riser had been added, and a wraparound curtain hung from an oval-shaped stainless steel rod which, in turn, was suspended from the ceiling by a series of cables. The fixture was striking, adding an eloquent touch to an otherwise dull bathroom.

Robert Townsend assigned the group to the three outer cabins nearest the woods. He gave an informative speech (one which had likely been recited a hundred times over to previous guests) about the ins and outs of the grounds: where the commissary was located, what time meals would be served, the types of activities available (archery, fishing, canoeing, etc.) and the proper safety precautions which should be followed for each.

"You're it," the man announced, after Beth inquired as to the whereabouts of the other guests. "The season doesn't really get going until after Memorial Day weekend, once the schools have let out. Some places won't rent until then, but my wife and I are always here, anyway, so I figure, what the hell? If someone wants to come early and stay, I'll let them."

He paused, giving Beth and present company a long, hard look. "Speaking of which, you look like you should be in school yourself. Where'd you say you were from again?"

"Portland," Beth replied, squirming a little.

Would it matter to him that she and her friends had cut class for the day to get a head start on the weekend? Their parents knew about the getaway, of course, but were under the impression that the trip was to begin *after* school was out for the day. Beth hoped her curious nature hadn't just blown up in her face. She worried that the man, suddenly wise to their truancy, might send them all packing. Wouldn't that be the end all?

Robert continued to stare for several long seconds, his deadpan expression unreadable. Then, as if a switch in his brain had just been thrown, he smiled a broad smile and handed over the three sets of keys.

"Well, lucky you," he said, in a way that was almost congratulatory. "Kids here still have a few weeks left before they get a reprieve for the summer. Looks like you'll have the run of the place. Let me know if you need anything at all, hear?"

Beth breathed an inward sigh of relief when the man started to leave, then tensed again when he came to an abrupt halt and spun around, waving his hands about in a mad fit.

"Oh! One more thing. During the off-season, the creatures of the forest get mighty used to this place being empty and a few find their way into the camp looking for food. It's not much of an issue once the place fills up, but with you being the first arrivals, I wouldn't recommend wandering too far from your cabin after dark. Wouldn't want anything to get you now, would we?"

A reticent grin spread across Robert's face. It was an enigmatic mug, suggestive of one who was privy to a secret of which he was not allowed to speak. The manner in which he'd conveyed the words, however, was so exuberant and cheerful that it belied any real sense of danger, sounding, instead, as if the forest were made up of kittens and cotton candy.

"Well, too-da-loo, now," he said, giving a small wave and shuffling down the path.

Dagger eyed the man with puzzlement. *Funny little dude*, he thought to himself.

Beth glanced over at her boyfriend and shrugged. "Lions, and tigers, and bears?"

"Yeah, something like that."

"You won't let me get ravaged by some wild animal, will you?"

A playful finger poke to the chest derailed Dagger's thought train. He stopped watching the old man teeter away and focused his attention on Beth. A wide, ornery smirk crossed his face.

"You've got nothing to worry about. They don't like vegetarians. Besides, the only thing you'll be ravaged by this weekend is me."

With a low growl, he swooped forward and grabbed his girlfriend by the waist. She screamed with delighted surprise, breaking free and bounding towards the cabin with Dagger close in tow.

John nodded in the couple's direction. "Guess we know what they'll be up to all weekend."

"I think I'd rather take my chances with the bears," Amy said, in a matter of fact tone.

John began to laugh. "Good one, Ames."

He pulled up on the strap of his travel bag and slung the piece of luggage over one of his broad shoulders. "I suppose we should get unpacked before the day wastes away."

He was still laughing when he entered his cabin and closed the door behind him.

....

She heard someone whisper her name.

Beth stopped fiddling with her cell phone and glanced up at the observation tower.

Two flights of stairs zigzagged in a switchback fashion and led to the first of two railed decks. From there, three more sets of stairs climbed upwards, exiting onto a narrow platform comprising the smaller top deck.

Her friends were on the upper section of stairs, and Beth could hear the tenuous laughter of the group as they ascended ever higher.

The tower, a soaring skeleton of rusting steel, provided the only sure way to view Crystal Falls. Due to the geography of the land on this side of the gorge, one could only catch partial glimpses from various points on the ground. To see all of it, you either had to scale the mountain to get a birds-eye view of the falls rushing over the lip of the ridge and dropping into Cooper's Canyon below, or you climbed the tower to watch the full-on show.

Not a fan of heights, Beth chose to stay on the ground while everyone else went to ogle the waterfall. It was no loss as far as she was concerned. Growing up in Oregon, she had seen her fair share already. How different could this one be? Besides, her phone was finally pulling a decent signal up here on the hill and she thought she could use the time to catch up on social media; find out what was happening amongst the unfortunate souls who were, at this very minute, stuck in third period at Lincoln High. She had just started reading about a new prank that Freddy Carter was plotting on poor, unsuspecting Ms. Brunetti, when she heard the voice.

It rode in on a breeze, like the first harbinger of autumn chasing away the sweltering heat of summer. At first, Beth thought one of her friends was calling from atop the tower, but looking in their direction now, it was clear they were paying her no mind whatsoever. Thinking it her imagination, she turned her attention back to the phone and the devious antics of Freddy Carter.

The voice came again.

"Beth." It was thin but well-defined.

Beth turned and scanned the empty path behind her. The sound seemed to emanate from all around. It was everywhere and nowhere at the same time.

"Beth, please," the entity whispered. Sharper and more distinct, the tone possessed a sense of urgency.

"Over here, Beth."

And there he was. Near the edge of the forest, a measured distance away, stood a young boy. A pair of glasses rested at a slanted angle, obscuring the eyes, while his remaining features appeared muddied and indistinguishable. It was as if he had no face at all.

Just the distance, Beth assumed, thinking that she might need glasses herself.

The boy lifted an arm and pointed a crooked finger into the woods.

"Beth."

He took a sideways step and disappeared behind the trees.

....

Metal rattled and clanged under Dagger's feet. He pounded up the stairs and emerged on the top deck with his arms raised in a show of victory. "Boom, baby!" he yelled.

Amy trailed a few steps behind. "I should have known better than to compete with someone who runs track *and* plays on the football squad."

"You held your own, and came in a respectable second place." He gestured towards a visibly exhausted John, who was just beginning to appear over the top riser with trails of perspiration tracking across his face. "At least you're not on the TV dinner squad."

"Hey, smart-ass, I made it, didn't I?" John was huffing and puffing. He staggered over to the railing and steadied himself, looking as if he were mere seconds away from puking.

"You okay, big guy?" Dagger asked. "You know I'm just messing with you."

"Yeah, yeah, I know. I'll be the first to admit I'm out of shape. You're still a smart-ass though."

Dagger clapped his friend on the back and laughed. "Indeed I am! A bona fide asshole some would say."

Amy placed a hand over one of John's bear-sized paws and gave a gentle squeeze. "Sorry. I shouldn't have turned it into a race."

"No worries. I could stand a bit of exercise." He raised an arm and flexed a bicep. While his arms possessed the girth of a young oak, the actual muscle tone had more in common with a block of cream cheese.

"I guess I've spent too much time turning these guns into cannons and may have neglected my cardio in the process," John teased. Dimples touched his features and Amy smiled back.

"I'd say it was worth it, though. You see that?" he continued, pointing towards the west.

In the distance, a wall of gray rock jutted above the treetops and reached high into a hard-blue sky. A wide veil of white poured from a granite mouth down a long and steep precipitous face, the clear water glistening in the sunlight as if it were studded with diamonds.

"Stunning," Amy said, with a gasp of astonishment.

Even Dagger stood in quiet amazement, which was something of a rare sight. "Beth has no idea what she's missing," he remarked, upon finding his voice. “How is this place not on everyone’s radar?”

"Not sure." John’s gaze never shifted from the falls. "But a guy could get used to this sort of thing. Imagine waking up to that every day?"

"I can dig it," Dagger replied. He fumbled his hands around in his pockets and brought them away empty. "Shit! I left my phone at the cabin. I wanted to get a picture of this for Beth."

"I’ve got it," John said, pulling his own phone from a pocket on his shorts. The pasty white hue he’d exhibited moments ago was starting to subside, a healthy pink taking its place. He snapped a few shots and passed them to Dagger to inspect.

"Nice job, bud. These are great. Now, let's get Beth to take one of all of us."

"Good idea," Amy said, taking her turn to look over the pictures.

Dagger walked around to the opposite end of the deck overlooking the trail below and peered down.

“Beth! Angel! Love of my life. I need you to take our picture.”

There was no answer.

“Beth?”

Dagger looked both left and right along the narrow path and called out again. He was met with only a paralyzed silence.

Beth was gone.

6

Scraps of sunlight streamed through lofty pine branches and lit the forest floor in a disjointed array, making the ground appear as a patchwork quilt which had become fodder for moths. The terrain was scabrous and uneven, and Beth treaded carefully. She was trying to keep up, but a misplaced step could prove treacherous.

The boy, still holding a sizable lead, seemed to glide on invisible wings. He was either accustomed to this parcel of land and its potential pitfalls, or simply had no fear of twisted ankles and broken bones.

"Beth . . . here."

He was stopped near a deadfall roughly one hundred yards ahead.

Beth eased herself down a sharply graded slope, her feet sliding and catching in the roughhewn soil. She wondered how it was the boy knew her name, and why, for that matter, she was following him at all. These were questions which she had not thought to ask herself until now.

She supposed the boy might have overheard the group talking as they had made their way to the tower (Dagger's voice echoed loud enough to be detected half a mile away) and set out to find them.

The answer to her other question was more complex. Was it blind impulse that had brought her here? As a rule, she always erred on the side of caution. So, no, she didn't think it was that. It was something else. Something deeper and more reflexive.

Perhaps it was an inherent maternal instinct at play. After all, this was a child crying out, whereas, had it been a grown man calling to her from the edge of the woods, she would have wasted no time climbing right up on top of that tower with the rest of her friends, heights be damned.

But she wasn't convinced that it was a budding maternal proclivity, either. If the boy were in immediate peril, that would have made sense, but she realized she had no idea where he was leading her, nor for what purpose. Certainly, something had made her assume he needed help, setting her in motion without question. But what?

It came to her in a flash. A memory—one she had long tried to bury—pried itself loose from that part of the brain where bad remembrances are abandoned and left to rot. Only this one had refused to die, and was presently clawing its way back to the forefront of her mind. Its name was Richie Miller.

Richie, a former neighbor and childhood friend, had been eleven years old to her eight when he'd smuggled his father's shotgun out of the house and carried it out to the field behind his rural home. It was unclear as to why he had taken it to begin with, but his mother later surmised that he may have been going after the coyote that had slunk off with the family's puppy a day prior.

Beth had just returned home from school the day Richie set out for the field. Making her way to the kitchen in search of a snack, she had seen the top of his head bobbing through the tall grass just beyond her dining room window. She was spreading peanut butter over crackers when she heard the blast from the rifle.

The grisly discovery came a few minutes later. Most of Richie's head was gone. What remained looked like the serrated edges of a pumpkin after having been thrown to the ground and smashed to pieces. Parts of his brain clung to crimson soaked stalks of prairie grass, while the rest had been scattered God knows where.

A traumatized young Beth had tried to flee, but her legs turned to rubber and faulted beneath her. She subsequently collapsed in the field where, for over an hour, she'd lain next to Richie while he glared back at her with his one dead eye. When her father finally found her there some time later, he'd had to pick her up and carry her home in his arms.

A cold shock settled over Beth as the memory of that day galvanized her all over again. She hadn't been able to speak for several days following Richie's death, and it had taken two years of therapy before she could sleep through the night without waking up in a fevered pitch, screaming incessantly in the dark.

Eventually, through either extensive counseling, the remarkable ability of the human psyche to repress trauma, or some combination of the two, she'd been able to move past the horror of the incident and live a normal life again (although even now, there were nights when Richie would come calling).

In a roundabout way, Beth blamed herself for what had happened to Richie. He'd asked her over to play games on that fateful afternoon, but she had declined for reasons she could no longer recall. She couldn't help but think that if she'd made a different decision, Richie might still be alive. Sure, he could have gone out with the gun the following day, or the day after that. But, then again, maybe he wouldn't have. Maybe the itch to shoot a dog-snatching coyote would have passed. And, if not, then perhaps he would have taken a different path and avoided the hole which had caused him to stumble and pull the trigger.

Speculation, of course, and Beth had been told repeatedly that you should never dwell on the what-if's. What happened, happened. End of story.

But still . . .

Beth reached the deadfall and made her way around it. The boy was on the move again and was well ahead of her. He swerved up and to the right, disappearing on the other side of a small hill.

She wondered if the accident was the reason she was so quick to pursue the boy. On some level, she thought that aiding another child in peril might lessen the lingering guilt she felt over Richie. Maybe it would and maybe it wouldn't. To her, the logic seemed sound enough.

"Beth."

There were multiple voices now. High and sexless they drifted up, waxing and waning in intensity as they moved in and out of the trees.

"This way, Beth."

Airy and ethereal, they bore an almost hypnotic quality.

"Help us."

The ground began to ramp upwards and Beth pitched forward, digging the toe of her shoe into the rocky soil for traction. As she started her climb, another utterance cropped up in the far corners of her mind, telling her to turn back; to run as far away from this place as possible. But the sound of it was small and delicate, like the papery wings of a mosquito whining in her ear. A minor distraction at most; one which was quickly drowned out by the chorus of disembodied chants swirling about. No longer propelled by instinct, impulse, nor the convicted memories of Ritchie Miller, Beth was held spellbound, fully consumed by the whispers around her.

She trudged forward in a mindless crawl, drawn like a moth to the flame. When she crested the hill moments later, her eyes went wide with curious wonder.

Resting in the valley below, far removed from any road, was a derelict school bus.

The voices called out once more.

"We're here, Beth."

7

Dark coppery splotches bubbled up under the metal, eating away at a sunflower tinted skin that had long ago lost its luster. Beneath the rusted shell, the deflated remains of tires hung like loose flesh over wheels encrusted with thick clumps of dirt and moss. At the head of the bus, tentacles of ivy looped around the latticework of the metal grille, producing an army of spindly new tendrils that snaked their way across the hood towards a cracked and hazy windshield.

A cold chill settled over Beth as she approached the yellow beast. The high voices encircling her had started to wane, becoming ever softer as she drew near.

"*Bethhh . . .*"

They were but whispers now, yet their pull would not be denied.

Closer. Just a little closer.

She stood upon the threshold, gazing up at the decaying bus. The accordion style door was collapsed slightly inward, leaving a small gap between the frame and the rubber seal; an opening just wide enough to accommodate the lanky form of a child.

Beth reached in and opened the door fully.

The voices ceased.

"Hello?"

A drowsy curtain of air—the shallow exhale from a dying heap of metal—drifted out from within the cavernous vehicle with a sharp, rancid odor on its back. Reminiscent of spoiled meat, the stench stung the inside of Beth's nostrils and made her eyes water. She held the back of her hand to her nose and took a tentative step backwards.

"Hello?" she asked again, thinking the boy must surely be anywhere but in the belly of the bus.

A thin cry faltered from somewhere inside.

Without trepidation, Beth mounted the high steps and peered down the narrow walkway between the rows of seats. Though she saw no one, the cries continued to ebb throughout the cabin. Small and muffled, they seemed to originate from somewhere near the back of the bus.

"Hello? Are you there?"

Beth began to ease herself down the aisle, searching behind each seat as she passed.

Many of the seat bottoms had wide gashes in them, the dry vinyl upholstery ripped open to expose the coiled metal bones and yellow foam guts beneath. A tattered Raggedy Ann doll was splayed out across another, its face blotched with grungy tea-colored water stains.

The sobs were growing stronger now.

"Little boy, are you hurt?"

There was a brief respite, followed by a few seconds of stillness; then the weeping resumed.

The old vehicle shuddered and moaned, sounding like the creaking hull of a ship battered by waves the breadth of houses. Black mold grew heavy around the window sills. It trailed upwards along the metal seams before branching out across a ceiling stippled with narrow strips of peeling paint.

Beth thought what a horrific place this was for anyone, least of all a child, to be living in. How had the boy come to be here? Was he all alone? And for how long? The thought of it was heart wrenching.

"Hey, what's your name?" she asked gently.

The sobs quivered a few times and then hushed.

"Don't be afraid. I want to help you."

There was no answer. In the moments following, a great silence rang out, playing not a familiar recital of serenity, but rather a disquieting anthem that was jarring to the senses. The sudden stillness struck a chord of fear in Beth. Concerned for the child's welfare, she hurried to the back row and peered behind both sets of seats.

She found no one.

"Where . . . where are you?" she stammered.

"Heeere," a voice hissed from over her shoulder. The sound was spectral and shrill, like gales of wind whistling under the eaves of a ramshackle house.

Turning around, Beth's mouth fell open in stilted shock.

Richie was there in the aisle, his one good eye doggedly fixed upon her. He grinned through pallid lips pulled back over fractured teeth and fissured gums, while pulpy bits of red slopped out over a jagged, open skull and ran like rivulets down his cadaverous face.

The image of her deceased friend remained but for a moment, seeming to be nothing more than a simple manifestation of her tormented subconscious. But then the thing in the aisle began to change, its bones stretching and shifting as it morphed into its true form. What stood there in that next instant was inconceivable; worse even, than the ghastly visage of Richie Miller and his soupy brains. Something much worse.

A scream lodged itself in the back of Beth's throat.

The bus doors swung closed with a jolt.

....

A dance of shadow and light played against her shuttered eyelids.

Beth saw children with monstrous features: two individuals with a common resemblance cleaved down the middle, one half of each of the two bodies lashed together with crude stitching to form one soul; another with a face that had slipped far down over the bone and drooped to one side, as if the skin were made of wax and had partially melted and disfigured before hardening again. The last wore a pair of shattered glasses, yet possessed no eyes from which to see out of, his mouth slit open ear-to-ear; carved into a ghastly grin by a curved blade that resided where his hand should have been.

Behind the children, shrouded in partial darkness, stood a woman clad in primitive garments of straw and animal hide. Beneath her cloak was withered skin the color of midnight, offset by eyes which burned like white hot marbles. She spoke of things which were a mystery, in a tongue that Beth did not understand, yet somehow the words scorched like fire. They seeped deep into her psyche, where they would fester like an old wound until their purpose should be known.

The children began to amble forward, their movements erratic and shaky. An odor of death preceded them, turning from rancid, to almost sweet, then back again. The hideous forms hobbled closer until they were but an arm's length away. The one with no eyes cocked his head to one side and let his jaw fall slack. The gashes across his cheeks split open, arcing upwards from the corners of his mouth to form a wide, perverse smile. He lifted the arm which was capped with a sickle and began to laugh.

Darkness came over Beth and she fell into a sea of forgetfulness.

....

Sometime later she came to on the trail near the edge of the forest, having no recollection of the boy she had chased into the woods, the bus she'd found at its heart, nor the nightmarish sights and sounds that followed. She held in her hand a phone, the musings of Freddy Carter splashed across the screen, and when her friends found her and asked where she had gone off to, she simply shrugged and said she had followed the cell signal.

After, as the group made their way back down to the camp, a single word sprang to the edge of Beth's mind, where it caught and began to play over and over like a vinyl record stuck in a loop:

EAT . . . EAT . . . EAT!

8

"Someone's in the house!"

Dagger leaned forward in his chair, where his face caught the soft glow of the campfire blazing nearby. Deep shadows rose and fell across the young man's features, making his eyes appear as black holes which elongated whenever he shifted from side to side.

"Sounds creepy, already," Beth replied. She sat next to Dagger in a folding chair of her own and took a tug from a bottle of cheap beer (one of the many that her underage boyfriend had managed to acquire before leaving Portland). The stuff tasted like piss, but it did the job alright. She was on her second bottle, and already the pleasant side effects were beginning to swim through her head. "I like a good scary story."

"It's more of a poem, really; one my dad used to tell me growing up," John said from the other side of the campfire. He was stretched out on a blanket, propped up on his elbows, while Amy sat beside him, knees pulled up to her chest and hands clasped around her shins. "We were both into the horror stuff. This is the sort of thing he would put me to bed with."

"Poems are good, too, I suppose," said Beth.

"And Johnny here kills!" Dagger added. "So, come on. Let's hear it."

"Well, alright," John replied, flashing his trademark dimples. "It's been awhile. Let's see if I can remember how it goes."

In the dim, shadowy light his face appeared devilish and his grin took on a sinister quality (an effect which, one could argue, was likely the reason ghost stories and campfires had become synonymous with one another in the first place). John cleared his throat and began to narrate in a low and ominous tone:

Entering the room, she's wrought with fear
The monster has come back
He is here, so very near
Hiding, waiting, ready to attack
Anchored now with paralyzing dread
Visions of death dance through her head
Panic born by nightmares roused
Scrawled in blood above the bed:
Someone's in the house

Yonder comes his haunting stride
There's nowhere to run, no place to hide
Hither now the monster creeps
She tries to scream, but only weeps
Thump on the stairs, shadow moving down the hall
Foretold this night by blood upon the wall
Tap, tap, tapping on the door
She falters now, collapses to the floor
Oh, dear God, now it's in the room
These four walls have sealed her doom
Terror strikes, tears stain her blouse
Death has come, there is no doubt
For someone's in the house

John lifted his hands in the air, shaped them into claws, and loosed a diabolical laugh.

Amy buried her face in her hands and shook her head. "Stop! No more!" she cried.

"What's the matter?" Dagger asked. "Too much for you? It's only a poem."

"Right," Amy murmured, peeking out between the small gaps in her fingers. "And Cujo was just a dog. Listen, you know I'm a big chicken. Always have been."

"I thought you were getting better with that sort of thing. You handled yourself like a champ when we went and saw *The Haunting of Lancaster Lane*," John noted.

"That wasn't too bad. I do alright with ghosts, aliens, monsters; things that are make believe. But *that*?" she shrieked, referring to the poem, ". . . or slasher stuff? No way. If it can happen in real life, it terrifies me beyond belief."

"It's all scary to me, real or not," Beth said. "I can't believe your dad read that to you when you were a kid, John. How were you not scarred for life?" As she spoke, another troubling vision of Richie Miller materialized in her mind. He stood at the edge of the field, bloodied and brainless, while motioning for her to follow. She pushed the image away with a shiver.

"I don't know," John laughed. "Like I said, my father is a big horror fan, which in turn rubbed off on me. I suppose being raised on a steady diet of the stuff desensitized me somewhat. Don't get me wrong, there were still things that could scare me—ghosts and zombies mostly. But not that poem. We had this ritual of checking under the bed each night and, as weird as it sounds, that was all the comfort I needed. Now that I'm older, I've stopped believing in zombies and, while I still believe in ghosts, the thought of them doesn't frighten me all that much anymore. In fact, there's a part of me that hopes to see one someday. I think being in a haunted house would be a heck of an adrenaline rush."

Dagger nodded. "Staying in a haunted house would be pretty bad ass, I've gotta admit."

"I think you're both out of your damn minds," Amy said. "I don't know if ghosts exist or not, but I certainly wouldn't go looking for them, that's for sure."

"I guess it's just you and me then, Dagger," John remarked.

"Right on. I'm with you, bud." He chugged the last bit of beer from the bottle in his hand and tossed it aside before reaching into a small backpack at the foot of his chair and producing a bag of beef jerky. With a quick motion, he ripped the pouch open and retrieved a strip of the dried meat.

The pungent odor wafted towards Beth. Normally, the smell would have made her sick and she would have moved away, chastising Dagger in the process. But now, as the aroma filled her nostrils, her stomach began to rumble, while her mouth salivated with a wanting anticipation. The reaction left her stunned, leaving her feeling betrayed by her own body.

What the hell is wrong with you? It's meat. You don't eat meat!

No matter how much she rationalized, however, the craving would not abate. Her stomach twisted and churned, and she yearned for sustenance. But why? She had eaten dinner no more than an hour and a half ago. Robert had been kind enough to cook up a vegetarian pasta and a salad just for her, and she'd enjoyed both until she was full. Now, however, it was as if she hadn't had a thing to eat all day. A hunger, deep and insatiable, filled her. She wanted—*needed*—food. And not just any food. She desired only one thing; that one thing which she had sworn off long ago. She yearned for the taste of meat.

Stop it, Beth. Just stop.

She closed her eyes and tried to will away the hunger.

"What else you got? Any stories that are more Amy appropriate?" Dagger asked. "Maybe something with adorable furry monsters that spread happiness and shoot glitter out of their asses?"

"Real cute." Amy smiled a sardonic smile. "Remind me again why we're friends?"

Dagger spread his arms out in the manner of a Japanese sensei dispensing valuable wisdom. “Because it is awesomeness you seek, my child.”

Amy rolled her eyes. “Yeah, whatever. You keep telling yourself that.”

John sat up straight, a pensive look upon his face. He began to shake a finger in Dagger’s direction. “You know, I might have one for you. Ever hear of a Windigo?”

“Wind-a-what?” Sounds like a kite or an airplane,” Dagger replied.

“I think I’ve heard of it. A type of mythical creature along the lines of Bigfoot, right?” Amy asked.

“Somewhat,” John said. “But Bigfoot tends to shy away from people. With only a few exceptions, encounters with the creature have never proven to be dangerous. The Windigo, on the other hand, is not something you’d want to cross paths with.”

“Okay,” Dagger nodded. The attentive posture he held indicated he was all ears. He tugged on a piece of jerky and gave it a vigorous chew. “I’m listening.”

John leaned forward and began his story. “The Windigo was a legend of the Algonquian-speaking tribes along the upper East coast and Canada. A cannibalistic creature with a ravenous appetite for human flesh, it shares many similarities with the Skinwalkers of Utah and the Kwakiutl Man-Eater of the Pacific Northwest— “

“Man-eaters? I like it already,” Dagger interjected. He grinned like a pubescent boy getting his first look at a girly mag.

“The appearance of the Windigo varies,” John continued. “It’s been described as everything from a giant skeleton made of ice, a yellow-skinned monster covered in pale fur, to an emaciated corpse with large claws and fanged teeth. Some say it is a shape-shifter which can take the appearance of both animal and human. Who can say, though, as those who encountered a Windigo seldom lived to tell about it. Natives more often heard the blood-curdling screams of the monster deep within the forest and reported a smell like rotten meat whenever the thing was near."

"Wicked," Dagger muttered. "If I were them, I think I'd have just stayed out of the woods. Am I right?"

"Sensible, but not plausible," Amy replied. "These were primitive tribes. To eat, they had to hunt."

"Exactly," John agreed. "But what made the Windigo even more deadly was its cunning. It didn't just wait for some poor soul to enter the woods so it could pounce. Legend says it could mimic human speech and would often call to people outside the walls of the forest. If the person answered the call, it was believed they would come back to devour those they loved. Afterwards, they would often go mad, running back into the woods never to be heard from again; likely consumed by the creature upon their return.

"The Navajo people saw the Windigo as a curse rather than an actual monster. They held the opinion that those who were killed at the hands of this dark spirit became an empty shell to be inhabited by the wicked force. But, regardless of whether a tribe believed the creature to be physical or supernatural in nature, it was widely accepted among all that a bad spirit called an 'otshee monetoo', or manitou, was responsible. This spirit was capable of all manner of deception and was not taken lightly. Even now, some claim to hear voices calling from some unseen spot inside the forest. If you should hear your name whispered on the wind, beware, and do not enter the woods, for the Windigo may await you there!"

Dagger began to clap his hands together. "Bravo, buddy. That's some mind-melting shit right there. Way to go!"

"Thanks, but it's not really my story. I'm just repeating the legend."

"Perhaps. But you told it well," Amy said. "It didn't bother me as much as the poem, which is good, but it was definitely creepy. You're a natural storyteller."

"Here, here!" Dagger added, raising a fresh bottle of beer in a toast. John and Amy raised their own bottles in like fashion.

Dagger glanced in Beth's direction and frowned. Rather than toasting, she appeared to be in some sort of a trance, staring straight ahead in his direction. He followed her gaze and realized she was fixated on the bag of jerky. "Care for some?" he asked with a sly smirk, pushing the bag in her direction. To his surprise, she reached forward in a slow and tentative manner.

"Beth?" Amy asked in quizzical shock.

Beth stopped. She looked around, momentarily lost, and then just as quickly found her bearings. When she noticed her boyfriend extending the bag of jerky her direction, she blinked in astonishment. A brief second later, her brows furled together and she fumed.

"Fuck you!" she screamed, slapping the bag out of Dagger's hand. She stood up and stormed towards the cabins.

Dagger sat in stunned silence for a moment. "Ah, hell," he mumbled.

"What were you thinking?" John asked.

"I dunno. I was just messing around. I didn't think she'd get so bent out of shape."

"Appears you thought wrong. And since there are no florists nearby to deliver flowers, I hope your apology is on point."

"I suppose I'd better go after her."

"I think that's the smartest thing you've said all day," Amy remarked.

Dagger stood and, without another word, jogged off in the direction Beth had gone.

"How long do you think he'll be in the doghouse this time?" John asked.

"Not long enough. I'll bet you they'll be banging like bunnies before the ten o'clock news."

"I don't know. She seemed pretty pissed. You're probably right, though. No matter how many wrongs are committed, those two always make up. They're either going to be the death of each other, or they'll end up married. I'm not sure which."

"Maybe both," Amy chuckled.

"Right. There's always that," John agreed. He took a long, slow sip from his beer and watched as Dagger disappeared into the night.

9

Amy opened her eyes and stared at the ceiling.

Something had awakened her.

She had not been dreaming, nor had she suffered from the dreaded falling sensation which was known to strike on rare occasions, violently wrenching her from a peaceful sleep and leaving her gripping the sheets in a panic. She hated when that happened, always welcoming the sweet relief that came with the realization that she was safe in a warm bed.

But this had been neither of those. She considered that it might have been a noise. She vaguely recalled hearing a strange sound while she was drifting out of sleep, although now the room was silent.

She held her breath and listened.

There. She heard it again.

Her eyes scanned the room. Streaks of moonbeam slanted through the window nearby, bathing the top of the quilt she was under with thin slices of silver light. The only things Amy could make out were her blanketed feet and the shimmery brass bed frame that lie just beyond. The rest was darkness, pure and absolute.

The sound rose and fell. Scratching . . . coming from underneath the floor.

Amy sat up and clicked on the lamp next to the bed.

The noise stopped.

She sat and listened for another minute or two, hearing nothing more.

Probably just a small animal. A raccoon, perhaps, taking shelter under the crawlspace beneath the cabin.

The sounds hadn't been all that loud, and Amy figured that the fullness she felt in her bladder may have been the real reason she had awoke. Crawling out of bed, she paused to look out the window, peering out over the worn pathway which she and her friends had taken to reach the lookout tower earlier in the day. Tall pines stood like sentries along each side of the dirt walkway, reaching high into the dim night sky. A heavy gust of wind kicked up and the tree tops bowed in quiet submission. Somewhere on the dark porch, a loose board began to rattle.

To Amy, the night suddenly took on a cold and lonely feel, and a stab of heartache washed over her. She missed Scott and wished he were there to share the bed with her.

No. Don't do this. You promised yourself, remember? He doesn't love you, so he's not worth crying over anymore.

The pep talk didn't help much. The nights—those damned lonely nights—were still the hardest. She knew Scott was a selfish prick who only cared for himself. She also knew she was better off without him. But, for now, the hurt still lingered. Regardless of what she knew to be true in her head, her heart refused to listen. Stubborn in nature, the damn thing was hell-bent on recovering in its own time. She just wished it would hurry up already.

Amy turned to go, hearing a new noise then: a distant cry echoing from within the forest. The sound was shrill and thin; unlike anything she had ever heard before. It was like the bugling of an elk, but with something else mixed in. Something which sounded . . . almost human.

The cries were strange enough in their own right, but now Amy also saw a light moving within the trees. Like a single star that had fallen to earth and continued to burn, the point of light cut through the dark and moved in a sideways trajectory through the woods.

Who was out there tonight? She knew John slept like the dead, so he wasn't even a consideration. Dagger and Beth? Not likely, given that Beth wasn't the type to parade around in a dark forest, even if her boyfriend were crazy enough to suggest it.

Robert, perhaps? He certainly knew the layout of the land, but what would he possibly be doing in the middle of the woods at three o'clock in the morning? Likewise, she doubted that Robert's wife, Catherine, was traipsing around way out there, either. Even if one of them *had* gone for a late-night stroll through the woods, it still didn't explain the bizarre cries she'd heard. So, who?

There was one other option, albeit, not a very plausible one: what if it weren't a person at all?

Amy recalled the story John had told and a cold shiver ran down her spine. Her imagination started running wild with images of goblins, phantoms, Windigos, and other assorted monstrosities. She was quick to reel it back in, chastising herself for being ridiculous. She didn't believe in that sort of thing after all.

Her thoughts were interrupted by drops of rain beginning to tap dance along the roof of the cabin. Amy glanced up toward the sky. A long line of fat clouds slipped past the moon at a brisk pace, resembling a commuter train whisking home a load of nine-to-fivers after a long day's work. Seconds later, the *tap-tap* melody of raindrops began to give way, escalating into the white noise of a steady downpour.

Amy turned her gaze back to the forest and saw that the mysterious light had gone out. With a small sigh, she let the curtain fall back over the window and retreated into her room.

In the distance a peal of thunder mounted.

A storm was coming.

10

She stepped out onto the front porch and squinted in the bright morning sun. The storms had passed sometime during the night, leaving the air smelling new and freshly scrubbed. Breathing in the sweet aroma, Amy felt instantly invigorated. She looked in the direction of her friends' cabins and knew she was the first one up. No surprise there.

She had always been an early riser; never able to sleep until noon like most her age. Her parents were both the same way, so maybe the trait was an inherited one.

As a child, Amy would shuffle barefoot into the kitchen each Saturday morning, decked out in her pink Hello Kitty pajamas, to find her mom tending to several pans on the stove.

Looks like the early bird has come for her worm, her father would often remark from behind his copy of the *Oregonian* whenever he'd hear her enter the room. And while there were never any real worms to be had (thankfully), there was never a lack of food. The dining room table would be decorated with platters and bowls filled with scrambled eggs, bacon, hash brown potatoes and, sometimes, even biscuits and gravy to boot.

That alone was an awful lot for a family of three (Dad could eat a fair amount, Mom ate like a bird, and how much could a little girl really eat?), but then there was also Amy's favorite: French toast. There was *always* French toast, and she loved it so. Her mom's secret, she later learned, was dipping the thick slices of bread in eggnog before frying them up in a buttered skillet and slathering warm maple syrup over the top. Who wouldn't want to wake up early for that?

Thinking on her mother's exquisite French toast, Amy realized she was quite hungry. She didn't want to eat breakfast without her friends, but understood it could be another hour or two before they were up and ready to start their day. She knew better than to try and wake Dagger, as it would result in him being a bigger pain in the ass than usual (a department he most certainly needed no help in). John wouldn't mind if she woke him, but there was no reason to do so. Let the big guy get his rest. She would saunter over to the commissary and find something small to nibble on while she waited; maybe scrounge up some fruit or a piece of toast to tide her over until breakfast.

Amy made her way down the pathway leading to the commissary building, listening as sparrow song played all around her. Whenever one bird would stop singing, another would pick up the refrain from a tree nearby. And so it went throughout the forest. Further on, a gentle breeze stirred, drifting lazily through the valley and creating tiny ripples across the surface of the lake. When the air touched Amy's cheek, it was warm and pleasant, tinged with the scent of clean mountain water and pine. A contented smile graced her face and she thought what a beautiful day it was shaping up to be.

Nearing the office a few minutes later, Amy noticed Catherine running a broom across the wooden decking of the porch. The woman was still dressed in the same white cotton nightgown that she had worn the day before. She appeared even thinner now, the gown hanging loose and swinging like a bell over her emaciated frame. When she saw Amy approach, she stopped what she was doing and eyed the girl with acute curiosity.

"Good morning," Amy said, with a wave.

The woman's expression became more severe. "Who are you? What is it you want?"

"I'm Amy. My friends and I arrived yesterday, remember? We're renting the cabins up on the hill."

Catherine's bottom lip twitched in a nervous manner. She regarded Amy in a cautious way, as if the girl were somehow up to no good. "If you say so. I already answered all your questions. Why won't you just leave me be?"

Amy was puzzled by Catherine's response. The old woman was worse off than she'd imagined. Dementia, perhaps? Her grandfather had suffered from the same condition and she knew what a cruel thing it was. To be robbed of your memories, of your very identity, was the worst thing imaginable. Amy had never given much thought to her own mortality, but after her grandfather had passed a few years back, she'd prayed that death would come sooner rather than later, if it meant she could be spared the fate of mental decay and go out with a sound mind instead.

"I was just on my way to the commissary and thought I would say hello. I'm very sorry to have bothered you." Amy gave a sympathetic grin and turned to leave.

"Wait—"

Catherine's brow drew down into a hard line. It was as if she were remembering something important; something which now rested on the tip of her tongue, yet remained just out of reach. A curtain of sadness fell upon bloodshot eyes, and the woman's arms went slack by her side. The broom hit the deck with a sharp crack.

"Are you alright?" Amy asked.

Catherine said not a word. She glanced over at a pair of rocking chairs a few feet away. Propped up in one of them was the worn porcelain doll in the dirty dress. One eye was closed; the other, a glassy pupil of bright blue, gazed out at the world with an abandoned stare. The old woman coddled the doll in her arms and bent over to kiss her on the forehead. She looked lovingly down upon the pale porcelain face and spoke in soothing tones. "It's alright, Eleanora. Don't cry, now. It's just a little bump. That's all it is. Nothing to worry about."

Amy, like most girls, had her share of dolls growing up, but this damn thing was just plain creepy. And the way Catherine treated her, as if she were a real live child, was even more disturbing.

The woman paced back and forth now, bouncing the doll in her arms. She continued to prattle on, becoming more agitated—almost frantic—as she spoke. "Mommy's going to take good care of you. I won't let you get hurt. No, not again. I won't! I won't! I won't!"

Amy began to inch backwards, thinking she might be able to slip away unnoticed. It didn't work. She had taken no more than two steps when the old lady's head snapped up with the quickness of a springing mousetrap.

Amy froze. Catherine examined her up and down with the same curious look she had exhibited moments earlier. Was it possible the woman had already forgotten their initial encounter? Amy considered it was. Regardless, she was ready to leave. It wasn't that she was afraid, per se (she felt pity for the woman), but the whole situation was awkward.

Catherine's eyes widened and her mouth fell open in a gasp. "You heard them, didn't you?"

"Who?" Amy asked. The awkwardness continued.

"THEM! HER! And the glow! Did you see the glow?"

It dawned on Amy that Catherine was referring to the strange noises and the light coming from the woods the night before. "I did," she replied. "Do you know who was out there?"

"The people of the lake. *She's* been watching. And now *they* are coming!"

Amy was as confused as ever by the woman's nonsensical ramblings. "*She?* And who exactly are *they*?"

"She of the lake. That lake, it takes whomever it wants; claims their very souls. Oh, yes, it does. And when they rise, the lucky ones come back much as they were before. But the others . . . the others become something else entirely."

"I'm sorry, but I don't really understand what you're saying."

Catherine studied Amy through narrow slits of eyes, her upper lip pulling back in a snarl. "Stupid girl!" she hissed. "You have no idea what they can do to you. Best to stay out of the woods altogether. And if you see them, run. Run fast, dear."

Amy felt a knot in the pit of her stomach. She thought the old woman to be out of her mind. Anyone could see that. But there was the matter of the light in the woods, and the eerie cries which had accompanied it. That much was real. She had seen it with her own eyes; heard with her own ears. The thought that there could be even a small amount of truth in what Catherine spoke of was terrifying. Could there really be someone out in the woods watching? Could this be the thing Eric had tried to warn them away from?

The knot tightened in Amy's stomach as she started up the hill. She didn't bother to say goodbye to Catherine. What would be the point? She knew the response would just be more cryptic mumblings. There hadn't been a shred of normalcy to the conversation since it had begun. And right now, she just wanted to get away from the woman.

Halfway up the hill, Amy heard Catherine call out: "The lake, it takes what it wants, young lady. Best be hoping that it doesn't want you."

Amy quickened her step and hurried toward the commissary.

Behind her, the old woman cackled hysterically.

11

It was his third day on the job, and Landon Stephens had been at the station less than ten minutes when the call came in. Seconds after dispatch sent word out over the radio, his phone buzzed. It was Sheriff Frank Andrews. "Stay put. I'll be there in five," he told the rookie officer.

Twelve minutes later, a black Crown Victoria—the words MONTGOMERY COUNTY SHERIFF emblazoned in gold along the front doors—rolled up to the station. "Get in and buckle up," Frank barked, as if Landon had somehow been the one responsible for holding up the show.

Once the young deputy was securely strapped in the passenger seat, the sheriff flicked the switch which turned on the flashing reds and blues and gunned the accelerator. "You know where we are headed, Stephens?"

"Old 19. On the far eastern end of town."

"Do you know what for?"

"Car accident, I believe."

"That's correct. But this is the worst kind, son. A 12-16A."

"Fatality?" the deputy asked, his voice rising an octave.

Landon had graduated from the academy in Los Angeles, after which he'd served the briefest of stints with the L.A.P.D. before his new wife had convinced him to give it up and move somewhere safer. During that time, an incident involving a deceased had not presented itself. Yet now, here in the sleepy little burg of Shadow Lake, one was slapping him square in the face before he'd even had a chance to get his feet wet. The inevitability of such an event was a given, of course, he just hadn't expected it quite so soon.

"You ready for this?" Frank asked.

"Is one ever really prepared?" Landon punctuated his response with a nervous laugh.

The sheriff didn't answer, which was of no consequence to the deputy. After all, the question had been rhetorical. Obviously, no one could predict how they would react to working their first fatality. A big part of the equation, Landon had always assumed, was the grisliness of the scene. A bit of blood and a limp corpse was one thing. Finding pieces of the body strewn about was quite another. But, ready or not, the deputy knew he would get no sympathy from Frank.

His boss was a gruff man; a loud, outspoken, tactless, three-hundred-pound bag of flint that always spoke his mind and catered to no one. Frank knew his job, though, and he expected the same of those in his employ. To him, *suck it up* wasn't just a catchphrase. In this line of work, it was a motto. If you weren't cut out for the grittier aspects of the position, Frank had no problem telling you to hit the road. When it came down to it, the man wasn't that far removed from a drill sergeant.

It mattered little to Landon. High-minded, with an easy-going nature, he was adept at getting along with just about anyone. And the way he saw it, having a boss like Frank Andrews kept him on his toes, which is what every rookie officer needed. Not to mention, it was bound to keep things interesting.

Frank stared at the road ahead from behind a pair of large brown Aviators and took a sip—actually, it was more a slurp—of coffee from a paper cup. He smacked his lips together under a thick push broom mustache and let out an audible *ahh* of satisfaction.

It occurred to Landon that between the mustache, the heavy jowls, and a more than ample frame, Frank Andrews was exactly what a walrus might look like if it were to take human form.

The sheriff swallowed another mouthful of coffee and, after his lips had performed an encore, dropped the drink into a cup holder. Resting on the console next to the cup holder was a small bag with MABEL'S MORNING GLORY printed across the front.

"Donuts, sir?"

Frank took his eyes off the road long enough to shoot Landon a hard glare. "You got something to say about it?"

"I . . . uh . . . I mean, no. Nothing comes to mind."

"You had a tone."

"A tone, sir?"

"Yes, Stephens. After thirty years on the force, I know when someone is insinuating something with their tone."

"I wasn't intending to insinuate anything. I was merely asking about the contents of your bag. Just trying to make small talk, sir."

"Uh-huh. The asking is usually code to say that I'm perpetuating a stereotype."

"Oh, I wasn't trying to—"

"Do you like donuts, Stephens?"

"I suppose so, yes."

"Of course you do," Frank snapped. "Who *doesn't* like donuts? This notion that cops desire them more than any other run-of-the-mill schmuck is ludicrous."

Landon tipped his head to the side and considered the sheriff's remark. "I always believed most stereotypes had some foundation of truth to them, however small that may be. Isn't that how they became stereotypes in the first place?" he asked.

"I'm calling BS on this one. It's not like we have some sordid donut addiction, buying the things by the dozens and stashing them all over the place so there's always a fix handy. If you do see a cop loading up, it's because he or she is taking them back to the station to share with everyone. We aren't the only ones who do that. Plenty of office workers do the same. Regardless, do you know *why* I end up eating donuts most mornings?"

"Because they are damn good, sir?"

"Don't be a smart ass, son. I would have preferred an omelet from the Two Skillets Café this morning. The reason I didn't go there is because whenever I try to sit down and enjoy a real breakfast, I always get a call. It's like Murphy's Law. If I'm lucky, I'll get a few bites in me before I've got to run. But, no matter how you roll the dice, I end up going hungry. And I get cranky when I'm hungry."

You're cranky when you're not hungry, Landon wanted to say, but he had the fortitude to know that for the sake of his career, it was best to keep his mouth shut.

"They can't box it for you, sir?"

The question elicited another curt glance from his boss. "You ever try to eat an omelet in the car, Stephens? It's not exactly finger food. And I don't fancy a lapful of hot ham and cheese. Do you?"

Landon opened his mouth to answer, but the sheriff cut him off. "Don't tell me I could take it to reheat, either. Damn thing could end up sitting in the car for several hours before I get to it. And that, son, is how you end up with a nice bout of food poisoning. Now, maybe you've never experienced your meal coming back out of you from both ends at the same time, but I can assure you it's no picnic."

"I get it," the deputy said, trying to shake the picture Frank had just painted. "Donuts are easy to eat on the run, with no worry of them going bad in a matter of hours. Doesn't quite compare to an omelet, although I suppose it's better than having nothing at all."

He wasn't sure how much truth there was in that last statement, but it seemed to pacify his boss. The redness in the sheriff's puffed-up face had started to subside and the mustache, which had taken on a life of its own while the man was worked up, twerking more than an oversexed college student at some tawdry nightclub, was slowing to a slight twitch.

Landon had never seen anyone become so twisted over a donut before. Did it matter if people thought Frank (or any cop for that matter) ate them all the time? It wasn't like the general public held deep animosities or prejudices towards officers who frequented donut shops. Certainly no one was hurling Molotov cocktails through the sheriff's window because of it. In the end, who cared?

An image of his boss clapping his arms together like the trained animals at Sea World, wedged itself in Landon's mind. He imagined Frank catching a donut in his mouth, gobbling it up, then clapping for another, all while barking and snorting like the aquatic mammal he approximated. The deputy turned to the window and stifled a smile.

"You been to Mabel's yet?" the sheriff asked.

"No, sir."

"I'm partial to the old fashioned, or sour cream donuts, as some would say. Whatever you want to call them, Mabel's are the finest in the state. I'm not into those fancy ones with sprinkles or sugary breakfast cereals all over the top, but if that's your bag, I hear those are good as well. Had I known that we would be on this call together, I would have grabbed you something."

"Oh, no worries. I ate before I left the house. My wife made a great quiche this morning."

"Quiche?" The alarm in the sheriff's voice was akin to a stunned parent whose two-year old child had just uttered their first curse word. "By God, Stephens. I'm going to have to keep an eye on you."

Landon laughed. "It's really not bad, sir. My wife is an amazing cook. And she also packs a mean lunch. Never just a boring sandwich and a tired bag of chips."

"Isn't that nice?" Frank grunted. "Do you know what my wife gave me?

"What's that, sir?

"Eight years of hell, a divorce, and a dependence on Xanax."

Landon wasn't sure if the sheriff was being serious or simply pulling his leg. He settled on the former, which explained a lot.

"First rule of marriage, kid," Frank continued, "Don't marry a bitch."

"Oh, I'm sure she was nice in the beginning, right? Why else would you have married her?"

"She was never nice," the old guy bellowed. "She was a challenge, that's what she was. And I always liked a good challenge. Damned if I didn't get more than I bargained for with her though. Every day was like wrestling with a hyena. Lesson learned, I suppose. Maybe I need to find a woman who will make me a quiche."

"Yeah, maybe so," Landon said through a broad smile. "It's worked out well for me so far."

"Well, good luck to you, son. I—"

The sheriff went quiet and his mouth drew down into a scowl. "Ah, hell. Not this again," he cried, giving the steering wheel a good slap.

"Sir?"

Frank motioned towards the front of the car. "*There!* Pay attention, Stephens!"

The cruiser had just crested a hill on Old Highway 19 where, roughly a quarter of a mile ahead, a bridge crossed the waters of Shadow Lake. A pair of black and whites were positioned across the road on each end, restricting any through traffic from passing. In the middle of the bridge, a large truck holding a crane assembly was parked butt end against one side of the road, its boom extended out over the water.

"The car is . . . in the lake?" Landon asked.

"That it is," the sheriff replied.

"And this happens a lot?" The deputy's voice reverberated with surprise.

"More often than it should. Funny thing is, there are never skid marks on the road; no signs of erratic driving, nor anything to indicate the drivers ever even slowed down. It's like they purposely drove full speed ahead, right smack dab into the water."

"Why would they do such a thing?"

"Beats the hell out of me. No one has ever been pulled out of the water alive for me to ask them. One might assume they had been drinking or were high on drugs, but toxicology always comes back clean."

"That seems a bit odd."

Frank slowed the cruiser and brought it to a stop near the crane, where two other officers were peering over the side of the bridge. He grabbed his campaign hat off the dash and popped the car door open.

"Better get used to it, Stephens. A lot of weird shit happens in this town; with no rhyme or reason that I can tell. I've given up trying to make any kind of sense of it. Bottom line is, there are a disproportionate number of crazies that live in these parts. The old asylum down the road is a testament to that. Place is full of townspeople who have gone mental."

Wasting no more time with words, the sheriff perched the hat atop his slicked back gray hair, paused to grab his coffee and donut, and climbed out of the car.

"Huh," Landon muttered, exiting the vehicle after his boss. "And here I thought Los Angeles was bad."

Nearby, a motor began to squeal as the steel load cable on the crane began inching upwards in a slow and steady crawl. One of the officers from the bridge—Arwood was his last name—approached. "Morning, gentlemen. Looks like we've got us another ugly one."

"How much do you know about this?" Frank asked.

Deputy Arwood raised his voice to be heard over the rumbling of the crane engine. "It was called in by a Wes Tomlinson. He was out here fishing this morning when his canoe collided with something. He didn't pay it any mind at first; thought it to be a stump or a piece of driftwood. But then he heard scraping along the hull of the boat and knew whatever he'd hit had to be made of metal. That's when he saw the car. Said most of it was submerged, but there was no doubt as to what it was. Suffice it to say, Mr. Tomlinson was alarmed at the sight of the vehicle, but it was what he saw *in* the car that prompted him to call emergency services."

"The unlucky occupant," the sheriff surmised.

"Yes, sir. Guy said the corpse was all kinds of chewed up. And it was staring right at him."

"I bet that put a good stain in his Hanes."

"You know it," Arwood laughed.

Frank set the cup of coffee on the roof of his car, fished around inside the bag from Mabel's, and retrieved the old fashioned he was so fond of. After admiring the way the top of the pastry formed a tiny canyon for the glaze to pool in, he lifted the donut to his lips and tore off a small hunk with his front teeth. A moment of quiet ecstasy followed.

Over at the edge of the bridge, the back of the vehicle was slowly coming into view. It looked to be one of those oversized luxury sedans with a big V8; the type usually driven by some geriatric with a cruising speed of thirty miles per hour.

Landon's nerves jangled as he watched the rest of the sedan slide into view. Water poured from the windows in furious gushes and spilled into the lake below. A body was visible in the front seat, still restrained by a seatbelt. Its head was slumped forward and resting on the wheel. Much of the flesh around it had either decayed or been picked clean by the creatures of the lake. What remained hung like tissue paper from dirty, algae-encrusted bone.

Landon felt the contents of his stomach rise, the sweet alkaline taste of vomit lingering near the back of his throat. *Don't get sick . . . don't get sick.*

The deputy remained poised and upright, but had to look away from the corpse in the car. He took a deep breath and swallowed hard. The hot liquid in his throat receded a bit.

Another deep breath.

That's it, suck it up. You can handle this.

Although his tongue still felt thick between his teeth, the sensation of nausea was beginning to let up. Landon was fairly confident that he would not embarrass himself in front of Frank Andrews, at least not on this day.

The churning of the crane motor stopped, leaving the car dangling in midair. A moment later, another engine whirred, and the boom began to swing the vehicle over the road.

"We've got another one!" the deputy at the edge of the bridge yelled.

Landon stiffened. *Seriously? I haven't acclimated to the first one yet.*

The sedan twirled at the end of the cable, bringing the other side of the car into the officers' line of sight. Another body could be seen hanging partway out of the passenger window. Its state of decay was much like the other, only this one had an eyeball still partly intact. The cloudy white orb bulged from beneath lids which had been relegated to thin strands of tissue. Patches of hair clung to the right side of the scalp, while the other side of the head had been chipped away, exposing what looked to be a wormlike section of brain bobbing up and down inside the waterlogged skull cavity.

Deputy Arwood whistled between his teeth. "Looks as though those guys were down there for quite a while."

Frank nodded in agreement. "Whatever was holding her down, I suspect last night's storms must have knocked it free." Without taking his eyes off the vehicle, he polished off another bite of his donut.

How the hell can he do that? Landon thought, his own stomach commencing another round of backflips at the sight of the second victim.

"Call the M.E. and tell him we'll need a toxicology report and cause of death on these two," Frank muttered through a mouthful of food. "Run the tags on the car and check for anything on their persons that might give us a preliminary ID. We'll have to check dental records to get a positive."

Arwood understood the orders clear enough. He hollered at the other officer to check the tag on the sedan once it was grounded, then headed over to his own squad car to radio dispatch and notify the coroner.

The sheriff moved to get a closer look at the body hanging from the window. He stood beneath the weeping rusted-out-shell of a vehicle and shook his head. After some time had passed, he remarked: "Didn't quite make it out in time, did you? I'd sure like to know what your partner was thinking to make him drive off into the lake the way he did."

The corpse hung in stilted silence, grinning back at the officer with a wide, toothy smile.

"I know. Dead men tell no tales, right? They do seem to smile an awful lot though." Frank snorted in amusement. "But, hey, what else can you do when you have no lips?" He started to take another bite when his lips froze around the donut.

The jaw of the corpse had started to move, hinging open and closed ever so slightly. Frank watched, his eyes like saucers, as the head shifted and the mouth opened even wider.

"What in God's name— "

There was a flash of movement near the back of the throat. Something was in there . . . something alive.

The sheriff shuffled backwards, nearly tripping over his own feet as a thick black water snake slithered out from the open mouth and writhed up along the decaying face.

"You've got to be kidding me!" he heard someone behind him shout.

Frank looked over at the squad car, where his new deputy was now crouched behind the trunk. He heard gagging, followed by the wet echo of partially digested quiche splattering across the pavement. The sheriff scrunched up his nose, glanced back at the body hanging from the car, and then down at the half-eaten donut in his hands. "Christ," he mumbled, chucking the donut over the bridge in disgust. He stood, mumbling something unintelligible under his breath for several long seconds. Then, with a sigh: "You alright back there, kid?"

"Fine, sir," the deputy called out. "Just a little motion sickness, I think."

"Sure, kid. Don't worry, you get a pass on this one. Damn thing even got to me a little."

Landon raised his head up over the trunk of the car, peering at the sheriff through red, watery eyes. "What was that you said?"

Frank didn't turn around. He didn't care to see the road which had just been redecorated with Landon's wife's famous quiche. "I said, suck it up, rookie! There's work to be done."

"Yes, sir. I'll be right there."

Back at the sedan, one of the dead continued to watch over the men through its ravaged remnant of an eye. The sheriff leaned back against the cruiser, folded his arms across his chest, and studied the deceased. "Now, what's your story?" he asked, in the hardboiled voice of a seasoned interrogator.

Exercising its right to remain silent, the corpse only grinned.

12

"Please forgive my wife. She's not well." Robert shifted his gaze away from Amy and looked down at the mug clasped between his hands.

When she'd first arrived, the man had been in great spirits. He'd remarked that breakfast wouldn't be ready for a while yet, but asked if he could offer her a danish and a coffee. Amy had said that would be fine. After bringing the warmed pastry, he returned a minute later with a thermos of piping hot coffee and poured each of them a cup. It wasn't until after he'd heard about Amy's encounter with Catherine that his jovial mood had turned somber.

"She wasn't always that way," he said now. This was followed by a throaty chuckle which exuded a sense of raw pain more than it did pleasure. "Would you believe she was homecoming queen once?"

Amy couldn't.

"Really?" she asked. Her intent had been to sound cheerfully inquisitive, but the question came out reeking of astonishment. Amy's cheeks flushed with embarrassment. I'm sorry, I didn't mean to sound—"

"It's alright," Robert replied. "If I were meeting her for the first time, I'd have a hard time believing it as well. All I can say is, she's not the woman she once was."

An uncomfortable silence followed before Amy asked the inevitable: "What happened to her?"

"Tragedy, my dear. Life dealt her a hand which she could not trump. The depression issues were always there, mind you, but she dealt with those just fine. The medicines worked well enough, and if you didn't know she'd been diagnosed with the condition, you'd have been none the wiser. She suffered some dark days from time to time, but then who doesn't? We married just out of college, settled into new jobs, bought a modest home; all the things you would expect from a couple of newlyweds as they begin their journey into adulthood.

"The following ten years were all I could have hoped for. There were job promotions, vacations to exotic locales, and a wonderful group of close friends. It seemed as if we had it all, and I suppose we did. Catherine and I had our share of disagreements, but like most arguments, they were over things which were petty and inconsequential. We never stayed angry for long, and those moments were far outnumbered by the good times we shared. I can say without a doubt that we were completely, madly in love with one another . . . and we were happy."

Robert looked up for the first time since he'd started talking and smiled. His eyes held a cheerful glint from the recollection of those early years with his wife. Amy couldn't help but to smile back.

"I remember the day Catherine told me she was pregnant," he mused. "God, I was beside myself with joy. We'd wanted a family from day one, but had agreed to wait until we were financially stable enough to provide a good life. After a year and some months of trying, Catherine gave me the good news. It didn't take us long to clear out the room I had been using as an office and turn it into a nursery. It was a wonderland of pastel pinks and creams with touches of gray. Catherine, always the consummate artist, painted a tree on the wall behind the crib. Full of flowering blooms and butterflies circling about, she said it was about the loveliest piece of work she'd done, and I had to agree. I don't think I'd seen her smile as much as I did during the months leading up to our daughter's birth.

"Come the following March, she delivered the most beautiful seven-pound little girl I had ever laid eyes on. We named her Eleanora, after my grandmother, and she filled my heart with an enchantment that was unlike anything I'd known in all my life. A father's love, I suppose. Catherine adored her in equal measure but, even so, things started to derail soon after we'd returned home with Eleanora."

Robert turned his attention to the window, where he looked not at the wooded view outside, but far beyond, to a place in time that only he could see. The winsome expression on his face began to wane and the gleam in his eyes faded into tiny embers before disappearing altogether.

"The doctors said it was postpartum depression, compounded by the clinical depression she already suffered from. All I know is, for the first time since we'd been together, Catherine had more bad days than she did good. The medicines she had taken for years weren't working anymore, so she was given a new cocktail of pills. They seemed to help a bit at first, but then I noticed her becoming forgetful—a side effect of the medication I was told. It was little things at first: misplaced items, forgotten essentials at the store, placing the baby's clothes in my dresser drawer and vice versa. But then it became more serious.

"She would forget to change Eleanora, or miss a feeding. I would come home to the baby crying and find Catherine passed out in the bedroom, or sitting in front of the television with a blank stare. When she would come around and realize what she'd done, she would burst into tears and swear she hadn't meant for it to happen. I knew it wasn't intentional, but what I didn't know was that she was also forgetting to take her medicine on a regular basis. The day I came to that realization was the same day she left the baby on the changing table and walked away. There were bruises on Eleanora's forehead and legs from where she'd hit the ground. Catherine acted as if she hadn't noticed, and when I questioned her, she broke down again and said she couldn't remember what happened.

"I made the decision to stay home from work after that, at least until I could find a nanny to be at the house while I was away. It pained me to think it, but Catherine wasn't fit to be alone with our daughter. Maybe she would be one day, but not until she was mentally and emotionally sound again. Anyway, I thought things would be alright with me being at home, but I was wrong.

"A few weeks later, I heard Eleanora cry in the night. Catherine slipped out of bed to tend to her. I saw the light come on in the baby's room down the hall and heard Catherine singing a lullaby. A few minutes later the crying subsided, the light went out, and my wife came back to bed."

Robert paused and swallowed hard. All the color had drained from his face; his eyes were glassy pools of pain. Amy, certain of what was to come, knew the story would not end well. That knowledge stirred in her a mix of dread, empathy, and heartache, so it came as no surprise when she felt tears budding in her own eyes as well.

"I was awakened the next morning by Catherine's screams," Robert continued. "I raced down the hall and into the nursery. Eleanora was lying in the crib, eyes closed, looking as peaceful as any sleeping child would. Only, she wasn't asleep. I knew from the moment I saw her complexion that she was gone. Catherine was howling, pleading for me to do something, but there was nothing that could be done. I took my wife in my arms and we both cried for I don't know how long. At some point, I was able to dial 911 and, when the paramedics came, they took my baby girl away; carted her out like some old appliance that no longer worked. I can't begin to express how much that tore me up inside."

A single tear ran down Amy's cheek. She'd had little experience in dealing with a loss as tragic as this one, but told Robert she was sorry in the best way she knew how. The man responded with a heartfelt thank you and sat in quiet introspection.

Not knowing what else to say or do, Amy picked at the danish in front of her. It was good. Cherry and cream cheese. Not one of those prepackaged jobs that came off an assembly line somewhere. This one had been made from scratch. If not here, then from a bakery in town perhaps.

"Trying to hold it together after that was the hardest thing I've ever had to do. But I had to be strong for Catherine. You see, the police questioned us both, but her much more so. Because of her condition, and the events of which I spoke of previously, they thought she might have played a part in Eleanora's death. They were unable to come up with anything conclusive, and the coroner ultimately ruled it a case of Sudden Infant Death Syndrome.

"Catherine was never the same afterward. Something inside of her broke beyond repair. She stopped taking care of her appearance, completely withdrew from society, and became locked in a prison of her own making. Her mind remains stuck twenty-five years in the past. She believes Eleanora is still alive, which is why she carries that doll around. To her, the doll *is* Eleanora. But people don't know how to deal with that. Our own friends and family couldn't accept it. They wanted me to put her away; stick her in one of those institutions for crazy people, like that Elmhurst asylum on the opposite end of town. But I couldn't do that. She's still my wife, even if she's not the same person she used to be, and she's all I have left. That's why we moved out here from Michigan. I had to find a quiet place far away from the naysayers where I could take care of her."

Amy broke off a piece of the danish and took a small bite. Her appetite was not what it was when she had entered the commissary, yet the food offered some small measure of comfort. It had been much the same after she and Scott first broke up; a candy bar here and there, or a pint of cookies and cream, went a long way in providing a brief respite from the anguish. "Do you think Catherine will get better someday?"

"I don't know. After this much time, I doubt it." Robert took a sip of coffee and placed the mug back on the table. He watched an errant drop of the liquid slide down the side of the cup and wiped it away with his thumb just before it reached the table. "We all go to dark places sometimes. And those places always have locked doors. Most of us find that we hold within ourselves the key to unlock those doors and walk back out into the light. Some people, though, seem to have lost their key along the way. Or maybe they just never had one to begin with."

"Perhaps she'll find hers," Amy replied. "I would think it would do her good to be in such a beautiful place as this. In the end, maybe things will improve."

Robert grunted. "I'm sorry. Amy, was it?"

"Yes. Amy Grainger."

"Right. Well, Miss Grainger, it's been my experience that happy endings exist only in fairytales and storybooks. Now, I suppose on occasion one might befall a lucky few elsewhere, but not here. There are no happy endings in Shadow Lake. Of that I'm certain."

"I know it might seem that way, but don't give up. Something good could still happen."

Robert grinned at that. "Oh, to be young again, with a head full of dreams and a belly full of optimism. Hang on to it for as long as you can. Who knows, maybe you'll be one of those lucky few."

His story having been told, Robert rose from the chair and collected his coffee cup. "Now, I'd best be tending to my work or I'll have to stop making breakfast and start fixing lunch. Tell your friends that I'll have everything ready within the hour."

He crossed the dining room and had just pushed open the door to the kitchen when he heard Amy call after him.

"Wait!" she hollered. "I almost forgot. What about that light I saw last night? And those noises?"

"Probably just an elk. If it were injured, or even a calf that had gotten separated from its mother, that would explain why it sounded a bit unusual. As for the light, my best guess is that it was a reflection coming off one or more of the feeders. Either way, I'll go up and have a look around. It's nothing to worry about, I'm sure."

"Thank you. That makes me feel a little better." Amy paused for a moment before cracking a slight smile and adding, "Remember what I said, okay? Someday, good things might still happen."

Robert nodded in appreciation. "One could hope, Miss Grainger. One could certainly hope."

13

The water was cold. In the Pacific Northwest, the water was always cold, rarely eking above seventy-four degrees Fahrenheit on its best day. That's just the way it was; how it had always been. If you hailed from the region, you were used to swimming in the crisp waters. It was always a frigid experience at the onset, to be certain, but before long it was no different than splashing around in a tepid bath. The trick, any resident would tell you, was to jump in all at once rather than attempting to ease yourself in a little at a time, for the latter was nothing more than a form of prolonged torture, practiced only by the likes of oblivious tourists, transplants from the South, or the occasional sadist.

Amy sat at the end of the wooden dock, decked out in a black Mediterranean swim dress, her bare feet swishing back and forth in the shallows of the lake. The chill she felt at present stemmed not from the icy waters encircling her ankles, but from within her own despondent soul. For once, the emotional state she found herself in had nothing to do with Scott. She hadn't given him so much as a single thought since she'd crawled out of bed that morning. No, it was Robert's story which now weighed heavy on her mind.

Amy was the empathetic sort, and whether she could directly relate to a situation (which, based on her limited experiences, was more often a not), she was quite adept at putting herself in other people's shoes, the culmination of which almost always propagated an impassioned response. It couldn't be helped.

She imagined what it must have been like for Robert to lose an infant daughter; to watch the woman he loved slip into a state of mental decay, and to then have the authorities infer that Eleanora was killed by Catherine's own hand.

Tragic.

Of course, the possibility that Catherine *had* inadvertently caused the girl's death—and then been none the wiser the next morning—was not inconceivable given her history.

Amy was certain Robert wrestled with that very thing. While it was apparent he wished to maintain his wife's innocence, there had been a flicker of doubt in the man's eyes when he'd told his story. Not to mention, it was Robert himself who'd stated that Catherine had become unfit to be alone with Eleanora. It was the whole reason he'd started working from home in the first place. What if Catherine hadn't been lucid the night she went to check on the baby, and had done the unthinkable? To know for certain, the memory of that night would have to jog itself loose in Catherine's head, ending in either confirmation that she'd left the baby sleeping soundly, or with a tearful admission of guilt. Until such a day came (if it ever did), the truth would remain a mystery.

It was all too much.

"What are you doing over here by yourself?" Beth plunked herself down on the dock and sat cross-legged next to Amy.

"Just thinking."

"Scott again?"

"No," Amy replied. "About what Robert shared with me. You know, the story I told everyone after breakfast this morning."

Beth looked out across the lake. The telling of Eleanora's demise had once again stirred up uncomfortable memories of Richie and the shotgun accident. God, she hated death. She could accept the fact that everyone's ticket would be punched someday, just not when you were so young. If our existence was like the proverbial roller coaster that some made it out to be, then people like Richie and Eleanora never even topped the first hill. And that just didn't seem fair at all. "Life really blows sometimes," she finally said. Not very profound, but it was the best she could come up with.

"Think of what Robert has had to go through; what he is *still* going through. Can you imagine having to shoulder such a burden?"

As a matter of fact, I can, Beth thought. She considered telling Amy about Richie, but then discarded the idea. The story wasn't one which was going to elevate anyone's mood. And since her friend was already down, why turn a smoldering ember into a full-on bonfire? "I know. It's very sad. I feel bad for him."

"He's such a nice guy, too."

"I don't think being nice matters all that much. Sometimes shit just happens to the best of us." Again, not very profound, but it was the truth. "And no matter how much we would like to at times, there's no way to change the past."

"Yeah," Amy agreed. "I think I'm just too soft-hearted for my own good."

"That's not a bad thing." Beth gave her friend a pat of reassurance and her mouth turned up in a sideways grin. "There is one silver lining in all of this, though."

"What's that?"

"At least you're not dwelling on that douchebag ex-boyfriend of yours anymore."

A smile spread across Amy's face. She looked down at her lap and shook her head, laughing in spite of everything. "I suppose you're right. To be honest, I don't want to think about him, Robert, or that poor little girl anymore. It's all too depressing."

"Then don't!" Beth asserted. She jumped up and took Amy by the arm. "C'mon."

"Where are we going?"

"You see that rock sticking out of the water over there?"

Amy looked in the direction Beth was pointing and nodded.

"Let's see who can reach it first."

Amy's eyes moved from the rock, over to Beth, and then back to the rock. "Okay, I'll be the first to admit that I suck when it comes to a foot race, but you do realize I'm on the swim team, don't you?

"Well, yeah! I mean, that's what makes this a challenge. You down?"

"You bet your ass, I am." Amy slipped into the water with a hollow splash.

"What are you doing?" John called out from the other end of the dock, where he and Dagger were busy loading an ice chest into a waiting canoe. "I thought we were going out on the boat."

"We are!" Amy yelled back. "Just getting in a quick swim."

"Paddle out and pick us up," Beth added. She undid the zipper on her faded denim and lace shorts and sidled them down over her hips, revealing a pair of white Brazilian bikini bottoms which rode high on her buttocks.

A warm rush of blood washed over John's face and he averted his gaze. Dagger appeared at his side, holding two bottles of beer he'd just popped the tops on. He handed one of them to John without ever taking his eyes off Beth. "Hey, man. It's alright. I can't blame you for wanting to look."

John harrumphed. "I wasn't trying to check her out. I just didn't expect her to be wearing something like . . . *that!*"

"Oh, she's full of surprises," Dagger replied. He raised his voice and shouted over at Beth, "Show us what you've got, girl. I've been waiting all morning to see that sexy ass."

Beth turned and flipped Dagger the bird.

"And tenacious too, I see," John muttered.

"What? Again? We just did it last night. You're wearing me out. I suppose I could go another round, though. Anything for you, babe."

"Give it a rest," Beth hollered back.

"Hold up, now. I wasn't even talking to you. I was talking to John, here." Dagger took a swill of beer and laughed.

John grimaced. "Now, that's just wrong."

"I know better than that," Beth chided. "Do you think about anything other than sex?"

"Well, sure I do. Sometimes I think about pizza and a good football game."

"I can drink to that," John said, raising his beer.

Dagger followed suit, and the two bottles met in the air with a sharp clink. Beth gave a dismissive wave and then went to work shedding the tank top she was wearing.

John swung one leg into the canoe, using his foot to bring the vessel flush with the edge of the dock before climbing inside. "Sounds like the two of you made up last night, although I think she might still be holding on to a bit of animosity."

"You have no idea," Dagger replied. He climbed aboard, stretching out his arms to steady himself as the boat rocked from side to side. Once the swaying subsided, he took a seat across from John. "She yelled and cried for a while when I got back to the cabin. After that came the usual make-up sex. But it wasn't great. I could tell she was still angry; probably just going through the motions and hoping it would somehow make her feel better. I don't think it did. When we were done, she yelled some more, and then went to shower while I tried to find something good on TV. A few minutes later, I heard the water turn off in the bathroom and out she came in all of her majesty, if you know what I mean."

John gave a nod to signal he did.

"She had this expression on her face that was pure sexual energy," Dagger went on. "Sort of like those swimsuit models in the magazines who look as if they're about to eat you up and spit you out. But you're down, of course, because you know it'll be the best sex of your life. Am I right?"

Another nod from John.

"Anyway, I didn't even get a word out of my mouth before she was on top of me; taking charge and riding like she had something to prove. It's not like her to go more than one round in the same night. And *never* like that. It was off the charts, dude! Hell, I'm getting horny just thinking about it. She even did this one thing where—"

"Okay, man," John replied, waving his hands about. "No need to give all the details. I think I get the picture."

"And what a picture it was. That is, until she started crying again. She said she was hungry, so I told her there were still plenty of snacks left from that gas station we stopped at. You figure that would have been good news, but no. She starts in with the waterworks again. Says she doesn't want to eat. I told her the only way to stop being hungry was to eat something. Then she's mad. Telling me I'm trying to make her fat. Can you believe that?"

"Hmm." John shifted his eyes upward and appeared in deep thought. He let a few seconds pass and then said, "Nope. I can't help you with this one."

"I don't know what's gotten into her. Ever since we came back from that tower yesterday she's been moodier than usual; hot one minute, cold the next. And get this: after I dozed off, she goes and eats up almost every bit of that shit from the store. That after saying *I'm* the one trying to make her fat."

"Seriously?"

"No joke, my friend. She's had her moments before, but nothing as crazy as this."

"What can you do?" John shrugged.

"Not a damn thing," Dagger replied. "Man will never understand the workings of a woman . . . which is probably the reason God gave us beer."

John chuckled. "No better therapy, I suppose."

"Words of truth, brother."

The two bottles came together in another toast.

....

The race was a short one. Despite a respectable effort on Beth's part, Amy was first to reach the rock formation by a good twenty seconds. It was the outcome Beth had expected. She'd known all along there wasn't a chance in hell of her winning. The whole thing had been a rouse to help Amy take her mind off things. And it seemed to have worked.

"Not bad for a first attempt. Race you back to the dock?" There was a gleeful enthusiasm in Amy's voice.

Beth clung to the side of the rock, her chest rising and falling in rapid succession. She held up a finger, closed her eyes, and swallowed. "One second. Let me rest a minute." The reply came between heavy breaths.

"Take your time. I think I'll do another lap real quick. Be right back."

Beth nodded before hoisting herself out of the water, where she perched atop an outcrop in the rock.

Amy doubled over and disappeared beneath the water, her legs opening and closing in scissor-like fashion as she propelled herself forward. While there were those in her circle of friends who would attest to her often clumsy nature on land, none could argue the sheer grace she possessed when in the water. Amy had always loved the water, taking to swimming before she was even old enough to walk. And although reincarnation was not something she gave credence to, many of those same friends liked to joke that she must have been a fish in another life.

When she came near to the dock (something she seemed to sense without seeing), Amy eased up on her strokes and came to a stop, her legs dropping like anchors. Something foreign grazed her right ankle. It wasn't a rock, nor was it the slimy underwater flora that she was used to feeling underfoot. This was something man-made which had been lost to the depths. The only question now was: *trash or treasure?*

Curious, Amy dug around in the dirt with her toes. The thing was metallic, box-shaped, and hollow. It was also wedged in the ground tight, so there would be no gripping it between her feet and swinging it to the surface. With a deep breath, she somersaulted over, her legs rising out of the water in a perfect straight line before slinking down and out of sight.

Visibility in the lake wasn't great, with the waters tending to run on the murky side. Here in the shallows, however, not only was the water clearer, but the bright rays of the sun penetrated all the way to the lake's floor. It took but a second for Amy to find what she was looking for.

She brushed a thin layer of mud from what turned out to be a vintage lunch box; the kind which featured a motif from a popular movie or television show and came packaged with a matching thermos. She had never owned one like this (they were all made of plastic by the time she was in grade school), but her father still had the *Star Wars* themed lunch box that he'd carted around in the third grade. *You never know when something might turn out to be worth a lot of money*, he would say on occasion. In his case, he'd been right.

Unfortunately, the box at hand was not of the *Star Wars* variety. And even if it had been, it probably wouldn't have fetched much in its current condition. There was a considerable amount of rust, but Amy was still able to make out the words, *Six Million* and *Man*. Had that been a TV show? She wasn't certain, but it must have been a big enough pop culture sensation to grace the front of a child's lunch box. Either way, it wasn't interesting enough to warrant digging up.

Amy moved to return to the surface, when a glimmer of light caught her peripheral vision. Looking up, she spied something in the cloudy waters ahead. The thing waved back and forth with the current, its movements lithesome and agile; almost hypnotic. There was another flash then, and it became apparent that the twinkle of light had come from within the swirling mass.

Her curiosity piqued, Amy moved closer. When she came to within a couple feet of the flashing object, she dug her feet into the muddy ground and brought herself to an abrupt halt. A silver barrette twirled just below the surface of the water, catching the sun's rays and reflecting them back. But it wasn't the barrette which had stopped Amy. It was the fact that the metal clip was still pinned to a long strand of auburn hair.

The water grew colder then. Much colder. Or maybe it was only the blood racing through her veins at a brisk pace—blood which felt as though it had thickened into an icy slush. Amy was certain that had she been above water, her breath would have spilled out in thick white plumes, much as it did every December with the arrival of winter's first frost.

She didn't make a conscious decision to look down, but found her eyes wandering in that direction nevertheless. In a mindless crawl, they traced the billowy wisps of hair to their roots, and to the child lying motionless in the sand. It was a girl, probably no more than eight years old, positioned between two young boys of close to the same age. The three of them were lined up side by side on their backs in a neat little row, as if they had been placed there just so. Their skin was the color of bone china; glassy smooth with no signs of decay, and each of their mouths hung open in a wide O-shape, as though they were singing *Silent Night* in the school Christmas pageant.

There was something about the children lying there in such a serene state which held Amy transfixed. She saw in their cherubic faces a kind of strange and intrinsic beauty. The moment was fleeting, however, and in the next instant the dreadful reality of what lie before her stormed the gates of her mind with a swiftness that rattled her senses. Just as the first razor-sharp inklings of panic began to cut deep into her soul, the unimaginable happened: the dead girl opened her eyes.

14

John slipped out of Amy's cabin and eased the door shut. He stood on the front porch for a long moment, replaying the events of earlier in his mind. He could still hear Amy's screams ringing in his ears, and recalled the stark terror he'd seen in her eyes. Just the thought of it caused him to tense, sending a surge of adrenaline coursing through his body all over again. If the race up the tower the day before had worn him out, the swim over to where Amy was thrashing in the water should have done the same, especially given the speed at which he'd moved. But it hadn't. That part of the incident was nothing but a blur now, and all he could remember was the panic; both Amy's and his own.

"How is she?" The voice startled him.

John turned to see Dagger walking up the path, with Beth trailing a few paces behind.

"Okay for now. We'll see how she is after she wakes up."

"She was able to fall asleep after all of that?"

"I gave her one of my Ambien. She should be out for a while. Who'd have ever guessed that my insomnia would one day come in handy?"

"That's good. I didn't think we were ever going to get her calmed down."

"Me neither. My hands are just now starting to get some circulation back in them. That girl has got a grip like the jaws of a snapping turtle."

"Did you hear what she was saying?" Dagger asked. "All that going on about dead kids in the water?"

John frowned. "I did."

"But there was nothing there, man. Not one thing. I swam around the area at least a dozen times; no dead kids. None that were alive, either. Not that they could have held their breath for that long, but I'd have found them if they'd been there to find."

"I know." John's look was a troubled one. It was clear he was still trying to wrap his head around what had happened. "She had to have seen something."

"You're not suggesting there are zombie preschoolers paddling around under the water—"

"No, of course not. It's just . . . something scared her. Who knows? Maybe something in the haze of the water was playing tricks on her eyes."

"What else is going to look like a row of little kids? That would be one hell of an illusion."

"I don't know." There was agitation in John's voice now. "I wish I had an explanation, but I don't. Even so, she's not crazy, Dylan. You should know that."

Dagger raised his hands in defense. "Whoa, big man. I didn't say she was. I'm just saying, she couldn't have seen what she said she did. The only crazy person around here is that old bat with the doll. When you've got psycho Sally running around raving about the people of the lake, who can blame Amy for thinking she saw a few of them? Poor girl is just having her impressionable head filled with bullshit, that's all."

John ran a hand through his hair and released a deep breath. "I'm sorry. I didn't mean to sound like I was irritated with you. I just feel like between the breakup, and now all of this, that Amy's not exactly having the best time, you know? I probably shouldn't have brought her out here."

"Don't blame yourself, John," Beth said. "I know Amy doesn't. You're doing what any good friend would. If she had stayed behind, she'd just be holed up in her bedroom all weekend crying over Scott. In the end, I'm sure she'll be glad she came along."

"Yeah, what she said." Dagger nodded.

"I don't know. Maybe you're right. I just hope she's okay."

"I'm sure she'll be fine," Dagger said. "Anyway, we just came back from the kitchen looking for some grub, but there was no sign of the old man. Guess lunch is going to be late. I thought I'd see if I could get the keys to the Jeep so Beth and I could run back up to that store and refill the snack supply."

"Just use the spare I keep under the driver seat. I was about to run down to the office for some clean towels anyway, so I'll walk with you. And if I see Robert while I'm there, I'll ask him about lunch."

"Please, do," Beth said, in a way that came across as a desperate plea rather than a casual request. "I'm starving."

....

The office was empty. John had expected to find Catherine tucked away in her corner of the large room, but the rocker sat vacant. The place seemed darker than it had the day before. Save for a few patches of sunlight streaming through the windows and the soft glow from the television, the room was otherwise bleak. The air hadn't improved in here, either. The faint sour odor was now sharper and more pronounced.

John wrinkled his nose at the smell, thinking that something must have died under the crawlspace of the cabin. "Hello?" he called out near the door leading to the living quarters.

No one stirred.

He called out a few more times, his voice steadily increasing in volume, but there was still no answer.

Weird. Why would they have left while there were guests on the premises?

John reckoned the pair might have had cause to go into town, but found it odd that Robert hadn't informed any of them. Come to think of it, neither he nor Catherine had come out to investigate Amy's screams earlier. Surely they would have heard the commotion if they'd been anywhere near the office at the time.

Another thought struck John then. He had been over the grounds several times since arriving, and the only vehicle he recalled seeing was his own. Where did Robert keep his car? He had to have a car, right? This place was too secluded to not have a means of transportation for getting into town.

Not knowing how long the pair would be away, John decided he would try to find the towels himself. He'd taken his last clean one with him on the canoe and had used it to wrap around Amy before he'd carried her back to her cabin. Now he needed a shower, and the small hand towel which remained in his bathroom wasn't going to cut it.

He stepped around the front desk and began opening the cabinets. They were empty, each and every one. Not only that, but they were also filthy; caked with a visible layer of dust and riddled with cobwebs.

"What the hell?"

John rifled through the papers scattered across the counter. The pages were blank; nothing but naked sheets which were brittle and yellowing from age. But how could that be? Where were the reservations Robert had combed through yesterday? And the keys to the other cabins?

At the far end of the counter, another set of papers were stacked. At a glance, these appeared to have something marked on them.

John walked over to investigate. Written in red crayon, and scrawled in the large misshapen penmanship of a child, was a single word: YAUBA. Shuffling through the stack, John discovered that each sheet held the same strange word—YAUBA—written over and over. What did it mean?

Turning to scan the room behind him, John felt something slick under foot. Camp brochures, like those he had seen fanned out on the lobby table the day before, were strewn about the floor. He squatted down and picked one up. Yesterday, he'd only given them a casual glance, but as he studied the one in his hands now, the mystery around him only deepened.

Splashed across the front in bold font, the heading read:

Wrap yourself in the pristine beauty of Crystal Falls.
Where good times await, and adventure is all around you!

Underneath the words, a boy and a girl were posed with their arms around one another, implying that they had become the best of friends over the course of their camping experience. Throughout the rest of the pamphlet, more images depicted the various activities which campers could engage in during their stay. In each, the children and counselors wore smiles as wide as the Grand Canyon, while seeming to have the times of their lives.

That would be the norm for any marketing material meant to entice one to open their wallet and purchase the product or service being advertised. What was odd here, though, were the styles of clothing and the hairdos worn by the subjects in the photographs. The boys had long hair, high-legged shorts, and socks up to their knees, while the girls, some with straight hair parted down the center and others with feathered wing styles, sported flare bottom jeans and strap sandals with high cushion crepe soles—all fashions which were decades old. Why would an active camp still be using brochures that had been created nearly forty years ago?

The front door opened. It was Dagger. "You find the old dude?" he asked.

"No. Something isn't right. Everything is bare. What little I did find is garbage. Other than the television running, it looks as though no one has been back here in years. There's no phone, either. With cell reception sucking the way it does here, you'd think a landline would be a necessity. And check out these brochures. They're ancient."

"Later, man. We've got bigger problems." There was an urgency in Dagger's voice that John rarely ever heard.

"What is it?"

"The bridge is out."

"How can the bridge be out?"

"I don't know, but it is. Come see for yourself."

A bad feeling began to creep over John. Thoughts, like dozens of darts hitting a backboard all at once, pelted his brain. For a few seconds, he could only stand in silent shock. He was anxious to make sense of everything, but right now his thinking was a jumbled mess.

"You coming?" Dagger asked.

The question snapped John back into singular focus. He shoved the brochure into the back pocket of his shorts, hurried across the lobby, and pulled the door shut behind him with more force than he'd intended. The slam rattled the walls and echoed throughout the deserted room.

Moments later, a new sound pierced the empty space. From the small speaker on the television came the jingle of a local news broadcast. The *Station-5* logo faded out and the camera cut to a curvaceous blonde anchor sitting behind a desk.

> *"Good afternoon, this is 5 news at noon, Pamela Sheridan reporting. Following up on the story we first brought you involving the car which was pulled from Shadow Lake early this morning, we have now learned that the vehicle's plates are registered to a Robert Townsend of Grand Rapids, Michigan. Unnamed sources also tell us that identification for both Robert and his wife, Catherine Townsend, was discovered inside the vehicle. When we contacted police chief Franklin Andrews about the case, he said that his office had yet to release any official statement, and that positive identification of the bodies was still pending the coroner's findings. When asked what forms of I.D. had been recovered from inside the vehicle, the police chief had no further comment."*

15

Beth stood on the hill near the observation tower. Yesterday, this spot had proven conducive to good cell phone reception, allowing her to connect to Facebook where she'd been able to read about the devious trickery of Freddy Carter before becoming distracted. What exactly that distraction had been, she could not recall. Nor did she care. The simple fact of the matter was she no longer wanted to be here. And not just up here on the hill, but away from this place entirely.

The bridge they had crossed to enter the camp was no more. The only evidence of it ever existing were the heaps of concrete and twisted rebar resting at the bottom of Cooper Canyon. On top of that, the caretakers had gone missing, the office was in disarray, and the commissary was empty. Whatever food had been stocked there earlier was now gone, with not so much as a slice of bread or a can of soup remaining in the whole place. Even the salt and pepper shakers had been removed.

Dagger had said it would have taken a truck to cart out the number of goods which had been in that kitchen just hours ago, yet no one had heard a vehicle come into the camp, much less seen one. And why would the food have been removed in the first place? If anything, the level of stock should have been increasing with the start of the busy season just around the corner.

Whatever was going on was more than Beth could comprehend. Even John, the most rational one of the group, was at a loss to explain what was happening. For reasons unknown, the group had been abandoned with no easy means of leaving the camp. The best they could hope for now was to be able to reach someone on the outside who could assist in getting them out.

Beth stood on the trail, listening, while scanning the tree line of the forest. She had the distinct sense that she was being watched. That, coupled with the other occurrences of the day, had set her on edge, and she could feel a heavy weight of fear pressing against her, its icy fingers scaling the length of her spine in a slow, agonizing ascension.

There was a visible tremble in her hands as she lifted the cell phone and clicked the button to bring up the screen. A single signal bar was illuminated. Not much to work with, but better than no service at all.

Beth struggled to hold the phone steady while she input her home phone number, hitting a wrong digit on more than one occasion. Once the number had been entered correctly, she punched the green call button and held her breath. The word *CALLING* came up on the screen, while a series of dots flashed in succession behind it.

The seconds ticked by in an insufferable crawl.

"Please!" Beth pleaded.

The word on the screen changed to *CONNECTED* and a call timer began counting.

A small whimper of relief escaped Beth as she moved the phone close to her ear. Several hollow rings later, someone picked up.

"Hello," said a familiar voice.

It was her father. Not since the day he'd carried her out of the field behind their house—and away from the bloody heap of bone and tissue that was once Richie Miller—had she ever been so glad to hear his voice.

"Daddy!" she cried.

"Beth? I didn't expect to hear from you until you got back into town. Is everything alright?"

"No. They left us. We can't get out of here."

"Out of where? Where are you, honey?"

"Shadow Lake. They left us, daddy."

The line clicked and began to fill with static.

"Daddy?"

"Hello? Beth, are you still there?"

"Yes. We're at a camp called Crystal Springs."

"If you're there Beth, I can't hear you."

"I'm here. Help us. Please, daddy."

"I think we have a bad connection. I'll have to call you back."

Beth panicked. If her father got off the line, she feared she wouldn't be able to get him back. In desperation, she scrambled further up the hill.

"Can you hear me? Please, don't go. Help us!"

The line went dead.

"No!" Beth screamed. She tried to redial, but the singular reception bar—all the bars, in fact—were gone. The words *NO SERVICE* now resided in their place.

"What's wrong?" Dagger yelled, peering over the top deck of the observation tower. "No luck?"

Beth appeared ready to burst into tears. "I had my dad on the line for a moment, but I lost him."

"You're doing better than me. I'm not getting shit up here with my phone. Just try him again."

"I did. The service is gone."

"Hmm. Okay, I'll come down and get your phone. If I bring it up here, maybe that'll do the trick." Dagger retreated out of sight, and the faint sounds of footsteps clanging against metal stairs could be heard in the distance.

Beth sat down in the dirt and buried her face in her hands. The clutches of fear were gripping ever tighter, bringing with them an overwhelming hopelessness. Something—whether it was instinct or premonition—told her that they would not be able to dial out again, no matter how many times they tried. She was also certain that no one would be coming for them.

Why was this happening? She thought about the mechanic back at the service station and how she had regarded him as a quack. Now she wished she'd have heeded his words. As it turned out, Eric wasn't the one to be concerned with, as it seemed he had been right in trying to steer them away. Without a doubt, there was something quite wrong with this place.

The cell phone rang then, pulling Beth out of her thoughts with a start. She picked the phone up off the ground and stared at the screen in disbelief. The display read: *HOME*. Without haste, she accepted the call.

"Hello? Daddy? Can you hear me?"

The voice on the other end resonated in a high-pitched squeal. "Daaa-dy. Help me, daddy," it teased.

"Who is this?"

There were several seconds of soft breathing, followed by laughter. It was the sound of a child giggling in amusement. "You know us, silly. We played together yesterday. And we get to play again tonight. Yauba says we can play together forever."

Another chord of fear struck Beth. She didn't know who this child was, yet for some reason thought they had indeed crossed paths. And recently, at that.

But how? And when?

She wanted to dismiss the whole thing as simply a moment of déjà vu, but on a deeper level she suspected it to be more. There was a truth buried in there. How much, she did not know, for she remembered nothing of the meeting. And *that* scared the hell out of her.

"What do you want?" Her voice was softer now, and she tasted the saltiness of tears on her trembling lips.

"You . . . Beth."

"Just leave me alone. *Please*. I just want to go home."

"You are home. And we are going to be friends . . . such good friends."

Beth pulled the phone away from her ear and tried to hang up, but the screen remained lit. She pressed the button several more times to no avail.

When the child spoke again, his voice encompassed a space beyond that of the tiny speaker on the phone, filling the air and swirling about; enveloping Beth in an ethereal dance of whispered chants.

It happened then—that which had been seeded inside of her by virtue of the old woman on the bus, awoke. The dark force was like a living being, yawning and stretching from out of its slumber. Beth could feel the thing squirming beneath her skin; could feel it turning in her belly. She knew she should be terrified, revolted even, but she wasn't. A wave of serenity washed over her, making her feel stronger, purposeful, and more alive.

As the entity eased its way into the driver's seat of her mind and took control, Beth's sense of reasoning relaxed, bit by bit, until her consciousness slipped down into a remote valley of obscurity. There it would remain, independent and unaware of her physical actions, until the thing which possessed her body rescinded control.

The final recollection she had before her free will withered away, was of the hunger—that deep insatiable urge which was now building at an exponential pace, the pangs growing in intensity until they were tenfold what they had been before.

God, the hunger.

Just as the last dying flames of conscious thought were being extinguished, the other voice inside of her spoke. "*I will ease your torment,*" it said, "*. . . and you shall feed. It won't be long, my dear. No, not much longer at all. Now, sleep, Beth.*"

And she did.

16

Landon wadded up the food wrapper and dropped it inside the *Baxter's Burgers* branded paper sack at his feet. As far as hamburgers went, Baxter's made a good one. There was a nice seasoned crust on the thick patty, the buns tasted homemade, and the sweetness from the caramelized onions piled atop a meaty wedge of melted Swiss made for a nice touch. If he had been in the mood for a burger, Landon surmised that it would have been a stellar meal. But he hadn't. His mind was still on the dinner his wife had prepared; a meal he was having to miss because, as was often the case in his line of work, duty had called.

After the grisly find in the water that morning, Landon had spent most of the afternoon tagging and processing evidence, after which he had been tasked with writing a detailed report of the incident. Any of the other officers on the scene could have handled the report, but Frank thought it would be a good experience for the rookie officer. And when you're the new kid on the block, it's never a good idea to argue otherwise.

With the report done and filed, Landon had been looking forward to a nice dinner at home. His wife was making her famous smothered pork chops which, of the many star quality dishes she prepared, just so happened to be his personal favorite. Then, a mere ten minutes prior to the end of his shift, his gastro-fantasies were crushed.

Sheriff Andrews had received a call from a concerned parent in Portland claiming that his teenaged daughter and her three traveling companions were in dire straits. The girl's phone had cut out before she could specify her exact location, and the only thing the worried father knew for certain was that the group was camping somewhere around Shadow Lake. That didn't exactly narrow things down, as there were a plenitude of campgrounds dotting the hills around the expansive lake. That being the case, Andrews had called on every officer to assist with scouring the outlying areas, and Landon found himself once again riding shotgun with his irascible superior officer. At least the man had stopped and bought them both something to eat before heading into the foothills. Though it was no smothered pork chop, it was commendable on the part of the sheriff to have picked up the tab, a fact which was not lost on the young rookie.

"Thank you, sir," Landon said. "I missed lunch today with all that was going on, and breakfast . . . well, we both know what happened there. Didn't realize just how famished I was until I started eating."

Sheriff Andrews nodded. "Sorry about your quiche, kid," he replied in his graveled voice. "I know that must have been a tragic loss for you. Dinner was the least I could do."

Landon could have taken exception to yet another remark about the quiche, but didn't. In the span of only a few days, he was already becoming accustomed to the man, having learned that rarely was there any real contempt behind the sheriff's words. There was a saying: *If you ever want to know if you've gotten fat, ask a child to draw you.* It's funny because everyone knows that kids speak with such blistering honesty. There's no hurtful agenda or malice intended; they just call the world as they see it. And so it was with Frank Andrews. He wasn't trying to be offensive, but in the off chance you were to take exception with something he'd said, he would likely tell you to put on your big boy pants and grow a pair, because the world was no place for sissies.

"Much appreciated. It was very good." Landon smiled.

"Stick with me, kid. I'll point you to all the best grub in town." Frank gave his belly a couple of pats. "This here is a testament to all of the fine cooking in our little burg."

"You mean to tell me there's no six-pack under that jacket?" Landon said. He was teasing, yet maintained his best poker face.

The sheriff glanced over at the officer as if the young man had just told him he'd seen Bigfoot. "Hell, son. I've never had a six-pack in my life, and you know it. I went straight for the keg. Listen, I don't know if you were just being a smart ass or trying to make me feel better about my physical state, but I'm not your wife, so you don't have to dance around your words with me. I'm not the type who'd get in a twist if you said my pants made me look fat. You know why? Because I'm fat. And there's not a pair of pants on this planet that's going to make me look otherwise."

Landon couldn't help but to laugh at the remark. "Noted," he replied. "And yes, I was just being a bit of a smart ass, sir."

"That's alright. I like that in a deputy. Keeps things interesting. Just don't be a dumb ass. If you're a dumb ass we're going to have some problems."

"Of course. I don't think that will be an issue."

"Six-pack," Frank scoffed. "That's rich." The sheriff chuckled once, then turned his attention back to the road and fell silent.

Landon followed suit, watching out the window as the last of the city street lights whizzed by. Before long they were but distant reflections in the side mirror, twinkling like the stars of some far-off galaxy. Moments later, the cruiser coasted around a bend in the road where the grade steepened, becoming a series of twists and turns leading up into the mountains. On the radio, the Stones sang about wanting to paint their world black. When the deputy glanced in the mirror again, it was if Mother Nature had granted them their wish. The lights; the stars, were all gone, and in their place resided only darkness.

17

When Dagger joined his friends around the fire that evening, he was markedly agitated. His hurried gait, along with the dive-bomb method he utilized to drop his ass into one of the folding chairs, were clear indicators of this. The real telltale sign, however, was his silence. Once seated, he proceeded to stare at the campfire without speaking a word.

The mood was already somber prior to his arrival, with John bringing a still groggy Amy up to speed on all that had transpired since her fright in the water. Needless to say, she didn't take the news well (although she was coping better than expected, which John attributed to traces of Ambien still lingering in her system).

After a long silence, Amy broke the ice. "Everything okay?" she asked. "Where's Beth?"

"She's being a bitch. Actually, bitch isn't even the right word. Psycho is more like it. I don't know what's gotten into her. All she wants to do is eat and argue. She's acting weirder by the minute, man. Girl has always had her moods, but nothing like this."

"I've noticed the appetite," John said. "She's been talking nonstop about being hungry. I still can't believe she ate all of that food last night while you were asleep."

"Well, not all of it. She didn't touch the beef jerky. The rest is history, though. Speaking of which, if you guys are hungry we could split the jerky."

John glanced over at Amy. "I'm okay, right now," she answered. "Save my portion for tomorrow?"

John nodded. "Good idea. Same goes for me."

"Right on," Dagger replied. He turned to Amy and asked, "He tell you our plan for getting out of here?"

"Yes. Just before you walked up." Her voice was low and flat, almost melancholy.

"What's the matter? You don't think it will work?"

"Oh, it's not that. I'm sure it will. I just wish we could leave now. I hate the idea of spending another night in this place."

"Wouldn't be a good idea," Dagger replied, pointing up at the sky. "There's no moon tonight. Hell, with these clouds rolling in, you can't even see any stars. If we launched those canoes now, I wouldn't be able to see you if you were two inches from my face."

"Not to mention, with no moon, or anything else to use as a point of reference, we'd have no idea what direction we were headed. We could end up going in wide circles and not even know it," John added. "Better to head out early in the morning when there will be plenty of light."

Amy lowered her gaze and picked at the blanket she sat upon. "I'm just ready to be far away from here."

"I think we all are. I just wish I'd have listened to you yesterday and gone over to Mary's Bend. I'd be willing to lose my deposit three times over if it meant we were out of this mess. All I wanted was for everyone to have a good time. I'm sorry, Ames."

"It's no one's fault. Besides, you asked me if I was okay with staying here, and I said I was. Up until the swim this morning, everything was fine. This sounds crazy, I know, since neither of you found anything in the water, but I would swear by what I saw. There were two boys and a girl. I can remember the clothes they were wearing, the color of their hair, and those faces . . . I can still see those faces. They had to be real.

"The rational part of me says otherwise, of course. Maybe what I saw under the water was nothing. Maybe it was my own anxiety and overactive imagination kicking into overdrive after all the things Catherine talked about. That's what I *want* to believe. But I can't believe it, rational or not, because how do you rationalize any of what's happened today? Something about this place doesn't feel right, and frankly, I'm scared."

"Yeah. I feel it, too." John put an arm around Amy's shoulder and gave it a light squeeze. "It's going to be alright though. Nothing's going to happen to you. I won't let it."

"Oh, gawd!" Dagger groaned. "This is getting out of hand. Either consummate this thing between you two, in which case I'd be happy to watch," he said, with a wry smile, "or let's get this party started."

He reached into the cooler beside his chair and pulled out two beers. Even though most of the ice had melted, the bottles were still good and cold. He extended them towards his friends. "Interest you in a little dinner?"

"I'll bite," John said with a reticent laugh. The previous comment had caught him off guard and he fought to shake off the nervous heat which was creeping into his cheeks.

Dagger tossed the bottles over to John, who caught them and twisted the caps off before handing one over to Amy. When she took it, she smiled one of those mysterious smiles—the type which may have meant something, or nothing at all. John also thought there was a different quality to her eyes when she met his gaze. They appeared softer, more alluring. It was as if they were trying to tell him in their own subtle way that the room option sounded rather appealing, and didn't he agree? Or maybe not. He had always been terrible at reading women, never knowing whether they were trying to say *fuck me* or *fuck off*.

"Now we're talking," Dagger said. He took a long swig and gave a nod of satisfaction. "Let's loosen up and laugh a little.

Forget about that old bat and her crazy talk. There's nothing to be afraid of out here."

As was his fashion, he raised a bottle in the air, offering up a toast which was every bit as unsophisticated and unpretentious as the man himself: "Cheers, bitches!"

....

Beth started with the jerky, ripping into both packages and shoving the dried beef into her mouth by the handfuls. Her breathing was frantic, her pupils were wide, and strands of saliva ran down her chin as she chewed. The meat was good, sending shivers of delight through her body as it slid down her throat and into her stomach. But it wasn't enough to extinguish the fire in her belly.

She needed more.

Much more.

She tore through the grocery bags in search of additional food.

There was none.

In a frenzy, she rummaged through the luggage, tossing the contents of the cases every which way. When she found nothing, she turned her attention to the drawers, opening each and every one in desperation.

Still nothing.

Beth clawed at her face in agony. The hunger was relentless, scorching her insides with its intensity. She began to tear at her clothes, not taking the time to remove them properly, but ripping both seam and fabric as she shed them from her body. When she had finished, she fell upon the bed, screaming like a petulant child in the heat of a tantrum. That was when she saw Dagger's knife resting on the nightstand.

She sat up on the edge of the bed, picking up the oversized pocketknife and turning it over in her hands several times before prying it open. The cold steel gleamed under the light from the table lamp. Beth ran a finger along the sharp blade in one long, contemplative stroke until she reached the curved tip. Without hesitation, she jabbed the knife into her skin. The gasp which followed sounded more like a cry of ecstasy rather than one of pain. She watched with morbid fascination as blood trickled down her palm and splashed onto her bare thigh. The full measure of what she was meant to do dawned on her then, and a wide smile spread across her face. She clicked off the lights and retreated into the small space between the nightstand and the corner of the room.

Huddled in the darkness, Beth bounced the tip of the knife up and down her leg. Not hard enough to break the skin, but with enough force to feel the sting from each stick. The pain was a welcome distraction, helping to take her mind off the hunger. She turned her thoughts to Dagger and his imminent return. Once he arrived, everything would be alright. Oh, yes, it would. All she had to do was wait just a little bit longer.

And then . . .

The very idea of what was to come made her delirious with excitement, so much so that she fell into a state of arousal. In the cover of darkness, she slipped one hand between her legs, letting her fingers glide over the thin strip of manicured pubic hair to the smooth, wet skin just beyond. She pictured herself straddling Dagger, her mouth on his naked body, and a soft moan escaped her.

"Come to me. Come to me, now," she whispered, licking her lips in sweet anticipation.

....

"Okay, tell me another one," Amy said through a burst of laughter. "I can't believe I've known you guys all of my life and have never heard these stories."

"Maybe because most of them are too embarrassing," John replied.

While there was some truth to his statement, it was of no consequence. He'd swallowed his pride once before for Amy's sake, and was more than willing to do it again if it kept her in good spirits. And really, what story could possibly trump the pickles and onions debacle during his night of passion with Cindy Wilson? Not a one. At least none that he could think of now.

"I don't know," Amy said. "I think they are funny more than anything else. Besides, we've embarrassed ourselves in front of each other countless times before. Especially when we were kids."

"This is true." John agreed. He thought for a minute and said, "Did you hear about the time Dagger and I were on the flight to Cancun? That was spring break of last year, I believe, when the pilot forgot to shut off the intercom after his take-off announcement."

Amy shook her head. "I don't think so. I was sick then, remember? I had to spend the week in bed with the flu while you two jetted off to paradise without me."

Dagger raised his hands as if he'd just had a revelation. "Dude! I forgot about that. Not the trip, just what happened on the ride over. That whole week was a blast. Sucks that you missed out, Amy. If it makes you feel better, we thought about you an awful lot while we were there."

"Sure you did. I bet you were all kinds of broken up. Which explains why I didn't hear from anyone the entire time." Amy smirked.

John rubbed the nape of his neck and grimaced, looking like a boy whose mother just caught him in the cookie jar right before dinner. "Sorry about that, Ames. We might have had a bit too much to drink. I'm surprised we remember as much as we do."

"I'm just giving you crap," Amy smiled. As if to validate her statement, she gave John several quick pats on the knee. "So, tell me what happened on the plane."

"Okay. After take-off, the pilot made his usual announcement, but forgot to shut off the microphone when he was finished. He starts talking to the co-pilot and says to him, *"You know what I could use right now?"* The co-pilot answers, *"What's that?"* And the pilot comes back with . . . are you ready for this? *"A cup of coffee and a blowjob."*

Amy's eyes widened with surprise. "Seriously? Oh, my God! I can only imagine the reactions on the passengers' faces." She was laughing now.

"Oh, but wait. It gets better," John said. "One of the flight attendants goes rushing down the aisle towards the cockpit, presumably to get to the captain to turn off his mic before he says something even worse. Anyway, as she passes us, Dagger yells after her, loud enough for the entire plane to hear, *"Hey, miss. Don't forget the coffee!"*

"No way!" Amy shrieked. She nearly fell over laughing, barely able to keep a grip on the bottle in her hand.

Dagger and John were laughing as well, with Dagger looking proud of himself for coming up with such a clever remark on that day. "That gal wasn't so thrilled with my comment. I got the stink-eye later when she served the drinks. And she more or less threw the bag of peanuts at me."

There were tears streaming from the corners of Amy's eyes. Her face was bright red and she clutched her side. "Oh, stop. It hurts!" she tried to say, although it came out as more of a wheeze. This was followed by a snort, which only made her—and the guys—laugh all the harder.

A few minutes later, after the belly laughs had tempered, Amy fanned her face with her hand and wiped at her eyes. "I can guarantee you I'll never forget that story. Probably still be telling it when I'm old."

"That's for sure," John said. "Although not around the grandkids."

"Maybe when they're grown," Dagger replied. "But let's not jump so far ahead. I can't even imagine myself with kids right now, let alone grandkids." He shuddered.

"That makes two of us." Amy added. "Can you picture a bunch of little Daggers running around?"

"Heaven help us," John said.

Dagger dropped his spent bottle back into the cooler and stood up to leave. "Hey, at least you know they would be handsome little bastards. Anyway, I'm going to go check on

Beth and see what kind of fresh hell awaits me. Who knows, maybe she'll feel like coming down and joining the party.

"Yes, tell her to come hang out. She's missing all the fun," Amy replied.

"I will. But if I'm not back in the next fifteen minutes or so, that means she's still in major bitch mode. If that's the case, I'll spare you the agony and stay away." He motioned toward the cooler. "Plenty of beverage left in there, so you guys enjoy."

"Thanks. I wish you luck, my friend." John waved. "See you bright and early?"

Dagger gave a tip of his head and a mock salute, then turned and stumbled up the hill. Midway up the rocky path, an old number by the rock band KISS—aptly titled, *Beth*—popped into his head. *Oh, the irony* he thought, and started belting out the words to the popular ballad.

A short time later, still laughing and crooning, Dagger navigated the narrow steps leading to his darkened cabin. Unaware of the impending danger looming within its walls, he opened the front door and stepped inside.

18

Amy lay back on the blanket, peering up at the starless night and marveling at just how much wonder and romanticism were lost when a sky was void of its celestial bodies. The very presence of such trivial thoughts, she realized, was a testament to how much good the time spent telling stories around the campfire had done for her. The unrest which had crept into her upon learning that she and her friends were stranded at the camp without food—and no signs of Robert or Catherine—was nothing but a faint glimmer in the back of her mind now. It could (and probably would) return at some point, but between the bouts of laughter and the numbing effects of the alcohol, right now she was content. And content felt wonderful.

“Do you think we'll laugh about this someday?” she asked.

“God, I hope so,” John replied. “It'll be one for the books, that's for sure. Not many can say they went to camp and ran off the directors. I blame Dagger.”

Amy laughed. “Well, who wouldn't? If anyone were to guess which of us was most capable of scaring them away, he'd be the obvious choice.” She laughed again, briefly, and sat up. “Do you think he and Beth are going to be okay?”

“Oh, I imagine so. I mean, she's the only one who could put up with him for longer than a month. And she calls him out on his bullshit, which is exactly what he needs. Even during their rough patches he's never strayed. That's a big deal for a guy who was never a fan of monogamy. I remember him saying once that he'd already sown more oats than the Quaker Oats man. That was an exaggeration, since we were only twelve at the time, but still—"

Amy was smiling. "Seeing as how the Quaker guy is a Puritan, or something along those lines, I don't think that's much of a brag. Pretty sure the only oats he ever sowed were the ones going in the box."

"Good point," John said. "He may not admit it, but I believe that son of a bitch has gone and fallen in love."

Amy fell back onto the blanket. "Love," she resounded, in a tone that was anything but amorous.

"Sorry, Ames. I didn't mean to open a wound."

"It's fine. I'm happy for Dagger. If he does love her, and I think he might, then I wish him nothing but the best. Just because my story had a bad ending doesn't mean his will. Wouldn't it be an ironic twist of fate if the one member of our group, whose biggest desire in life was to sow his oats, ended up being the person with the happily ever after?"

John took a swill of beer and nodded. "Just like Cinderella."

"No, not at all." Amy raised up, took the bottle from John, and swallowed several long gulps. When she finished, she wiped her mouth with the back of her hand and said, "I was thinking more along the lines of Beauty and the Beast."

She met John's eyes, which were already twinkling with amusement, and the pair doubled over with laughter.

....

The lights were out inside the cabin, with the only illumination coming from a trio of pillar candles burning on the nightstand. The small flames appeared to tremble, sending up little curls of black smoke which disappeared into an even blacker room.

"I've been waiting for you."

Dagger knew the voice well. And based on the tone, had a good idea of what was about to occur. His eyes moved from the candles to the shadowy figure hiding in the corner of the room. He watched, transfixed, as Beth rose from her seated posture. She was naked.

Hands behind her back, head cocked sheepishly to the side, she hunched her shoulders as if to beg the question: *What do you think?*

The soft, flickering candlelight bathed every curve of her body in warm golden tones, and Dagger's eyes darted from her breasts to her hips, and back again, like he was seeing her without clothes for the very first time.

"My night just got a hell of a lot better," he said.

"I've been waiting for so long," Beth cooed. She pulled one hand from behind her back and ran an index finger in little circles around the raised nipple of her left breast.

Dagger's mouth hung agape, and he stood as motionless as if he'd been carved out of marble. Beth never did this sort of thing. Not that she wasn't ever adventurous in the sack (she could always give him a good run), but stripteases and playing with herself were not her usual idea of foreplay. She was a bit more modest, leaving the touching of her body to him.

Beth dropped the finger from her breast and ran it down along her naval, causing her stomach muscles to quiver. She tossed her head back and loosed a gasp of pleasure.

Dagger felt himself getting hard. He watched as Beth's finger continued south, where it played over the smooth, glistening mound between her legs. Even in the dim light he could see that she was wet, and this aroused him even more.

"Do you want me, baby?" Her voice was honey.

"You better believe I do." Dagger moved in Beth's direction, but she held up a hand and motioned for him to stop. He did.

"Take off your shirt," she said in her silken voice.

She didn't have to ask twice. Dagger reached hand over hand, grabbing the bottom hem of his shirt and pulling it up over his head. He tossed it to the floor amidst the rest of the contents of their luggage, which he had failed to notice was scattered about the room.

Beth stared at his chiseled torso and licked her lips in a slow, deliberate manner. "Now, take off those pants and lie down on the bed."

Dagger let out a shuddered breath. "Damn, Beth. I don't know what's gotten into you, but this is hot. *You're* hot. So fuckin' hot!"

Beth's lips parted in a sultry smile. There was wanting in her eyes. "Hurry, baby. I want to feel you," she moaned. "I want to . . . taste you."

Dagger kicked off his shoes and undid his pants, sliding them down with his boxers and freeing his erection.

Beth moved away from the wall, keeping one hand behind her back to conceal what she hid there. She walked over to Dagger, rocking her hips from side to side. Once she reached him, she brought her face close, as if she were going in for a kiss. When her lips were almost touching his, she turned away, running the tip of her tongue along his cheek and up along his ear. The sensation drove Dagger wild.

"Now, lie down," she whispered.

He perched on the edge of the mattress and tugged the pants from around his ankles, letting them fall to the ground before lying back on the bed.

Beth hovered over him now. Strands of damp strawberry-tinted hair hung across her forehead. Dagger could make out the perfumed aroma of the shampoo she had showered with, and felt moisture emanating from her still balmy skin. She studied him with rapturous eyes the color of the Caribbean seas.

Dagger saw something else in those eyes as well. Something wild, almost feral. Desire, perhaps? Whatever it was, it raged deep; an all-consuming passion which shone through her baby blues like fire and ice. He lifted his head to kiss her, but she pushed back, pinning him to the bed with a strength which surprised even him.

That turned him on, notching up his excitement to another level. Every inch of his body burned with a desire so intense that he was on the verge of begging her to take him.

As if she had heard his thoughts, Beth reached down and gripped his member in her hand. It throbbed against her palm, keeping time with the rapid drum beat of his heart.

Dagger arched his back and drew a salacious breath at her touch.

Beth climbed upon the bed and straddled her boyfriend's naked body. She worked her hand up and down his shaft a few times before placing him inside of her.

An exhilarating warmth enveloped Dagger as his girlfriend began to grind, inviting him to go deeper. Once he was all the way in, she tightened. Already in a heightened state of arousal, it was all he could do not to come. He placed his hands upon Beth's hips, feeling a thin layer of perspiration on her skin, and watched her small, firm breasts bounce with every back and forth gyration.

The joining of her body with his own was intoxicating. Dagger closed his eyes, keenly aware of Beth's every sensual movement. Without conscious thought, his own body responded in kind, synchronizing his thrusting with her downward strokes.

Something about this tryst was different compared to their previous unions. The way Beth spoke, the forceful, almost carnal, way in which she moved, and the sheer level of passion she exhibited were deeply erotic. He felt as if the moment were transcendent, going beyond the physical to something much deeper; almost spiritual. It was, in his opinion, pure heaven.

Then came the pain.

It rushed in like a whirlwind, turning his brief glimpse of heaven into a boundless hell.

Dagger's eyes flew open. He saw the handle of a knife—his knife—poking out from between his ribs. At first, his brain refused to accept what he was seeing, and several seconds passed before the realization came that the blade was buried beneath skin and tissue.

In a panic, he tried to sit up, but sharp stabbing pangs knocked him back down. Sheer and absolute in torment, the affliction branded him, much like someone ripping open his chest and shoveling hot coals inside. He gasped for air, but found little. Adrenaline surged through his body, quickening his pulse. This only exacerbated the pain, with the knife seeming to slice deeper into his heart with each frenzied beat.

His gaze found Beth, still sitting on top of him; the feral quality of her stare now more pronounced. Where her eyes were typically soft and vulnerable, exhibiting kindness under a thin veil of unspoken insecurities, they now teemed with a wicked ferocity. Hard and emotionless, they pulsated with an unquenchable thirst for blood. They were no longer Beth's eyes at all, but the cold, unfeeling eyes of a predator killing its prey.

Dagger tried to speak, but all he could muster was a thin gurgle. He wanted to cry out for help, but it was too late for that. His expression was one of pain, shock and disbelief; his face resonated with suffering, both physical and emotional. He wanted to know why. Wanted to know how the girl he loved—and who had claimed to love him in return—could be capable of such a heinous act.

Dagger began to thrash about, his head snapping back in a desperate struggle for breath. The veins in his neck bulged and his face turned a dark shade of purple. He coughed, expelling a shower of blood which spattered across Beth's face.

She smiled.

Why? Dear, God, why?

The agony was spreading now, radiating up through his shoulders and down his back. He gripped the sheets until his knuckles were as white as the fabric he held onto. Little by little, the fight ebbed out of his body as precious lifeblood flowed from the wound and soaked the mattress beneath him.

The room became a blur. Ice was settling into his bones. His pulse slowed to a crawl.

The pain was leaving him, but he was cold . . . so very cold.

Beth leaned in close, running her lips alongside Dagger's face until they were poised just above his ear. "I am Yauba," she whispered, "and I am Windigo." She dropped her head, letting her lips graze his neck until they found the soft cleft just above the clavicle.

Dagger's fitful breathing shifted into a languid series of jagged wheezes. His pupils started to dilate, the pale brown irises giving way to wide, dark circles, as the light within them began to tarnish. With darkness creeping in, Dagger acknowledged the fate which had befallen him. A single tear escaped the corner of one eye and rolled down his cheek. Death, he knew, was at hand. His body twitched once before falling slack, yet there was still a thread of life in him when Beth opened her mouth wide and began to eat.

. . . .

The wood crackled and popped, creating a spray of glowing embers that danced about in the summer night like fireflies. The laughter and conversation which had ruled most of the evening had waned over the last few minutes, and now a comfortable afterglow of silence had settled in, leaving the close friends to their own thoughts.

Amy stared into the flames. She was growing tired and her thoughts had begun to drift, sliding into the same listless state as her body. "We were never going to make it," she mumbled.

"What's that?" John asked.

"I'm sorry. I'm sleepy, and starting to think out loud. Walk me back to my room? I can tell you on the way."

"Sure," John replied. He stood and extended a hand to help Amy up. Once she was on her feet, he walked over to the cooler, flipped open the top, and carried it to the campfire, where he doused the wood with a generous splash of cold water. The burning logs hissed in protest. John couldn't blame them. After all, he'd have done the same had it been him on the receiving end of an unexpected ice bath. With the flames extinguished, the pair found themselves in utter darkness.

Amy giggled. "This is going to be interesting."

"Damn. I didn't think this one through, did I? Hold your arms out in my direction. I'll do the same and walk towards you until we find each other."

John stumbled along, swinging his outstretched arms left and right while groping at the air. After several verbal cues—and more than a few laughs along the way—their arms collided, and Amy slid her palm down John's forearm until she found his hand. She entwined her fingers with his and clutched tight.

John's expression was one of pure bliss. What had started as an embarrassing gaff now seemed a happy accident. It would take a bit more time to reach the cabins under such ill-lit conditions, but now that Amy's hand was in his, John didn't mind if it took all night. With the utmost care, he led her away from their spot near the water's edge, and the two of them started up the trail.

"As I was saying," Amy continued after several steps, "we were never going to make it, Scott and I. If I'm being honest, I think some small part of me always knew that, but I was too wrapped up in my feelings to see it. The thing is, Scott never had the same devotion to me that I had for him. I was just a pretty face in his little corner of the world, and now that his world is about to get much bigger, he'll find another, possibly even prettier, face to stroke his ego and give him what he wants, whenever he wants it. He made me feel important for so long, and I interpreted that as love on his part. But, it never was, was it? I can see that now, but it doesn't ease the loneliness. I hate the thought of being alone."

"You'll find someone, Ames. Girls like you are never alone. At least, not for long anyway."

John could tell by the way Amy squeezed his hand that his words had found their mark.

"And what about you?" she asked. "When will you stop being alone?"

"Whenever I can learn to talk to a girl without looking like an idiot, I suppose."

"I don't think you have any problem making conversation. Besides, you talk to me all the time."

"That's different." John refuted. "I've known you almost my entire life."

"Maybe so. But every relationship starts with a hello. Ours was no different. And trust me, we all say stupid stuff at times. I'm probably the queen of sticking my foot in my mouth. Even you should know that. You've just gotta shrug it off and keep going."

John sighed. "I know, but when you're shy, that's not so easy. I've made some strides, but it's still a struggle making new friends. Couple that with the pressure of asking a girl out, and I'm a real disaster. Even when people know I'm shy, it seems most of them don't want to take the time to break through my walls. Starting a new school is going to be a real joy. Come senior year, I'll be bald from anxiety."

"No," Amy lamented, "It won't be that bad. College is a lot different than high school. Find a group or club that appeals to you and, voila! Their shared interest becomes an instant topic of conversation. Before you know it, you'll have friends almost as cool as me."

That made John grin. "New friends? Maybe. As cool as you? Never! People like you are few and far between."

"Thanks, J. I'm glad we could agree on that." Amy leaned over and gave John a playful nudge. His grin grew wider.

"We can always agree on that count. You are, as my grandfather used to say, a bona fide original."

"Oh? And that means what exactly?"

It means you're legit," John replied. "The real deal. Authentic. Genuine. One of a kind. Should I go on?"

"Please do. It's working wonders on my self-esteem," Amy giggled.

John was laughing now. "That's good. It worked for my grandmother's as well."

"Your grandmother was a lucky lady."

"I think my grandfather would say it was the other way around. I had to ask him what bona fide meant the first time I heard him use the word. He told me that bona fide people were the best of the best. They were the ones that you could be yourself with; the ones you could tell your deepest secrets to without fear of judgement. They possess the biggest hearts of all, always bringing out the best in others. He compared them to a lighthouse in the storm, saying if you spent enough time in their presence, you'd find that you could tackle anything life threw at you with grace. They are the ones you can't ever imagine having to live without, he told me, and if you are lucky enough to find such a soul, your life will be infinitely better for it."

"That's beautiful." Amy said. "Your grandfather sounds like a wise man."

"He was." John nodded. "He was both wise and lucky. I realized I'm lucky also, because you are all the things he spoke of. You're that person for me, Ames. You're my lighthouse."

With the words out of his mouth, John was surprised by their candor. Perhaps it had been Amy's own openness which made him want to be equally forthcoming. Or perhaps the time was simply right for saying what needed to be said.

Amy came to a halt. She turned to the dark form beside her and took his other hand.

"I think that's the sweetest thing anyone has ever said to me."

In the blackness, John could make out the dark outlines of the cabins just ahead, yet was unable to see the wistful expression on Amy's face, nor the tears which were budding in her eyes. He lowered his head and muttered a sincere word of thanks. "It's true. All of it."

"It's true for me as well. You know that, right?" She tightened her grip on his hands and gave them a gentle shake.

In that moment, John wanted to tell Amy that he loved her; had for a very long time now, but still his words, and his nerve, failed him. What she asked him next, however, was something he never could have expected: "Why didn't you ever ask me out?"

Surprised by the question, John went rigid. He tried to speak, but stumbled over his words.

"Come on." Amy prodded. "I know you have feelings for me. I've known for a long time now. A girl can tell these things."

A barrage of words rumbled through John's mind like a freight train running at full throttle. He just hoped the train wouldn't derail once he opened his mouth to speak.

"I guess I was afraid. Not just that you would say no, but of what it might do to our friendship if things didn't pan out. I never wanted to jeopardize that, so even though I'd hoped it could be more, I told myself that having you as my best friend was better than not having you at all. But, since we're being completely honest here, I never thought Cindy Wilson hung the moon. It was you all along. It was always you."

There. It was out. *Finally!*

Although John felt a deep sense of relief over letting go of the secret which he'd kept locked inside of himself for years now—something which, as it turns out, was no secret at all to Amy—he was still holding his breath over what her reaction might be. Would she reciprocate, telling him that she, too, had loved him all along? *God, wouldn't that be something?* Or would she say what he'd always imagined she would—that as much as she cared for him, and thought he was a great guy, she didn't . . .

Amy's mouth met his then, and the rambling voice inside his head fell silent, allowing him to focus solely on the kiss. Mouth slightly agape, Amy pressed against him with lips that were gentle, yet firm. They were moist with lip balm, the candy-coated sweetness of which permeated John's senses. She exhaled, slow and purposeful, and when she did, a small, fervent moan escaped the back of her throat. It was all enough to send John into outer space.

Was this really happening? The thought that this might be nothing more than a grand dream from which he could awaken from at any moment did cross his mind. He knew better, though, because his dreams were never this lucid. Nor had they ever been this good, come to think of it.

When Amy pulled away, John was still in orbit. Speaking in her softest voice, she said, "Maybe you should have."

With that, she slipped her hands from around his and took a step back. "Anyway, I'm feeling tired, and I should probably sleep since we have to get an early start in the morning. Thank you for tonight. I had a lot of fun."

"Yeah, me too."

"Goodnight, John."

Even though he was still unable to make out her features, John could hear the smile in Amy's voice. He smiled back, dimples and all. "Night, Ames."

She was halfway up the stairs leading to her cabin when he called after her. "All of this time . . . would you have really said yes?"

"I've got some things I need to work through right now. But, once I have, maybe you should find out."

Amy bid goodnight again and left John where he was standing. His cheek remained damp from her tears, while the taste of berry lip balm lingered on his mouth. He touched his tongue to his lips while he replayed the kiss several times over in his mind.

I think she likes me. By God, I think she likes me!

He ascended the stairs and crossed the front porch with a snap in his step, feeling more alive than ever. With all the endorphins and excitement coursing through his body, John wondered if he would find sleep at all this night. In the end, he decided it didn't matter. Tomorrow was the start of a new day, and with it came the very real possibility of a future with Amy.

19

They began their search on the far eastern end of Black Water Pass, investigating a campsite situated just across the county line in Mary's Bend. While the resort was technically not a part of his jurisdiction (even though it billed itself as being a part of Shadow Lake), Frank decided it was worth a look, due to the camp's proximity to their location. Having found nothing there, the officers continued their search in earnest, following the pass through the mountains which would bring them back to the western edge of Shadow Lake.

A few miles into the journey, they passed a small green sign signaling a return to their home territory of Montgomery County. At about the same time, a glossy piece of bubblegum pop exploded across the airwaves, eliciting a string of colorful words from the sheriff. He reached over and punched a button on the radio to select another station.

"Not your cup of tea?" Landon asked.

"Sure, if I took my tea with a lump of shit. You like this garbage?"

"Not particularly."

"Good. I might have to wonder about you otherwise. The stuff on the radio these days flat out stinks, Stephens. They start with turds, polish them up, give them a coat of paint, even bedazzle them, but it doesn't change the fact that they're still turds. Now the greats like Zeppelin, Pink Floyd, The Who, Aerosmith, Queen; even the Beatles—what those guys created back then, *that* was music. None of those bands sounded the same and that was the beauty of it. They created their own sound. Granted, most of them didn't have the sort of face worthy of the cover of Teen Beat like these pop stars today, but no one cared, because they had talent. Hell, I can think of a few who were about as handsome as my uncle's ass, but do you think they ever had a problem getting laid?"

"Doubtful, sir," Landon said.

"I'm certain these kids on the radio now don't have that problem either, because they look like they were created in Photoshop," Frank continued, "but most of them couldn't write a song or play an instrument to save their life. The record companies just produce a bunch of synthesized cookie cutter shit and then find some no-talent teen masturbatory fantasy to sell it for them. It's a damn travesty, I tell you."

Landon remained quiet, letting a couple of seconds pass before speaking. Another thing he knew about the sheriff was, when the man got on a rant, it was often impossible to squeeze a word in until he'd climbed off his soapbox. The deputy found these frequent—and always impassioned—outbursts to be quite amusing, especially given the trivial nature of their source: the price of a cup of black coffee was nearing two dollars, Twinkies didn't taste the same as they did before Hostess sold out, some tabloid reported that Dolly Parton had decided to get a breast reduction, and so on. Landon couldn't even fathom what would happen if Mabel's ever went under and the sheriff could no longer get his old-fashioned. But what was one to do? Frank was the way he was, and all you could do was sit back and enjoy the show . . . for however long it may last.

"Well, sir," Landon said, clearing his throat. "I think rock and roll has always been geared toward the young since its inception. The groups you mentioned were hot when you were growing up, but for me, it was bands like Nirvana, Pearl Jam, and the Smashing Pumpkins. My parents hated them, yet loved the rock bands of their youth. It's a cycle; the way it has always been and probably always will be. Having said that, I do see your point. The bands I just mentioned, like them or not, still made their own music. The manufactured pop of today is pretty awful."

Frank exhaled a hearty grunt. "You're a good man, Stephens."

"Thank you, sir." Landon grinned. He directed his attention back to the long stretch of blacktop ahead just in time to see the cruiser speed past a road on their left. "Shouldn't we check down there?"

"No need," Frank answered. "You won't find anything but potholes and a collapsed bridge. A camp existed there once, but there was a bit of an incident during their second summer in business. That was back in the late seventies. Place was shuttered and hasn't operated since."

"Must have been a pretty serious incident."

"One of the town's worst. A bus carrying a bunch of kids left the camp one evening and never made it back to town. They found the bus a couple of miles down that road, but no one was on it. The initial hunch was that it had broken down and the lot of them were trekking back to the camp on foot. But it hadn't, and they weren't. The engine fired right up, and not a one of those kids was ever seen again. They never found the driver either."

"That's a bit alarming," Landon said. His eyes were wide, and one could see the cogs of his mind turning beneath them. "How do that many people just disappear into thin air? Did they have any leads?"

"I don't believe so. That was before my time here. And you must remember that, back then, forensics were about as useful as reading glasses to a blind man. We had fingerprints and ballistics, but DNA profiling was still a few years away. It's a shame, really. If they'd had those techniques at their disposal, they might have found those kids. At the very least, they could have shown foul play on the part of a real person and kept all the superstitious nut jobs from claiming the witch was behind it all."

Landon's eyes stretched open even wider. "The witch?" he cried out. "You have an insane asylum, people committing suicide by spontaneously driving into the lake, and now witches also? What kind of town is this?"

"It sure as shit isn't Mayberry, son. What were you expecting?"

"I don't know. Something a little less like Salem's Lot?"

"Not to worry. We don't have any vampires around here. Not even any of them sparkling ones." Frank wiggled his fingers for added effect.

"Are you sure about that?"

The sheriff nodded. "Fairly. But listen, regardless of all the stories swirling about, I don't buy into any of it. Just an old legend that people won't let die. Every weird or tragic event that crops up, people want to start blaming it on some old hag that's been dead for over a hundred years. I suppose that's easier than facing the truth."

"Which is what?" Landon asked.

"That people are just bat shit crazy. Don't ask me why. I'm a transplant just like you. Maybe it's genetic. A bunch of folks who were light in the head settled this area way back when and have been making generations of crazies ever since. Or, perhaps they've been using the legend as a bedtime story for their children. Poor little tykes lying there in the dark and pissing themselves over every sound in the night, thinking that old witch is coming for them, until finally their fragile minds snap like twigs. Who knows? Thank God it's not something in the water, or we'd all be up in that asylum."

"So who was she? The witch, I mean," Landon asked.

"She was a spiritualist; a member of one of the indigenous Native American tribes that used to call this area home. The locals often refer to her as the lost lady of the lake. I'm not sure if anyone knew her real name outside of her own people, but she was called Yauba. And because I know you're going to ask, Yauba is an Indian word which translates to devil," Frank remarked. He glanced over at his deputy and raised an eyebrow.

"She sounds lovely so far," Landon replied, his mouth turning up in a sarcastic grin.

"I think the opposing tribes and the homesteaders of that time might disagree. One of the first mentions of Yauba came from a group of Chilwitz Indians. They rode into the Chinook camp one day while the men were away on a hunt and made off with some of their women. The next morning, the Chilwitz found every one of their warriors hanging by their wrists from the trees at the edge of the forest. They had been skinned from head to toe and their eyes plucked out of their sockets. The Chinook women they had captured were gone as well, reclaimed by their own."

"Who's to say that the Chinook didn't send their own men over in the cover of night to recapture their women and take out those who'd made off with them?" Landon asked.

"Logic would dictate that, yes. But, allegedly, the Chilwitz had scouts posted around the camp all night who swore they saw no one enter or leave. They did hear things, however—wails and screams coming from within the forest. They believed it to be a dark cannibalistic creature known as a Windigo. These people were a superstitious bunch, and finding their men in the condition they did the next morning served as confirmation of their beliefs. Supposedly, skinned bodies and missing eyeballs were a part of this thing's M.O."

"If this monster was their suspect, how does that implicate the old woman and make her the devil?"

Sheriff Andrews studied the deputy with a hard look. His eyes narrowed and the corners of his mouth briefly twitched upwards. It was the closest thing Landon had seen to a smile since he'd started working with the man.

"Thinking like a true detective, Stephens. Remember, this woman was a spiritualist and, if you believe the stories about her, a very powerful one at that. These tribes came to believe that she could become the Windigo or, at the very least, had the ability to summon it to do her bidding. Either way, they soon learned not to trifle with her or her people."

"Interesting," Landon replied. "I suppose she wasn't such a lovely woman after all. I'm still curious as to how she factors into any of the terrible events that occur in the here and now?"

Frank grunted. "That's where the story gets gruesome. Legend has it that a group of men from Shadow Lake were out scouting the woods one afternoon and came across a young Native American girl collecting water. They had their way with her, the whole lot of them. Passed her back and forth like a bottle of cheap whiskey. Only fourteen, she was."

Landon was horrified. "Dear, God," he whispered, his mouth going dry. "And we called *them* savages. Seems to me it was mostly the other way around."

"You're not wrong about that, son," the sheriff said. "They should have hung for it, and knew they likely would if anyone back in town were to find out what they'd done. Afraid the girl might talk, they bashed her head in with a rock, threw her body in the water, and went back home to their families as if nothing had happened."

"How people can do a thing like that I will never understand. It makes me sick to my stomach. I'm guessing they got found out then?"

"That they did. But not by the people of Shadow Lake. It was Yauba who knew. Now, I don't know how she knew, but she did. See, that girl was her daughter; her one and only child. And if you thought what happened to those tribesmen was bad, it was nothing compared to what was about to come down the pike. Problem is, the witch didn't just exact revenge on those men, but on the entire town."

"Sins of the fathers," Landon said.

"Exactly," Frank replied. "And it's those sins that some believe are the reason for everything bad that happens in this town."

"That answers that. I'm a little afraid to ask what happened to those men."

"As I'm sure you can guess; it didn't end well. They were found strung up in a woodshed, cut open stem to stern and gutted like hogs. Well, two of them were. They got a good cut on the third but didn't finish the job. Must have heard someone coming and split. Didn't matter though. The truth came out. And when it did, it was ugly. Seems it was their own kids that did it to them."

"Are you kidding me?" Landon asked.

"Nah. One of the men, the one who hadn't been disemboweled yet, still had a bit of life in him when he was discovered. He claimed the kids had done it. But he didn't lay the blame on them. Said it was the witch that made them do it. Claims she was there when it happened, watching from the doorway."

Landon shook his head. "Quite a story," he remarked.

"Oh, it doesn't end there. That same evening, the town awoke to find the schoolhouse ablaze . . . and every child old enough to walk burning up inside of it. Crazy part is, the doors weren't latched from the outside, so those kids could have let themselves out at any time. But they didn't. It was as if they'd collectively decided to leave their beds in the middle of the night, barricade themselves inside the schoolhouse and set the building on fire, all of their own free will. Like a mass suicide. But you ever hear of children committing mass suicide? Hell of a thing."

"And all of this really happened?" Landon asked.

"So it would seem. The murders of those men and the school fire are documented in the town's historical records. The only mention of the witch, however, is in the transcript of the dying man's last words. Most of what we know of her is pure legend."

"How is it then the people knew about the young girl that those men raped and killed? They were all dead before they could confess, right?"

"They were, yes. Story goes that the tribal chief met with the leaders of the town and told them about the girl. Said Yauba had been angered. The deaths of the three men, he claimed, was punishment from the great spirits, while those of the town's children were Yauba's own vengeance. The chief went on to nullify the peace treaty and made an ultimatum: the inhabitants of Shadow Lake would agree to pack up and abandon the land, in which case Yauba would allow them to leave in peace, or stay and face her wrath."

"I guess it goes without saying, they chose to stay," Landon said.

"Not only that, but the men of the town banded together, pulling in reinforcements from nearby settlements. They attacked the tribe, killing nearly everyone, including the chief. The witch fled into the mountains and the men followed. They cornered her at the edge of Crystal Falls, intending to capture and do God-knows-what before killing her. She wasn't about to let that happen. Old gal threw herself over the falls, but not before cursing the town of Shadow Lake and all of its descendants."

Landon nodded, considering all the sheriff had just told him. "Now I get why people want to blame the unexplainable on the witch. You'd think it would have ended with her death, though. Unless, of course, the people were ruled by superstition."

"I'm sure that accounts for most of it, coupled with the fact that they never found Yauba's body. Those men traveled to the bottom of the falls and searched the river below, presumably still hell bent on committing violence upon her corpse, but found nothing. Not long after, strange and deadly occurrences began to vex the town. Of course, that's all conjecture based on stories that have been passed down for generations. How much is true is up for debate. If you ask me," the sheriff scoffed, "that's probably little to none."

"You think so?" Landon asked. "I mean, from what I've already seen and heard, there are an awful lot of bizarre goings on around here."

Frank shot a perturbed look in the young officer's direction. "Don't tell me you buy into all of this hocus-pocus supernatural bullshit, Stephens."

"I don't know," the deputy replied, unfazed by the sheriff's annoyed demeanor. "I've had an experience or two in my own life that I can't explain. I'm a God-fearing man, sir, and I believe there are things out there which are beyond the realm of what we can see with the naked eye."

"I see where you're going," the sheriff replied. "And despite what you might think, I'm no heathen. My momma, rest her soul, raised me to believe in the Almighty also, which is all the more reason I *don't* believe some crazy witch is running around with the power to wreak havoc on whomever she pleases."

Landon could see the cords beginning to strain in the sheriff's neck and knew if an argument ensued that an eruption the likes of Mount St. Helens was imminent. Not one to back down from a debate, the young deputy continued to make his case, but did so in the politest way possible. "With all due respect, we both know there is good and evil coexisting in this world. If there is an entity responsible for the good, then it stands to reason there must also be an entity responsible for the flip side of the coin. Would you say that's a fair assessment?"

"I think man is quite capable of evil without much assistance," Frank barked. "But if there is a devil, I have a hard time believing he exists in the form of a Native American woman with an axe to grind."

"Fair assumption, and one I agree with. But, be it black magic, witchcraft, or whatever, she may have found a way to tap into that dark force we call evil and wield it like a sword. Now, before you blow a gasket on me, I will say that, while I'm open to the idea of the supernatural, I've never put much stock in curses per se. I'm sure it's just like you said; superstitious settlers passing along a string of tales which have become taller over time. But, fictitious or not, I'll admit I do enjoy a good scary story. They're rather fun. I remember hearing some doozies as a kid, sitting in a circle of friends with nothing but a flashlight. Surely you had similar experiences growing up?"

Another grunt from the sheriff. "Fun, huh? When I was little, those kinds of stories always tied me in knots until I was ready to shit my pants, so I avoided them at all costs. But if that's your idea of a good time, then I imagine the last five minutes have been a real hoot."

Landon laughed. "I don't know if I'd go that far, but it was enjoyable in a creepy sort of way."

"You're an odd one, Stephens. But at least you speak your mind. I can respect that. Most agree with everything I say, or tell me what they think I want to hear. It's like they're afraid of me or something."

"I can't imagine why," Landon said, a wide grin plastered across his face.

"You really are a smart-ass, aren't you boy?"

The deputy raised his hand, pinching his thumb and forefinger together. "Only a little. Not enough for any concern."

"No, of course not." Frank grunted again, this time in mild amusement. "At least we can both agree that whatever trouble these kids we're looking for have gotten themselves into, has nothing to do with some century-old deceased witch. They're most likely holed up somewhere right at this very moment; drunk, stoned, and laughing at the trouble they've caused."

20

The knocking roused him from a light slumber. John sat up, sending the book he'd been reading tumbling to the floor. He rubbed at his eyes and glanced over at the clock on the nightstand. It was just past eleven. When he'd last checked, it had been a quarter till. He must have dozed off. And here he'd been worried that his daydream prone mind would keep him up half the night or more. Had he not decided to pass the time by reading, perhaps it would have. As much as he loved a good book, he did his best reading when he was vertical. Lying down with one was akin to the proverbial counting of sheep, and he was lucky if he could finish more than a single chapter before nodding off.

The knock came again.

John climbed out of bed, picking the book off the floor and tossing it on top of the dresser. He wondered who was calling this late. His first thought was that Robert had found his way back to the camp and was coming to apologize for his unexpected leave. But that wasn't likely, was it? Having made off with all the food and the office furniture, chances were good that old Mr. Townsend planned on staying gone for a long while, if not indefinitely. No, it was most likely Dagger coming to say that Beth was still in a mood, and wanting to know if there were any beers left.

Opening the door, John saw he was wrong on both counts.

"Amy?" There was a noticeable measure of surprise in his voice.

"Hi," she said, sounding almost bashful. Standing barefoot and clad in an oversized T-shirt that stopped mid-thigh, Amy could have just crawled out of bed herself. With arms draped in a V across her torso, she looked even more demure under the dim light. "May I come in?"

"Uh . . . yeah. I mean, yes. Sure," John stuttered. "Everything okay?"

Amy stepped inside and pushed the door closed behind her. She turned back to John and nodded. "I guess I'm still a bit scared after everything today, so—"

She paused, as if afraid that what she was about to ask of her friend was something he would never concede.

"What is it?" John asked.

Amy raised the heel of her right foot and pivoted it back and forth in a timid fashion. "I was wondering if maybe I could stay with you tonight?"

"Of course," John replied. "No way I'm going to let you be afraid. You take the bed. I'll be fine on the floor. All I need is a pillow and—"

"No," Amy interrupted. "You're not hearing me."

If the candor of her words was not enough, Amy's body language and the wanting in her eyes should have told John all he needed to know. Even so, he was having a hard time accepting the reality of it all. "Are you saying what I think you're saying?"

Amy smiled and dropped her gaze to the floor.

John couldn't help but take her all in. He admired the smooth form of her long legs, could see the outline of her breasts beneath the thin cotton shirt, and marveled at the way the fabric hugged the curvature of her hips. With no noticeable panty line, it appeared she might not be wearing anything underneath the oversized tee. A dizzying feeling swept over him at the thought, and a warm rush of blood raced to his extremities.

Amy looked back up at him with wide hazel eyes—intoxicating eyes—and nodded twice.

"Oh, boy," John muttered, going weak in the knees. He rubbed the nape of his neck where a thin layer of nervous perspiration had already metastasized. For the briefest of seconds, he considered that he might still be asleep, but knew that this was no more a dream than was the kiss earlier. It was just hard to believe that this much good fortune was befalling a guy who had, more often than not, drawn the short end of the stick in life. What he asked next was something most guys in his position never would have, as it could quite possibly lessen their chances of getting laid. But John loved Amy, which was precisely the reason the question had to be asked. "Are you sure about this?"

Saying not a word, Amy walked over and placed her hands upon John's chest, locking eyes with him for a long moment before reaching one hand behind his head. She pulled gently forward, guiding his mouth to hers.

John closed his eyes and let himself become lost in the moment. The warmth of her kiss, the softness of her breasts pinned against his body, and the way the tip of her tongue grazed his own, was nothing short of rapturous.

Amy pulled away, regarding John through soft green eyes which were now resplendent with longing. She took him by the hand and led him toward the bed. Once there, she slipped out of the long shirt she'd been wearing and tossed it aside.

Looking upon her nakedness, John exuded a wistful breath. He wanted so badly to take her in that moment and feel her body mesh with his own. He longed to touch her; to know her in the deepest way possible. Yet, even now, his mind somersaulted, torn between desire and trepidation. What would tomorrow bring? Would she regret her decision, second guessing everything that happened between them this night? If so, he would end up right back in the friend zone, and John understood that one night with Amy, no matter how amazing, could never be enough. It would be but a single drop of water for a heart languishing in thirst. Not to mention, if Amy were to end up in someone else's arms after they had been intimate, how much more would he ache then?

"What about the things you said earlier? About needing to work through stuff first?" he asked.

Amy's mouth drew down into a pout. "I'm lonely, John. I don't want to be lonely anymore. Don't you want me?"

"Yes, of course I do. More than anything!" John exclaimed. "I just don't want you to wake up tomorrow and feel like this was a mistake."

Amy pressed her palms to John's face and looked him square in the eye. "I've thought about this, and it's what I want. I couldn't stop thinking about you after our kiss tonight, nor all the things you said to me. I've made some mistakes in my life, that's for sure, but you are not one of them. Nobody has ever cared for me the way you have. I love you, John."

"Really?"

Amy nodded. "Really," she whispered, her eyes glassy with emotion. She smiled and slid into bed, pulling John in beside her. Their lips met once more, harder and more passionate than before.

This is happening, John thought. *Oh, my God. This is really happening!*

Amy reached back and took John by the hair, thrusting his head down until his mouth found her breast. She arched her back and moaned, simultaneously taking his hand and placing it between her legs.

If John had been enraptured just moments ago, he was now drunk with euphoria. Whatever reservations he'd initially held regarding this union were long gone, replaced by carnal desires which he could no longer ignore.

"Take me," Amy whispered in his ear. "Please. Take me now," she pleaded.

With that, the last of John's resolve melted away like ice cream dropped on a sun baked sidewalk. He went to remove his boxers when a flash of light on the nightstand caught his attention. Someone was calling his phone, which should have been nothing more than a minor distraction at a most inopportune time. But what John saw on the screen chilled his blood.

It was the caller's picture—a fresh-faced young girl with a beautiful smile. And near the top of the screen, superimposed in bold white letters, was the girl's name . . . Amy.

....

FIVE MINUTES EARLIER:

Amy knew it was a dream. She knew the moment she found herself standing outside of her cabin in the cool evening air. She'd always had a propensity for lucid dreaming, but when those dreams turned into nightmares, as she felt this one would, cognizance did little in the way of making the experience any less terrifying.

It was dark outside, save for a thin sliver of moonlight hanging high in the night sky. Amy had no recollection of leaving her room to get to the spot where she now stood, but then that was the nature of a dream wasn't it? They started at whatever point in time they pleased, caring little for proper introductions.

From somewhere ahead, a high-pitched squeak split the air. The rhythmic *cree-craw* was like the sound Catherine's chair had made when she rocked in it, only sharper. The noise rose and fell, starting softly, growing louder, then becoming soft again.

As if drawn by some unseen force, Amy started down the path toward the strange sound. To her, this action was yet another indication she was dreaming. Had this been real, she would have said to hell with it, and stayed in her warm bed. Of course, the reality was she was technically in her bed at this very moment, and therein lie the irony.

The path ahead was a maze of long shadows borne of tall pines and moonbeam. Something stirred in the fallen leaves nearby, though it was impossible for Amy to tell whether it was moving closer or further away. A harmless woodland creature most likely, but she quickened her pace nonetheless. Somewhere deeper in the forest, an owl screeched, either unfazed by the caustic *cree-craw* that was growing louder by the second, or believing the source of the sound to be a kindred spirit and answering its call.

A sense of apprehension was building in Amy and she wanted more than anything just to wake up. Never able to simply will herself awake, she had read that committing a suicidal act while in a dream—say, leaping from a tall building or jumping in front of a train—would do the trick, but she had neither of those resources currently at her disposal. Even if she had, Amy knew she wouldn't have the courage to follow through, real or no. In a dream state, there is still a survival instinct. One still possesses a fear of pain, has a healthy respect for danger, and doesn't hesitate to run from whatever terrors stalk them in their slumber.

The hellish dirge played on, poisoning the air with its shrill, malevolent melody. Something horrible waited just around the bend. Amy could feel it. Her pulse quickened and the breath sprung from her body in short, agitated bursts.

Wake up! Wake up! Wake up!

She pleaded to no avail while her legs marched forward against her will. When it came time to face the terrible thing lingering ahead, she knew her eyes would refuse to close, leaving her no choice but to look upon the horror.

Amy came around the bend and could see the office straight ahead. At first glance, the place appeared to be deserted. Then she saw movement. There, in the hard-yellow stare of the distant porch light, a silhouetted figure pivoted back and forth.

It was Catherine. The old woman stood behind a rusted metal swing set, pushing one of the small bucket seats. The decaying steel frame stood like a fossilized skeleton, slanting to one side as if tired and ready to collapse. Dry, rusty hinges served as worn joints, and with each forward and back pass of the swing, they cried out in agony, filling the air with a sharp reverb.

Cree-craw

As she neared, Amy detected a pale white form propped up in the seat, which she took to be the tattered porcelain doll that Catherine believed to be her daughter. She could also hear the old woman singing a lullaby in her arid, uneven voice: "Hush, little baby,"

Cree-craw

". . . don't say a word."

Amy moved closer, though Catherine took no notice of her and continued to sing.

"Papa's gonna buy you a mockingbird."

The squealing hinges grew louder; harsher.

CREE-craw

"And if that mockingbird don't sing,"

The shrill screams were becoming maddening, jangling Amy's nerves with each piercing howl. *Something isn't right. I need to wake up!*

CREE-craw

". . . papa's gonna buy you a diamond ring."

Something is wrong. So very wrong.

CREEE . . .

Oh, God. No!

Amy stood aghast in front of the swing. The figure that she had taken to be the disheveled doll was not a doll at all. It was a flesh and blood child. And there was no life in the thing.

The small form was slumped back in the seat, head angled to one side, its complexion pasty and blue. The eyes were wide open and empty, and a wet milky substance dribbled from one corner of the mouth, dripping from the chin and pooling in a wide circle on the child's pink Onesie. This was Eleanora, the real Eleanora. Or at least some semblance of her.

Catherine stopped pushing the swing and spoke. "The people of the lake have awoken. She has seen to it, she has. And now the children are here, too. Have you seen them yet, Amy? They are so looking forward to playing with you." The old woman began to laugh.

Before Amy could reply, a sudden movement from the swing caught her eye. She looked down at Eleanora. The child remained cold and stiff, the eyes were still vacant and unblinking, but the mouth began to open. Wider and wider it stretched, becoming a gaping crater of inconceivable proportions. When it seemed the jaw had no more give and was in danger of snapping clean off, the stretching stopped, making the infant appear as some sort of gruesome statue. Then, to Amy's horror, the child screamed.

She shot upright in bed, a panicked cry lodged in the back of her throat. A rapid pulse pounded at her temples and her body was covered in a thin layer of sweat. She exhaled slowly, trying to calm her erratic breathing.

It was a dream. Just a dream. Regardless, the bloodcurdling, preternatural scream from the dead baby still echoed in the blackness of her mind, sending goose pimples springing up on her arms.

Amy lay back on the bed and tried to still her mind. The image of that child was one she doubted she'd ever be able to shake. Nightmares had never been commonplace for her, especially ones of this magnitude. She knew they reflected one's own subconscious fears, which made sense, especially when her bad dreams typically consisted of losing her parents, falling out of a rollercoaster mid-inversion, or showing up to a public place with no clothes on. But *this*? What she had just experienced was straight out of a Stephen King novel. Of course, so was what she'd seen (or thought she'd seen) beneath the water earlier in the day. And she hadn't been asleep then.

With another deep breath, Amy closed her eyes and tried to clear her thoughts. It was then that the noise returned: the same abrasive sound she had heard the night prior, only louder. Long and measured the scratches came, as if something hard and sharp was being dragged across the wood floor.

The noises seemed to move closer before coming to an abrupt halt.

Amy held her breath and waited. Time ticked by in her head until she felt she would break from the mounting tension.

Nothing.

She considered going for the door and running to John's cabin. But to reach the exit, she would have to enter the darkness. What if the unseen source of the noise was standing in the corner next to the door, waiting for her to do just that very thing?

Amy eased one hand out from under the blanket and reached toward the nightstand. She fumbled about until her fingers felt the cold metal of the lamp. Tracing the curvature of the base upwards, she found the switch and gave it a click. In an instant, light pushed back the shadows and illuminated the room.

No one was there.

The absence of something tangible lurking in the shadows of the room broke the tension, but even so, between the odd noises, her nightmare, and the rest of the unsettling events of the day, Amy was in no state of mind to be alone the rest of the evening. She reached for her phone and dialed John.

....

It wasn't possible. How could Amy be calling if she was already here?

John stared at the phone with a mixture of confusion and disbelief. The passage of time between his brain registering the caller ID and his eyes darting back to the girl lying next to him in bed was only milliseconds, yet it seemed much longer. Within that span, innumerable questions knocked around in his head as his brain grappled in vain for some sort of explanation. When he finally turned to face his newfound lover, John was still at a loss. He expected to find Amy, giggling in her cute, effervescent way at his dumbfounded expression before giving him one of those '*it's so obvious I can't believe you missed it*' answers. What he found instead, was a monster.

An old woman, looking like something straight out of a zombie flick, stared back. Her eyes were cloudy white orbs set within deep sunken sockets. The skin was dark, leathery, and decayed, with a few patches worn down to expose the underlying bone. Intermittent clumps of hair stood like cornstalks across a mostly barren scalp, spilling around the face and past the shoulders in a tangled cascade of silver and gray.

Thin, cracked lips opened wide to reveal teeth which were almost as black as the gums around them. The crooked, gnarled nubs of bone exuded a pungent odor and were covered with a thick, wet goo, making them appear as if they had been bathed in crude oil.

The cadaverous jaw hinged open and the woman spoke in a voice that was harsh, throaty, and far from the effeminate cadence of Amy. "What's the matter, John? Don't you want me anymore?"

Horrified, John launched himself off the bed, catching one foot in the sheets and falling to the ground with a thud. He rolled over on his back and worked to loosen the fabric from around his ankle.

The thing in the bed sat upright and swung its legs over the side of the mattress.

John pumped his own leg up and down in a fit, but the sheet would not let go of its grasp.

The woman stood up, took one step, then another.

Hands trembling, John tugged at the sheet, creating enough slack for him pull his foot free. A cry of panic escaped him as he pedaled backwards on hands and elbows.

The monster was positioned between the end of the bed and the front door now. Flaps of skin dangled from her emaciated frame, while dirt encrusted bone poked through at the shoulders and knees. Her breasts, which had appeared full and firm while taking the form of Amy, were now sagging curtains of withered flesh. Then there was the smell: a sharp, rancid odor that perfumed the air with death. It was, John imagined, what a body might smell like during the early stages of decomposition. The putrid aroma it gave off was repugnant enough to sting the insides of the young man's nostrils with every frantic breath he drew.

"What are you?" John asked in a tortured whisper. "What do you want?"

The old hag tipped her head to the side and studied the boy through eyes that burned with a white-hot intensity. Without speaking, she lifted a gangly arm and pointed a skeletal finger, twisting her leathery lips into a makeshift smile that was as unsettling as it was malicious.

John shook his head and inched backwards.

The creature, in turn, closed the distance. Each time it raised a foot to take a step, long strands of shimmery mucus stretched from the bottom of its soles to the floor, creating a gelatinous peal that rang through the room in a grotesque refrain.

"There's nowhere to run," the thing hissed. "Tonight my children shall feast on your flesh . . . and I will devour your soul."

With those words, the woman craned her neck forward and gnashed her teeth in rapid bursts, much like those wind-up toy choppers that bounced around on a table while clacking together at lightning speed.

A new wave of fear hammered John's insides. He pulled himself up and bolted for the bathroom. Once inside, he slammed the door shut behind him and turned the latch. At first, he considered sitting with his back against the door for reinforcement, but he had seen enough horror films to know there was a good chance something could punch a hole in the door, impaling him in the process. An image of him looking down and seeing the rotting arm of the old woman sticking out of his chest and clutching his still-beating heart was enough to change his mind. He braced himself against the vanity and fortified the door with his feet.

Seconds later, the handle began to jiggle. John wondered how much strength this monstrosity possessed. Her overall appearance suggested her to be feeble, though that did little to console him. After all, someone in her condition shouldn't be walking around at all, yet here she was. It was enough to push his mind to the breaking point.

The handle stopped moving.

Silence.

John listened, hearing only his own ragged breathing.

BAM!

The noise sounded like a grizzly bear had just charged the door, and the sudden jolt nearly made John piss himself.

"Go away," he screamed, realizing how stupid the words sounded as soon as he'd said them. Did he think this thing was going to listen and just leave? Not a chance.

BAM! BAM! BAM!

The pounding intensified.

John squeezed his eyes closed and pressed harder against the door. Behind him, the shower curtain glided open with a whisper. A shadowy figure emerged.

BAM!

The door shook on its hinges and the monster loosed a cry that sounded inhuman.

John raised his hands to his ears and began to wail. A moment later, when he was sure he would go mad from the unrelenting terror, the screams—and the pounding—fell silent.

Seconds ticked by without a sound. *Was it over? Had she given up?*

John lowered his hands and waited, mentally preparing himself for another assault.

When the attack did not come, he figured it best not to open the door for a good while. But then the thought came: What about his friends? What if that thing was knocking on Amy's door right now, pretending to be him?

No, I can't stay here and let that happen. I have to open the door and find something to arm myself with. Prepare to fight this thing head on and . . .

A rustling sound caused John to stiffen. Whatever had made the noise was in the room with him. A cold consternation hit him like a thousand tiny pin pricks jabbing into his body. He held his breath, afraid to turn around; afraid *she* would be there.

Sweat began to pour from his brow in steady streams as he waited, consumed by a suffocating fear over what he felt would be the inevitable outcome of his situation.

There was the sound of breathing other than his own; quick and jagged it resonated. John sensed the presence slipping up ever closer behind him. An involuntary shudder raked across his body and he hunched over, a grown man driven to the brink of tears.

There was laughter now as the shrill, jubilant giggling of a child echoed throughout the tiny room.

John was stunned, taken aback by this unexpected turn. Where had a child come from? Without conscious thought, he whipped his head around to look, coming face to face with a presence that was even more hellish than the old woman—a young boy, wearing a pair of glasses with cracked lenses, yet possessing no eyes from which to see out of. Patches of smooth skin, encircled with crude stitching, had been sewn over his sockets, and a deep gash, wide and bloodied, ran from the corners of his mouth all the way up to his ears, giving him a ghastly everlasting smile. The boy's jaw started to clap up and down in a herky-jerky fashion, looking like the mouth on one of those old wooden ventriloquist dolls, as he squealed with delight.

"God, help me!" John cried, his voice shaking.

By the time he noticed the curved blade of the boy's right hand, it was already coming toward his neck in a rapid downward swing.

21

"Beth . . ."

The faintness of it ebbed throughout the darkness and then faded. Within the abyss, somewhere below the noise, she stirred.

"Beth," the voice sounded again, but it came in like a whisper on the wind, and she had no understanding of what had been said, only that she'd heard something in the far away.

Who am I? Where am I?

Those questions pierced the fog of her existence, yet she had answers for neither.

A hodgepodge of scattered memories circled at a dizzying pace. The girl knew that within the swirling vortex were the things she could not remember, and everything about who she was. Although she groped with all her might at the spinning pictures around her, they moved too quickly for her to latch onto.

The unseen voice drifted up through the void again, uttering a single word.

What was it?

She strained to listen.

Nothing.

Then it was there.

"Beth."

A name. *Her* name.

Still, it was some time before the spinning wheel slowed, allowing her to catch that first flash of recollection—sitting upon the dusty ground, face buried in her hands; crying out for her father. And the memory was gone.

"Beth. It's time . . . Beth."

That voice. Or was it more than one? It seemed so. Delicate and unworldly, they rose and fell like tides of winter wind whistling under the eaves. She knew the sound; had heard these voices before. But from where?

Rising from the black void and moving into a state of semi consciousness, Beth had a feeling reminiscent of coming out of a drunken stupor, where the memories of the prior evening always came together in a steady patchwork of vague images and dull pain, mingled with the foul, skunky taste from a mouth desiccated by an excess of rum, gin, tequila, or whatever poison she'd used on said occasion to numb her senses. But even in the current cloudy haze of her awakening, Beth knew on some intuitive level that she had not imbibed. The malodorous flavor registering on her tongue now was quite different from the stale, mucky essence left over from a night of binge drinking. This was saltwater tainted with copper and there was something familiar about its taste.

The spinning carousel continued to slow as Beth plumbed the depths of her subconscious, bringing the memories into sharper focus. Within seconds, countless images of her youth paraded through her mind's eye. She saw her parents, family and friends; relived a myriad of holidays, birthdays, special occasions, and every other event which her brain had seen fit to catalog. These elicited a wide gamut of emotions—joy, laughter, love, sadness, anxiety, jealousy, accomplishment . . . and fear.

Beginning with her arrival at Shadow Lake, the pictures in her mind took on a dreary cast, as if she were viewing the world through glass which had been tarnished with a dull film. She saw clearly that first night around the campfire with her friends, with John reciting his creepy poem. Beyond that, however, the cloudy veneer over the window of her soul grew thicker and heavier until she could barely see anything at all.

The memory of lying on the ground and weeping came to her again.

What was I crying about?

She heard her father's voice. "Beth, are you still there? I can't hear you."

"Daddy?" she heard herself ask.

A cellphone rested on her lap. It started to ring and she answered.

"Daddy, can you hear me?"

Stark terror now, worming through her insides like a parasite.

"Daaa-dy . . ."

That voice. I know that voice.

Her eyes flew open. The world around her was dark and in motion, and she moved with it, bobbing up and down. There were noises within this new blackness as well: a cyclical rhythm of churning and sloshing.

"Beth." The voices again.

Why was she still hearing them now that she was awake? She had no doubt that she'd awoken from her sleep, as there was a perceptible sense of reality touching her senses: the coolness of a breeze drifting lazily across her skin, the faint musky odor of lake water, and the wretched metallic taste which lingered on her palate in the same way that the presence of soured garbage was discernible long after it had been removed from the house.

Beth sat up, her eyes darting this way and that while they took in her surroundings. She was alone, floating roughly ten yards from the shore in one of the canoes belonging to the camp. The sound she'd heard upon waking, she concluded now, was that of water washing against the hull of the boat.

How did I get here? Is this Dagger's idea of a joke?

A gust of wind skimmed across the lake, biting at her skin. It was then Beth realized she was naked. "Oh, what the fuck?" she muttered. *If Dagger left me out here like this, he is so dead!*

She crossed her arms over her bare chest, only to pull them back a split second later. Her skin was wet, coated in some sort of viscous fluid. Scrunching up her face in disgust, Beth extended both arms out in front of her and gave them a shake. She strained to see what it was she had on her, but was unable to identify the substance. In the blackness of night, her body—and everything around it—was gilded only in shades of onyx and coal.

Damn you, Dagger. This is not funny. When I get ahold of you—

"Beth." The spectral whispers corkscrewed around the canoe from every angle.

She gasped, whipping her head left and right to locate the source of the voices. If someone was out there, they were masked by the inky darkness.

This is not cool. Not cool at all.

"If you're trying to scare me, Dagger, it's not working," Beth shouted, hoping that her boyfriend would believe she was onto him and give up the game. It didn't work. With her bluff called, the worm of fear inside of her body went on the move again, twisting and turning its way through her gut.

Back at shore, a geyser of flames erupted from the ground with a cavernous rumble, forming an impromptu campfire in the spot where Beth and her friends had congregated the night before. Standing along the water's edge, silhouetted by the flames, was the vaporous form of a woman. Positioned around her were other smaller forms. One held a sickle at his side, another was slumped over at an unnatural angle, but all of them, to some degree, appeared contorted or misshapen. And while Beth could not observe their faces, she could sense eyes on her and knew they were watching.

"Beth," a voice called.

"We're here," came another.

The sounds originated with those children. Of this, Beth was certain. Yet the voices were disembodied, coming from all directions, as if they'd been projected onto the backs of the insects flying erratic circles around the canoe.

"We like playing with you," they echoed. "Stay with us."

It wasn't just one worm writhing its way through Beth's gut now. It was many. The fear had become an infestation of thousands upon thousands of tiny little worms that crawled over her body, chewing on muscle and organ with their diminutive jaws and squirming their way inside, where they would feast until the last bits of tissue had been picked clean from her bones.

Beth could no longer look upon the shadowy figures in front of her. She had to get away; row as far from the shore as possible until her arms fatigued and she could go no more. She turned her attention back to the boat in search of oars.

The roaring bonfire on the banks burned with a blistering ferocity, the brightness of which illuminated a wide band of the lake and shone inside the canoe.

Beth scanned the boat's bottom until she spotted the oar handles protruding from under the bow. She reached for the paddles, stopping cold. Her arms were painted a deep shade of crimson. The slick substance her body was covered in was blood; blood which was still shiny and wet.

Alarmed, Beth traced along the soles of her feet all the way to the top of her head. She found nothing more than a small cut on one of her fingers. Hardly the type of injury that would produce this kind of blood loss. If it hadn't come from her, then where?

"Beth . . ."

The voices called her name, but she did not heed them. She was back on the carousel of memories, only this time she was on the outside of the window, looking through the cloudy panes and seeing a dull reflection of herself on the other side. The girl she saw behind the glass, the one stuck in a room with a filthy window, was her true self. The person on the outside, whose eyes she saw out of at present, was an imposter; a doppelgänger that was but an outward shell of who she was, and whose desires were far from her own.

The brief ride she took within this foreign form—and the things she witnessed through its eyes—was like taking an express trip through hell. She saw herself devouring meat like a ravenous animal, while saliva dripped from her chin in long, frothy ribbons. Her teeth ripped and tore at raw flesh, turning her lips the color of rubies. And the blood. There was so much blood. Yet she reveled in it. Soaked her hands in the stuff and rubbed long cherry-red streaks from neck to naval. The last thing she saw as the ride stopped spinning and the vile melody of the calliope ground to a halt, were a pair of burned out eyes within a milky, bucolic face that was as cold and still as a porcelain doll. It was the face of her prey; the face of the man who'd loved her.

She looked back at the window and the person standing just beyond. The glass was no longer dirty, but clear to the point of near invisibility, like someone had taken ammonia and newspaper to it while the carousel was busy twirling through a nightmare.

There were no more barriers, no more secrets. All the cards had been laid out on the table. The girl on the other side understood the fullness of what she had done. She had seen everything and now her mind was on the verge of coming unhinged. She started to scream.

"Dagger!" Beth cried, hurling her body against the gunwale of the canoe and ripping at her hair. "No. Oh, god. No, no, no, no . . ."

She doubled over, her body convulsing with tortured sobs. "Why? It's not . . . I can't . . ." she murmured, unable to form a whole thought or sentence. She balled her hands into fists and began banging at her temples. She wanted desperately to believe that none of this was happening. But it was. And the reality of it was more than she could process.

"Don't cry, Beth," the voices urged. "Stay with us forever."

A primal scream erupted from Beth's lungs. It was too much. All of it. She looked at her arms and saw the cardinal streaks running down them. The images—those brutal images—played through her mind over and over, while the awareness of what it was in her mouth that tasted like copper brought with it a sudden wave of nausea.

Without haste, Beth leaned over the side of the canoe and opened her mouth to be sick. What she saw just beneath the surface of the water made her eyes grow wide, displacing the vomiting reflex in the pit of her stomach.

At first glance, Beth mistook the pale visage in the water for her reflection, yet upon closer inspection, the face staring back belonged to another. The features were much like her own: lush lips, a slender nose, and a small jaw. But faint creases around the eyes and mouth suggested a face which was older by at least ten years. The hair was different, too. Lighter than Beth's, the long strands hung in curled ringlets around the shoulders and waved about under the water in a serene, hypnotic dance.

"Come with us," the voices whispered, their call going unnoticed by Beth, who was still transfixed by the pair of light blue eyes peering up at her from the lake. Without thought, she reached a hand toward the water, hesitating just before the tips of her fingers broke the surface.

What am I doing? This isn't normal. Who, or what, is this thing?

The woman's eyes stared straight ahead, unblinking, while the face remained stoic, with not so much as a single bubble of air escaping the nose or mouth.

She's dead . . . or something else altogether.

With that thought, the dawning of everything which had led up to this moment crashed down upon Beth and she snatched her hand back inside the boat.

"Beth."

She looked upon the dark figures dotting the shoreline. One by one the gaunt forms raised their cadaverous arms and stretched their hands in the direction of the canoe.

"It's time," they declared.

Beth sensed the movement in the water before ever glimpsing it. She turned back just in time to watch the face of the pretty young woman change into a gnarled mass of flesh-colored putty. It pulsed and stretched over moving bone before settling into a picture-perfect vision of Richie Miller. His one good eye found Beth and he grinned at her through a broken smile.

Before she had time to react, a pair of arms shot out of the water and gripped her by the back of the head, pulling her into the murky deep.

Up on the shore, the raging fire snuffed out as fast as it had been ignited, plunging the land once more into darkness.

The shadowy figures vanished.

The surface of the lake went still.

And there was only silence.

22

When John did not answer his phone, Amy—still in a state of unrest after the experience of the nightmare—slipped into jeans, pulled on a pair of shoes, and made her way to her friend's cabin. She didn't have far to walk, but the short trek rattled her nerves. Every sound, every rustle of wind, had her looking back over her shoulder to make sure no one was following.

"The people of the lake have awoken . . . and now the children are here, too. Have you seen them yet?"

The sensible part of Amy's brain argued that those were but words spoken in a dream, yet she was haunted by them nevertheless. No amount of logic, regardless of how sound, could alleviate the disquiet in her soul. She was beyond that now.

John's cabin was steeped in darkness, the space appearing as a gaping black hole within the caliginous night. There were no sounds; no welcoming porch light or warm lamp glow emanating from behind the window to greet Amy. But why should there be? It was late, and John was no doubt sleeping. Under normal circumstances, she would have let him be. But fear held her in its mighty grip, and the thought of spending the rest of the evening alone in her own cabin was not appealing in the least.

Still, Amy hesitated at the threshold before rapping on the door. But only for a moment. She let her knuckles fly, thumping at least half a dozen times, and then waited.

There was no answer.

She knocked again, harder this time.

No one stirred.

Amy, knowing John might be sleeping heavily if he'd taken one of his Ambien, decided to give it her all.

Third time's the charm, right?

She pounded against the door with the sides of her fists, loud enough that she wondered if it might also wake Dagger and Beth in the adjacent cabin.

Still nothing.

He *had* to have heard that. Unless he wasn't inside. But then where else would he be?

"Amy." The voice was distant, coming from somewhere behind her.

She whirled around and scanned the night.

"Up here, Amy."

Her eyes traversed the foothills until she spotted a dim glow midway up the trail. The old dormitories which had once housed large numbers of adolescent campers were situated there. There were four of them: buildings A and B for the boys, and buildings C and D, set a bit further down the path, for the girls. The entrance to building A stood open, and a faint light flickered from inside. Out front, a sullied form loomed.

"We're in here, Amy. Come on up." The figure waved.

"John?" Amy muttered under her breath. The voice had sounded like his, but from this distance the dark shape was ambiguous and could have belonged to anyone.

The veiled form beckoned once more and stepped inside, where a bout of laughter rang out.

Amy stood on the porch, befuddled. From the sound of it, all her friends were up in the dormitory, seemingly having a good time. Perhaps none of them could find sleep. Or, like her, maybe they'd chosen not to be alone in this God-forsaken place. *But why there* she wondered, then shrugged. They had full run of the camp now, so nowhere was off limits. It would be just like Dagger to decide it was worth investigating every nook and cranny of the grounds for no reason other than he could.

Amy wished John had come down and escorted her up to the dorm, as she didn't savor the idea of making the walk up the dark trail by herself. Of course, staying down here alone was even less agreeable.

"Here goes nothing," she said, exhaling a deep breath.

Firming her shoulders, she trotted down the steps and headed toward the company of her friends.

....

The police cruiser turned off Black Water Pass and veered into the lot of an antiquated convenience store. Frank brought the car to a stop in front of a worn wooden bench near the store's entrance and shut off the engine.

Landon craned his neck to see the name painted across the front façade of the building:

EASLEY'S ROADSIDE SERVICE

"What are we doing here?" he asked, glancing out the window at the deserted parking lot. "I mean, are they even open? Place looks like a ghost town."

"They are," Frank assured. "Customers are just sparse this time of night. I'm not sure why Doug keeps the place open so late when camping season hasn't even begun, but he must have his reasons. That's fine by me, because I could use a snack right about now, and this is the only place within miles to grab one."

"Donuts again, sir?" Landon inquired.

Frank gave the deputy a cool stare. "You're a real ball buster, aren't you, Stephens?"

"Sorry, sir. I didn't mean to—"

"Yes, you did," Frank bellowed. "I'm wise to your ways, son. You're a good kid; a smart kid. But you're also a self-professed smart ass who is knee deep in bullshit. And you enjoy shoveling that bullshit at other people's feet because you like seeing their reactions when they step in it."

"What if I were to tell you I was only concerned about your health?" Landon's expression was as deadpan as they come.

"Then I'd say you're not knee dip in shit after all. You're chin deep in it."

The deputy cracked a smile. "Okay, you got me. But, sometimes less really is more."

"Is that right? Well, I'll be sure and remember that when I'm writing your paycheck," the sheriff barked. He popped the car door open, mumbling something unintelligible under his breath as he climbed out. After hitching up his pants and perching his campaign hat atop his head, he leaned over and peered back at the deputy still seated inside the vehicle. "I can't believe I'm asking this, but would you like something to drink? Or are you coming inside?"

"I'm good, but thank you for asking." Landon replied. "You're a good man; like the father I never had. I think I love you, sir."

"Oh, good God," the sheriff grumbled. He held one hand flat beneath his chin, raising it upwards like the level indicator on a thermometer until it was positioned just above his head. "Drowning in it now, Stephens. Drowning."

Frank flung the door closed and turned to go inside. He had only gone a few steps when a small grin spread across his face. *You've met your match in this one, Franklin. That damn kid is likely to be Sheriff one day, just you wait and see.*

....

It's too quiet.

That was Amy's first thought upon reaching the old dormitory. Where was the laughter she'd heard just minutes ago? Or the sounds of voices engaged in conversation? And where was John for that matter? Considering that she had just opened the door to a relationship between the two of them, she figured he'd have dusted the trail like a horse running the Kentucky Derby to get down to where she was. At the very least, she'd expected him to be waiting to greet her, grinning in the same jubilant manner as that boy from the movie *A Christmas Story* after he'd been gifted with his long coveted Red Ryder BB gun.

Gosh, that made her seem hoity-toity, didn't it? She thought of those uber-popular girls at school who acted as if they'd been touched by the hand of God; gifted with such remarkable beauty that every guy who looked upon them would give his left nut just to be in their presence.

But this wasn't like that. And it wasn't her intention to come across as some smug bitch, even if only to herself. It's just that John had loved her in his shy and silent way for the better part of his young life. She could have done something as trite as dropping a bag of groceries and he'd have come running to her aid. Given that, it surprised her that he would act so indifferent now, especially after the kiss they'd shared earlier in the evening. That didn't seem like him; didn't seem normal. Then again, what exactly had been normal about this day?

The door to the bunk house stood ajar, allowing a thin strip of light to escape from within. Dry, neglected hinges let out a protracted squeal as Amy nudged the door open.

A cold draft assaulted her senses right away, pushing past her and leaving a stale odor in its wake. At the outset, the smell was damp and musty, reminiscent of an underground storage cellar. Amy attributed this to the numerous beds which flanked the walls on each side of the room. The metal frames were lined up in a neat and evenly-spaced fashion, with a mattress atop each one, as if a new batch of campers were expected any day now. Only, these mattresses looked to be as old as the building in which they resided. Even under the low light, the brownish-yellow tinged rings staining their cushioned surfaces could be seen clearly. Some of them even had deep indentions in their middles where the springs and padding had worn, forming an outline of the smallish bodies that had once rested there.

On the heels of the stagnant, mildew-ridden gust, a new and stronger odor presented itself. It was the same rancid smell that she'd detected in the office upon her arrival, only much more pronounced. It was so bad that Amy cupped her hand over her nose and took a step backward. She considered leaving altogether before remembering what it was that had brought her up here in the first place. It was the comfort of her friends she sought. But where were they?

"Amy." The voice was low, but recognizable.

"Beth?"

"Back here, Amy."

Further down the aisle, between the rows of beds near the rear of the dorm, candlelight flickered, illuminating two forms sitting side by side upon one of the mattresses. Amy identified the shapes as those of Dagger and Beth.

Finally! She still didn't understand why her friends had chosen this spot to congregate or why, for that matter, they were huddled together at the back of a dark room, but at least she wasn't alone, and that in and of itself was a great consolation.

Amy made her way across the room at a brisk pace. "This is weird, guys. What the hell made you want to come up here? And where's Joh—"

She halted just steps away from her friends. Something was wrong.

The couple sat with their backs to her, not moving. At their feet, in the middle of the aisle, an oversized antique jack-in-the-box was positioned on the floor, surrounded by half a dozen pillar candles. The burning candles were the only source of light within an otherwise pitch black room, adding yet another layer of strangeness to an already bizarre situation.

Then there was the buzzing. It wasn't so much audible as it was tactile, moving across her body like a current of electricity. An icy drop of perspiration trickled down the small of Amy's back and she felt the skin draw tighter over her bones.

"Beth?" There was a tremor in her voice. "Dagger?"

The dark forms of her friends remained rigid, their heads positioned in the direction of the box on the floor.

Amy felt the sudden urge to run, but to where? And to whom? By some unknown means—be it an inner strength and the desire to conquer her newfound fear, or simply the type of intrinsic curiosity which has landed many a man in dire straits throughout the course of history—she willed herself forward.

As the faces of her friends came into view, tears welled up in Amy's eyes.

Beth sat naked, staring at the floor through a pair of eyes which were vacant and dilated wide. Her complexion was pasty, with skin the color of milk, and her bloated lips were kissed with a deep shade of blue.

Dagger was seated beside her. His eyes were gone, with only wet, crimson sockets remaining as placeholders. His head was tipped back slightly, the corners of his mouth slit open to the tops of his cheekbones. With his jaw slack and his teeth visible, he appeared to accept death with a permanent smile.

A small whimper escaped the back of Amy's throat. A part of her mind refused to accept what she was seeing, reasoning that it must be yet another dream. Though she knew better, her brain would not accept the full truth, for to do so all at once would have sent her on a sure descent into madness, the likes from which she might never return.

The handle on the side of the jack-in-the-box began to crank of its own accord, emitting a plucky chime which jerked Amy back to her cruel reality with a start.

All around the mulberry bush.

She recognized the melody.

The monkey chased the weasel.

A heavy dread ratcheted up her terror.

The monkey stopped to pull up his sock.

This isn't right. There's something in there. Something bad.

POP!

The trap door flew open.

. . . goes the weasel.

Amy's knees buckled and she nearly collapsed. Her breathing was erratic now, coming in short, rapid fire bursts.

What popped out of the box was not the customary puppet wearing a whimsical grin, but rather a human head. The noggin bounced up and down on the end of a large spring, exhibiting a look of cloying amusement from a mouth that had been molded to emulate a smile. The head in the box belonged to John.

A scream formed at the back of Amy's throat, but her vocal cords were paralyzed, causing her to exhale only air.

In the darkness beyond the ring of candles, something solid hit the floor, bouncing twice before rolling along the hardwoods in a steady arc of sound. A rubber ball entered the circle of light and came to a stop near Amy's feet.

"My children have been busy," a jagged voice said. "They do love their toys."

Tears streaked down Amy's face, while her chest convulsed with sobs.

"Now, don't cry, child. The children have been looking forward to playing with you for such a long time now. You mustn't let them down."

In one quick simultaneous burst, at least a dozen more candles ignited beyond the circle, bringing the unseen into view. At the back of the room, veiled in shadow, stood a woman. Her eyes reflected white, burning like two small torches beneath a matted and tangled mass of hair, while the bones of her hands were gnarled and twisted, making her gangling fingers appear as talons.

Three of the beds near the woman were occupied. On each, a single child appeared to be sleeping. Or maybe they were dead. Amy was unsure which, as their features were obscured under the low light. She wondered if these might be the same children she had encountered at the bottom of the lake. The words from her dream rattled through her brain once again: *"The people of the lake have awoken . . . and now the children are here, too. Have you seen them yet?"*

Were these the children foretold in the nightmare? And was this woman the 'she of the lake' whom Catherine had spoken of?

A flash of movement captured Amy's attention. She turned to find Beth staring at her through empty raven-colored eyes. The girl's head tipped forward in a jerky motion and her mouth dropped open, allowing a gush of dirty lake water to escape. The liquid fell from her chin like a waterfall, snaking down her clammy skin and soaking the mattress between her thighs. When the last bit of water had dribbled from the corners of Beth's mouth, her head pivoted back and her soulless eyes shifted until they found Amy.

"I've been to the playground in the deep," she croaked, her voice thin and water-logged. "There's darkness there, but no need for sleep."

Someone giggled then. The children had awoken from their slumber, all three now sitting upright in their beds. But these were not the same cherubic faces Amy had seen in the lake this morning. No, these were monsters.

One of them wore a blade for a hand, his mouth slit open in the same manner as Dagger's.

And his eyes. What had happened to his eyes?

Another had a face like molten lava, the skin slipping and sliding over misshapen bone, contorting his features into a living abstract nightmare. The last was half boy and half girl—two bodies that had been crudely stitched down the middle and were somehow still moving.

The boy with the sickle for a hand laughed, spurring excitement in the lava-faced kid. He bounced up and down on the bed, arms flapping wildly. His sideways mouth parted and he exuded what could only be described as an elated moan. Three times he howled, each cry more zealous than the last. When he'd finished, the boy-girl spoke, with two separate voices emanating from the single mouth. "Would you like to play with us in the deep, Amy?"

"Take my hand," Beth chimed in. "Come with us, Amy. It will only hurt for a second." At that her cold blue lips peeled back in a perverse smile, revealing teeth which were speckled with slimy green algae.

The words Catherine had spoken came back in that moment, resounding with a newfound sense of clarity. "*The lake, it takes whomever it wants; claims their very souls. Oh, yes, it does. And when they rise, the lucky ones come back much as they were before. But the others . . . the others become something else entirely.*"

Sheer terror ripped Amy from where she stood and she bolted for the door. Once outside, she sped up her pace, moving down the path as fast as her legs would allow. Behind her, she heard the crack of the dormitory door being pushed open several times as, one by one, the monstrosities filed out of the building. The dead were coming for her.

She reached the main trail near her cabin and rounded the corner at full speed. The sudden shift threw her off balance and she fell backwards, sliding partway down the incline on ass and elbows. She dug her heels into the ground and came to a halt in a swirl of dust.

"A-meee. We're gonna get you, Amy," one of the children called. Another laughed.

The sound of pounding feet echoed close behind. The children were gaining ground.

Amy righted herself and pressed onward, pawing at her eyes to brush away the tears which had formed there.

Thump-thump-thump.

The stampede of small feet rattled Amy's teeth with their intensity. She willed herself to go faster, but her legs were already running at full tilt. Even that didn't seem to be enough. She imagined the lava-faced boy, his features shifting like a living Picasso as he drew down on her, mewling with that perverse, animalistic squeal of his. The thought of it turned Amy's arms to goose flesh.

Whoops and hollers filled the space around her, the voices coming from every direction. They were on the trail, in the woods, situated to her left, to her right, from behind, and everywhere in between. It was almost dizzying. There had been only three children in the bunkhouse, yet now it sounded as if there were legions of them.

John's Jeep came into view and Amy felt a new surge of energy at the sight of it. Some part of her saw this as a finish line; a place of safety. But as she barreled toward the vehicle she had rode in on, the thought occurred: even if she were to find the spare keys and get the engine started, where was she to go? With the bridge out, the only driving she would be doing was in circles.

The office seemed a safer place of refuge, but she didn't like the idea of holing up in there anymore than she did her own cabin (which was the very reason she had run right past it). There were too many places of entry and no time to properly secure them all. Not to mention, even if nothing could get inside, she would be surrounded with no way out, and no means of calling for help.

Still, she couldn't run indefinitely. Already her throat was dry and her sides were exhibiting the first telltale signs of cramping. And those children—those things—which were chasing her showed no signs of slowing down. As much as she disliked the idea, getting inside the office seemed her only chance for survival. At the very least, she could rest, catch her breath, and have some time to think. Come morning, if she could find a way to get to the canoes, she could follow John's plan and paddle to safety.

Amy reached the office and threw herself at the door. She grappled with the handle and pushed, but it did not open. She jiggled the knob and tried again. Still nothing.

Amy glanced over her shoulder. The children were just rounding the corner. They slowed, as if knowing they had just won the race and were about to collect their prize. The stitched monstrosity smiled, the clammy skin around its mouth tugging at the loose threads binding the lips together. It squealed with satisfaction.

Trembling, Amy twisted the knob while throwing her full weight against the door. Several times she tried this, yet the door would not budge.

Another glance over her shoulder. The dead kids were close. Too close.

A peal of wicked laughter split the air.

It was of no use. There would be no making it inside. She had no choice but to run. Amy turned and lit off the porch, running past the Jeep and toward the road leading out of the camp. The air in her lungs was heavy. With every rise and fall of breath, an aching radiated throughout her chest. In the panic, she hadn't thought about what she would do when the road ended at the fallen bridge. Her survival instincts simply told her to run.

Roughly thirty feet down the path, Amy hit a small dip in the road. Rock slid underfoot and she pitched forward, losing her balance and crashing to the ground. On the way down, something popped in her left ankle. A sharp pain followed.

Not now. Oh, God, not now!

She looked up and saw two white orbs shining in the distance. They were on the road ahead, moving closer. The old woman. It had to be her. Amy remembered how her eyes had shone a bright white, glowing as brilliant as if they were lit from behind by incandescent bulbs.

She turned her gaze back toward the office in time to see the boy with a sickle for a hand step out from behind the Jeep. "Red rover, red rover, let Amy come over," he chanted, just before flashing his eternal bloodied grin.

There was no hope, was there? The old woman was in front of her and the children were closing in from behind.

"It will only hurt for a second."

Amy remembered Beth's words and began to sob.

The boy ran his blade along the side of the Jeep in a slow, steady motion, causing the metal to scream as long ribbons of yellow paint peeled away from its body.

Tears clouded Amy's vision. She pulled herself into a tight ball and looked away. The pain would come soon and nothing could prepare her for it. How much would it hurt? How much would she have to endure before death released her from the agony? And in death, what would she become? Would the horrors end there?

Light seeped beneath her closed lids and a new noise broke through the shrill screeching of metal on metal. Low, guttural, and rhythmic it came. It sounded almost like a—

"Car," Amy mumbled, opening her eyes. The white orbs she had seen previously were almost upon her. They were much larger than before—too large to be eyeballs—and burned a hundred times brighter. A faint noxious odor of exhaust filled Amy's nostrils.

It *was* a car. *But the bridge? How?*

When Amy saw the face of the driver, her questioning ceased. She pulled herself up off the ground, blubbering with relief as she hobbled forward on her one good leg. A new hope had arrived, and his name was Eric.

The old Mustang pulled up in a cloud of dust and swerved to a stop beside the girl. From the open passenger window, the mechanic looked upon Amy with wide anxious eyes as he leaned over and popped the door open.

"Get in," he shouted. "Quickly!"

23

The wooden screen door announced the officer's presence with fanfare, springing shut with a loud clap. *Who needs a bell when you've got that thing?* the sheriff surmised. No sooner had he finished the thought when a familiar black dog appeared from around the counter.

"Hello, Boo," Frank said. "I believe this is the first time I've seen you out of your bed. Did you finally decide I was worth getting up for?"

The old dog gave Frank no more than a cursory glance as he trotted past. He stopped at the screen door, stared out into the night, and whimpered.

"I guess not," the sheriff muttered.

The clerk, yet another recognizable face, entered from the back room. Dressed in a button-down shirt and sporting his trademark suspenders, he carried a box of nails in one hand and a hammer in the other. "What do you know, Frank?"

"Evening, Doug. Didn't expect to see you here this late."

"Stephanie called in. Says she isn't feeling well, but it wouldn't surprise me none to see her car parked out front of the Whiskey Wagon on my way home. She's a good worker, but her priorities can get a little skewed on the weekends."

"What is she . . . early twenties?" Frank asked. "Still a kid, really. Not trying to make excuses for her, but I was certainly guilty of playing hooky once or twice back in my younger days."

"As did I," the clerk nodded. He walked over to the wall behind the counter where several framed black and white photos hung in a large grouping and began tapping a new nail into the sheetrock. "She hasn't made it too much of a habit, which is why I haven't fired her. Well, that and she's family, of course."

Frank grimaced. "Yes, that always complicates matters, doesn't it?" He turned his attention back to the front door, where Boo continued to whine. "Say, what's gotten into him?"

Doug Easley looked toward the entrance. "I'm not sure. He's been agitated most of the day. He gets that way every now and then. Must be something in the air." He watched his dog for a moment longer and then averted his gaze back to the sheriff. "So, what brings you in? You needing some bait? It's a tad late in the evening for fishing, isn't it?"

"No, nothing like that. I'm still on duty. Got a call from a concerned parent saying his daughter and her friends were in some kind of trouble. Four teens—two girls; two boys. Driving a yellow Jeep Wrangler. You by chance seen them?"

"As a matter of fact, I have," the clerk replied, his tone one of concern. "They were in here yesterday morning. Filled up, grabbed some food, and headed east, I believe. Seemed like a nice bunch of kids. What kind of trouble are they in?"

"The father said his daughter claimed she was stranded before the call cut out on him. He's tried calling her back throughout the evening, but you know how good the cell service is up this way. Anyhow, my deputy and I have been searching campgrounds, but haven't found a thing thus far. If you ask me, it's just another prank. For every legitimate missing person, there seems to be about three or four more that are hoaxes; usually carried out by teenagers trying to make folks believe the witch got them. Why they think it's fun to worry their loved ones, I'll never know. I wish that damned legend would just die already."

"If that's the case here, they'll be home soon enough," the clerk said. "For their sakes, I hope it is a prank. Would hate to see them missing for real." He picked up a framed photograph and went to work positioning the wire backing over the nail he'd just pounded into the wall.

The sheriff nodded in agreement. "As much as false alarms chap my ass, you're right. I'd much prefer to call that father back with good news rather than the alternative."

With the picture hung, Doug Easley took a step back and surveyed his work. "Look straight to you?"

Frank studied the photograph. In it, a fisherman stood tall and proud next to a monster of a chinook salmon. The fish stretched from the top of the man's head all the way down to his knees. The shot had been captured just outside the store, with the Easley name prominent in the background. Like every other picture on the wall, it formed a patchwork piece of the family's humble legacy. The wall itself was a time capsule, depicting in photographs the people and events that had played a prominent part of the store's past. In a sense, it was its own museum, and any local with an appreciation of history would have felt it an honor to see their mug up on that wall.

"Looks good to me," the sheriff replied. "How much did that salmon weigh in at?"

"A hair over eighty-five. And caught with bait purchased right here."

Frank whistled through his teeth. "Impressive." To that he added: "When are you going to put my picture up there?"

Doug, in the middle of hanging another frame, turned his head and said with a smile, "When you catch one bigger, I suppose."

Frank laughed and took a gander at the second addition to the photo gallery. The slightly tattered black and white showed a young man with tousled, mid-length hair wearing a t-shirt emblazoned with the Rolling Stone's lips and tongue badge. He was propped up against a ’69 Mustang. The smudges of grease on his forearms and pant legs suggested he may have been one of the mechanics who’d worked at the now defunct service garage next door.

“There’s a classic. When was that taken?” the sheriff inquired.

“Well, let’s see,” Doug said, scratching his chin in thought. “The car was a ’69 model, and the Stones debuted that logo in ’71. That means the picture had to have been taken sometime between ‘71 and December of ‘72. It couldn’t have been any later than that.”

“How do you figure?” Frank asked.

“The man in the picture is my uncle. He passed in mid-December of ’72, just two months before I was born. His car went off the road about three miles from here. He lost control and collided with a tree. Killed him on impact. It was a very hard time for the family. My father later told me that my arrival was the only thing that kept him together. Dad always spoke well of his brother. It’s just a shame I never got to meet him.”

“I’m very sorry to hear it, Doug. What was your uncle’s name?”

“Eric,” the clerk replied, eyeing the photograph on the wall. “His name was Eric.”

24

There was a hardness to the night which even the headlights had a hard time cutting. Whether this heightened darkness was real or merely a reflection of her bleak emotional state at present, Amy could not say. Either way, she currently found herself unable to speak. She sat in stunned silence, staring at the road ahead, while tears cut glistening trails across her cheeks.

The Mustang's engine rumbled beneath a polished black hood, its intensity waxing and waning as the car navigated the switchbacks at high speeds.

Eric kept his focus on his driving, alternating his gaze between the road ahead and the rearview mirror, all the while tapping the wheel in a nervous fervor. "Your friends," he said, without averting his eyes. "Are they—"

Amy could only offer a faint nod before dropping her face in her palms and sobbing. *I'm sorry*, she heard Eric say, and when she sat up again, the young man was looking at her. His eyes held hers for a brief second before turning back to the road, but in them radiated a heavy sorrow.

Amy's voice came to her then. It was weak and thin and she barely recognized it as her own. "What were those things?"

"Abominations," Eric said flatly. He gave the steering wheel a twist, whipped the car around another turn, and jammed on the accelerator.

While the reply was an accurate description of the monstrosities back at the camp, it wasn't the answer Amy had been looking for, as it offered little in the way of any real explanation. "Where did they come from," she asked, probing deeper.

"They came from her, from that witch. She's the reason for everything in this town. Everything bad, that is."

"The old woman I saw back in the cabin, was it her?"

"I would imagine so," Eric replied. He gripped the wheel tight and pressed harder on the gas. "Now, you might want to hang on."

Amy turned her attention back to the road where the wide ravine of Cooper's Canyon was just coming into view beyond the narrow arc of the high beams. "The bridge!" she screamed, but it was too late.

At its current rate of speed, the vehicle wouldn't have stopped even if Eric had stood on the brakes. Yet, he didn't even attempt to slow down. Instead, he floored the gas pedal, sending the needle on the tachometer soaring.

He's going to jump, Amy realized. But the span between here and the other side of the canyon was too great. No car could traverse that distance, no matter how fast it was going. The realization that Eric had somehow made it to the campground in the first place did not strike Amy in that moment. Her only thought was that she was about to die.

The crunch of tires on gravel gave way to a sickening silence as the ground dropped from beneath the wheels. Amy clamped her eyes shut and gripped the door handle with enough force that she feared it might snap. Her breathing stopped and she waited for the inevitable impact which was sure to end her life. When the wheels found ground again, she screamed, squeezing her eyelids tighter.

Then she heard it: the growl of the engine spinning up and tires humming against pavement. Somehow, for reasons she could not yet fathom, the car was still in one piece. And she was alive.

"Are you alright?" Eric asked.

Amy drew a tentative breath and opened her eyes. She loosened her death grip on the door handle and looked around, half in a daze. Turning in her seat, she saw the road spooling out behind her; the lip of the canyon fading into obscurity.

"How?" The question came out in a partial whisper. "How did you make it across without the bridge?"

"There hasn't been a bridge there for years," Eric asserted. "I know you believe you crossed one coming in, but you didn't."

"That's . . . not possible," Amy stammered, wide-eyed and confused.

"It works like a wormhole. You enter one side and come out the other, bypassing everything in between. Anyone can cross, but if it appears the bridge is out, why would they try?"

Amy shook her head. "But it *was* there when I arrived. I saw it."

"You thought you saw it," Eric replied. "But it was an illusion, like so many other things you've encountered since you've been here. For instance, I'm sure you're not thinking about eating at a time like this, but I'd be willing to bet that if you did, you'd find you're a bit famished."

Amy hadn't thought about it. However, turning her attention to the matter, she could indeed feel the hollow pangs of hunger gnawing at her stomach. "I guess I am, but that's not much of an illusion. I haven't eaten since breakfast."

"It's been longer than that. You didn't eat breakfast at all," Eric stated. His boldness and manner of certainty took Amy by surprise. "You only *thought* you had breakfast. Except for whatever food or drink you may have bought at my uncle's store, you haven't had a thing to eat since you arrived here."

"That's not true. Robert cooked dinner last night and a big breakfast this morning."

Eric shot a quick glance in her direction. "And how much food is in that kitchen right now?"

The question stopped Amy cold. Her mind began to somersault over the full measure of what the young mechanic was suggesting. After a long silence, she finally uttered a reply. "There's none."

Eric nodded. "Because there was never any to begin with. The food you thought you ate; the feeling of being satiated, was just another illusion."

"This is crazy," Amy said. "What about Robert and Catherine? Or the old lady and those kids? Were they illusions also?"

Eric opened his mouth to speak, but Amy wasn't finished. "And how about my friends?" she asked, tears spilling down the sides of her face. "They're dead. Cut open and murdered by those things. Is that an illusion also? Because it looked awfully fucking real to me!"

Eric lowered his head and spoke softly. "No. That wasn't part of any illusion."

A new stab of pain came on Amy like a nail being pressed into her chest. Her friends were gone. She knew that to be real no matter what other sleight of hand had occurred in this hellhole. Eric's reply was just another confirmation of it; one which drove the nail even deeper into her heart. She wiped at her eyes and let out another cry.

"Around here, it's hard to trust your senses. What you see isn't always there. Sometimes it is. Other times, it's only a mirage; a projection of what scares you most. It's the witch's way of playing on your deepest fears," Eric went on. "Robert, Catherine, and those children, I guess you could say they're real. At least in some sense of the word."

"What does that even mean?" Amy blubbered. "I don't understand any of this."

Eric sighed. "I'm sorry. I know this is a lot to take in, and it's complicated, so I'll try to explain as best I can."

Amy nodded.

"This town was cursed by a witch. Those of us that grew up in these parts have all heard the tales about her. To be honest, I used to think they were all bunk. You know, like some sort of urban legend. But I was wrong. She's very real. And ever since she put a hex on this place, bad things have become the norm—disappearances, odd deaths, strange happenings, people going insane. Those sorts of things occur over the entirety of Shadow Lake. But that camp back there, that's ground zero. That's where she jumped to her death, and that's where she still dwells.

"All of those that have gone missing are because of her. They are the ones who wandered into the woods to hike, fish, hunt, or whatever, and ended up crossing her path by happenstance. Others have encountered her on the roads near the lake and found themselves catapulted into the water. Then there are those—people like you and your friends—that she lures here on purpose."

"Just to kill us?" Amy asked. "Why go through all the trouble if so many already stumble into her path?"

"It's not to kill you, so much as it is to turn you *into* a killer," Eric replied. "After her daughter was murdered by some of the town's settlers, she reciprocated by wiping out most of the children in Shadow Lake. Afterwards, there were reports of some of those children returning from the dead to claim more souls. And so it has been throughout the years. She uses the descendants of the cursed people to carry out her dirty work. Those kids you saw back there were once like you and me, up until she made them into something from a horror show. She seems to have a fondness for the little tykes. I don't know why other than maybe she gets her jollies by destroying their innocence; taking what should be good and twisting it into something wholly evil.

"Anyway, best I can figure is those she draws here could probably trace their lineage back to one of Shadow Lake's originals. She gets the most pleasure out of their deaths. They are the trophies. And after they're dead, she uses them to inflict all kinds of savagery against others."

Amy pawed at her eyes again. She thought about the faces of those children and shuddered. What had been done to them; what they had become, was unthinkable. “So, those kids, they’re not ghosts?"

Eric shook his head. “Not at all. I mean, they're dead and they don’t live and breathe like you do, but their physical presence is real enough. You can touch them and they can touch you, which is what makes them so dangerous.”

“What about Robert and his wife? You said they were here in a sense, but not really.”

“That’s why I said things are complicated. Those kids you saw—the ones she did a Frankenstein number on—have been reanimated by whatever dark magic the witch possesses. They are like zombies, in a sense, and I’m not so sure they even possess souls.

“The rest, their corpses lie scattered under the waters of the lake, mostly in that cove near the camp. The curse keeps their souls bound here and it is their spirits which are used for her bidding. Only when their bodies have been removed from the lake can the souls move on. Some seem to be aware of their death and of the things they are made to do. Others are not. Their purpose is often more obscure and they tend to live in a sort of loop, unaware of the hand they’ve been dealt.

“That was the case with Robert and Catherine. They, too, were at the bottom of the lake up until this morning, when police recovered their bodies. As far as Robert knew, I think he truly believed he oversaw that camp. Catherine saw more; understood more, but her thoughts and conversations remained as disjointed and muddied as they had been in life, so Robert paid no mind to her ramblings. I can only hope they’ve found their peace now.”

“Robert didn’t remember going into the lake? And had no idea of what was happening to the people coming to the camp?” Amy inquired.

Eric shrugged. “I wish I could say. If he did, it never showed. He and his wife were pawns; a part of the illusion that brought and kept you here long enough for that hag to sink her teeth into at least one of you. After they were pulled from the water, a big part of the charade was broken, but by that time your fates were already sealed. Robert and Catherine weren't the first souls used to man that old camp, and they won't be the last. It's a cycle; one big spider-web to lure those whom the witch wishes to ensnare."

"When does it stop?" Amy asked, her expression grim. "When is it enough?"

"Never," Eric answered without hesitation. "It'll never be over." His tone was as weary as his passenger's countenance. He slowed the Mustang at a junction in the road before swerving out onto Black Water Pass heading eastbound.

Amy sat in a languid silence for a long spell while she absorbed all that had been said. It was in those moments of quiet contemplation that a new question presented itself; one which jolted her out of her lethargic state with the same force as being violently shaken awake from a peaceful sleep. Even as the words spilled from her mouth, Amy detected a tremor in her voice and could feel her heart beginning to strum against her ribcage.

"How is it that you know all of this? I mean, how could you possibly?"

Eric glanced at Amy and saw a different kind of fear in the girl's eyes. No longer was it the picture of despair he'd seen upon first picking her up at the camp, nor was it the mixture of horror and revulsion she'd exhibited during the telling of his story. No, the look at present was directed his way. She was afraid of him.

"Wait," he said. "You don't think I'm a part of all this, do you?"

"I didn't. Not at first." Amy hesitated. "But now, I . . . I don't know anymore."

"I can assure you—"

Amy cut him off in mid-sentence. "No, you knew. Back at the garage, you knew. And now . . . now you show up and tell me things that no one could know. People here, they might have heard the stories, sure. But intricate details? That stuff about the witch and those things and Robert and Catherine; what happens to the lost souls in the lake, and how she uses the camp to trap people; even that wormhole—you know all of it."

"Amy," Eric said, low and calm. He extended a hand of solidarity towards her, but she shrunk back as if he were afflicted with leprosy.

"No!" she cried. "How do you explain that? You'd have to be close to her. It's the only way to know. And how do you get close without her killing you and making you a part of her game, unless . . . are there others who've done that? People who have escaped her?"

"None that I know of," Eric replied.

"Then you shouldn't know the things you do. Tell me how that's possible."

"Listen, it doesn't matter. What matters is I'm trying to help—"

"It does matter. My friends are all dead because of something you knew and did nothing about."

Eric's eyes grew wide and he went rigid. "I warned you," he growled. "I told you not to come here and you did it anyway. Why didn't you listen? Why didn't you just leave?"

Amy flinched as if she had just been struck. Tears brimmed beneath her lids and she shook her head in disbelief. "I should have. *We* should have. But we didn't know you. Imagine some stranger telling you the town you're visiting is cursed and to run away. Seems a little dramatic, doesn't it? Still, I thought about it; tried to convince my friends you weren't crazy. But when I got here, everything seemed so . . . normal. What would you have done? Would you have believed? Would you have run away if you were in my shoes?"

Eric was silent. His hardened expression began to soften, little by little, until it was one of remorse. When he spoke again, his mood was somber. "I'm sorry. I shouldn't have said that. I didn't mean to infer that what happened back there tonight was in any way your fault. And you're right. If someone had come at me the way I did you, I would have thought they belonged in the loony bin. Probably would have told them as much, too. It's just that . . . I don't know what else to do. I don't want to see people get hurt, but I'm not sure how to get them to take me seriously."

"My God, Eric." Amy gasped, cupping a hand over her mouth. "How many have there been? How many others have you watched drive away, knowing they were going to their deaths?"

Eric made a fist and pounded lightly against the steering wheel. "Too many," he answered through pursed lips. "Too damn many over the years."

"*Years*?" Amy was stunned. "If you aren't a part of that witch's scheme then why haven't you done something to stop it. Why haven't you gone to the police?"

Eric shook his head. "The police can't see her. They wouldn't be able to see any of them. People only see what she wants them to see."

"But you said the bodies of the dead were in the lake. You could show the police where they're at. Or send them to the camp whenever a new group goes down. If the place isn't operational, the officers could get them to leave by threatening trespassing charges, or something to that effect."

Eric grinned a melancholy grin. It was the same half-cocked smile Amy had seen the day before when she'd watched him wave goodbye. Just as it had then, his face displayed the same tired expression of defeat.

"It's not that simple. I wish it were."

"Why not? Are you afraid they won't believe you? Or that they will, and you'll be their number one suspect?"

"No, it's none of that."

"I don't get it then. Why can't you go to the police?"

"Because. . ."

Eric paused. There was apprehension on his face, and Amy wondered if he was only now trying to come up with something believable; something which would pardon his negligence and exonerate him from being an unwitting accessory to murder. She wasn't at all prepared for what came next. “Because the police can’t see me, either,” the young man blurted out.

25

A torrent of emotion rumbled through Amy's being, leaving her breathless and more shaken than she already was. "What do you mean they can't see you?" she asked, the question coming out in stops and starts.

"To you, I still look to be twenty-three, but I haven't been that age in a very long time. When the car accident occurred, I didn't think I'd been hurt; didn't feel any pain at all, actually. I was just angry at the guy who ran me off the road. I jumped out of the car and started towards him, but he just ran right past like I wasn't even there. I heard him ask someone if they were alright and, next thing I knew, he was freaking out. That's when I turned around. And that's when I realized I was . . . dead."

"No," Amy mumbled, shaking her head at a dizzying pace. "No, no, no. Stop the car. I need to get out. Let me out."

"I can't stop here. If I let you out, she'll come for you. She's probably already coming for you."

Amy was pressed against the door, fumbling with the latch and not hearing.

Ever so gently, Eric touched her arm. When she looked back at him, he could see that the initial fear in her eyes had blossomed into something more. Stark terror now raged there.

"What are you going to do to me?" She tugged at her hair, seeming on the verge of hysteria. "Please. Please, don't hurt me."

"Amy, if I wanted to see you hurt, I'd have left you back there with *her*. But I came for you. Why would I do that only to hurt you?"

"I don't know," Amy wailed. "I don't you, or what you might want to do to me. Maybe you don't want to kill me. Maybe you'd hurt me in other ways."

Eric winced, and his face became as pale and bereft as one would expect of someone who was already deceased. "Oh, God, no," he said, his voice barely registering above a whisper. "I would never. I don't want you to fear me, Amy. Please, don't be afraid."

"Why me?" Amy asked, after a long pause. "What made you come for me?"

"I couldn't sit back and let you die. My hope was to arrive in time to save all of you. I'm only sorry I didn't."

"But why now? Why didn't you come to the aid of others?"

"I couldn't. It's a one-way ticket, you see."

"What do you mean? Can the witch hurt you, even though you're—"

"Dead. It's okay, you can say it. I've had over four decades to come to grips with the fact that I'm checked out," Eric replied. "To answer your question, no, she can't do anything to me. She didn't punch my ticket, which means she didn't lay claim to my soul. I shouldn't still be here; don't know why I am, but I've seen it happen to a few others besides me. We just sort of wander around, going through the motions of our previous life and waiting for who knows what. For some, maybe they needed some sort of closure. In my case, I don't know, unless it was so I could be here now, trying to save someone from that damn witch and her curse."

Amy appeared more at ease now. She had stopped fidgeting with the door and was sitting upright in her seat. "If she can't hurt you, why is this a one-way ticket?"

Eric glanced in the rearview. "You see that?"

Amy looked out the back window, where a dense fog blanketed the road, jutting upwards some twenty or thirty feet into the air and appearing like a misty gray wall. Within the swirling mass, a light flickered.

"What is that?" Amy asked.

"It's her," Eric stated. "She's coming, just as I knew she would. I need to get you over the county line to save you. Her curse stops there. If she were to cross, it would be the end of her. The thing is, when we cross that line, it's the end of me as well."

"How can that be if you're already dead?"

"I'm not even sure how I was able to stick around in the first place. What I do know is, if I cut out of here, there's no coming back. Ever."

"Then don't go over," Amy said. "Let me out at the sign."

Eric shook his head. "Again, not so simple. That curse has given the witch free roam of Shadow Lake right up to the edge of the county line. But for a lost soul not bound by her magic, there's a point of no return which begins before that. The others like me, they wandered too close. Now they're gone. A few tried to turn away when they realized what was happening, but once the change begins, there's no stopping it."

"Do you know where that boundary is for you?"

"There is a sensation as I draw close, so I have a general idea."

"Okay, so let me out before then. I'll walk across on my own."

"If I could do that, I'd have been doing it for the others long before now. That witch is coming for you, Amy, and coming fast. I wouldn't be able to get you close enough. Letting you out of this car could be a death sentence. I only have one shot here, and I'm not about to chance that to save my own hide."

"What happens to you? Where do you go?"

"That's the million-dollar question, isn't it?" Eric smiled. "I cross over, I suppose. Although I have no more knowledge of what that means than I did when I was alive. Maybe there's a heaven, maybe it's the mysterious cosmic white light some claim to see, or maybe I cease to be anything at all. I think that's what scares me most—the fear of becoming nothing; of consciousness slipping away and never returning. We're all afraid of the unknown, and that didn't end with my death. Seems funny to me that I can be dead, yet still have a will to live."

Eric chuckled, but there was an uneasy edge to his laugh. He turned to Amy with a pained expression. "Now you know why I never acted before tonight. It was selfish of me. I was a coward, plain and simple. So, if there's a hell, maybe that's where I belong, because I stood by while all those people died. I had my time on this earth, no matter how short. It wasn't right of me to deny them theirs."

"From what you've just told me, you couldn't have saved them all, anyway, even though I know you would have liked to. If you had already made your run, those who came after still would still have died, including me."

Eric nodded. "I'm still sorry I didn't get to your friends in time."

"I know you are." Amy whispered, misty-eyed. "I'm sorry, too." She sat, contemplating, and then asked: "How is it that I can see you when the cops can't? You also said you'd warned others, which means you had to be visible to them as well."

Eric shrugged. "I have no idea. But those brought here by the witch always could. Must have something to do with her lifting the veil and allowing them to see things others can't. That's how I came to— "

"Look out!" Amy screamed.

Eric turned in time to see an obstacle in the road. Instinctively, and without knowing what he was in danger of colliding with, he slammed on the brakes, bringing the car to a screeching halt.

Fanned out across both lanes, facing the pair head on, were the dead children from the camp. Under the bright glow of the headlights, their pasty skin shone as white as new fallen snow, while their eyes (save for the sickle handed boy who had none) resembled chips of solid black coal. All of them had wild grins on their faces, their thin lips pulled back over slivers of broken teeth. The worst of these was the lava-faced boy, whose gaping hole of a mouth stretched like an apostrophe across his misshapen skull, carving away his nose, chin, and all semblance of anything remotely human.

Amy stared in horror as the children came on, ambling forward with their mad grins. "What are you going to do?" she asked of Eric.

"What I should have done a long time ago." He dropped the clutch, threw the shifter into first, and punched the gas.

The vehicle lurched forward like cannon shot, taking out the lava-faced boy first. His expression twisted into something like a scream before he was dragged beneath the car. A hollow, sickening thud followed as the wheels rolled over his body.

The remaining two were struck at about the same time. The one with the sickle disappeared under the car almost immediately, but the stitched boy-girl held on. Upon impact, its head snapped back on its shoulders with such force that it seemed in danger of detaching. Instead, it whipped forward with equal measure, slamming face first against the hood of the car. When the creature lifted its head again, Amy could see that the stitching which held the two faces together had ripped at the seams, exposing cracked bone and dry, brittle brain. The monstrosity did not bleed red, but rather oozed a substance resembling used motor oil. The stuff coursed from the open wound in spades, splashing against the windshield and skating across the glass in dark, oily ribbons.

Initially, Amy had believed the creature to have purposely latched onto the car, but now it appeared as if it were stuck there against its will. The thing writhed against the front of the vehicle, it's arms lashing out and beating on the hood in a frenzy. The mouth stretched open, tearing away more stitching as it began to shriek. The high-pitched cry was much like the one Amy had heard in the forest during her first night at the camp, only now it was louder; more intense, sounding like an instrument straight out of hell. Shriek after shriek, the peal resonated throughout the Mustang's cabin. It came again and again . . . and again.

Icy tremors raced down Amy's spine. She pressed her hands to her ears and cried out, "Make it stop."

Eric stomped on the brakes and brought the car to a stop.

The twitching form on the hood ceased its screaming and crumbled to the ground in a heap.

"Are you okay?" Eric asked.

Amy nodded. "Let's just go before it gets back up."

Eric shifted into reverse when something hit the back of the car—something with the force of a Mack truck.

Amy was thrown from her seat, hitting her head on the dash before falling to the floor. She pressed a hand to her head as a warm trickle of blood flowed from her hairline and dripped from her brow. "What's happening?" she howled.

Eric twisted around and peered behind the car. The witch was on them.

From out of the mist, a gangling arm emerged. The withered appendage stretched forward like a tree branch, snapping and popping as it extended beyond what was humanly possible. When the fingers lit upon the rear window, it was if there were no barrier between the cabin and the outside world. The windshield had changed. While still exhibiting the appearance of glass, it no longer possessed the same properties. The clear, gelatinous stew it had become emitted a wet sucking sound as the witch's gnarled hand passed through the thick substrate and entered the vehicle. Her bony fingers gripped the top of the seat cushion, the long talon-like nails gouging and tearing through the black leather.

Eric threw the shifter into first and mashed on the gas. The engine revved hard, causing the hood of the car to tremble. At the rear of the vehicle, tires screamed against pavement, filling the cabin with the acrid odor of burning rubber as they spun up ever faster. “Hold on,” Eric said, just before letting off the clutch. The rear tires bit into the pavement with a yelp, propelling the car forward with a jerk.

Glancing in the rearview, Eric watched as the witch fell from view, sheathed once more behind a misty gray wall. From out of the fog, a distant howl emerged. High and savage in nature, it was a cry of unrelenting fury.

With the witch once more behind them, and nothing else standing in his way, Eric believed the chase to be over.

It wasn't.

26

"Is it bad?"

"I don't think so." Amy crawled back into her seat, still holding one hand against her forehead. "May need a stitch or two though."

"No worse for the wear, I guess," Eric said. "But you might want to buckle up just in case things get bumpy again."

Amy pulled the belt over her shoulder and inserted the tongue into the latch until she heard the obligatory click. She peered behind the car, where the rolling currents of fog had set themselves in motion once more, bubbling and boiling with a feverish intensity. "How much further?"

"Not much," Eric replied. He glanced in the side mirror where he could see the mist closing the distance. The engine gave a throaty growl as the young man shifted into fourth and accelerated. He watched the speedometer climb, rocketing the car forward until it was running a brisk 80 mph. *Let's see if you can keep up with that*, he thought, moving to check his side mirror again.

A scant whimper diverted his attention. He turned to see Amy, still staring out the back, her eyes wide with shock.

"It's alright," Eric assured. "She's fast, I know, but so am I."

"Not her" Amy choked. She lifted a shaky finger and pointed. "There."

In the reflection of the rearview mirror, a small figure could be seen slipping up over the back of the car. Under the crimson flare of the tail lights, the creature's bladed hand appeared like a blood red crescent moon rising over the horizon. The sickle came down in a gleaming arc, it's tip punching through the sheet metal and anchoring to the vehicle. The boy leveraged himself up, where his thin frame began to squirm along the trunk and towards the rear windshield.

"You've got to be kidding me," Eric muttered. He whipped the car from side to side, trying to shake the child.

The boy remained glued to the vehicle like a parasite embedded in its host. He worked his way to the windshield and beat down on the glass. This time it held solid, not altering in structure as it had when the witch touched it. The monstrous form ran his blade up and down the clear glass, unleashing a screech which quivered Amy's insides.

"He can't get in," Eric mused. "He doesn't have the same abilities as her."

"I don't care," Amy replied. "I just want to be away from him; from all of them."

"Don't worry. We're getting close. I can feel it."

Sure enough, Eric's complexion had undergone a change. His skin was becoming thinner, taking on a translucent quality and unmasking grayish bone underneath. The process had started, just as he'd said it would.

The enormity of what Eric was doing struck Amy then. One could argue that he wasn't *really* giving his life to save her, seeing as how, in the physical sense, he was already dead. And, while he was only doing what was right by saving the living, one could also surmise that whatever force of good was keeping him here had done so for that very purpose. Still, he could have chosen complacency, conscience be damned. He could have been selfish; turned a blind eye to the atrocities around him while continuing to avoid going into that great unknown which he so feared. But he hadn't. Even though it had taken him a good deal of time to build up the courage to do something, here he was, fighting to save her, while simultaneously casting away his own life force on this earth.

New tears crept into the corners of Amy's eyes, tears borne of compassion and a grateful heart rather than out of fear. She touched the sleeve of Eric's t-shirt. When his eyes met hers, she noticed the color in them had already started to fade. "Thank you," she said.

A laconic smile graced his lips before he turned back to the road. "Thank me after I've gotten you over the line."

"I won't be able to then, will I?"

Eric considered, and gave a humble tilt of his head. "Yeah, well . . . "

A series of hollow thumps interrupted the conversation. It was the dead child. He scampered up the back windshield to the top of the car. A noise like nails being scraped across a chalkboard pierced the air as the boy raked his blade repeatedly across the metal roof, his shrill, spectral cries filling the spaces between each frenzied beat. A few of his blows were powerful enough to perforate the metal, allowing the sharp tip of the blade to protrude into the cabin.

Amy ducked in her seat, distress having returned to her face.

"We're going to make it, Amy. *You're* going to make it. I promise," Eric said. He alternated between gunning the accelerator and slamming on the brakes, hoping to buck the boy off the car. The monster didn't budge.

Eric worked the shifter and punched the gas again, attempting to regain the speed lost by his maneuvers. As he hit second gear, the mist caught up to them, billowing past the windows in inky plumes.

The witch rammed the back of the car, sending it spinning out of control. The Mustang veered off the road, tearing through dirt and gravel.

Eric spun the wheel, tossing Amy hard against the door, as the car rocked to the left and back onto the pavement. It crossed the center line before making a hard one eighty and skidding to a stop.

The witch drifted out of the fog and stood in the middle of the road, her opaque eyes burning with rage. She drew her shriveled mouth into a ghastly, skeletal grin and pointed a bony finger at Amy.

Turbulent voices filled the air, undulating within the confines of the vehicle. They spoke to Amy, whispering of torture and death, while opening her mind's eye to view things which had been seen through the eyes of Yauba. She saw the knife twisting in Dagger's chest; saw a bloodied Beth being pulled into the depths of Shadow Lake by a shape-shifting phantom, and lastly, she beheld the face of John. At first, his expression was soft; his eyes, lovesick and filled with longing, gazing upon what he thought was Amy. Then she saw his panic and experienced the terror which had snaked through his body. She saw him barricaded in the bathroom and watched as a cold steel blade wheeled towards his neck.

Amy was sobbing when her vision returned to the here and now. Her lips trembled and her eyes were once again clouded with tears.

The witch clacked her teeth together and lumbered forward, emitting a sound that might have been demented laughter. "I'll have your soul," she hissed.

Eric dropped the car into reverse and shot backwards, yanking the wheel hard and spinning the vehicle back around before shifting into a forward gear.

Amy noticed that the ends of his fingers were nothing but bone now. Skin was slowly drawing back and curling up along his arms, the edges smoldering with tendrils of ebbing blue flame.

The Mustang began to shake—the dash, seats, and frame rattling as if the ground on which they rested were in the throes of a mighty earthquake.

A hand appeared at the side of the passenger window, followed by the face of the dead boy. His lower jaw was missing, having been torn away when the Mustang ran him over. As frightening as his appearance had been then, it was nothing compared to the ghoulish visage pressed against the window now. His glasses were gone, and one of the patches of skin sewn over the eyes had a long gash running through it, out of which flowed a brackish substance like stagnant green swamp water. He gurgled and hissed, and Amy screamed when she saw him.

"Almost there." Eric's voice sounded strained. His face was haggard, dark circles had pooled beneath his eyes, and hair was falling from his head in clumps.

"Eric," Amy bawled, fearing he might fade away completely before reaching the county line.

The blue flame wriggled over his entire body. Like sulfuric acid on bare skin, it formed a series of holes which began to pool outwards. While he didn't seem to be suffering any pain, it was obvious that Eric was becoming markedly weaker and less present by the second.

A loud clatter startled Amy and she cried out again.

The dead boy pounded against the window with his blade. A dull crunch could be heard on the third swing, with a visible crack forming in the glass. Amy watched with dread as the narrow split distended, creating a jagged trail across the length of the window. Another blow or two like that and there would be nothing between her and that monster.

The rumbling inside the car intensified, eliciting moans of anguish from the stressed welds. Another noise, like that of metal on metal, came on the heels of the creaking joints. The Mustang was coming apart.

"There," Eric said. "There's the sign."

Another thud hit the window, followed by the brittle sound of glass splitting. A series of cracks fanned out from the center of the impact like a spider web. The sickle came down in one more arc before the window gave out completely, crashing inward and falling at Amy's feet.

"Oh, God!" she screamed.

Eric pushed the gas pedal to the floor.

The boy swiped inside the vehicle, nicking Amy's cheek with the tip of his blade. She howled in a terror.

"Almost . . ." Eric hollered.

The child leaned in and swung again, but Amy moved just out of reach.

A raspy gurgle came from the dead boy as he started to wiggle his way inside, all while swinging at the girl in front of him.

"He's coming inside, Eric. He's going to—"

A hand gripped her left arm, and she heard Eric say, "It's done. You can go home now."

What followed happened in a kind of stop-motion slowness. Amy looked up just as the sign for Newfield County zoomed by. Almost immediately, a sound like rushing water filled her ears and radiant blue light filled the car.

The dead boy was consumed by fire. He flailed and screamed as flames licked at his skull, the putrid substance within his eye sockets boiling out from the cavernous pits and cascading down his mangled face.

Everything which had been in motion—the car, the boy, and Eric—came to a sudden halt. All that is, except for the girl. The seatbelt thinned, becoming like wet paper, before dissolving away completely. Amy felt her body leave the seat, realizing with a sudden and dire presence of mind that she was about to be hurled, unrestrained, down the road at over ninety miles an hour. When gravity brought her crashing down, the force of her head hitting the ground would kill her. And if by some miracle it didn't, she would likely end up severely brain damaged and missing half of her face from the long skid into the home stretch.

Panic settled into her bones as she went airborne. Then, the unexpected happened: the hand which had gripped her arm, held on. It faltered initially, and Amy could feel her arm slipping from Eric's grasp. When she looked at him, his facial features had mostly diminished, save for his eyes. In them remained the tiniest spark of life which, upon seeing the terrified plea on Amy's face, ignited with color. For a fleeting moment, he became whole again, mustering one final roar of determination. His hand tightened around Amy's arm long enough to pull her to him and then lower her to the ground unharmed.

Eric's grip fell away. He bowed his back and floated upwards, now fully suspended in the ball of blue light. Amy watched while that which remained of the man and his car broke into thousands of tiny pieces. Like embers mixed with hot ash, the pieces wafted upwards, spinning through the air before faltering and disappearing altogether. A brilliant flash followed, and then the blue light was gone as well.

Amy ran her hand along the ground, letting her fingers play against the rough pavement. Her breathing was ragged, and her heart was still racing, but she was safe. As if she needed further confirmation, she fished her phone out of her jeans pocket and pressed the home button. The top of the screen indicated a full signal. Her chest heaved with emotion, while bittersweet tears crept into the corners of her eyes.

She tried to stand, but her knees buckled, sending her back to the pavement. The adrenaline, the shock, and the myriad of emotional highs and lows of the past half hour had left her dizzy and light headed. She decided to sit for a spell to let the delirium pass. She could wait for someone to drive by; maybe even let them take her into town, providing, of course, that the town was Mary's Bend and not Shadow Lake. For now, she would call home, let her parents know she was alive and well, and ask them to send help.

With trembling hands, Amy navigated her contacts until she found the one that said HOME. She raised the phone to her ear and waited for the first ring.

Not far from where she sat, a child giggled.

Amy gasped and her body fell slack. She lost her grip on the phone, which clattered to the ground. "No," she cried in disbelief. Another bout of lightheadedness weaved its way through her, bringing with it a wave of nausea. With trepidation, she slowly lifted her head.

Standing no more than fifteen feet away, on the Montgomery County side of the road, was the witch and the remaining children. The lava-faced boy clutched the old woman's cloak, resting his head on her hip in the manner of a shy child clinging to the safety of its mother. The boy-girl rocked back and forth, grinning, as if ready to play a game. Both appeared to have recovered from their earlier injuries, looking just as they had before being mowed over with Eric's car. The old woman only glared, her glowing white eyes burning with hatred and malice.

Amy held her breath and waited. Several seconds ticked by before she remembered that the old woman and her monstrosities could not come over to where she was. The realization brought with it a deep sense of relief, but the sick feeling stemming from the traumatic course of the evening continued to mount. She had only ever fainted once in her life (taking a less than classy early bow during a third-grade dance recital), but remembered well the sensations leading up to it.

Feeling certain that she was on the verge of a repeat performance, Amy locked eyes with the old witch and sneered. "Rot in hell!" The words came out in a strangled cry. "Every last one of you."

If the witch ever uttered a response, Amy did not hear it. With darkness storming her vision, she slumped to the ground in a state of unconsciousness.

27

At just past nine the following morning, Frank Andrews charged across the parking lot at County General Hospital in Mary's Bend.

Landon quickened his pace to keep up. The deputy surmised that this was probably the most exercise the sheriff had had in months, maybe even years. His boss was irritated, which wasn't an uncommon sight, but the level of agitation the man was experiencing now was either a great motivator, or a potential heart attack inducer likely to land him back in the very building he'd just walked out of.

"Hold up, sir," Landon called out. "I'm not the trained athlete you are."

"Can it, son. I'm not in the mood."

"Fair enough. But what's eating you?"

Frank stopped and faced the deputy. "This close, Stephens," he said, holding his thumb and forefinger together. "In the long history of missing people in Shadow Lake, there has never been one turn up alive, until now."

"And . . . that's a bad thing?"

"No. It's grand, Stephens. I'm glad she's alive. I couldn't wait to get here and talk to her. But I got my hopes up for nothing."

"I'm not following," Landon said. "What were you expecting from her? A hug?"

"Damnit, Stephens! You should know what I'm talking about. You were there. You heard what she said."

"She didn't say much of anything at all."

"Exactly my point," Frank replied. As if he had provided satisfactory answers to all of Landon's questions, he turned and resumed his march across the parking lot.

"Wait. You're upset because she can't remember what happened to her?"

"Yes!"

"How is that her fault? It's not like she's lying to you about it. You heard the doctor."

"I did." Between the curt answers and his hurried gait, the sheriff seemed like a child on the cusp of a tantrum.

"It's basic psychology," Landon said. "Sometimes the brain represses memories after a traumatic event."

"They teach you that at the fancy police academy you went to?" Frank snapped.

"Yes, they did," Landon replied. "Didn't they teach you? Or was that so long ago they didn't cover mental health?"

The sheriff spun on his heels. His face was drawn tight and there was fire in his eyes. He lifted a finger and wagged it at the deputy in a scolding manner. "You're on thin ice, Stephens."

"I apologize. That was out of line. It's just hard to have a conversation if you're biting my head off. I'm only trying to understand your position here."

Landon watched as the boiling pots which were the sheriff's eyes gradually reduced to a low simmer. After what seemed like an eternity, Frank cupped his hand around the deputy's shoulder and gave it a firm squeeze. "Let's go, kid," he said with a nod.

Landon figured that was the closest he'd get to an apology from the sheriff, but it would do. "Right behind you."

"Listen," Frank continued, walking at a more leisurely pace now. "It's not that I'm upset with the girl. God knows, she's been through something awful. I'd just hoped she would be able to give us some insight."

"Maybe she still will. Sometimes these memory lapses are temporary. And if she doesn't remember on her own, regression therapy might help."

The sheriff grunted. "I like your optimism, but I wouldn't count on it."

"Why not?" Landon asked.

"You're new to these parts, so you haven't seen enough of what goes on just yet. Some of what we get is normal, but most of it isn't so cut and dry. That's the weird shit I was telling you about. Those are the cases that never give up their secrets; the ones that end up being one dead end after another. Work enough of those and you become jaded. It's like that car we pulled out of the water yesterday. I can guarantee you we'll never know how those people ended up in the lake. Same goes for this. That gal doesn't remember what happened and I'm willing to bet she never will, therapy or not. And her three friends? Based on my experience, we won't see hide nor hair of them ever again. Mark my words, Stephens.

Landon hoped the sheriff might be wrong in this instance. While he didn't view his boss as entirely pessimistic, the deputy could understand how not finding answers to so many cases could get to the man after a while. After all, without answers there could be no solutions. And in that respect the sheriff might have felt that he was not making enough of a difference; that he was, in many ways, failing both his profession and the community at large.

The two officers had just reached the patrol car when Landon spoke. "I know this is frustrating, but try not to let it get you down. The answers we're looking for may be hard to find, but I'm up for the challenge."

"Of course you are," Frank replied, reaching for the door handle. "Why the hell else would I have hired you?"

"Good point," Landon laughed. "Say, it's still early and neither of us has had breakfast. What do you say we head over to Mabel's? I haven't been there yet, although I have it on good authority that it's the place to beat."

Frank stopped, eyeing the deputy on the opposite side of the vehicle with suspicion. "Are you pulling my leg, Stephens? They don't serve quiche over there, you know."

"No joke, sir. I thought it might take our minds off things for a while. And forget the quiche. I was actually looking forward to trying the donuts."

The sheriff appeared flabbergasted. "You? A donut? After the grief you've given me over those things, now you want one?"

"With coffee, sir. Yes."

After a moment of quiet astonishment, a wide grin spread across Frank's face. "By God, son, there's hope for you yet." He gave the roof of the squad car a hearty slap. "Well, don't just stand there, deputy. Get your ass in."

Landon obliged.

28

Amy stepped out between the sliding glass entry doors of the hospital's entrance and squinted under the bright mid-day sun. A light breeze stirred, teasing the ends of her hair, while the clear summer afternoon enveloped her like a warm blanket. It was a nice change from the cold, sterile room she had occupied on the second floor, but the pleasantness of the day was not enough to quell her insipid mood.

The fact that her closest friends were missing was disheartening on its own, but having been told she'd been with them, and was now unable to remember anything about what had happened over the past couple of days, made Amy feel even more dismal.

"Now, where is your father?" her mother said impatiently. She stood at the entrance, craning her neck and scanning the wide expanse of the parking lot. "I sent him down here ten minutes ago. He should have already been here with the car. Probably stopped to talk to someone. I swear, it's a wonder he ever makes it anywhere on time."

Why? Why can't I remember?

Amy had asked that question countless times over the last twelve hours. Her parents would point to the six stitches running across the top of her skull. *You just hit your head,* they would say. *Thank God, that's all it was. We're just happy you're okay.*

But she wasn't okay. Even if the gash on her head were to blame for the memory loss, there were still too many lingering questions. How had she hit her head in the first place? What had she been doing? What if her friends had hit theirs also . . . or worse? Suppose they needed medical attention? She had no way of knowing where to send help.

Such thoughts brought with them a surge of anxiety which only worsened the longer she thought on them. In fact, the very act of trying to remember anything at all ended up giving her fits. The doctor had anticipated as much, sending her home with a cocktail of scripts for sleeping pills, painkillers, and antidepressants, among other things. The thought of taking those only made Amy more anxious. She didn't want to be doped up. She just wanted to remember.

"There he is," her mother said, pointing to the gray Lexus sedan which had just turned into the circular patient loading zone. She waved like a woman hailing a cab at rush hour, as if her husband might not have seen her otherwise and kept on driving. Harold Grainger tooted the horn in response, a gesture which was every bit as unnecessary as the wave.

Mrs. Grainger patted her daughter on the back and the two of them started towards the car. They were halfway there when Amy, still lost in thought, collided with someone walking the opposite direction. "Oh, I'm sorry," she said.

"No, pardon me," the man replied. "I was trying to read this text my wife sent and should have been paying closer attention to where I was walking. Are you alright?"

Amy didn't answer. She stared at the man's shirt with rising curiosity. The tee was old, the ink fading, but the lips and tongue printed across the front were still distinguishable enough. Amy knew it to be the iconic logo of the Rolling Stones. She had seen it many times throughout her life, but something about it now gave her pause.

"Miss?" the man prodded. When Amy still didn't answer, he shrugged, mumbled something about kids these days, and went on his way.

"Amy, sweetheart, is something the matter?" her mother asked.

"No," Amy replied. "I just saw that guy's shirt and . . . I don't know. It's like there was something there for a second. A memory, maybe?"

"Don't fret about it," her mother replied. "If it's important, you'll remember in time. Let's get you home."

You can go home now.

Images of a young man and a car flashed through Amy's mind, then retreated just as quickly. Who was he? Was there some kind of association between him and the words she'd just remembered? What did it all mean?

Amy's father walked around the vehicle and opened the door for his daughter. "Are you hungry? One of the doctors was telling me about a great burger joint over in Shadow Lake. Baxter's, I think he said it was called."

Amy stiffened. "I don't want to go back there."

"You've been there already? Well, alright. We can eat somewhere else."

"No, I mean I don't want to go through Shadow Lake. I don't know why. I wish I did, but I'm afraid. Please, don't go home that way."

Her father scrunched his brow together and scowled. "That's the quickest way back to Portland. Any other route will take us at least an hour out of our way. Besides, going back through there might help you remember something. That's good, right?"

Amy could feel her eyes welling with tears. She didn't understand why the thought of Shadow Lake terrified her so, only that she never wanted to step foot there again. "I just can't. Daddy, please."

"Harold," her mother said, in that grave tone which makes every husband cringe.

"Fine, fine," he waved. "We'll go north. But, we're stopping for a burger somewhere between here and home. I'm going to need some lunch."

Some moments later, driving along the main road which would take them out of Mary's Bend, Amy turned and looked in the vicinity of Shadow Lake. Even now, her stomach remained knotted over her father's suggestion that they travel through there. Whatever had happened; whatever it was she couldn't remember, was ugly and terrible. That sense had been with her ever since coming to in her hospital bed, but it had been faint and not at all prevalent. It was akin to waking from a dream you suspected of being dark and unsettling, even though you could not recall what it had been about. You knew, because there was an underlying splinter of fear woven through your consciousness; a splinter belonging to one of the hidden doors of the mind which only ever allows a fleeting glimpse of what lies behind it. But sometimes a glimpse, even an obscure one, is enough to discern that some doors are better left unopened.

Such was the case now. The mere mention of Shadow Lake had fully awakened that sense in Amy, setting off alarms without providing any insight into why. As much as a part of her wanted to peek into the memories of the past two days, if for no other reason than to know that her friends were okay, another part of her wondered if the amnesia might be the only link to her sanity.

Amy continued to stare out the rear window with a blank and far away stare. She was numb; her insides wrapped in a murky haze—alive, but feeling mostly dead. All she could think about were John, Beth, and Dagger. She wanted to believe they were out there, safe and waiting to be reunited, yet feared they were still behind the hidden door with whatever horrors lurked there.

Amy's vision clouded and a solitary tear escaped the corner of one eye. She stretched out across the backseat and wept, the steady hum of tires lapping against the highway masking her low sobs. It wasn't long before she slipped into a dreamless sleep.

29

ONE YEAR LATER . . .

The boys were still squabbling when the red Chrysler minivan they were riding in pulled to a stop in front of the office. The younger of the two, bespectacled with short, spiky hair, was lamenting the fact that his older brother was already trying to lay claim to the front seat of one of the canoes.

"You can't call shotgun in a canoe, dummy!"

"Shut up. What do you know? You've never even been to camp. I've been twice. That gives me first dibs."

"No it doesn't!"

"Both of you listen," their mother scolded, turning in her seat. "If you wake your sister, there won't be a canoe ride for either of you. Understand?"

The boys gave a reluctant nod. As soon as their mother's eyes were no longer on them, the eldest stuck his tongue out, which earned him an immediate slug to the arm from his younger brother.

"Dad, Jason hit me."

"You started it, jackass!"

"That's enough from both of you," their father said. He kept his voice low, but his tone was as severe as ever. "I'm not going to put up with this all weekend. We came here to have a good time. If you two can't do that, and insist on fighting the whole time we're here, you can each sit in separate cabins by yourselves while the rest of us enjoy ourselves. Now get your butts out of the van and start acting civil towards one another."

Sour-faced, the brothers pulled open the van door and stepped outside. Neither of them spoke, but their cool stares indicated that the animosity level was still high. The older of the two grabbed the handle to pull the door shut.

"Easy," the mother said. "Don't slam the—"

WHAM!

". . . door," she finished. She sighed in exasperation as the baby began to wail.

"Sorry, hon," the father said. "I'll deal with them after we get checked in. You want to grab Olivia and come inside?"

"It's okay. I'll stay here and see if I can get her back in good spirits. But next time we want to take a relaxing trip to the mountains, let's get a sitter."

"I'm sure once we get settled the boys will calm down. You know how it is when they are cooped up together on long car rides. Probably should have given them some Dramamine before we left."

"Or given it to me," the mother smiled. "I'd have been more than happy to have slept all the way here."

"Right," the father laughed, climbing out of the van. "Be back in a jiffy."

Stepping inside the musty confines of the office, the older boy remarked: "It's freezing in here. Kinda stinks, too."

"Probably just smelling your own underwear," Jason laughed.

"Your underwear, half-wit," his brother retorted.

"Your face!"

"What? That doesn't even make sense."

"Knock it off," their father warned. "There are some brochures over on that table. Why don't you take a gander at those? It'll give you an idea of the activities available. That way you can start thinking about what you'd like to do later. I'm going to grab the keys to the cabin."

With the boys occupied, the man stepped to the counter and tapped the service bell. While he waited, he surveyed the interior of the office. It was dated, to be certain, but also quaint. *Gives the place character* he thought. And despite the antiquated appearance of the office, the scenery outside was stunning, which was exactly what he had been looking for. He'd done well in finding this place, if he did say so. And to think, he'd almost missed it during his online search. Fate must have been on his side, however, as the camp seemed ideal, exceeding all his expectations thus far. Yes, sir. This was going to be a vacation to remember.

He was reaching for the bell again, when an attractive young woman stepped out from the back room. Thin, with strawberry-blonde hair pulled up in a loose bun, she smiled a warm smile as she stepped up to the counter.

"Hello," she beamed. "My name is Beth. Welcome to Shadow Lake."

DARK NIGHTS ON SHADOW LAKE

FEAR ALONE

"Monsters are curious things. We imagine them as grotesque forms lurking under beds or in dark places, waiting to prey on anyone who wanders near. But in truth, we needn't fear such things. For the worst horrors are not those which are imagined in fiction, but rather the ones suffered at the hands of men."

- Kevin Carpenter, Montgomery County District Attorney

1

For Gillian Adams, November 3rd was the coldest day of the year. There was a chill in the air, the sky was overcast, and the world was painted in steel gray hues. Weather, however, wasn't her issue. Wearing a pair of corduroys and a long-sleeved zip neck fleece, she was dressed appropriately enough to keep warm. The cold, rather, was rising from within her soul. Once warm and full of life, it was now a place of desolation; a black, barren landscape ravaged by ghosts from the past. Though there had been a long stretch of dark days in her life, Gillian thought she had finally put them behind her and that, little by little, what was broken would mend. But ghosts, as everyone knows, don't die easy, and Gillian was about to realize that this day would be her darkest yet.

The morning had started just like any other. She was up before dawn, packing a lunch for her son, Connor, and starting a pot of coffee before showering and dressing. Once she had herself put together, it was Connor's turn. It usually took several minutes to roust him out of bed and get him moving of his own volition. He was even less of a morning person than she was and it required nothing short of an act of God to get him up before he was good and ready. Today was no exception. It was a full fifteen minutes before he finally shuffled down the hall and into the bathroom. His eyes were half closed and he moved like a zombie, but at least he was awake.

Gillian made her way back to the kitchen where she clicked on a small portable radio and poured a cup of coffee. She collected a few eggs and a carton of milk from the refrigerator before grabbing one of the only remaining pans from the cabinet. There was very little to work with, as most everything in the house had already been packed for the move, but she had left just enough out to do the most basic cooking.

Turning the dial on the gas stove, the familiar clicking of the igniter was followed by an emphatic whooshing sound as the burner roared to life. Gillian flinched. The sound was always expected, yet she couldn't help but be startled. For a moment, she was lost, looking at the dancing blue flames and then down at the raised pink splotches on the palms of her hands. They didn't hurt—not anymore—but they would always be there. Like the other scars on her body, they were constant reminders of the past.

"Don't overcook the eggs, Gillian," she muttered aloud. Then, with the changing of songs on the radio, her trance was broken and she quickly pushed the memories out of her head. While the Verve played their *Bittersweet Symphony*, Gillian placed the skillet on the stove, dropped in a dollop of butter, and began whisking eggs together in a bowl. Once they were sufficiently mixed, she grabbed her coffee mug for a couple of sips while she searched the refrigerator for some cheese.

The song on the radio stopped, replaced by an emergency bulletin:

> "We interrupt this programming with an urgent news flash. Law enforcement officials in Montgomery County indicated that at approximately 11:52 p.m. last night, three inmates escaped from the Westbrook Correctional Facility and are still at large. They are believed to be on foot and were last spotted heading east. Residents of Havencrest and the Shadow Lake area are urged to be on the lookout and exercise extreme caution. Authorities are urging motorists not to stop for hitchhikers and to

immediately report any suspicious persons or activity. Escaped are John Taylor Rhodes, Michael Anthony Morrison, and Billy Wayne Adams..."

Gillian felt her breath catch in her throat. She lost her grip on the mug she held, which tipped forward, spilling coffee on the floor before falling to the ground and shattering. Her knees went weak and she latched onto the refrigerator door for support. Questions flew through her mind at a furious pace. *How? How could this be happening?*

She was just days from leaving this town and moving far away to a place that would provide a fresh start. So why now, when she was so close to being free? There were no answers, of course, other than the fact that this life—this place she called home—had dealt her a shit hand. The only thing she knew for certain was that if Billy Wayne Adams was no longer behind bars, he would be coming for her.

"Mama, are you alright?" Connor asked. He stood just a few feet away, a towel wrapped around his skinny waist and his hair still wet from the shower.

Gillian tried to restore her composure, wiping at the warm tears which had pooled at the corners of her eyes. "Yeah, I'm fine. Just a little clumsy is all," she replied, feigning a smile.

But truth be told, all she wanted to do was cry. She was shaken, and the sudden flood of emotion made it hard for her to think. Regardless, she still had enough presence of mind to know that she did not want to alarm Connor. She clicked off the radio and knelt on the floor, where she began collecting the broken bits of ceramic mug that were scattered about.

"You know, I was thinking," Gillian continued, trying to mask the tremor in her voice, "Perhaps we could get a jump on things and leave town a little early. It would be about lunch time once we reached the city and we could stop at that pizza place you like so much. What do you say?"

Connor looked at her as if she had just asked him to eat nothing but broccoli for an entire year. "We can't go. I have school. Besides, you're still watching grandma and grandpa's house," he said.

It was true that she had been picking up the mail and keeping an eye on her parent's house while they were away. They had gone to Seattle, where Gillian's aunt was undergoing knee replacement surgery, and were due to return sometime late next week. If Gillian were to leave, the mail and the house would be left unattended for several days. With the current turn of events, however, she was sure her parents would understand.

"Your grandparents will be back soon enough. I'm sure I can get Mr. Davis from next door to watch the house for a few days. Besides, when did you become so concerned about missing a day of school?"

"Ms. Miller said she was giving me a party today since this is the last time I'll see any of my friends. You're already making me move a thousand miles away, and now you want to leave before I can even say good-bye? That's not fair, Mom," Connor huffed.

A sense of guilt began to gnaw at Gillian and she let out a defeated sigh. It was an emotion she knew well, as it had been her constant companion for almost a decade, beginning with her marriage to Billy.

When the beatings first started, Billy had convinced her that they were her fault; if she had been a better wife and had done things right—the way *he* wanted them done—he wouldn't have lost his temper, and the marriage would have turned out the way she had always hoped it would. She knew now that was a lie and had long ago stopped blaming herself for Billy's actions. But, when it came to Connor, things were different.

Though he had never been a target of Billy's rage (that was always reserved for her), he had witnessed things that no child should ever have to see. It's a mother's job to protect her children, not just from physical harm, but from all manner of cruelty in the world. On that front, Gillian felt she had failed. Thus, she now found herself bending to her son's wishes (within reason, of course). It was difficult not to, as she was constantly plagued by remorse. Allowing Connor to have his way felt like a necessary penance, although she knew deep down it would never grant her absolution. Even if Connor had forgiven her, she wasn't yet able to forgive herself.

"You're right. You should have the chance to say your good-byes. I didn't realize Ms. Miller was giving you a party. We wouldn't want all of her hard work to go to waste now, would we?"

Connor grinned and shook his head.

"Well then, you'd better get dressed and eat up so you can get to school. You've got a big day ahead of you," Gillian said, smiling back.

As Connor darted back down the hall towards his room, Gillian's cheerful façade fell away. Now, instead of being on the road before noon, it would be closer to 3:00 pm before she could put Shadow Lake in her rearview.

She hoped and prayed that it wouldn't be too late.

2

Gillian turned her silver Honda CRV left onto Main Street and headed north towards the elementary school. The anxiety within her continued to mount, and she had to make a conscious effort to guide her thoughts away from the fearful scenarios clouding her mind. If only she could sleep the hours away and have someone wake her up when it was time to leave town. She had briefly considered taking a sedative, but decided it wasn't a viable solution to relieving her mental anguish. Not only did it pose the risk of oversleeping, but it would also make her that much easier for Billy to find.

"Mama, look!" Connor exclaimed, pointing out the car window and pressing his nose to the glass.

"It's your favorite place, huh? Mine, too," Gillian said. "That's one of the things I'm going to miss when we're gone."

They were coming up on Baxter's Drive-in. Since its founding by Melvin Baxter back in the late fifties, the drive-in had become a Shadow Lake institution and was, to this day, still the most popular hangout for teens cruising the strip.

A monolithic sign out front flashed like a carnival ride, with an arrow directing drivers towards a structure awash in blue and pink neon. Flanking the building on both sides were long rows of car stalls, each with menus encased in polished stainless steel.

Unlike their modern counterparts, the menu boards here did not contain two-way intercoms. Mr. Baxter had always insisted on more personal service, with staff going to each car and scribbling the orders on pads of paper. On any given night, the restaurant resembled a beehive as the carhops, dressed in their uniforms of pink, blue and yellow, swarmed in and out of the kitchen.

Gillian had worked at Baxter's during her last two years of high school and relished the memories of those days. They were, undoubtedly, some of the best of her life.

Being a bookish type who was a bit on the shy side, Gillian certainly hadn't been the most popular girl in school. On Friday nights, while her classmates were at parties or football games, she would have been at home by herself. For all practical purposes, she'd been invisible—a flesh and blood ghost that walked the halls of the high school without ever being noticed. But that all changed during her junior year. It started with her job at Baxter's.

Melvin Baxter was warm and charismatic; the type of guy who could engage anyone in conversation and make them feel like the most interesting person he'd ever talked to. Gillian thought he would have made a great car salesman had he not been so honest.

"Hot and cheesy, not too greasy!" he used to bellow each time he'd place a tray of burgers in the window. The man loved what he did and it showed. Everything was made from scratch to exacting standards, and if the food wasn't perfect, it didn't go out.

Melvin's doggedness to quality paid off. The place was always packed. People would drive from Havencrest and further just to have a Baxter burger and a slice of his famous black bottom pie. The pie was so good that Reverend Nelson once mentioned it in a sermon, saying: *"If the manna God sent from heaven had been Melvin's black bottom pie, the*

Israelites would have been content to stay in the wilderness, having thought they had already reached the Promised Land."

As good as the food was, however, that was not the thing which brought change to Gillian's life. Rather, it was the man behind it. Mr. Baxter was like a wise old uncle, treating his staff like family and becoming both an inspiration and a mentor to many. He instinctively knew how to bring out the best in others and had helped to draw Gillian out of her shell. He praised her work ethic and, for the first time in her life, made her feel like she was a part of something.

At Baxter's, she was one of the team. She was liked by her co-workers and, most importantly, she was seen. She smiled more, was less uptight, and making conversation with strangers soon became second nature. She was happy, and the confidence and cheerful energy she exuded soon caught the eye of a handsome young man—a boy by the name of Billy Wayne Adams.

3

It was a Saturday night in late September when Julia Davidson, a fellow carhop at Baxter's, took Gillian by the arm and pulled her over to a black Mustang convertible parked in one of the stalls. *"I'd like you to meet some of my friends from Havencrest,"* she'd said.

There were five people in the car: two guys up front and three girls in the backseat. The men all wore lettered jackets (football players as it turned out) and the girls, Gillian assumed, were probably cheerleaders. They were all friendly enough—much nicer than the jocks at Shadow Lake High—but after the traditional introductions and a bit of small talk, the attention and chatter turned towards Julia. All except for the driver, that is, who remained fixated on Gillian.

Billy seemed interested in learning all about Gillian. *Had she always lived in Shadow Lake? How long had she worked at the drive-in? Did she enjoy it? What did she like to do for fun? Did she have a boyfriend?*

The last question caught Gillian by surprise and rendered her speechless. Though she prayed it wasn't noticeable, she imagined her face was the color of the cherry fizz which Billy held in his hand. She wasn't used to this kind of attention, certainly not from boys, and especially not from boys as attractive and charming as the one in front of her now.

"No," she finally mustered with a bashful grin, evading his gaze and staring down at the ground.

"Good to know," Billy replied, flashing his perfect straight teeth and giving her a wink. "I'll be sure and remember that."

....

He didn't ask her out immediately. In fact, he came back to Baxter's alone at least a half dozen more times before doing so. It wasn't because he was timid at all but, as Gillian would later realize, he was calculating. Each stolen glance was as much about sizing up the type of girl she was as it was a form of flirtation. In hindsight, it was as if he were a predator stalking prey; thinning out the weakest in the herd, so to speak. Of course, at the time, how was she to know the kind of man he would turn out to be?

Looking back, it was hard to believe that those eyes of his—those deep, piercing eyes which had once made her weak in the knees—would later fill her with so much terror. Back then, she only saw a boy who liked her. And she liked him back. As such, it came as no surprise when Billy finally did get around to asking Gillian out, that she'd accepted without hesitation.

Like most relationships, things were wonderful in the beginning, especially for someone who had never been in one. The feeling of being wanted; the affection and words of adoration, were euphoric. Gillian couldn't get enough, and things progressed quickly.

The first time they had sex was in early December. Billy had driven her to the same secluded spot near the lake where they had made out several times before. It was cold that night, so Billy left the car and the heater running. They'd wrapped themselves in a blanket in the backseat and, on that occasion, she allowed his hands to explore her in places that she never had previously.

The sensation was exhilarating. Her entire body had gone flush and, as her pants slid down around her ankles and dropped to the floorboard, the realization of what was about to happen had her heart thrumming so hard that she'd wondered for a moment if it might burst.

The intercourse itself, however, did not live up to the anticipation. There was some pain, which Gillian had expected her first time out, but the whole experience was over almost as fast as it had begun. It wasn't awful, by any means, she'd just expected some sort of life-altering climax. After all, it always seemed so much more exciting and passionate in the movies.

Regardless, there was still something blissful about her naked body being intertwined with Billy's, and she'd enjoyed the sense of closeness and depth of the emotion that had come with it. It may not have been the fireworks show she had been hoping for, but Gillian was certain she was in love.

4

Soon after that night in December, the earliest signs of possessive and controlling behavior began to appear. Billy had a problem with every guy Gillian went to school with or worked alongside, convinced that they wanted to steal her away. In more subtle ways he began to dictate what kind of clothes she wore in public, how much make-up she used, and who she should or shouldn't be talking with.

There were other things as well—smaller heavy-handed acts such as putting butter on their popcorn at the movies, even though he knew she didn't like it. If she protested, he would turn the tables, as if she were the one in the wrong. "*Relationships are about compromise,*" he'd said. "*You can't just think about yourself all of the time.*"

Initially, Gillian shrugged it off. *That's just how he is. He doesn't mean anything by it.*

As a matter of fact, the jealousy was somewhat endearing at first. It just meant that he loved her and didn't want to lose her. What could be wrong with that? Besides, everyone has a few flaws. She could certainly be worse off.

More often, Gillian focused on the things other people were saying. Girls would remark on how handsome Billy was and how lucky Gillian was to have someone like that. Others mentioned how great the two of them looked together, what a perfect couple they made, and what beautiful children they could have together. It was all music to Gillian's ears. She'd felt she was living a dream and had begun to imagine what married life would be like with Billy.

She was reminded of something Mr. Baxter had once said, shortly after his 50th wedding anniversary. Even after all those years together, one could always see the love in Melvin's eyes whenever he spoke of his wife. When asked the secret for such a long happy marriage, the response Mr. Baxter gave was one Gillian would never forget:

"Every man has a passion in his life; that one thing which drives his enthusiasm and, in some sense, helps to define him. For some it's sports. For others, it may be cars, hunting, or building things. For me personally, it's cooking. But no matter what it is, if every man would devote the same care and attention to his wife as he does that life passion, I doubt there would be much in the way of divorce."

Those words had been both beautiful and wise. What woman wouldn't want someone to love them the way Mr. Baxter loved his wife? In Gillian's mind, she thought she'd found such a man in Billy. She couldn't have been more wrong.

5

They were married the following autumn. It was sooner than expected, but Gillian had discovered she was pregnant two days prior to graduation. Billy was thrilled with the news of a baby; her parents much less so. They had wanted Gillian to attend college and start a career before binding herself to the obligations of marriage and family.

There were also concerns on their part as to how the young couple would support themselves; worries which were quickly put to rest by Billy's father. His business, Devlin-Pacific Logging, had made him one of the wealthiest residents of Havencrest and he appointed his son to the position of crew foreman. The income had been more than sufficient, allowing Billy to purchase a small house and keep food on the table without placing any undue financial burdens on the newlyweds.

The first few months of marriage went well enough, but it wasn't long before Gillian noticed the full measure of Billy's control issues. He'd instructed that everything in the house had its place and needed to be aligned a certain way. In the kitchen cupboards, food labels all had to face outward, with cans stacked just so. Glassware was to be arranged by size and lined up in precise rows, and mugs were required to have their handles positioned to the right.

In the bathroom, it was much the same, with toilet tissue always feeding over the roll rather than under, while towels needed to be folded in a precise fashion. Billy also expected a clean house at all times and wanted dinner precisely at 6:00 pm. If any of these things were out of sort, then so was he.

Gillian thought it all seemed a bit anal retentive, but had accommodated him, figuring it was the least she could do since she stayed at home all day while he went off to work. But after Connor arrived, the demands of a newborn made it much harder to keep up with Billy's expectations, and that's when the abuse started.

The first time he had come home to dinner not being ready, he'd shoved Gillian against the refrigerator so hard that her teeth rattled. She'd started to explain that Connor had been fussy all day, but Billy cupped a hand over her mouth and told her to shut up.

"You're just going to have to let the baby cry sometimes. I have to eat too, you know?"

The experience had left Gillian stunned, and it was she who'd spent the next half hour crying while preparing dinner. Billy hadn't inflicted any physical harm—not then—but he had left a deep emotional wound.

Later that night he apologized, blaming the stresses of work for his outburst which, in his words, was unacceptable. *"Could she ever forgive him?"* he'd asked.

Of course she could.

Once Billy had turned out the lamp on the nightstand and rolled over to sleep, Gillian stared at the ceiling for what felt like hours. Though she'd done her best to keep the tears inside, one or two escaped, wetting the pillow beneath her cheek. All she could think about was the way Billy had looked at her while she was pinned against the refrigerator. It was as if the man she loved had retreated to someplace else, while a stranger took his place.

Gillian had tried to convince herself she was overreacting, and that Billy's actions were a one-off and would never happen again. But something in his gaze said otherwise. She'd never seen such a rage in her husband's stare. It unnerved her. For the first time since she and Billy had been together, she'd felt afraid.

6

As much as she could recall that night by the refrigerator, it was difficult for Gillian to pinpoint the moment Billy had first struck her. She was sure it had been over something petty, although there'd been so much physical abuse throughout the years that it was hard to say. The only episodes she still remembered with any real clarity were those in which Billy had inflicted the most pain or humiliation.

He had followed her around the house on several occasions, poking her repeatedly with an electric cattle prod until everything was cleaned and tidied to his liking. She'd been kicked, stomped, strangled, and beaten with anything that was within Billy's reach.

Once, while tending to her sick son, she'd accidentally scorched dinner. As punishment, Billy had fired up the gas stove and held her hand in the flames. The intense searing pain, the sizzling skin, and the smell of scorched flesh remained branded upon Gillian's memory in much the same fashion as the hypertrophic scars on the palms of her hands. And that had only been the beginning.

Some of the more severe abuse stemmed from Billy's increasing jealousy, beginning with an offhand remark made during a television program. When a veteran movie star appeared on an episode of the *Tonight Show*, Gillian had casually observed that the man was aging well and still looked quite good. That led to her being yanked off the couch by the hair and having a pocket knife pressed against her face.

She could still remember the sensation of the blade being drawn across the thin skin of her eyelid, all the while Billy threatening to carve out both of her eyeballs. He'd been drunk that evening, and Gillian had thought for some time after just how badly that night could have ended.

If he had stumbled, even just a bit, while the tip of that blade was pressing into my eye…

The thought always made her cringe.

In another instance, she had walked outside to retrieve the paper in a pair of shorts and the silk laced camisole that she'd slept in the previous night. While kneeling to pick up the paper, she'd noticed the old man across the street pulling into his driveway and had waved. When she'd gone back inside the house, Billy was standing just inside the door, his eyes once again teeming with anger.

"*What do you think you're doing going out like that?*" he'd yelled. "*Were you waiting until the neighbor was outside so you could flaunt your body like some whore? Do you want him to see your tits? Is that it?*"

Before Gillian could form an answer, Billy had her by the throat, ripping the camisole off her body by the seams.

"*If you're gonna act like a whore, I'm gonna treat you like one!*"

He'd then forced her to remove the rest of her clothing. After she was completely nude, Billy tossed her outside and latched the door, leaving her exposed on the front porch.

Though the neighbor had already gone inside, Gillian was mortified. Cupping a hand between her legs and crossing an arm over her bare breasts, she ran around to the rear of the house, hoping that none of the other neighbors were standing in their yards or walking down the sidewalk. The back entry was locked as well. Billy had made her stand outside for over half an hour before relenting to her incessant pounding on the door and allowing entry.

After he had calmed down, Gillian received the same teary-eyed apology that always followed one of his outbursts. On both occasions, she'd asked him why he did what he did. And in both instances, the answer was the same:

"Fear alone can blind a man; make him do things he would never imagine . . . terrible things. If it's strong enough, it can make you crazy. I love you, and the thought of you with another man is more than I can bear. I don't mean to do the things I do, I'm just afraid of losing you."

But no matter how many times—or how many assurances—Gillian gave him that she was neither leaving nor had any desire to be with another man, Billy's jealousy never abated. It only escalated.

7

Gillian made a right onto Parkhurst Avenue towards Connor's school. With every turn, she caught herself looking in the rearview mirror. She hated the feeling of paranoia that was building inside of her, but for however long she remained in this town with Billy on the loose, there would be no reprieve.

He was out there right now. Maybe he was still hours away, or maybe, just maybe, he was right around the corner. The news of his escape had brought back everything she'd tried so hard to forget, ripping through her insides and tearing away the scabs from the emotional and psychological scars until they bled profusely. She tried not to dwell on the past, but the memories paraded through her mind nevertheless.

She wondered again why she had stayed with him as long as she had. Why hadn't she packed herself and Connor up the night Billy had first raised his hand towards her? But she already knew the answer. There had been a few times, early on, that she had considered it, yet could never bring herself to do so.

In the beginning, it had been all about her love for Billy and her belief in the institution of marriage. It wasn't just a sense of obligation that compelled her to not give up, but it had been her desire as well. She did love Billy, after all. She had believed him when he was down on one knee, crying and telling her how sorry he was; swearing it would never happen again. He'd seemed genuine in his apologies, always stressing how lost he would be without her. In some instances, he even went so far as to talk about killing himself if she were to leave, saying that life would no longer be worth living. In those moments, her heart would break and she'd felt certain he would change. By the time she realized he never would, it wasn't love or a devotion to marriage which had kept her where she was. It was fear.

Later, instead of threatening to kill himself if she left, Billy was threatening to kill her. And though he'd never laid a hand on Connor, he used the threat of it to keep Gillian right where he wanted her. After a while, she'd accepted the abuse, taking the beatings when they came and learning the best ways to avoid inciting Billy's wrath.

For a time, things improved and Gillian had some semblance of happiness, however small it may have been. But it was only the calm before a crushing storm. On one ordinary Friday night, just over a year ago, the clouds broke and the flood waters poured. It was the beginning of the end.

8

THE PREVIOUS SEPTEMBER . . .

It was good to be out. No, it was *great* to be out.

Once a month, a few ladies from the block would meet up at a local restaurant for a girls' night. It was about the only time that Gillian could go anywhere without Billy at her side, and she looked forward to these evenings with tremendous zeal.

The sense of freedom was indescribable. In those moments, she could be herself, without worry of doing or saying anything wrong. She could laugh (something she rarely ever did at home), and here amongst her friends, there was plenty to go around.

Judith was the unofficial ringleader of the group. Boisterous and loud (but not annoyingly so), she was as quick with a witty comment as Wyatt Earp was with a Buntline Special. While not a heavy woman by any means, she was, in her own words, considerably stacked in the back. She would often say that her caboose was *the reason for the shadow on Shadow Lake,* or that she *put the ass in sass.*

Sharon, on the other hand, was the complete opposite. A quintessential soccer mom, she spent most of her time shuttling her three children between school and extracurricular activities. She was involved in the PTA, volunteered at her church, and was arguably the most conservative of the bunch.

Tricia was a successful author of children's books and the only one of the lot who was still single. Always dressed to the nines and well-manicured, she was also a bit of a cougar, with much of her personal life revolving around events which would never be able to grace the pages of her books. To know her, one would have thought she'd have been better suited for erotica rather than writing about the adventures of cuddly talking animals. The subject had come up once, and Tricia had explained that the stories came from her own experiences while growing up on the family's farm (experiences which were clearly more G-rated than her current escapades).

On this night, the ladies were all meeting at Casa Del Fuego, one of the best Mexican eateries in town. Though Billy had always been agreeable to Gillian going out with the neighbors (for the sole reason that there were no other men in tow), he minded even less now. He was busy helping Judith's husband, Rick, with the restoration of a recently acquired classic Corvette that Rick had bought at an auction.

Whenever Billy was working with cars, he didn't like to be bothered. And while Gillian knew to stay out of his way, Judith would often go out to the garage and talk. Billy had come home from working on the car before, saying that he couldn't understand why Rick let his wife stand there and yammer on, and that he needed to learn how to keep her under control. That being the case, Billy was more than happy to see the ladies off on this evening, and with less prying at Gillian than was customary.

There were times when Gillian wondered if the ladies, or any of the neighbors for that matter, knew about the abuse. If so, they turned a blind eye. But she didn't think they did. Billy had always been careful not to damage her face. Cuts and bruises on the body could be concealed or blamed on any number of things. On the face, however, they raised questions and were more difficult to explain away. Additionally, her friends still seemed to envy her, always talking about how pleasant, how mannerly, and how good looking Billy was; remarking that he must certainly make a great husband. If only they knew.

Even as Gillian rode with Judith to the restaurant, she considered divulging all the things Billy had done. But, like every other time, she kept quiet. She was too afraid. Afraid of what he might do to Connor, of what he might do to Judith, or Rick, or anyone that confronted him on the matter. There were too many uncertainties, too many risks, so Gillian pushed the thought aside and focused on the evening ahead.

Now, as the group neared the end of a second round of margaritas, the conversation steered from the usual gamut of gossip and current affairs and turned, instead, to a discussion of an altogether different type of affair.

"Tell us about this new man of yours, Tricia," Judith said.

"Carlos, you mean?" Tricia asked, with a sly grin.

"Hell, I don't know. I can't keep up with their names anymore."

"Oh, come on now. There hasn't been that many."

"Trish, dear, trying to figure out how many men you've dated is like one of those contests where one has to guess how many jellybeans are in a big jar to win the grand prize. It's a daunting task," Judith replied.

Tricia's mouth dropped open in a look of pretend shock. "Well, some friend you are."

"None of us are putting your lifestyle on trial here. We just like to live vicariously through you. So, tell us about this Carlos. And spare no details."

"For your information, I think Carlos may be the one."

"Oh, that's wonderful, Tricia," Sharon said. "Congratulations!"

"We haven't discussed marriage or anything, but he's so charming and thoughtful. I don't think I've ever had anyone be so into me. I mean, he's extremely attentive, and shows such concern for my welfare."

"He sounds nice," Gillian said.

"He is that. And he is also . . . how shall I put it? Very accommodating." Tricia raised an eyebrow in a knowing manner, swirling her margarita before taking a sip.

Judith leaned forward and nodded. "Now we're getting somewhere."

"I don't think we need to hear about what goes on behind closed doors. That's so personal," Sharon said, shifting in her seat and appearing uncomfortable with the subject at hand.

"Oh, yes. Yes, we do!" Judith exclaimed, waving for Tricia to continue.

"Well, he often likes to blindfold me. Then he'll tease me with a feather . . . or his lips. I love when it's his lips. I can feel his breath on my skin, going lower and lower. And then there's the tongue. Oh, the things he can do with his tongue! Sometimes he'll even take me in his mouth and ever so gently bite down—"

There was a faint gasp from Sharon's side of the table. Red-faced, she fumbled for her margarita, took a gulp, and then tipped the glass over while trying to put it back down. There was a brief commotion as everyone scrambled to contain the spill, followed by an eruption of laughter.

"Oh, my, that's just . . . oh," Sharon stuttered, fanning her face with her hands.

"Never had it quite like that, I'm guessing?" Judith quipped. "That's alright, me neither, darling. These days, Rick stays on the toilet longer than he stays on me."

Gillian almost choked on a bite of her enchilada. "Judith," she whispered, "I'm sure people can hear you."

"You're right. I imagine anyone within earshot is now offended, amused, or aroused. We should probably change the subject, anyway, before Sharon over here starts sizzling like a plate of fajitas. I'm sure she didn't bring a change of clothes."

"Oh," Sharon gasped again. "Heaven, help me!"

"It's alright, sweetie. You haven't done anything wrong. It's all in fun. The good Lord has a sense of humor, too. If he didn't, he wouldn't have given me an ass the size of Texas," Judith jested.

There was another round of laughter, followed by another round of margaritas. Gillian knew the moment was fleeting and that soon she would have to return to the harsh realities of home. For the moment, she didn't care.

That was later. This was now.

And right now, she was having the time of her life.

....

"Is it true? What you said about Rick?" Gillian asked.

"I've said so many things," Judith replied, keeping her eyes fixed on the road in front of her. "You'll have to refresh my memory."

"That part about him spending more time in the bathroom than with you."

"Oh, that," Judith laughed. "It's not quite what it used to be, but it's not as bad as I make it out to be, either. I do tend to exaggerate sometimes. Why do you ask?"

Gillian had been reflecting on their dinner conversation ever since leaving the restaurant. Mostly, she thought about Tricia's sex life in comparison to her own. While Tricia's sounded adventurous and fun, Gillian's had become nothing more than a duty; something she endured rather than enjoyed. It had never gotten any better since that first night down by the lake, but at least back then she'd felt wanted.

Nowadays, it usually only happened when Billy was drunk. There was no foreplay and no affection, just him grunting on top of her until he either climaxed or exhausted himself and passed out. It was a far cry from what she saw depicted on television or in those magazines at the check-out counter of the grocery store, the ones whose headlines always promised *50 New Ways to Spice Up Your Love Life.*

Gillian had always thought those were just lies; flashy ways to play on women's fantasies and sell magazines. But now, she wondered if those articles were written by women like Tricia—women with a Carlos in their life.

"I guess," Gillian replied, fidgeting with the purse in her lap. "I just wondered if I was the only one whose husband wasn't at all like Tricia's boyfriend."

Judith laughed as if Gillian had just said the funniest thing all evening. "I forget how young you are, dear. Let me tell you a little secret. There's something wrong with just about every man, especially after they are married. Why do you think it is we go out for margaritas so often? We've got to get away from them and blow off some steam. Men are the reason that ladies' nights are a necessity."

"Do you think Carlos will change if he and Tricia were to marry?

"Who knows? I think there are some men who are as passionate about passion as others are about football. There are exceptions to every rule."

"I wouldn't mind if Billy were one of the exceptions," Gillian remarked.

"I've thought the same about Rick before, too. One thing I've learned about fantasies, though, is that when you get one, you often find that it doesn't measure up to what you had imagined in the first place. Not that I would let them all pass me by, but some fantasies are better left as fantasies. Rick may not bring blindfolds or feathers into the bedroom, but he still surprises me sometimes. He's a good man. And he loves me. I suppose what I'm saying is, you have to know when to separate fantasy from reality, and to know when the best things are already right in front of you."

Gillian nodded, pondering Judith's words in silence for a long moment. It was sound advice. The one thing that echoed in her mind, however, was Judith saying that Rick was a good man. She imagined that Sharon's husband, Paul, was also a good man. And Carlos, well, no one could argue against him being a good man, at least in some respects. In the end, it all seemed to come down to one thing: despite whatever flaws those guys possessed, they were still decent men; men who loved and respected the women they were with.

And that was the whole problem, wasn't it? Billy just wasn't a good man.

9

All the lights in the house were out.

It was the first thing Gillian noticed as she traversed the steps leading up to the front porch. She'd expected Connor to be in bed, as it was already past 10:00 pm, but had assumed her husband would still be up working on the car. On weekends, it wasn't out of the ordinary for him to tinker around in the garage with Rick until well after midnight. Billy had seemed more tired than usual upon returning home from work earlier, so he must have called it an early night and put himself to bed as well.

Fumbling through her purse for keys, Gillian could still feel the effects of the alcohol swimming through her head. Right now, it was an agreeable and pleasant sensation. Tomorrow would probably be a different story. *Oh, well. Tonight's been worth anything I might have to suffer through in the morning.*

She found the ring of keys at the bottom of her purse and tugged them free. After selecting the one to the house, it took her several attempts to insert it into the lock. She laughed as she pushed the front door open, both at herself and at the recollection of something Judith had said during dinner. She had no sooner stepped inside and pushed the door shut behind her, when she was startled by a voice rising out of the darkness.

"Amusing, is it?"

Gillian let out a faint gasp and strained to see in the pitch black of the room. "Billy?" she asked, groping for the light switch on the wall. In her slightly inebriated state, it was a futile attempt.

A lamp across the room clicked on and Gillian winced at the sudden brightness. Billy sat at one end of the couch with a blank look upon his face.

"Why are you sitting here in the dark? I thought you'd still be working on the car."

"Cars," he grunted, staring across the room in a bemused state. "You know what I like about cars?"

Gillian opened her mouth to speak but Billy cut her off.

"You can dress them up in any fashion you choose; make them your own. They're loyal to a fault. You hit the gas, they go. You hit the brake, they stop. They do what is expected of them. No questions. No complaints."

There was a cold edge to Billy's voice which made Gillian uneasy. That, coupled with his unusually calm demeanor, only added to her anxiousness. Something was wrong. She was sure of it.

"Where were you tonight?" Billy asked, still tranquil and composed.

Though she'd done nothing wrong, Gillian's heart began to hammer. She could feel the rush of blood turning her face to warm embers.

"I was at the restaurant."

Billy turned his head and made eye contact.

"With . . . *who*?"

There was anger in his eyes now. A deeper anger than Gillian had ever seen. It was as if every look of fury that had come before was only a precursor to this moment; the smoldering seed of violence within him having only rumbled prior, but now, like a volcano, ready to erupt in a firestorm of cruel ferocity.

Gillian began to tremble. Her voice shook when she answered.

"Wi . . .with . . . Judith . . . and the other girls," she stammered. It was the truth, but under the scrutiny of her husband, the words somehow sounded like a lie.

Billy's eyes narrowed, while one corner of his mouth lifted in a smirk. "Is that right?" he asked, his tone one of mock belief.

"Yes. You know I was. You saw us leave together. We went out for drinks like we do every month."

"Tell me, are you both fucking the same guy? Or, are you just a cover for that whore?"

"What?" Gillian asked, dumbfounded. This wasn't the first time he'd insinuated infidelity. She'd long ago learned never to comment on other men, or to even look at one for longer than a passing glance. She could think of nothing she had done recently to warrant this current accusation.

"Of course, the way I see it, you could be covering for each other. Yeah, that's it, isn't it? She goes to her guy. You go to yours. Probably even have adjoining hotel rooms."

"Billy, I don't know what you're talking about."

"No? That's funny, because you know what Rick said to me tonight?"

Gillian shook her head.

"He said he thought Judith might be having an affair."

Now it made sense. There had been a time or two, when Billy wasn't around, that Gillian had heard Rick joke with Judith just before she'd left the house to run errands.

"Headed out to see your boyfriend? You have fun. Just don't go making him your pot roast, you hear? That would really get my blood boiling," he'd jested.

And they'd all had a good laugh. But that's all it was—a joke. Nothing more.

Rick must have made a comment while he and Billy were working on the car tonight. He would have certainly intended for it to be a put-on, but Billy would have taken it to heart.

And because Gillian was in Judith's company, that made her guilty by association.

"Rick didn't mean it. Judith would never—"

"Who is it?" Billy asked, moving from the couch. As he stood, he loosened the belt from around his waist and pulled it free. "Is it that little league coach of Connor's? I've seen the way he looks at you."

"No. It's no one. Billy, please . . ." Gillian pleaded.

She raised her hands and backed away, imploring her husband to listen and to have mercy. But she had never received mercy at his hand. The only thing he knew was brutality.

"I'm only trying to make you a better wife. Don't you see that? I tried to make you understand before, but you just didn't get it. When this is all over; when you finally comprehend, you're going to thank me."

Gillian backed into a corner as Billy continued his march forward. When he was within striking distance, he did the one thing he'd always been careful not to do. Lifting his arm high in the air, he brought the belt down hard. There was a sharp crack as the leather strap connected with Gillian's right cheek. She let out a loud cry, one of both pain and surprise, before falling into a crouch against the wall.

Billy wrapped the belt around her neck. He looped the strap through the buckle and pulled taught, effectively turning the thing into a noose. Gillian pawed at the belt with both hands, struggling against the constricting tie that was cutting off her airway. She gagged, her tongue poking out between her lips as she fought for breath. With a sudden force that made her neck feel as it might pop off her shoulders, Billy yanked her back up into a standing position. He relaxed his grip, and Gillian began to cough and wheeze as she sucked in deep gulps of air.

There was a noise in the hallway, and Connor bounded into the living room. "Momma?" he asked, sounding as if he were ready to cry.

"Go to bed, boy," Billy rumbled, turning and meeting his son's gaze with a hard scowl.

Connor took a few timid steps backwards, his eyes wide and flooding with tears.

"Daddy, stop. You're hurting her."

"I said go to bed. Now!" Billy raged, sending little bits of spittle flying from his mouth.

Connor cowered down, bawling, and ran back towards his room.

Billy turned to Gillian, red-faced. "After I finish with you, it's his turn."

Gillian was horrified. She shook her head in defiance and began to beat her fists against Billy's chest. "Do whatever you want to me, kill me, but you don't touch him! Don't you dare touch him!" she screamed.

Billy placed his palm over Gillian's face and slammed her head against the wall. He tightened the belt once again and used it like a leash to drag his wife across the room. He led her through the kitchen and out into the garage, where he slung her down face first onto the cement floor.

While Gillian lay on the ground trying to collect her breath, Billy walked over to his work bench and looked up at the wooden pegboard on the wall containing his many tools.

"This should do just fine," he remarked, slipping an axe from one of the metal hangers. He gripped the wooden handle and bounced the instrument up and down a few times, as if considering its weight and ability to do the task at hand. Satisfied with his selection, he made his way back to Gillian.

She was on her elbows now, attempting to move into a sitting position. Before she could get upright, Billy brought the butt end of the axe down across the back of her head. She dropped like a rock, her face smashing into the hard concrete.

For a moment, Gillian blacked out. When she came to, the copper-tinged taste of blood filled her mouth. Fragments of broken teeth cut into her tongue. Her skull pounded with a relentless throb, sending ripples of pain shooting through her entire body as she tried to lift her head. With each movement, Gillian felt as if her brain were sloshing between her ears.

It took her several seconds to feel the sharp sting at the back of her skull where the skin had been splayed open. She reached back and touched the wound. The stinging increased ten-fold as her finger slipped into the wide gash there.

The agony made her stomach lurch. She was going to be sick. Her insides clenched and a fire rose in her chest. The liquid gunk lingered at the back of her throat, and she could taste the putrid sour mix of everything she'd had to eat and drink over the past few hours. She swallowed hard, trying to keep the sickness at bay, but at that moment, Billy delivered a blow to her side. The swift impact of the blade landing between her ribs caused both her stomach and bladder to release at the same time. When the regurgitating stopped, Gillian lay motionless in a pool of her own body fluids.

Billy grabbed her by the hair, lifting her face out of the muck. "You disgust me," he spat.

Gillian's right eye was swollen shut and her lips trembled uncontrollably. "Please," she whispered in an afflicted voice. "Please, don't hurt my son."

Billy yanked her head back and pressed the knife-edge of the axe against her throat, "I'll handle Connor. And if you so much as move from this spot, I'm going to take your head off. Do you understand that?" he asked, shoving her aside. He walked inside the house, axe still in hand, and slammed the door behind him.

Gillian let out a whimper, which turned into a full-on wail when the helpless cries of her son filtered into the room.

Oh, God. What is he doing? What is he doing to him?

Her mouth fell open in a scream, but only a muted sob escaped her lips. She stretched out a hand towards the door as hot tears poured down her face. With every bit of breath and fortitude within her, Gillian began to drag her mangled body across the cold floor, inch by slow inch. She only made it a few feet before her senses darkened and the world around her faded to black.

10

A long procession of cars snaked through the parking lot of Pine Ridge Elementary. Though it always took a fair amount of time for each vehicle to stop at the drop-off zone near the front entry of the school and unload its contents of children, today was taking much longer than usual.

Gillian had noticed several patrol cars parked in the lot when she'd pulled in. Presently, a handful of uniformed officers stood in a huddle conversing near the flagpole. One of them was Landon Stephens.

Fourteen months earlier, after Billy had left her for dead in the garage and fled with Connor, it was officer Stephens who'd apprehended her husband and made the arrest. Gillian hoped lightning might strike twice and that the deputy could be her hero once again, but the man's presence here now alongside the other officers suggested that Billy's whereabouts were still unknown.

Gillian nervously fidgeted with her hair while she watched the car in front of her. The passenger door swung open and a young girl, bundled up in a white coat and pink scarf, exited the vehicle and bounced towards the front doors of the school. As she did so, a portly man with a whistle around his neck approached the opposite side of the vehicle and began speaking with the driver.

"Ugh," Connor moaned, rolling his eyes. "Not Mr. Hoffman. What is he doing out here?"

Brian Hoffman was the gym teacher at Pine Ridge, which was ironic given his appearance. He had an odd sort of body shape, with a large head and an even larger waist, yet much smaller through the arms, legs, and chest. To Gillian, he resembled a can of refrigerated biscuit dough that had burst open in random places. Anyone with any degree of smarts could see that the man greeted exercise with the same amount of enthusiasm as he would an enema or a prostate exam.

It was also widely known that he still lived with his mother, despite being over the age of thirty and gainfully employed. That notwithstanding, the man held himself in a much higher regard than was warranted. Proud and boastful, he was quick to brag, flirting with women as if he were George Clooney himself. Unlike the famous actor, however, Brian Hoffman's methods were never successful. In fact, they were flat out painful to watch. If he were still a virgin, it would have surprised no one.

There was also the matter of the whistle around his neck, which he wore as faithfully as if it were a wedding ring. The thing was a source of contempt amongst all the children at Pine Ridge, as Mr. Hoffman seemed to delight in policing them with it daily. Whether moving through the halls of the school, eating in the cafeteria, or frolicking about on the playground during recess, some poor unsuspecting child was either walking too fast, eating too slow, or playing too rough. To say that Brian Hoffman was the least liked teacher for five years running—and perhaps even in the whole history of Pine Ridge Elementary—would have been an understatement.

The leading car pulled away and Mr. Hoffman puffed into his whistle, waving Gillian forward. Connor grabbed his backpack and popped the passenger door ajar before the vehicle came to a full stop, eliciting another ear-splitting screech from the whistle.

"Easy there, young man. Let's not be too hasty. Don't need any injuries to start the day," the doughy man barked.

"Thanks, Mom. I'll see you after school," Connor said, ignoring the gym teacher's admonition and climbing out of the passenger seat.

The excitement over seeing his friends and attending a party in his honor caused Connor to hasten his trek towards the school entrance, although he was mindful not to run, lest he once more draw the ire of the whistle.

Mr. Hoffman hitched up his pants and stepped towards the SUV. "I don't think I've ever seen anyone so anxious to come to school. The kids usually only move that fast when the bell rings at the end of the day. This old whistle really gets a workout then."

"Yes, well, his teacher is throwing him a party." Gillian smiled.

"Ah, I see. It must be the little guy's birthday. Good looking young man. Looks like he takes after his mother." The coach stood there with a stupid grin on his face.

Gillian just nodded. She didn't feel the need to go into explanations, nor did she want to acknowledge what she perceived to be a flirtatious remark. Besides, there was still a hefty string of cars waiting in line behind her.

"Right," Mr. Hoffman said, his smile waning. He cleared his throat before proceeding. "I suppose you've already heard about the incident involving the prison escapees?"

"I have. Is everything alright?"

"Oh, yes, absolutely. It's unlikely they would come this way, but we're still taking the necessary precautions. I'll have sheriff's deputies here throughout the day to assist me with patrols and surveillance. We don't want to alarm the little ones, so we're trying to downplay the situation as much as possible. I just wanted to apprise you of the matter and assure you that your son is in good hands."

"Thank you. Like you said, I doubt there is anything to worry about, but I'm glad to see the officers. I certainly feel better knowing they're here."

"Yes, ma'am," Mr. Hoffman replied. Then, in keeping with his boastful nature, he elaborated, holding his head high and puffing up his chest. Whether this was meant to impress her, or merely to serve as a reminder of his own self-importance, Gillian could not say. It was likely a bit of both.

"You know, I served on the volunteer police force back in Washington for a stint. Trained at one of the finest police academies in the nation," he crowed, "I can assure you, nothing will get past me. Those prison scums won't come around, not if they know what's good for them. I'm not too concerned, though. I'm sure they're far away from here by now."

11

Twenty miles northwest of Pine Ridge Elementary—and Brian Hoffman's interminable ego—Lindsay Wallace pulled her white Nissan Altima into a parking space at Thurman's department store. She shut off the engine and surveyed the empty lot.

First one here again. What a surprise. Had she said it aloud, one would have detected the bitterness in her tone and known that she was none too pleased.

As assistant manager, she was supposed to alternate opening duties with Vivian Green, the day manager. Vivian, however, pulled rank more often than a teenage boy played with his pecker, and Lindsay increasingly found herself saddled with more and more of the woman's responsibilities of late.

"Bitch," she mumbled, grabbing her purse and collecting her venti Starbucks soy vanilla latte from the cup holder. *Glad I got an extra shot this morning. I'm going to need it.*

She climbed out of the car and scurried across the lot, anxious to retreat into the warmth of the building. A storm was moving in and the wind blew in frigid gusts. Snowflakes swirled about, nipping and stinging the skin of her calves which poked out from her skirt.

Once she reached the store entrance, Lindsay juggled the latte and her purse in her right hand while she worked the heavy deadbolt on the front door with the keys in her left.

Of all the days. I mean, really, Vivian?

Having to pick up the woman's slack would have pissed her off on any given day, but it did so even more on this one. She was to be the maid of honor at her best friend's wedding in a couple of weeks and had been busy organizing the bachelorette party scheduled for that evening. She'd also found herself running all over town with the bride-to-be, who was busy in her own rite, fussing over all the last-minute details.

Lindsay was ready for it to all be done with. She was a no-frills type of girl. When the time came for her to wed, she wasn't going to go through the stress and expense of putting on a big dog and pony show. A simple justice of the peace, a few friends, some close family, and a long trip to the Caymans was her idea of perfect.

This current wedding was placing staggering demands on her free time and was also jeopardizing the potential future of her own marital bliss. She had barely seen her boyfriend, Jason, over the last few weeks. And when she'd had to decline another of his dinner invitations the night before, an argument had ensued. Not that she could blame the guy. After all, he missed having her around which, she had to admit, was rather nice.

In the end, she'd compromised and they'd met up for late drinks, which led to even later sex. It was fantastic, but now she was running on only a couple hours of sleep. She was tired, and certainly in no mood to do her boss's job, especially when the woman was making a good fifteen grand more than her each year.

Was she angry?

Yes.

Was it without merit?

Certainly not.

Latching the door behind her, she entered the dark confines of the cavernous department store, her heels clacking in time on the marble floor. She could still hear the whistling of the driving winds outside, coupled with the rumbling of metal, as the sturdy gales rattled the large air handlers atop the roof. She pressed on, working her way towards the offices at the rear of the building.

Entering the men's clothing department and passing the fragrance counter, Lindsay detected the aroma of Armani cologne and the adjacent scent of tanned leather. She thought of Jason and their tryst from the night before. The recollection sent a warm rush of excitement down her spine and made her smile.

If only I could be home with him right now, under the blankets, still wrapped in his warm embrace, feeling the prickly stubble of his neck resting on my shoulder . . .

She stopped.

Were those footsteps she'd heard?

Standing in the dim aisle, she listened. The wind howled for a moment and then abated. The silence of the empty store had never bothered her before, but now it seemed harsh and eerie. Perhaps it had been her imagination, but it had distinctly sounded like someone running.

With some degree of trepidation, she dismissed the noise and walked on.

Rounding a corner moments later, she froze. A garment rack had been knocked over and clothes were scattered across the floor. Even more alarming, was the orange jumpsuit nearby with the words DEPARTMENT OF CORRECTIONS stamped on the back.

"Oh, dear God," Lindsay muttered.

The prisoners I heard about on the radio this morning. They were here. They might still be here.

A paralyzing sense of terror bolted her to the ground. What if they were watching her right now? What would they do to her? All sorts of possibilities—none of them pleasant—

paraded through her mind, causing tears to well up in her eyes and stream down her cheeks.

An abrupt clatter erupted from the stock room near the back of the store. Lindsay nearly jumped out of her skin, but the ensuing adrenaline rush helped her to find her legs. She dropped the latte she held and raced back towards the front entrance. Her chest was tight, shuddering uncontrollably with each frantic breath.

Please, don't let me die. Oh, God, please!

The rapid clicking of her heels against the floor, the thundering of her heart, the howling of the wind—all sounded deafening in her ears. She wasn't positive, but she thought she heard footsteps again; footsteps other than her own. Were they in pursuit? Coming up behind her? Or perhaps somewhere ahead, waiting to lunge once she was near?

There was another crash from somewhere in the building.

A new surge of anxiety ripped through Lindsay and she screamed. No matter how fast she ran, it felt as if the she was going nowhere. The path to the exit, to her salvation, still seemed miles away. It was if she were running in place. At any second, she was certain a stranger's hands would bear down on her, but she kept moving, propelled by the will to survive.

When she reached the door, she fumbled for the right key. The forceful trembling in her fingers made it difficult and she feared she would drop the key ring. To her relief, she kept them in her grip and worked the deadbolt with relative ease considering her current state of mind.

Once the door was open, Lindsay vaulted through it. Gusts of wind and snow pelted her burning face as she raced out into the parking lot. No sooner was she out in the open, when she fell to her knees and emitted a shrill cry.

The parking space that had minutes earlier held a white Nissan Altima now sat empty.

Her car was gone.

12

Gillian sat in the waiting area of Murray's Tire Shop, thumbing through a worn issue of Better Homes and Gardens. With the wave of storms that were currently rolling across much of the Pacific Northwest, she knew she'd have some nasty road conditions to contend with by the time she and Conner started their journey. It wouldn't be anything she wasn't accustomed to driving in, but making sure the tires were in good shape would reduce the chances of becoming stranded on the side of the road somewhere or, worse yet, causing an accident.

Try as she might, Gillian was finding it impossible to focus on the magazine she held in her hands, or much of anything at all for that matter. Another storm—a darker one—had been developing in her mind, and it was getting stronger. She glanced up from the page she had been staring at over the last several minutes and gazed out the window. Thick clouds had stalled in the skies overhead, while driving winds whipped the snow into what looked like a wall of hazy gray cotton candy. It was a bleak spectacle, and just looking at it chilled her to the bone.

Billy is still out there. Maybe he'll freeze to death.

Was it wrong of her to think that? She reasoned not. After all, it was a foregone conclusion; the inevitable fate of any person unfortunate enough to be without shelter in this sort of weather. But she wasn't just thinking it in a logical sense. No, a part of her was hoping for it, the realization of which frightened her a bit. Not many people would have faulted her for thinking such a thing after what she'd suffered at Billy's hands, though she still felt a twinge of guilt. She wanted him to pay for what he'd done, sure, but wanting him dead made her feel like she was, in many ways, as much of a monster as he was.

But Billy wouldn't freeze. No, he was too clever for that. He would find a way out. He always did. For all she knew, the impending weather had even been a part of his plan.

The door leading to the shop opened, breaking Gillian's train of thought. A sixtyish-something man with a mop of salt-and-pepper hair and the name Jasper embroidered on the chest of his navy-blue button up shirt, stepped into the lobby carrying a clipboard.

"The silver bullet, she's ready to roll," he said, making his way behind the counter. "Checked her out from top to bottom. I went ahead and installed some new wiper blades and topped off your washer fluid. Other than that, everything looks good. I don't expect she'll give you any trouble."

"That's great," Gillian said, stepping up to the register. "I've got a long trip ahead of me."

"Oh? Where you headed?" the old man asked.

"Home . . . a new home," came the hushed response.

"Hmm," the mechanic murmured. He seemed to sense he'd struck a nerve and simply nodded in response. "Well, wherever home is, I hope it's warmer than here."

He sat the clipboard down next to the computer and started tapping on the touch screen, adding fresh black smudges to the already grease-streaked monitor. After a few moments of silence, he turned and looked Gillian square in the eye.

"He's coming for you."

Gillian felt a hitch in her chest. She stood in stilted silence as the words bounced around in her head like the metal ball in a pinball machine, their force striking her repeatedly. "What did you say?" she finally asked.

"That's $29.42," the man repeated, pushing a printed invoice towards Gillian.

"Right, sorry. Too much on my mind, I guess."

She pulled a credit card from her purse and slid it across the counter. It had been a false scare. She'd merely misheard the man, yet still her blood ran cold. There was a noticeable tremble in her hand as she signed the receipt.

Jasper may not have said what she thought he had, but it didn't change the truth of the matter. Billy was coming for her; coming just as sure as the snow was falling. Gillian believed it to be true with every fiber of her being.

She'd thought about going to the police, but even if she were surrounded by their protection she knew Billy would be patient. He would hide, watch, and wait, looking for just the right moment to strike. After all, she couldn't be guarded the rest of her life now, could she? And if they failed to catch him, and she and Connor were to leave this place, she was certain Billy would follow. The only chance she stood was to get out of town before he found her. But could she?

(He's coming for you)

The dark clouds inside of her grew blacker by the minute, unleashing winds which lashed against the shutters of her soul. She could feel them clattering on their hinges now.

(He's coming for you)

The storm was near.

Gillian walked towards the exit on unsteady legs, heart and mind racing, and reached for the door.

"You be careful, Miss," Jasper called after her. "It's a bad one out there. Nothing good ever comes of days like this . . . nothing at all."

Unable to muster a single word, and offering only a feeble nod in return, Gillian stepped into the frozen world outside and vanished behind a veil of icy gray.

13

It was warmer. The place they were going was much warmer, which was exactly why Gillian chose to move there. She was no fan of hot weather, but that was what made it so perfect. Billy knew how much she hated it, so Gillian reasoned the deep South—Baton Rouge, to be specific—would be the last place he would come looking for her.

Her only experience with the southern states had occurred in her early teens, when she'd accompanied her parents to Texas on a few occasions to visit an uncle on her father's side. The visits had always taken place during the month of August which was, coincidentally, the hottest damn month of the entire year.

The town he resided in, a place called Millford Springs, shared some similarities with Shadow Lake. Both were charming and somewhat small, but whereas the downtown area of Shadow Lake reflected an Old West feel from its origins as a gold mining town, Millford Springs was a Norman Rockwell slice of Americana that could have taken its cue straight from Mayberry. There was even a waitress at the local diner, Gillian recalled, that while a bit spunkier than the character portrayed on the *Andy Griffith Show*, was the quintessential Aunt Bea in both appearance and baking prowess.

Even back then, Gillian could see the appeal of the place and understood why Ray, her uncle, liked living there. She would have liked it too, except for two things: the summer heat and the bugs. If the hotter-than-Hades temperatures didn't get you, the legions of insects certainly would.

Miriam—her aunt and Ray's wife—had once said: "*Step outside for more than thirty seconds and the mosquitos will be on you like a pack of dogs on a pork chop. There are three things you'll need to survive the summers here: bug repellent, soap, and bug repellent.*"

She'd been right. The family had all gone to a drive-in movie one evening and Gillian, being at an age where she thought she knew more than most adults, failed to heed her aunt's advice. As such, she'd come home looking as if she'd broken out with a case of the measles, itching and scratching incessantly for days on end. Lesson learned.

That all seemed like another lifetime ago now. Gillian missed the girl she had been then. She longed for the sense of freedom and the carefree thoughts that had once filled her days. Back then, she'd had dreams, and the whole world had been hers. The future held promise and possibility rather than hopelessness and defeat. More than that, and perhaps most important, she'd felt safe. And that was the key, wasn't it? Without a sense of safety, it would be difficult, maybe even impossible, to be carefree, or to dream, or to possess any of the other attributes she'd lost along the way.

But it could be that way again someday. It would be. She couldn't let Connor be robbed of all the things which had been taken from her. He deserved a better life than what he'd had thus far. She could learn to live with the heat, the bugs, or whatever else she had to for his sake.

A car horn honked in the distance, snapping Gillian back to reality and pulling her from the stifling Texas heat and happy-go-lucky memories of summers' past, to the bitter chill and suffocating anxiety of the here and now.

The now also brought with it an oppressive weight of sorrow. It was not unlike waking from a marvelous dream, one in which all your troubles had melted away in the face of some serendipitous fortune, only to realize as the alarm jarred you from slumber that none of it had been real.

Seconds ago, Gillian had likewise dreamed—daydreamed anyway—of a time when all had been right with the world. In those short-lived moments, the grim truth of her situation had subsided. But now she found herself alone again, with only an unbearable sense of despair for company. As much as she kept trying to reassure herself everything was going to be alright, it was to no avail. All she could do was stare at the clock, counting down the hours until she could pick up Connor at school.

She'd been so shaken after leaving the tire shop that she had reconsidered letting her son stay in school all day. He would be angry with her, probably for some time, but it was in their best interest to leave sooner rather than later. She knew that now. But upon calling the school to inform them she was coming, she'd been told that a full lockdown was in place, with no one allowed in or out of the building until further notice.

The school official could not comment on what prompted the change, other than to say there were unconfirmed reports of the escapees having been spotted in the outlying area. The news had thrown Gillian into a tailspin.

"Mrs. Adams, I understand your concern, but rest assured your son, and every child in this school, is completely safe. There are police officers on site and there is no way for anyone to enter this building."

(Let me speak to him)

"I'm sorry, but we can't allow that right now. We don't want to cause any unnecessary alarm, and we need to keep the lines open for law enforcement."

(I want to talk to my child, dammit.)

"Mrs. Adams, please..."

(Let me speak to whomever is in charge, then. I have to pick up my son right away. We need to leave town. It's a family emergency.)

"Again, I'm sorry. Please understand, ma'am. It's policy. Your son is safe. We will call you just as soon as we have the all clear."

Gillian had told the official exactly what he could do with his policies and then slung her cell phone across the passenger seat. With tears clouding her vision, she'd pulled over to the curb and beat against the steering wheel with closed fists.

Why did you let him go to school at all? What were you thinking, Gillian? Now you're stuck. And there's not a damn thing you can do about it. Not one damn thing!

She'd sat with her head on the wheel, wondering why it was she always seemed to make such poor choices; wondering if her current plans were the right ones, or if they too would come back to slap her in the face one day. At some point, she'd zoned out, her mind drifting from a replay of the morning's events to the more pleasant daydream state she'd been in only moments ago.

Staring out at the town around her, Gillian concluded that there was nothing she could do but proceed with her errands. Sitting and crying was certainly not going to accomplish anything. And with any luck, the all clear would be given soon, maybe even before classes normally let out for the day.

With a sense of renewed vigor, albeit a very small one, Gillian threw the shift lever into DRIVE, turned on her blinker, and glanced over her shoulder. A red Dodge blistered past, but the next car, a white Nissan, slowed and allowed passage. She gave a courtesy wave before pulling away from the curb and merging into traffic.

The white Nissan Altima trailed close behind.

14

Five minutes later, the silver bullet (as Jasper had affectionately called it) arrived at HTM Pacific Capitol where, per the marquee outside, one could now obtain the *Lowest Rates on Holiday Loans.* Though the bank had been around longer than she could remember, Gillian was still unsure what HTM stood for, but *'happy to take your money'* came to mind.

Today, however, it was she who would be doing the taking, closing her account and receiving a lump sum payment. The funds would simply be moved to some other financial institution in Baton Rouge; one with an equally confounding, acronym-heavy name, no doubt, and presumably every bit as eager to take her money.

Despite the pall of gray outside, the bank interior was as bright as a sunny day in May. And though it was only early November, a lavishly adorned Christmas tree—twenty feet high if it were an inch—stood under the domed ceiling in the center of the lobby. Sounds of sleigh bells and holiday cheer droned over the sound system, while a seemingly amphetamine-fueled voice crooned about the joys of riding in a wonderland of snow.

Gillian groaned. Not that she had anything against the holiday, but right now it was the last thing she wanted to think about. In her mind, it was too soon for anyone to be concerned with Christmas. Although, if you needed a holiday loan from HTM Pacific, perhaps it wasn't.

There were a scant number of people inside the bank this morning, which Gillian attributed to the weather. That was just fine by her. No lines meant she could get in and out that much quicker. Like everyone else, she would have preferred to stay in the cozy confines of her vehicle and utilize the drive-thru, but closing an account, much like opening one, could take some time, and any poor sap that happened to pull up behind her would be sorry they had.

A trim, doe-eyed teller with long blonde locks spilling over her shoulders smiled as Gillian approached the counter, displaying a mouthful of pearly whites' worthy of a Hollywood close-up. The girl worked them like a seasoned game show host, beaming like she had just been proposed to by every A-list hunk in the movie biz.

For a moment, Gillian was envious. It wasn't the exceptional dental worked she coveted, but rather the relaxed, untroubled soul behind the smile. It was as if the girl had not a care in the world. Perhaps she didn't. Or, perhaps, she was merely too young to have made enough bad decisions to strip away the rose-colored tint from her world.

Either way, Gillian wished she could trade places with this young woman, if only for the day. But that wouldn't be fair, would it? Surely not for the teller, who would have to suffer instead.

No, it was a selfish and cowardice wish, and Gillian was ashamed for even thinking it. Yet in the face of such overwhelming fear, how many people wouldn't wish for an easy way out?

None of it mattered, anyhow. Even if such a thing were possible, who in their right mind would want to be saddled with the weight of her problems? Like it or not, this burden was hers, and hers alone.

"Hi, my name is Megan. Welcome to HTM Pacific," the teller recited. "How may I help you today?"

"I need to close out my account, please," Gillian answered.

At this, the teller's smile dropped away and her look turned to one of dismay, as if she'd just been told all those A-list proposals had been a ruse and she was, instead, on an episode of *Punk'd* or *Candid Camera*. "Oh, I'm sorry," she replied, "Do you mind if I ask the reason? I mean, I hope we haven't let you down in some way."

"No, nothing like that. I'm moving across the country and I'm afraid there are no HTM branches where I'm going."

"Of course," Megan said, her warm smile returning. "I'm sorry to hear you're leaving us, but congratulations on your move."

Gillian hoped the woman wouldn't ask her where she was going. It was a question which, for obvious reasons, she was unwilling to answer. She could lie and say she was moving to the East Coast, but she was a terrible liar; always had been. And dodging the question was no better, as it only made her feel like she had something to hide. In a manner of speaking, she did, but still she hated coming off as pretentious over such a simple query. It was certainly no one's business where she went, but they were only making conversation, after all, not trying to subject her to a criminal interrogation.

Fortunately, the only thing Megan asked for was a form of identification, which she examined before excusing herself to collect some paperwork.

While waiting for the woman to return, Gillian stared ahead, looking out through the wide panoramic teller window to the drive-thru lanes on the other side. It was a busy morning, with cars stacked at least four deep in every slot. The ATM lane fared a bit better, with only two vehicles in the stall. Of those, the one which held the second position in line stood out. It was the same white Nissan Altima that had let her into traffic earlier.

It's just coincidence. Must be, right? But what if it isn't? What if it's him? What if . . .

"Here we go, Ms. Adams."

The teller's voice surprised Gillian and she flinched.

"Oh, I'm so sorry. I didn't mean to—"

"It's alright," Gillian interjected, "I was just lost in thought, I guess."

Her mouth formed a smile which was meager at best and her eyes darted back to the Nissan. She tried to see the face of the driver, but the windows were too dark. A thought occurred: *what if the car's occupant was staring back, watching from behind the heavy tint?* A sickening sensation welled up in her gut.

"I just have a few forms for you to sign, then I can get you on your way," Megan announced, sliding several sheets of paper across the counter and holding out a pen.

The Nissan inched forward as the car in front of it pulled away. The side window began to slide down. The driver was a man. Gillian could see that from the short cropped hair; hair which was the same color as Billy's.

The window continued its descent.

A little more. Just a little bit more.

As the man's forehead came into view, the car slipped behind the ATM.

"Dammit," Gillian muttered.

"Ma'am?"

"I'm sorry, that wasn't directed at you. I just remembered something that I forgot to do this morning."

Gillian grabbed the pen and began scrawling her name on the signature line of each piece of paper, not taking the time to read the forms. Did anyone ever read all that stuff anyway?

"If you have your new account information, we could transfer the funds directly," Megan said.

"I'm afraid I don't. I'm not even sure which bank I'll be using just yet."

"No problem at all. I'll issue a cashier's check instead."

"That will do fine. Thank you."

Gillian finished signing and pushed the paperwork back across the desk.

"Alright," Megan replied, collecting the forms and flashing her trademark million-dollar smile. "Let me get this entered into our system and I'll process your check."

Gillian nodded, only half hearing the woman. Her fingers drummed nervously on the counter as she observed the car sitting at the ATM.

A panel of security monitors hung on a wall nearby, displaying the black and white video feeds from the cameras positioned at each drive-thru lane. There were more cameras than there were monitors and Gillian watched closely as, one by one, the images alternated on the screens.

There. That one.

She craned her neck to get a closer look. A man's arm was visible, bent at the elbow and resting on the sill of the door. The rest of him remained obscured inside the vehicle.

Seconds rolled by. Ten . . . twenty . . .

Why is he just sitting there? Do something. Show yourself.

The man shifted in his seat. Gillian held her breath.

The image flickered and the monitor changed to a different camera feed.

No!

Gillian's eyes widened. Sharp stabbing pains entered her conscious and she looked down to see her fists balled up tight. When she unclenched them, several deep purple grooves remained from where her nails had dug into the palms.

Megan returned with the cashier's check and placed it on the counter. "Alright, Ms. Adams, I believe you're all set."

Gillian gave a cursory glance back towards the monitors before inspecting the slip of paper in front of her. Everything appeared to be in order. The amount, although accurate, seemed a bit paltry considering it was all she had to her name. Still, it would be enough to get her where she was going and keep food on the table until she was earning a steady paycheck again.

A drop of something wet fell onto the face of the check, startling Gillian. A second drop fell, hitting the counter with a splash. A third drop of the liquid dotted her hand. It took a moment for her mind to register what it was seeing.

Blood.

She looked up at Megan. The right side of the woman's face had been smashed in. One eye dangled from its socket, swaying back and forth on the attached optic nerve like a yo-yo on a string, while sections of hair glistened red, plastered against a misshapen skull from which bone splintered and flaps of skin hung loose. Despite this, her smile endured, wide and gracious.

Horrified, Gillian let out an audible gasp and took a step back. Her eyes darted around the room to the other tellers. They all flitted about, doing their jobs without noticing anything out of the ordinary. One even looked in her direction, offering a grin and a tip of their head.

What's wrong with them? Don't they see what's going on?

"Is something the matter, Ms. Adams?" Megan asked. A thin trickle of blood streamed down one cheek and into the teller's mouth, pooling in the ridges between her teeth. The woman's smile remained fixed.

Gillian squeezed her eyes shut and shook her head. When she opened them again, the teller appeared normal. Had it been any different, it wouldn't have mattered, at least not then. For it was the security monitors in the corner of the room—one of them, anyway—which now held her gaze. For a long moment, she stood still, mouth agape. Then, in one quick movement, she scooped the check off the counter and hurried across the lobby.

"Ms. Adams, are you alright?" Megan called after her.

Gillian quickened her pace and didn't answer. She'd just seen the white car again, and this time, the face of the man sitting behind the wheel. He'd stared directly into the camera, looking not at his own reflection, or even the device itself, but seeming to gaze through the lens, as if he could see her standing on the other side.

It had been Billy. She was sure of it.

And he was smiling.

15

One wheel wobbled.

There was a small squeak also, but that wasn't what Gillian noticed, at least not at first. It was the quivering of the shopping cart beneath her grip which brought her mind back into focus.

She stopped the cart and looked around. A chorus of beeps rang out from the distant check-out lanes, while a voice on the public-address system requested manager assistance at register eleven. It was the local Save-a-lot, the one she came to nearly every weekend to purchase groceries.

How had she come to be here?

The explanation wasn't immediately apparent, and Gillian wasn't sure she even wanted to know the answer. She didn't know why that was exactly, but a gnawing in the pit of her stomach told her something was wrong.

The bank. She remembered going there to close her account and then . . .

The images came slowly, looping through her mind's eye like a series of pictures in an old nickelodeon. There was a female teller behind the counter. One side of the woman's face was smattered with blood, yet she just stood there, speaking in cheerful tones, oblivious to the fact that half of her head had been squashed like a melon.

It wasn't real. Of that Gillian was certain. She did recall seeing such a sight, right after the teller had handed over the check, but then the vision had left her. It had been more like a dream really, except she hadn't been asleep. Regardless, it was unsettling as hell.

There had been something else, too; something that had terrified her even more than the bloody teller, something that had reached down to her very core and held on tight, shaking her like a rag doll.

(He's coming for you)

Oh, God!

The white car at the ATM; the man on the monitor . . .

Billy!

It had been Billy behind the wheel of the Nissan.

And his smile . . . that horrible smile.

The thought sent a cold shiver down Gillian's spine and her mind reeled all over again.

Had Billy been an extension of her strange vision? Or had that part been real? She thought it to be the latter. Which meant everything was happening just as she'd feared. He'd found her. And now he wouldn't stop. No, of course he wouldn't.

So, then, where was he now?

She couldn't say. Try as she might, she was still unable to recall what had happened between leaving the bank and arriving at the grocery store. Given the amount of anxiety she'd experienced over the course of the morning, wasn't it plausible that the sight of Billy had pushed her over the edge; to the point that she'd suffered some form of short term memory loss? Such things were possible, weren't they? She told herself they were.

As bothersome as the missing time was, however, Gillian was more concerned with Billy's current whereabouts. She wondered if he might be somewhere in the store at this very moment?

Given that he was a wanted fugitive whose face had probably been plastered all over the television by now, it didn't seem likely. After all, walking into a public place just hours after escaping from prison wouldn't be a very prudent move.

Perhaps Billy wasn't all that concerned with returning to jail. Perhaps, he was only interested in getting back at the person who had put him there in the first place. If that were true, Gillian figured he wouldn't think twice about killing her right here in the aisle, in front of God and everyone.

I have to get out of here. I need to leave.

Another voice from somewhere inside of her asked the question: *And go where?*

She felt the prickly heat of nervous perspiration creep over her entire body. Her breathing quickened and her palms grew sweaty. She gripped the handle of the shopping cart, leaning into it for support.

"I don't know. Just have to go," she answered aloud.

She began pushing the cart down the aisle and towards the front of the store. The air seemed heavier, almost suffocating, and Gillian noticed that the environment around her appeared to be coated in a drab wash of yellow and green, as if she were seeing the world through a colored filter. It was a sickly hue—the type often seen in those gritty thrillers in which someone always ended up on the wrong end of a knife in some cheap motel room or filthy gas station bathroom with a failing fluorescent bulb flickering overhead.

Gillian blinked several times, but the dreary tone remained.

This isn't right. It's not supposed to look like this. What's wrong with me?

She continued her march forward, stopping in her tracks when she saw Billy come around the corner. He walked towards her with a diabolical smirk on his face, the same shit-eating grin he'd worn countless times before, just prior to exacting various forms of pain.

(He's coming for you)

Yes, dear, I AM coming for you. I'm HERE.

Gillian's heart leapt into her throat and she did an abrupt about face, running in the other direction.

A stock boy was positioned at the end of the aisle, turning a mop on the tiled floor.

"Help me," Gillian croaked. Her voice was thin and hoarse.

The young teenaged boy looked up from his task and smiled through a mouthful of tin. Something was off about him. His eyes appeared cold and lifeless, void of all emotion, and his smile was just as disconcerting. The mop he held shone a bright red at the bottom, and Gillian saw a large pool of blood beneath his feet.

He sat the mop in the wringer and pulled the handle down. A cascade of crimson gushed into the bucket below. The boy removed the mop, plopped it back onto the floor, and began working it back and forth. The wet cotton head made a vile squishing sound as it moved through the circle of blood, leaving a series of red streaks across the white tile.

"What is this? What's happening?" Gillian cried out.

The stock boy tilted his head; his icy gaze remained anchored on the woman before him. He opened his mouth and spoke in empty nightmarish monotones. "You moved. You moved from your spot. He told you not to, but you did it, anyway."

Wha—? Gillian exhaled, desperately trying to understand the sight before her. Turning, she saw Billy just a few feet away now, and moving fast. She looked back at the stock boy, her eyes wide and pleading.

He winked.

Gillian shrunk to the ground and screamed.

A pair of hands came down on her shoulders and she cried out again, her arms swinging against her attacker.

The hands fell away. She waited for them to clasp tight around her neck, or to curl up into hard fists and strike, pummeling her skull until it resembled that of the bank teller's—cracked open like an egg, with eyes dislodged and dangling from their sockets.

"Ma'am? Ma'am, are you alright?"

The voice was soft and calm. It was a voice of concern.

Crouched beside her, a respective distance away, was the stock boy. He still had the mouthful of braces over his teeth, but his eyes were not the lifeless ones Gillian had stared into moments ago. These were eyes filled with concern and compassion.

"The man," she blubbered, "the one that was behind me. Where did he go?"

"I didn't see anyone behind you, Miss."

"He was right there," Gillian said, pointing to the left of the boy. "You had to have seen him."

The teen turned and looked over his shoulder, as if doing so might somehow jog his memory. He raised his brow, considering, then shook his head and wiped at his mouth, "I'm really sorry. I understand something frightened you, but I didn't see anyone else on this aisle, no one at all other than you."

A small whimper escaped Gillian's throat as her head whipped back and forth in silent protest. She glanced over at the mop bucket. A wet floor sign was perched next to it. The floor was clear. No blood.

This can't be. I saw it . . . I did. I saw him. Am I crazy?

A small crowd had gathered now, a sea of strange faces staring with morbid curiosity, as if she were some sideshow attraction that they'd just plunked down good money for the privilege to gawk at. You're crazy alright, their looks seemed to suggest. Crazy as a loon.

"Is there someone I can call for you, ma'am?" the stock boy asked.

Gillian felt the hot burn of embarrassment in her cheeks and scrambled to her feet, "No, I'm alright."

"Are you sure? Would you like me to walk you to your car?"

"That's not necessary. Really, I'm fine. I just need to rest," she insisted, dashing down the aisle. She wanted to get away from the onlookers who had come to see the woman in aisle four, the woman who'd lost her composure and must certainly be on the verge of a breakdown.

So, no, she wasn't fine. How could she be?

There was still the crushing fear that Billy would find her before she could leave town.

Yes, there was that.

But now there were also the strange visions, the missing block of time (not knowing how she even got to this godforsaken grocery store in the first place), and wondering if she was cracking under the weight of it all.

Oh, and one more thing: she didn't have the slightest idea where she'd left the car.

(Crazy as a loon)

16

Gillian had circled the neighborhood three times before entering, and now, as she turned down the drive leading to the two-story Cape Cod belonging to her parents, she slowed the vehicle to a crawl and surveyed the main road from which she'd come. She waited, looking both to her left and right several times before proceeding. Everything was clear.

The only cars in sight were those parked at neighboring houses, and none happened to be a white Altima. If, by some chance, the Nissan had made another appearance, Gillian would have been ready to drop the pedal to the floor and, as her uncle Ray used to say, get out of Dodge. As for where she'd have gone, she wasn't exactly sure. That was another question entirely, and one which, happily, she wouldn't need to answer.

It was fortunate, because Gillian felt her options were limited at present. Going home was out of the question, as it would be the most obvious place Billy would go looking for her. A public place was no better, for although it may have seemed a safer bet, the added sense of security was nothing more than an illusion, offering about as much protection as a suit of armor plied out of cardboard. The incident at the Save-a-lot, real or imagined, attested to that. Even now, the visions from the grocery store—and the bank before it—continued to march through her mind in an infinite, bloody parade of suffering and death, the vivid images playing on her perceptions until they were as rich and tactile as the fat flakes of snow which now lit upon the windshield.

She was weary, emotional, and, it would seem, on the verge of losing all sense of reason. Perhaps the best thing was to find a quiet place and lay low until Connor was done with school. She wouldn't be able to escape the nagging sense of fear which had tormented her all morning, but she could at least attempt to suppress some of the anxiety. That alone might be enough to subdue the freakish visions and bring back some semblance of calm and rational thought.

Her parent's house seemed like just the place to find the serenity she needed. Not to mention, she still needed to ask Mr. Davis, the neighbor, if he minded taking over the duty of collecting the mail until her mother and father returned home from their trip.

Gillian drove on, continuing past the house towards a two-car detached garage nestled behind it. With gray shaker shingles, gables and doors painted in bright white, and black lantern style lighting, the garage was a miniature version of the main house. There was even a four-pane window under the eaves with a flower box set below the sill. Had it been summer, the planter would have been overflowing with colorful blooms in varying shades of red (her mother's favorite color).

The drive curved to the left and behind the house, where an additional canopy style carport was constructed. Originally used to house her father's boat (an item he'd sold over fifteen years ago), it now sat empty and unused.

The boat had been purchased when Gillian was just a little girl, shortly after the family moved to Shadow Lake from California. It had been her father's pride and joy. She remembered how much he'd loved that thing, and how she used to sit on an overturned plastic milk crate on pleasant summer nights, sipping pink lemonade and watching him polish the painted exterior to a brilliant shine.

"*Outside of you and your mother, she'll be the finest sight on the lake this weekend,*" he'd often say. The line had always made her mother groan and roll her eyes, but Gillian would just giggle through a mouthful of lemonade.

Then, a few years later, in the early dawn hours of an ordinary June morning in 1997, a close friend of the family had taken his son—a boy Gillian's age—out to fish on the lake. Neither were ever seen or heard from again.

The boat was found drifting on the water some five hundred feet from the shoreline. The fishing poles were baited and ready to cast. Close by, the tackle box sat open, each hook and lure in its rightful spot. Resting on one of the bench seats was the boy's cap, next to which sat an opened can of grape soda with a mere a sip or two missing. It was as if the boy and his father had stepped away for a moment, perhaps to take a dip in the cool water or to gather some forgotten supplies, and were set to return in due course. Only they never did.

There had always been stories in these parts; legends and lore of others who had vanished in like fashion. Shadow Lake was famous for producing the kinds of hair-raising tales told around campfires. The most prominent and oft told was that of a busload of children who disappeared during one such camping excursion in the summer of 1978. Everybody knew that one. No bodies were ever found, nor had there been any indication of foul play—nothing but an empty bus and a group of deserted cabins. *Poof! Gone! Just like that.*

In the subsequent years thereafter, handfuls of tourists had made similar reports of lost friends or relatives in the woods around Shadow Lake, but none of the assertions were ever substantiated due to a severe lack of evidence. Many believed that those making such claims were only trying to play on a myth.

But the loss of a local man and his young son struck a nerve in the community, and for the first time since the 1978 tragedy, residents, including Gillian's father, were genuinely spooked. After the incident, he'd grown leery of the lake. The cover was placed over the boat, where it stayed indefinitely, and the cans of wax sat idle on the shelf until their inner contents had cracked and yellowed from age.

In time, the boat was sold off, but the carport remained right where it was, like some monument erected to honor a piece of sacred ground. The blessed square of earth beneath her had become a derelict piece of terrain which had forgotten the simple delight of the sun's warmth on its surface, and whose spotty patches of grass had not tasted a cool drink of summer's rain on their parched roots in many long years. It was a sad sight. A symbol, perhaps, of innocence lost on that fateful day back in '97.

Gillian parked the CRV under the shelter of the carport. Today, at least, it would prove to be useful once again. She shut off the engine and sat, absorbing the world around her. There was only the faint, ever-so-slight melody of hundreds of thousands of falling snowflakes touching the earth in synchronized harmony. The peacefulness of it stilled her turbulent mind and helped to banish some of the unsettling apparitions from the visions. But could it last? Would it last?

She pulled the keys from the ignition and dropped them in her purse before collecting her phone from the passenger seat. A quick click of the home button lit up the screen for several seconds, displaying the current time in large white numbers.

No new messages or missed calls.

Tossing the phone in her purse and climbing out of the vehicle, she crossed the yard to Mr. Davis's residence. The snow was already deep enough as to totally obscure the line between driveway and lawn; nothing but one long stretch of white powder blanketing the ground. Normally, she would have found pleasure in the simplistic beauty of winter's first show, but today its splendor was lost on her. All she saw was a drab, colorless world which she was desperate to escape.

Stepping up to Mr. Davis's door, Gillian knocked several times, first with a rap of her knuckles, and then, when there was no answer, with the iron knocker affixed to the door. The fixture was molded in the shape of a lion's head, with the mouth acting as a hinge for the metal striking ring.

It reminded Gillian of the scene in Dicken's, *A Christmas Carol*, when Scrooge returned home to find that the knocker on his front door had morphed into the face of his long dead business partner. She imagined this one changing as well, mutating into the face of the man who, not long ago, had nearly ended her life. Though such supernatural phenomenon only ever occurred in tales of fiction, given her current fractured state and the things which she'd already bared witness to, Gillian didn't find it all that implausible.

She backed away from the door, feeling a sudden aversion towards the metal ornament, as if it had already changed into something altogether horrid. It was clear Mr. Davis was not at home. She'd have to come back if she wished to speak with him, which was just as well, given her new disdain towards the man's door knocker. Why couldn't he have just had a doorbell like everyone else? *Maybe*, Gillian thought, as she turned to leave, *instead of a return visit, a simple phone call will suffice.*

After trekking back across the lawn, she keyed open the back door to her parent's house. Before twisting the knob and letting herself in, she noticed a nearby axe resting against the side of the house, the handle partially buried under a thick tuft of snow. It was the one her father used for splitting logs every autumn.

She stared at the thing for some time, filled with a deep sense of dread. Like the door knocker, it seemed to have become more than the sum of its parts. Oddly enough, having been attacked with a similar tool was not what gave her pause. Rather, it was the knowledge that it was there for Billy to find, allowing him to finish the job he'd started, yet never finished.

Gillian picked up the axe, dusted the snow from the handle, and carried it inside, where she propped it against one of the chairs situated around the dining room table. Now she had a means of self-defense. Should Billy find her, it would be he who would find himself on the lethal end of the axe this time around.

After slipping off her wet shoes and placing them by the door, Gillian entered the kitchen and collected a teakettle, which she filled with cold tap water from the sink before placing it on the stove. She twisted the knob and lit the burner (subconsciously flinching at the sound of the gas igniting), then turned and fetched a mug from one of the cabinets and a box of herbal tea from the pantry, both of which she placed on the counter near the stove. Now came the waiting.

She walked back to the living room and clicked on the television before lying down on the couch. *The Price is Right* was airing, and a trio of contestants were getting ready to spin the big wheel. It wouldn't have mattered what was showing, as Gillian wasn't interested in watching TV. The sound of it was but a distraction. Too much silence allowed her mind to dwell on bad things, and she hoped the noise from the tube would help divert her thoughts away from such evils.

As she closed her eyes and breathed in a deep cleansing breath, the home's subtle bouquet filled her nostrils—a heady mix of herbs from her mother's window garden, fresh laundry, a brisk hint of pine from her father's hand-carved wooden clocks, and the warm aroma of cinnamon apples that she'd always found so intoxicating, all lingering within the walls of the old house. It was the smell of nostalgia; the sweet fragrance of her childhood.

The effect was soothing, and Gillian took several long comforting breaths. Remembrances of her youth floated to the forefront of her mind, momentarily displacing her fears. The slow, rhythmic ticking of the wooden clocks on the wall drew her deeper down into the sandbox of her adolescent memories.

Gillian felt the tension begin to melt away. Peace and tranquility had come.

Tick-tock.

(There were castles here, such beautiful castles!)

Her muscles relaxed, the corners of her mouth turned up in a grin, and her thoughts began to drift upwards, becoming light as air, until they floated away into that vague and faraway space between consciousness and dreaming. Somewhere, in another realm, the big wheel was spinning.

(Gillian Adams, come on down—)

She slept.

17

It was a foul taste.

That was the first thing Gillian thought as the world around her slowly came back into focus. Harsh and brassy, the flavor possessed a distinct quality, reminiscent of the time she'd been on an antibiotic stew for a particularly stubborn respiratory infection, a side effect of which had made everything she'd eaten over the course of a week taste like a roll of quarters. Yes, that was it. It was the tang of metal she was detecting.

With her cognizance returning, Gillian tried moving her tongue, but it resisted, lodged in place by something dense and weighty. Her cheek muscles ached, and her teeth were jammed against cold steel. The realization came quickly—there was a gun in her mouth.

Her eyes flew open, confirming what her mind already knew. Billy loomed over her, sheathed in a rancid stench of sour perspiration and stale tobacco odor.

"Well, hello there, baby. It's so good to see you again."

Gillian's flesh crawled as he leaned in close, the tip of his nose slowly and deliberately tracing the contours of her face. He lowered his head until his lips grazed her left ear. "Look whose finally home," he whispered.

A muffled sob escaped the back of her throat and she felt a tear slide down her cheek.

"Oh, now, what is this?" Billy cooed, wiping the dampness away with the pad of his thumb. "Aren't you happy to see me?"

The syrupy tone with which he delivered his words did little to mask the contempt behind them. There was an old familiar fire in his eyes and his lips were turned up in that same horrible grin which had always preceded his most violent outbursts. Gillian had no doubt that the one brewing within him now would likely be his opus; a masterpiece that would ultimately climax in her death.

"No, I don't suppose you are," Billy continued, his voice hardening. "You always were an ungrateful bitch. I should have buried you a long time ago. Now, I can. I can do whatever I want. I mean, what's the worst that could happen? They take me back to prison? Strap me to a table and put me to sleep? A small price to pay, if you ask me.

"Do you know what I'd be thinking while lying there waiting for that cocktail to move through my veins and do its dirty work? If you're inclined to believe it would have anything to do with dying, or regrets I may have, you'd be wrong. I couldn't give two shits about that. No, I'd be thinking about this moment right here; about the final minutes we spent together. And how much I enjoyed making you scream."

The muzzle of the gun pressed hard into Gillian's palate and a pained cry passed over her lips. There was a deafening click as the hammer pulled back. She squeezed her eyes shut, wondering if there would be any pain when the bullet left the chamber and tore through tissue and bone. Probably not, but still the thought of it was agonizing.

Billy laughed, easing up on the pressure he exerted on the gun. "You think I'm going to shoot you? No, I can't let you off that easy. I just wanted to make sure I had your undivided attention. You see, as much as I would love to see your brains splattered all over this couch, I want even more to see you suffer. I want you to suffer the way I have over the past year, ever since you took my freedom away and turned everyone, including my own family, against me. I want you to think about your actions and what you're forcing me to do, Then I want you to have to live with the consequences of that for the rest of your pathetic life."

He slipped the gun out of Gillian's mouth and swung it behind him, where Connor was down on both knees, bound at the wrist and ankles. There was a jagged strip of utility tape across his mouth and his face was pink and puffy from crying.

Gillian barely had time to register what was happening before Billy had the barrel of the gun pressed against his son's head.

"Just remember, you asked for this," he said, and pulled the trigger.

18

The teakettle was screaming. Gillian sat up with a start, heart thundering in her chest. Her head whipped back and forth while her eyes combed the room.

"Connor," she cried.

But he wasn't there. No one was there. It had only been a dream; a vivid and all-too-real nightmare, the impact of which still lingered, shredding her emotions until her heart had been reduced to tiny slivers of devastation.

She thought she heard the cries of her son even now, insufferable shrieks of terror identical to the ones she'd heard just over a year ago while lying on the garage floor in a pool of her own blood. He had cried out for her in desperation and she could do nothing to save him. That same feeling of helplessness rippled through her again and she doubled over in anguish, tears flooding her eyes. Was there any worse feeling a mother could have than to know she could do nothing to protect her child from harm?

Although she'd only been dreaming moments ago, she knew she'd have chosen to die to save Connor. But Billy had taken that choice away from her. Billy had always taken her choices away; had made her a prisoner to his will and a hostage in her own home.

Amidst the tears and the heartache, she felt another emotion rising to the surface: indignation. She felt anger and resentment towards Billy for all he had done, for the toll he'd exacted on she and Connor both, and for the constant state of fear that continued to plague her. Earlier, she'd felt bad for thinking he might perish out in the cold, but now she hoped for it; prayed for it, for only then, when she was no longer living in his shadow, could she truly be free.

The cries she heard droned on, ramping up in their intensity. Gillian realized they were not those of a person at all, but belonged, rather, to the teakettle boiling on the stove. She ran to the kitchen and turned off the flame under the pot. Almost immediately the shrill call began to subside, changing from a piercing shout to a low, sputtering chatter.

She leaned against the counter, gripping the edge with both hands. Her face was ashen, a cold sweat covered her brow, and there was a hollow drumming between her ears from a pulse that was sky-high. The sprint from the living room to the kitchen had only exacerbated the situation, sending an abrupt rush of blood to her head and triggering a bout of lightheadedness. While she stood there waiting for the feeling to pass, a thump came from upstairs.

Startled, Gillian shot upright and froze, listening with rapt attention. An unnatural stillness fell over the room, yet there was no tranquility to be found within the calm. There was only a mounting sense of trepidation.

Tick-tock

The sound of the ticking clocks seemed to amplify with each passing second, becoming a countdown to something ominous now rather than a steady progression of time.

TICK-tock

Somewhere a hinge creaked. More silence.

TICK-TOCK

There was a rattle and another thump from upstairs, louder this time.

Gillian wasn't alone. Someone else was in the house. Her heart began to hammer again, harder than before, rapping painfully against her chest and rising steadily up her throat.

It's not real...I'm imagining things, just like in the bank and the grocery store. It's not real.

A doorknob clicked and a dead latch scraped across the metal strike plate.

No. Please, God . . . no!

There were footfalls on the stairs now.

(He's coming for you)

Gillian's mind told her to run, yet her legs had become cinder blocks, locking her in place.

Bump . . . Bump . . . Bump. The footsteps were getting closer now. They were almost to the bottom of the stairs.

(He's coming)

Gillian's breathing quickened. She thought she heard Billy's voice calling, low and haunting, "Gillian—"

Heels rapped upon the wood floor, the footsteps coming down the hall towards the kitchen. There was a change in the air. She could feel his presence now. Her hand tightened around the handle of the teakettle.

(He's here)

Billy rounded the corner and smiled. "Well, hello, dear" he said.

A tremor rattled Gillian's insides and a powerful surge of adrenaline pushed through her. Like a cornered animal, she went on the defense, releasing a vicious primal shriek from deep down in her lungs. Her arm was in motion now, swinging the tea kettle with all its might.

Billy's smile wavered, replaced by a look of surprise, just before a flood of scalding water doused his face. There was an audible hiss as the skin turned fire engine red and began to blister. He threw his hands up in front of him, howling in pain.

Gillian swung again, the metal kettle connecting with Billy's left temple. The blow sent him spiraling backwards into the dining room table. He slumped to the ground, knocking over chairs on the way down, and came to rest in an unconscious heap.

With face flush and heart still racing, Gillian looked past the table to the back door. On the other side was freedom. She started towards it, keeping her back pressed against the wall so that she was as far away from Billy as possible. Thirty steps away. Maybe twenty-five.

She kept her eyes glued to the body on the floor as she inched forward. Twenty steps now.

Billy groaned. Gillian stopped, twitching from the start. She waited, watching for movement. When there was none, she took a cautious step. Then another.

Her mouth was dry and her eyes burned. The air she breathed felt dry and hot on the back of her throat. Her body trembled forcefully and she could hear the involuntary tapping of her fingers against the wall.

God, just please let me get to the door.

Only ten steps away now. The slow procession was torturous. She wanted to run. Why couldn't she? She had beaten him once already. If he came for her, couldn't she do it again? Maybe. Maybe not. This time he might get the kettle and go to work on her. But the longer she waited, the more the fear took hold, and the more paralyzed she became. She looked at the door again and then down at Billy. His eyes opened.

A jolt of terror slammed through Gillian. She had to go right now. With a deep breath, she made herself run. She had taken about four steps when she felt Billy's hand graze her ankle, causing her to stumble. She fell forward, smashing into the chair at the head of the table. The axe she had placed there earlier skittered across the floor, just out of reach.

She turned and looked behind her. Billy had rolled over on his stomach. One arm was extended, reaching for her. "Gillian," he muttered. There was displeasure in his voice. His hand touched her foot, the fingers clawing desperately.

Full panic set in. Gillian pushed up on all fours and scrambled forward, grabbing the axe. She stood, and without conscious thought or feeling, turned and brought the blade down, nearly severing the outstretched arm. She only vaguely heard the scream which followed, for while one part of her lashed out in a tempest of fury, the rest of her retreated far away to a safe place deep within her mind.

The room faded and Gillian was a girl again, sitting on her father's shoulders at the outdoor amphitheater that they frequented back in California. She was no more than seven or eight years old then. The sun was dropping on the horizon, painting the sky with bold shades of pink and purple, while a warm breeze blew in from the Bay side, bringing with it the rich briny smell of saltwater.

The philharmonic was playing on this summer evening, and Gillian was feeling electric. She'd always loved the lush instrumentals of the orchestra and tonight they were playing one of her favorite pieces, *Prokofiev's Symphony No. 5.* She loved the bright energy and heavy use of percussion in the second movement.

Clutching a wedge of cold watermelon with both hands and savoring the sweet taste of the meaty flesh, she sat, wide-eyed and spellbound, fixated on the performance in front of her.

While violins sang and snare drums rattled, there were other sounds, fainter ones, which weren't a part of the movement—hollow, disembodied screams that danced in the distance, conducted by hands orchestrating a symphony of death.

Cellos moaned deep and heavy, and horns began to trumpet in frenetic bursts as the tempo of the music increased—*BOM, BOM, BOM, BOM, BOMP!*

Somewhere an axe fell, again and again, the sharp end clogged with blood and mats of hair.

The music swelled. The conductor waved his arms in a mad fit. Tadpoles of excitement swam in the pit of Gillian's stomach, making her squeal with delight.

Bone crunched and flesh ripped under each leaden wallop of the blade.

Cymbals crashed and timpani boomed. The crescendo was coming. Every instrument was at work—the clarinets, the bassoons, the tubas and French horns, all of them soaring to a fevered pitch.

BOMP, BOMP, BOMP . . .

The timpanist raised his arms, holding the felt covered mallet high in the air. Gillian held her breath in anticipation.

The axe dropped in one final grand gesture.

The sticks fell, striking the timpani and producing a cannon shot of sound which Gillian felt deep in her bones. The soft end of the mallet tore through the skin of the drumhead, triggering a dazzling explosion of red confetti which sprayed out over the entire stage.

The audience was on their feet, cheering and applauding for what had to have been the most glorious spectacle Gillian had ever seen. The clapping continued for an interminable amount of time. After taking a bow, the conductor stretched out his arms, first to his right, and then his left, as he motioned towards the musicians behind him. Then, with the applause waning and the last note having been played, the lights dimmed and the stage went dark. The show was over.

....

The clocks on the wall continued their hypnotic ticking while, nearby, a man on television prattled on about a revolutionary new product not sold in stores. Across the room, Gillian sat on the floor with her back against one end of the couch, her legs stretched out in front of her. How long she had been like this was unknown even to her.

Billy was dead. She knew that. She also knew that she had killed him. Though she didn't remember doing it, she knew she had. Her muscles were fatigued, her arms were covered in someone else's blood, and she was emotionally numb. All things considered, she should be feeling something, but right now there was nothing. It would come. She knew it would. And when it did, who knew what would happen then.

The axe rested on the ground a fingers-length away, a split in the wood handle now. Gillian had seen it lying there, but had yet to look at whatever sight waited beneath the dining room table. Probably better if she didn't.

She would need to call the police at some point. Yes, she had to do that. She wondered if they might haul her off to jail, but what she'd done had been an act of self-defense. Billy had tried to kill her once, so certainly they would believe he would try again.

(Thank you for making our job easier, Ms. Adams. Are you alright?)

Yes, fine. And it's no longer Adams. It's Harvey now. Gillian Harvey.

She continued to sit there, half-dazed and in shock, when a familiar voice caught her attention. Pamela Sheridan (Plastic Pam, as she was called in some circles, due to the varied and obvious enhancements she had bestowed on herself throughout her illustrious career as a local news anchor), was reporting on television. Judith had always said of the woman, that her appearance had been so fabricated she ought to have MATTEL stamped on her ass. But why was she on now? It was too early for the news.

Gillian rolled her head to the side so that she could see the TV from where she sat. To the right of the anchor was a large graphic on the screen with the words BREAKING NEWS in bold letters. Pamela looked straight at the camera, speaking in her polished professional tone:

"Once again, for those just joining us, we have a breaking update on the prisoners who escaped from the Westbrook Correctional Facility late last night. Police apprehended the men just hours ago after they stole a Nissan Altima from the Thurman's department store parking lot in Havencrest. The men were headed north on Interstate 5 when they were spotted in the stolen vehicle. After a lengthy pursuit and a brief standoff, two of the prisoners, John Rhodes and Michael Morrison, were taken into custody. The third, Billy Wayne Adams, was killed during the standoff after he allegedly drew on the officers with what was believed to be a gun—"

Gillian was on her feet now, staring at the television in disbelief. “No,” she said weakly. It couldn’t be. If the police had killed Billy, then who had she—?

Oh, God, no!

Her hands cupped over her mouth and her body shook uncontrollably. She began to turn, pivoting in the direction of the dining room. Her eyes were closed, tears already brimming over the lids.

(Look. Look at what you’ve done, Gillian.)

No, I can’t. Please, stop.

Her heart rattled in her chest like an old motor running on its last cylinder. She had to see who it was on the kitchen floor, but she was afraid; terrified of what she would find. Maybe it was no one. Maybe it had only been a trick, another vision. Perhaps she had only imagined seeing Billy in the house and, in her frantic state, had done nothing more than reduce the kitchen table to firewood. As much as she wanted to believe that, in her heart, she knew better. There was also the small matter of the blood, which told another story entirely. And the blood didn’t lie.

With a hesitant groan, Gillian forced her eyes open. The table sat at an odd angle, the once white tablecloth on top now spattered with large splotches of red. Beneath it, a mangled body lie splayed out on the floor in a lake of crimson. What remained of the face wore a thick mask of blood, yet despite its grisly condition, it was one Gillian knew well. “Daddy?” she whispered, a discernible tremor in her voice.

He must have returned home early from Seattle. Mom probably decided to extend her visit, but he’d wanted to come back to send Connor and I off.

Gillian's knees wobbled and her legs gave beneath her. She collapsed to the ground in an emotional storm, her chest convulsing with heavy racking sobs. The world began to press in, constricting around her neck like a heavy, suffocating blanket. A sickly-sweet darkness, thick and impenetrable, clouded her mind—inky pillows expanding on themselves over and over, pulling Gillian down into a place of perpetual night.

As she descended into the blackness, something stirred outside. Shifting her gaze to the back door, her eyes bulged with unbridled horror at what she saw there. On the other side peering in, was Billy. He stared at her with cold eyes, smiling his horrible smile. His attention turned to her father lying on the ground. When he looked back up and met her stare, his smile had broadened, as if he approved of what she'd done. Then, in his cruel and heartless way, he did the unthinkable. He winked.

Gillian's sobs turned to screams; cries of terror, anguish, rage . . . and madness. With the last remnants of sanity crumbling around her, she recalled the words which Billy had spoken time and again, words which would become her torment and the epitaph inscribed upon her soul:

"Fear alone can blind a man; make him do things he would never imagine . . . terrible things. If it's strong enough, it can make you crazy. . ."

And then she was gone, slipping down into the darkness; forever lost within the black vortex of a ravaged mind.

DARK NIGHTS ON SHADOW LAKE

HALLOWEEN HOUSE

"We wish for the things we think will make our lives better, happier, or easier. Things which we believe will bring us contentment. Yet, when fate sees fit to give us our desires, we often discover the fruits of our wishes to be bitter, and not at all what we'd hoped."

- Rev. T.R Nelson, Shadow Lake

1

Marjorie Bennett was fussing again.

Mrs. Bennett was always fussing about something, or so it seemed. The issue at present revolved around a life-sized clown doll which her husband had purchased during his visit to the flea market some hours earlier. Lyle Bennett was always scouring the flea markets, sometimes making upwards of three or four trips per week. He was a collector, but not of rare antiquities, vintage clothing, tools, cookie jars and such. No, Lyle Bennett was a collector of the macabre.

As a child, he'd accompanied his father to many a Saturday matinee. It was there, sitting in the darkened theater with popcorn and Coke in hand, that he'd first discovered the likes of the *Creature from the Black Lagoon*, *The Blob*, and *House on Haunted Hill.* Ever since those days, he'd been an avid horror fan. In truth, avid might not be a strong enough word to describe Lyle's fascination with all things ghoulish and frightening. Rabid was probably a better fit. But whatever adjective one wanted to use to describe the man, it was no secret that he loved anything spooky, be it books, comics, movies, figures, costumes, and anything else which fit the bill. It should come as no surprise then, that the holiday Lyle loved most of all, was Halloween.

The dawning of October always brought an increased measure of cheer to Mr. Bennet, for it was the one month of the year when the world at large shared in his morbid pleasures. Even a trip to the market was rife with chilling sights: witch's cauldrons filled with mounds of sweet treats (the Choco-Whirls, Gummy Goobers, and Fruity Fizz Bangers that were adored by children the world over), creepy costumed mannequins lording over end cap displays, grocery shelves decked in orange and black, and jack-o-lanterns or skulls strategically positioned between boxes of Frosted Sugar Snaps and Cinnamon Crackle cereals. Why, it was just as common to spy a severed hand or two in a shopping cart as it was a Sunday pot roast. And it was just that sort of thing which put an extra sparkle in Lyle's eyes. Though the man was ten years retired, October, he'd be quick to tell you, was his busy month.

And for good reason.

The Bennett residence, affectionately referred to by locals as the Halloween House, was the ultimate trick-or-treat destination. Not only did Mr. Bennett give out some of the best candy in all of Shadow Lake, he'd made it his mission over the years to transform his property into something of a spectacle. Spider webs covered every nook and cranny of doorways and window soffits. Bats flitted about, flying between the gnarled branches of dead trees, while red, glowing eyes peered from behind the many bushes around the house. The front yard had been transformed into a cemetery, with crosses and tombstones jutting above a dense blanket of fog. Here and there, one could even find a crooked hand or mummified corpse poking out from beneath the damp earth.

And that was only the beginning.

There were eerie moans, ghostly holograms, and assorted monsters traipsing about. Coffins propped against walls would spring open at random intervals, revealing a member of the living dead or the pale visage of a vampire, either of which would try to grab any poor sap that happened to be walking by.

Weaving through the maze of horrors at the Halloween House could be a hair-raising experience, eliciting a multitude of screams and shrieks at every turn. But it was also a delightful amount of fun, with residents returning in droves every year to see what kind of new sights—and frights—awaited them.

For Lyle Bennett, the night of October 31st was met with the same childlike exuberance usually reserved for tiny tots waking to Christmas morning surprises. Though he enjoyed scaring people, he was most pleased by the smiles on the faces of those visiting his humble home.

Marjorie, on the other hand, did not share her husband's interests. While it was common for her to voice some form of displeasure over her husband's antics, she had at least tolerated them. With the arrival of the clown, however, that all seemed to have changed.

Standing in the doorway between the house and the garage, hands firmly on her hips, she wore a pair of frumpy brown plaid pants and a loose-fitting cream colored blouse which was too sheer, allowing one to see the cone-shaped bra she sported underneath. Her silver hair was wrapped in pink hot rollers, while her eyes appeared owl-like from behind thick horn-rimmed glasses. Nothing about Marjorie Bennet's wardrobe had changed much since the sixties which, one could argue, was not the most fashionable decade to be stuck in.

"Would you look at it?" she crowed. "It's vile. What the hell were you thinking dragging that thing home?"

Lyle *was* looking at it, and couldn't see what the fuss was about.

The wiry form stood a good six feet tall, one hand holding a cone of pink cotton candy; the other resting on a barrel which had been striped in red and yellow with the words ZIMBO THE AMAZING CLOWN painted in a white comic sans.

The face was sheet white, with a dab of red grease paint over the nose. The eyes were rimmed in black, the makeup forming broad triangles above the eyes. Smaller triangles sat below the lids, trailing downward and gradually narrowing into a thin straight line over each cheek. The lips, and much of the surrounding jaw, were painted a garish red, forming a larger than life mouth which was turned up in a broad smile. The top of the head was bald, save for three tufts of bright orange hair evenly spaced across the smooth dome of white. Each frizzy mass, wide at the base and tapering into a peak at the top, looked like the end of a burning torch.

Decked out in baggy purple pants, oversized shoes, a yellow shirt resplendent with polka dots in a kaleidoscope of different colors, and a green sleeveless vest dotted with jingle bells, Zimbo looked like your average clown.

"I am looking at it, dear," Lyle replied. He scratched his head, puzzled over Marjorie's hostility. "It's a . . . well, it's a clown is what it is. A rather nice looking fella, I think. And in such great condition, too. Are you worried about the size?"

"Lyle Bennet, I hate clowns!"

"I'm sorry, dear. I had no idea— "

"No? I've hated them all my life. Why do you think it is I never liked the circus?"

"I wouldn't know. You were thirty when we met; a little old for either of us to care about the circus. And since we don't have children, the subject never came up. Might I ask what you have against them?"

"The damn things give me the creeps. There's something unnatural about the way they paint up their faces with those exaggerated smiles. You can never tell what they're thinking. I've never found them amusing, not even when I was a kid. All they did was terrify me."

"Huh," Lyle mumbled under his breath. "My wife suffers from coulrophobia."

"What's that you're saying," Marjorie squawked.

"I was just thinking out loud. I mean, coulrophobic people are the reason I bought this thing. I thought it would make a nice addition to my Halloween show. Of all the gruesome props I've accumulated over the years, I didn't expect Zimbo here to be the one to scare you. It's a little funny, don't you think?" Lyle chuckled.

"I don't think it's funny at all," Marjorie scowled.

"It's a little bit funny," Lyle said, grinning a sheepish grin.

Marjorie wasn't laughing. In fact, the hardness in her expression became more severe, making her look like a pressure cooker on the verge of exploding.

On the other side of the garage, nine-year old Tommy Prescott listened to the exchange with a casual ear. Most children his age would have been afraid of a destructive force of nature such as Marjorie Bennett, but Tommy was used to it. For one, he lived across the street and had seen the woman huff and puff more times than he could count. Secondly, Marjorie was the head lunch lady at Pine Ridge Elementary, where he was presently attending the fourth grade.

The woman wasn't much different at work. Tommy had heard her yell at one of the other lunch ladies for cooking too many green beans, bark at classmates who were running through the cafeteria or not disposing of their trash properly, and grumble about kids always being so cheerful. She once even chided a girl for greeting her with a customary good morning, saying, *"There's nothing good about mornings at my age, missy."*

Marjorie Bennett was about as nice as a grizzly bear that had been tied up in a bag and poked repeatedly with a stick. Tommy sometimes wondered how a nice guy like Lyle could end up marrying someone like her. In the end, all he could figure was that it must be because Mr. Bennet was so fond of monsters and other scary things. It was the only explanation that made any sense.

"I've put up with your foolishness for thirty-five years, Lyle, but I won't have that thing here. Take it back where you got it," Marjorie went on, wagging her finger at her husband as if he were a child who'd tracked mud across her just mopped floor.

"I can't just take it back, dear," Lyle replied. "Sales at the flea market are final, I'm afraid."

"Well, he can't stay out here. I don't want to see him every time I come out to the car."

"That's no problem. I'll put him in the basement for the time being."

"Are you hearing me?" Marjorie wailed. "I don't want to have to look at it! And I sure as hell don't want it inside my house."

"It's just for a little while. After I clean out the shed today, I'll move him in there. Until then, try to stay out of the basement."

Marjorie threw up her hands in exasperation. "Make it quick. I've got laundry to do, and I don't want to find that thing staring at me while I'm doing it."

"Yes, dear. I'll get to work clearing the shed right away. I'm sure I can get Tommy to give me a hand. Isn't that right, Tommy?"

"Sure, Mr. Bennett," the boy muttered, only half hearing what had been asked of him. He was busy prodding at a glass jar filled with eyeballs, fascinated by the wet, squishing sound they produced with each poke of his finger.

Marjorie grunted once before disappearing inside the house. As soon as she was out of earshot, Lyle turned back to the boy, grinning as if he were only nine-years old himself. It was the type of mischievous smile which all young boys exhibited when they were up to no good, whether that be plotting against their little sisters, hatching a dangerous scheme, or simply in possession of something they wouldn't want their parents finding out about.

"Let me get Zimbo here put away and I'll be right back. I've got something very interesting to show you."

2

"What is it?" Tommy asked, staring at the strange object which Mr. Bennett had dropped into the palm of his hand. The boy had expected the man to show him something cool—a bloody set of entrails, some brains on a platter, or even a new monster for the front yard—but this just looked like something straight out of Mrs. Bennet's jewelry box.

"It's a pendant," Lyle replied. "Like what you'd see on a necklace. I'm fairly certain that at one time or another it did hang from a necklace."

"Oh," the boy said. He looked back down, wondering what was so special about the thing he clutched in his hand.

The pendant, as Mr. Bennet had called it, was an inch-long, teardrop-shaped stone which was marbled with iridescent ripples of blue, green and black. A strange symbol had been carved into the face of the object; one which bore a striking resemblance to a human skull. Tommy thought it looked kind of neat, as far as jewelry was concerned, but it still wasn't as cool as a set of bloody entrails.

Lyle chuckled, amused by his young friend's puzzled reaction. "It's made of abalone shell," he remarked, reaching over and plucking the pendant from the boy's hand. "The Native American tribes in these parts used to make jewelry out of the stuff. What you're looking at here is over one hundred years old."

"Is that close to when you were born, Mr. Bennet?"

Lyle eyed the boy with suspicion. "They still teach math in that school you go to?"

Tommy nodded. "Mm-hmm. My math teacher is Mrs. Kent. She's really nice."

"Is that so? Well, I'd say Mrs. Kent is either bad at her job, or you need to pay more attention in class. I'm sixty-five, which makes this pendant at least fifty years older than me. Besides, do I look to be over one hundred?"

"No, I think you look about forty." Tommy flashed a wide, cornball grin in an obvious attempt at worming his way back into Lyle's good graces.

"Boy doesn't pay attention in class, and then neglects his eye exams, too?" Mr. Bennett hesitated a moment before giving the boy a playful nudge. "Don't worry. I'm just ribbing you. Truth is, I am an old man. Just not *that* old."

Tommy grinned wider. "What do you think you'd look like if you *were* that old?"

Lyle rubbed his chin for several seconds, pondering the question. "I suppose more like Mrs. Bennett . . . or maybe that guy over there."

The boy shifted his attention across the yard, where an authentic reproduction of a desiccated corpse, its mouth hanging agape and its hands pressed firmly against the sides of the face, was strung over the top of a tombstone.

Tommy began to laugh, small at first, then escalating into a full-fledged, gut busting roar.

"Sort of looks like the Mummy trying out for the role of the kid in *Home Alone*, doesn't it?" Lyle added, beginning to chuckle himself.

"Or, maybe . . . the future sequel, " Tommy said, the words coming between fits of laughter. "Nursing Home Alone!"

Lyle howled with glee, and over the next couple of minutes, the pair fed off one another's energy, guffawing until they were both red in the face and clenching their sides.

Tommy liked Mr. Bennet, always enjoying the time he spent with the man. In truth, he loved the guy like family, which was easy to do given that he'd never known his biological father. He'd asked his mother about his dad once or twice, but her response had always been the same: chock full of fury and four letter words. Ironic, given that Tommy wasn't allowed to watch R-rated movies, for they were filled with too many of what his mother called, *red words*. Yet, she embraced those very words in her own life daily, spouting them as regular as Old Faithful.

Sherry Prescott wasn't like most of the mothers in town. She didn't dote on her son, nor did she espouse the joys of raising children. You wouldn't find her looking up casserole recipes on Pinterest, posting pictures and videos of her son on social media, volunteering for the PTA, or driving the ever-practical mini-van. And she certainly wouldn't be winning any parent of the year awards anytime soon.

For one, she wasn't home much. Part of this was out of necessity. She was a single mother working two jobs to make ends meet. By day, Sherry was a cashier at the local Save-a-lot. Her shift ended at three in the afternoon, giving her two hours before having to be at the Whiskey Wagon, where she performed cocktail waitress duties until eight or nine. Though she didn't work either job on Sundays or Mondays, she would often make her way up to the Whiskey Wagon on those evenings, hoping to pick up an additional shift. If there was no honest work to be had, she'd sidle up to the bar, where she'd look for some sad sack sitting alone seeking comfort at the bottom of his glass. Once she'd found her mark, the flirting would begin. If the conversations went well (as they typically always did), she'd offer up her own brand of comfort in the backseat of her car to earn a few extra bucks.

Even when Sherry was at home, she was either sleeping off the ill effects of the previous night, or lying in her bed watching television. She'd make Tommy fetch her food, drink, clean clothes, or whatever else she needed in the moment, rarely ever helping her son with schoolwork or engaging him in fun, family activities.

Despite his mother's neglect, Tommy seemed well adjusted, acting no different than any other young boy his age. He was precocious, full of personality, and had an innate curiosity of the world around him. He seemed to have accepted the cards life dealt him, going about as if the hand he'd drawn was a royal flush rather than a lousy pair of twos. In fact, Lyle had rarely ever heard the boy complain, not even after the loss of his sister two years back.

Robin Prescott had died from an overdose of heroin at the age of sixteen, a tragedy made all the worse in that it was Sherry's live-in boyfriend at the time who was implicated in the death. The man's name was Gus, and Lyle had sensed the guy was bad news from the moment he'd first seen him. According to Tommy, the man had been a hard disciplinarian, doling out punishments with greater frequency than real parents delivered affection or encouraging words.

"Come here and take your medicine," was the man's favorite phrase; one which was always said just before he'd cut loose with a paddle. Although it was Tommy who had incurred the brunt of the man's wrath, Robin wasn't spared just because she was a girl. She had feared the man, not only because of his temper, but also for the inappropriate way in which he'd ogled her whenever her mother wasn't around.

To this day, it was unclear whether Gus had given Robin the drugs for his own amusement, as a means of attempting to have his way with her (though the autopsy results found no conclusive evidence to support that popular theory), or if she had found and taken them voluntarily. Either way, the man fled town the night before Robin's body was discovered in the bathroom and hadn't been seen or heard from since. If he was innocent of the charges lobbed against him, he'd done himself no favors by running.

Prior to Robin's death, Lyle had only spoken with Tommy on infrequent occasions. Afterwards, the boy began to find his way over more often, confiding his intense dislike of Gus and his grief over losing his big sister. Those first few months were the only time Lyle had ever seen the boy dispirited. Since then, the two had become fast friends, bonding over each other's fondness of spooky things. Moreover, Tommy was like the son Lyle never had, and Lyle was the father Tommy had always wanted, so the benefits of the relationship were mutual.

"Now, as I was saying," Lyle went on, "This pendant came from one of the tribes that once roamed these parts."

"Where did you find it?" Tommy asked.

"I picked it up at the flea market today."

"Did someone lose it? How do you know it's so old?"

Lyle smiled. He glanced to his left and right, lowering his voice when he spoke as if he were about to share something of the utmost secrecy. "Listen up, and I'll tell you. I think you're going to be quite surprised at the end."

Tommy gave an eager nod, his interest piqued.

"I came across an elderly man out at the market this morning. He was an odd sort of fellow; short and scholarly looking, with a long grayish-white beard and an antique tobacco pipe with funny little markings etched into it. I'd never seen him there before today. He didn't have much of anything to sell, really. The only thing I saw was an old trunk sitting on top of a table. I almost walked right past him."

"What made you stop?"

"It was what he said," Lyle continued. *"You, sir, desire the mysterious and hope to discover the secrets of the dead. I have what you seek."*

"He really said that?" the boy asked, his eyes narrowing in disbelief.

"I told you, he was an odd sort of fellow. Yes, that's what he said. I had to stop at that point, because anyone who begins a pitch like that has got my interest. Anyway, I was intrigued. Skeptical, of course, but still intrigued. That's when the guy opens the trunk and pulls out this pendant. He said the symbol on the face designates it as having belonged to a spiritualist of the highest order. And here's the kicker: legend has it, that this thing has the power to bring to pass the desires of whomever possesses it."

"What does that mean?" Tommy asked.

"That it's essentially a genie in a bottle," Lyle replied.

Tommy's eyes widened. "Does it really work? Have you tried it yet?"

"I have not. It's a nice idea, but I don't give credence to that sort of thing."

"You don't?" The boy looked even more perplexed now than he had upon first seeing the pendant. "Why did you buy it then?"

Lyle's lips turned up in a familiar grin. It was the look which always preceded the reveal of his greatest finds.

Tommy held his breath in anticipation.

"It's not the wish granting part that sold me, but rather the identity of the pendant's original owner. This isn't some toy or movie prop. No, sir. This is a real piece of history, like something out of Ed Gein's house of horrors."

"Who, Mr. Bennet? Who did it belong to?"

Lyle licked his lips with exuberance. "My boy, this little gem right here belonged to none other than . . . the lost lady of the lake."

"The witch of Shadow Lake?"

"That's the one."

Tommy's eyes appeared ready to bug out of his head. How could he have been so indifferent earlier? This was far and away better than a stack of bloody entrails or some brains on a platter. The tales of the witch and her curse on the town were legendary; greater than any he had ever heard. And unlike Bigfoot or the Loch Ness Monster, the witch was real. That was a verifiable fact, for there was mention of her in the town's historical documents. Mr. Bennet had told him as much.

Tommy suddenly found himself in awe, and couldn't wait to have the pendant in his hands again. First things first, though. Before asking to hold the newfound treasure, there was one small matter to attend to—he'd need to think about what to wish for.

3

The spider sat in one corner of the web, fangs raised high and ready to strike. A pair of eyes like glossy black onyx stones watched the child draw near. The boy reached out, slow and steady. He stuck his fingers into the webbing, grabbed several of the silky strands, and began to tug.

Tommy could see his reflection in those eyes and it sent a shiver through his body. He hated spiders, and even though the one staring at him now was made of rubber and plastic, it still gave him the willies. Unlike monsters, Tommy knew spiders were everywhere. He'd read that there were approximately one million of them for every square acre of land, and that was way too many for his liking. So, while he had no problem hauling around fake body parts, dressing monsters, or even stringing the webs, he was quite content to let Mr. Bennett wrangle the spiders.

"Sorry, kid. I shouldn't have stuck that thing up there yet," Mr. Bennett said, gently prying the arachnid from the web. "I'll wait until you've finished. You're doing a great job, by the way. Just the way I like it."

The boy beamed with pride. Mr. Bennett would sometimes let other kids on the block assist with setting up the various displays, but Tommy was the only one he ever entrusted with the webs. He'd never forgotten what the old man had told him the first time they'd worked together: "*Authenticity is key. You've got to stretch the stuff out and make it nice and thin. You can't just throw it up there in big bunches, because then it looks like wads of cotton. And you ever seen a spider shoot cotton balls out its ass? Yeah, me neither.*"

Since that day, Tommy had become somewhat of a pro, now able to create intricate webs with all sorts of elaborate twists and tunnels. Having an adult recognize him for a job well done wasn't something he was accustomed to, though he had to admit, it was a good feeling.

"Want to take a break for a few minutes?" Lyle held up two glass bottles which were coated with a thin layer of frost. "I've got us some orange soda pop."

Tommy jumped down from the stepladder and took a seat next to Mr. Bennett on a vintage wooden coffin; the same type he'd seen in old Westerns and the classic Hammer horror films. He snatched up one of the sodas, brought it to his lips, and proceeded to take several greedy gulps. The bright orange liquid was cold and delicious, tickling the back of his mouth as it ran down his throat.

"Beautiful day, isn't it?" Lyle asked.

"Sure is." Tommy agreed.

"Can't beat these autumn days. They're my favorite. When that first fall day arrives each year, you can bet I've got a smile on my face."

"I think it's my favorite season, too. But, how do you know when it's the first day of fall?"

"The calendar would tell you late September, but Mother Nature never looks at calendars. She brings autumn when she's good and ready."

"How do you know when that is?"

Lyle took a swig of soda, pursed his lips together, and nodded with satisfaction. "For me, autumn begins when the morning air turns a bit colder, the caramel apple pies show up in the bakery case over at Mabel's, and every food at the market is suddenly laced with pumpkin spice."

"I love pumpkin stuff," Tommy remarked.

"Oh, I quite like it myself," Lyle replied. "Although it's gotten a little ridiculous, if you ask me. I don't need pumpkin spice milk to pour over a bowl of pumpkin spice cereal, that I'm then going to wash down with a mug of pumpkin spice coffee. That's a bit much, don't you think?"

Tommy giggled through a nose full of soda bubbles. "You're funny, Mr. Bennett."

Lyle stared off into the distance with a dreamy, faraway look in his eye. Whenever he got that look, Tommy knew the man was about to wax poetic. And that's exactly what he did.

"Wouldn't it be something if the trees always wore a kaleidoscope of color, the air smelled of sweet cider and crisp October mornings, and the winds whispered the spooky happenings of Halloween nights? That, my boy, would be my idea of heaven."

"Sounds okay to me. I'd hate it if there was no October."

"That makes two of us," Lyle replied. "A world without Octobers; without Halloween, is unimaginable, and certainly no place I'd want to live."

Tommy polished off the last bit of soda, wiped his mouth with the back of his hand, and let out a small belch. Lyle chuckled, and the two were silent for a long moment, basking in the glory of autumn afternoons and the afterglow of an orange soda high.

"Mr. Bennett?"

"Yeah, Tommy?"

"If you could be any monster, what would it be?"

"That's a good question." The old man scratched his head in thought for several seconds and then said, "I think I'd be the headless horseman."

"Huh?" Tommy scrunched up his cherubic nose. "Who is that?"

Lyle appeared genuinely surprised. "My boy, you haven't read *The Legend of Sleepy Hollow*? Never heard of Ichabod Crane? Why, I know they even made a movie version of the story some years back."

Tommy shook his head.

"It's a classic. Tell you what. You hang tight. I've got something for you."

With that, Mr. Bennett stood and hurried up the drive, tossing his soda bottle into a recycle bin in the garage before opening the door to the utility room and disappearing inside the house. When he returned several minutes later, he had a comic book in hand, which he placed next to the boy.

"Read this," Lyle said, giving the cover several taps with his finger. "It's not the actual book, but I think you'll find this version more to your liking. The artwork is fantastic and you won't have to muddle through a bunch of archaic text."

Tommy scanned the front cover, his eyes full of enchantment. Under the glow of an oversized full moon, stood a horse the color of cast iron. The animal was reared back on hindquarters, pawing at the air with its front hooves, while clouds of white vapor spewed from his nostrils in angry puffs. Upon the horse's back was the dark form of a man with no head. The rider wore a cape which billowed behind him like a flag rippling in the wind. In his raised right hand, he held a noggin of a different sort.

At first glance, it appeared to be an ordinary jack-o-lantern, but upon closer inspection, one realized it was much more. The jagged cuts of the eyes and mouth were hard and angular, creating a face which resonated with menace. A red-hot furnace burned within the belly of the gourd, with yellow flames escaping the carved orifices and licking at the air like a giant torch. Although wholly consumed by this flame, the pumpkin did not burn, an indication that the thing was made of everlasting hellfire; likely spawned by the same dark magic which had allowed a headless man to go on living.

"This is awesome!" the boy shouted. "I promise I won't get it dirty or bend any pages while I'm borrowing it."

Lyle gave a wave of his hand. "Not to worry. I've got another one just like it, so you go on ahead and keep that one. I hope you'll enjoy it."

"I will. Thank you."

"Always happy to help a budding horror enthusiast further their education."

Tommy thumbed through several pages of the comic, stopping here and there to gander over frames which were of particular interest. "So, why the headless horseman, Mr. Bennett? I mean, if you could be any monster."

"That's easy. Every other monster has a weakness. Take a vampire, for instance. A bath of holy water, a stake through the heart, or even opening the curtains at the wrong time of day, and he's toast. The headless horseman, however, is a ghost, which makes him bulletproof. He couldn't cross the water, but who cares about that? I could live with boundaries if there's nothing gonna kill me. Plus, you've gotta admit, he looks pretty cool."

"Yeah, he does. I like that he uses a pumpkin for a head." Tommy grinned.

"And what about you?" Lyle leaned into the coffin, propping up on one elbow. "What monster would you be?"

"I'd for sure be the wolfman," the boy replied without missing a beat.

"You've obviously thought this through already. Why the wolfman?"

"Because you don't have to always be a monster. You're only one some of the time. Otherwise, you can still go outside, even in the daytime, and you're still you."

"Hmm. . ." Lyle nodded. "I never thought of it like that. Aren't you afraid someone might take you out with a silver bullet?"

"Mr. Bennett!" Tommy exclaimed, waving his hands about in a grand show as if the man should have already known the answer to the question. "Who carries around bullets made of pure silver?"

"Who, indeed? I guess you got me there."

"It's okay. You can't think of *everything*."

Lyle belted out a hearty laugh. "I sure can't." He gave Tommy a gentle squeeze on the shoulder. "You ready to get back to it?"

The boy nodded. He had no sooner hopped off the coffin he'd been sitting on, when the creak of the utility room door opening echoed from the garage.

"Lyle? Lyle Bennett, where are you?" Marjorie hollered, her voice resonating with the same delicate cadence as a battalion of bullfrogs at the peak of mating season.

"Run," Lyle whispered. "Don't let her see us. We can hide on the side of the house."

Tommy shot down the driveway and rounded the corner at the end of the home. His elder counterpart stayed close behind, arms swinging in a mad arc as he teetered along. To anyone watching, it would have appeared that the pair had just engaged in a game of ding dong ditch and were now searching for a place to hide. They ended up taking refuge behind a section of U.F.O. fuselage which had been cut to give the illusion of having crash landed in the yard. Nearby, two gangly aliens with bulging eyes stood at attention. Both were armed with futuristic assault rifles, the words PROBE-O-MATIC stenciled along the barrels.

Tommy was laughing. "Did she see us?"

"I don't think so," Lyle replied. There was a breathless quality in the man's voice which was brought on by his jog across the property, but he was grinning like the devil.

"Lyle!" Marjorie screeched. When she didn't get a response in a timely manner, she yelled again. "Lyle, where are you?"

Tommy could hear the woman's slippers shuffling down the driveway. He cupped a hand over his mouth to stifle a giggle.

Lyle, still grinning, ducked down further behind the spacecraft to ensure he wouldn't be seen.

The slippers stopped moving and an exasperated Marjorie could be heard cursing under her breath. "I don't want to have to search all over God's green earth for you!" she exclaimed. "Just hear this . . . you come get these shrunken heads out of my bathroom sink before I throw them away."

There was a long silence, and then the slippers began to scoot back up the drive. Shortly thereafter, came the sound of the utility room door slamming shut.

Lyle exhaled sharply. "We dodged a bullet that time, didn't we, kid?"

Tommy fell back on the grass laughing. "We sure did. That was fun."

"It was, wasn't it? You know what *won't* be fun? Going back inside."

"You're gonna get it, aren't you, Mr. Bennett?"

"To some extent," the man replied. "But, I'll cross that bridge later. Right now, let's work on setting up the guillotine."

Tommy sat upright with a look of alarm on his face. "You're not going to go in and get your stuff?"

Lyle shook his head. "Nah, it can wait a bit."

"But . . . she said she was going to throw it all away."

"No, she won't. She'll just yammer on at me for an hour or so. She'd do the same thing if I went in there right now. It's what she always does. And I've got better things to do with my time at the moment."

Lyle stood and helped Tommy to his feet. As the pair made their way around the house towards the shed, the old man sighed. "God knows, I love that woman as much as anyone can love a woman like her, but I've got to tell you, son, there are days when I wish like anything that she just couldn't talk."

4

The first few footfalls on the stairs went unnoticed. Marjorie might have heard the dull thuds had she not been busy talking to herself. She was in her bedroom, still complaining out loud; wondering why it was that her husband, a grown man, still wanted to play with toys . . . and such appalling ones at that. He never had grown up, had he? Lyle Bennett was essentially a twelve-year-old boy in a sixty-five-year-old body. And the older Marjorie got, the less patience she had with the man's antics, especially around Halloween. *Damn holiday can't be over soon enough!*

She heard them then: footsteps trudging up the stairs.

They were slow and measured in their pace; three of them all told. Then nothing.

"Lyle?" Marjorie called out.

The silence continued for several seconds before the footsteps resumed—at least half a dozen of them—only this time they were quick and purposeful, pounding against the stairs with a sense of urgency.

He knows I heard him, and he's running away, Marjorie thought. *Probably headed to the kitchen to make a sandwich instead of coming to take care of his mess. We'll see about that!*

The woman tossed the container of hairpins she'd been using onto the bathroom vanity and stormed across the bedroom.

"Lyle Bennett!" There was thunder in her voice. She exited the bedroom at full tilt, rounding the corner into the hallway, before stopping short. The fury fell from her face in an instant, replaced by utter terror.

Standing at the top of the stairs was the clown Lyle had carried down to the basement not more than an hour ago. Only now the thing wasn't just a mannequin wearing rainbow-colored clothes. It was very much alive—moving, breathing, and grinning in its grotesque way.

How such a thing was possible did not enter Marjorie's mind at present. Waves of shock numbed her brain, squelching all manner of rational thought, while the horror of what she was seeing rooted her body in place.

The clown's saccharine smile broadened, his blood-red lips parting to reveal a mouthful of jagged yellow teeth. He began to dance a jig in puppet-like fashion, raising one leg and swinging it like a pendulum on an antique clock, before switching sides and repeating the process with the other leg. He did this several times before throwing his arms open wide and striking a pose.

"Ta-da!" The voice was low and garbled.

A feeble chirp escaped Marjorie's lips. *Those eyes. There was something terrible in them. And that smile . . . that horrid smile . . .*

Zimbo thrust the cone of cotton candy forward, holding up the index finger on his other hand as if to say, *prepare to be amazed.*

Dear God, help me!

The clown began pulling at the pink fluff, ripping away tuft after tuft of the candy and tossing it into the air, where it would explode in a burst of shimmery glitter. When the candy was no more, Zimbo waved his hand up and down over the empty cone three or four times. With a final quick upward motion, the red and white swirled cup disappeared and something else took its place.

Marjorie couldn't make out the new object. Whatever it was, whipped the clown into a frenzy. The monstrous creature bounced up and down with uncontainable excitement, not unlike a sixteen-year-old boy who'd just been handed the keys to a Ferrari.

Once the jumping had subsided, the clown leaned forward and waved the mysterious object back and forth in a methodical motion. *See what I have here*, the thing said, without uttering a single word.

Marjorie did see. Her mouth fell open in a silent scream.

Light bounced off the straight razor as it twisted about, cutting through the dim confines of the hallway—a hallway which now felt too narrow and restrictive.

The sudden knowledge of what was about to happen sucked the very air from the woman's lungs. She wheeled backwards, finding the wall behind her. It was probably Marjorie's own sense of equilibrium thrown awry, but the wall seemed to be moving forward, pushing her closer towards the freakishly cheerful monster ahead. She clawed at the sheetrock, pressing her body hard against the barrier as if it might somehow absorb her mass and whisk her out of harm's way. It held firm; as hard and unforgiving as a tax collector.

Zimbo rocked back on his heels and laughed. "Let's *cut* to the chase, shall we?"

"No. Please, go," the old woman protested. But the words were weak, registering as nothing more than a faltering whimper.

The grease-painted man formed his mouth into a wide O-shape and began to howl. He raised the blade and rushed forward, his devilish laugh morphing into a mad cackle.

Marjorie's trembling body went rigid, the cords in her neck straining until they appeared ready to snap. She tried to cry out, but the same fear which had kept her glued to the floor was also constricting her vocal cords. By the time the first inklings of a scream began to pry itself loose from the petrified walls of her throat, it was already too late.

Zimbo had her tongue.

....

The sun was nesting on the horizon when Lyle decided to call it a day. He and the boy had accomplished quite a bit over the past few hours, not only clearing out the shed and assembling the guillotine, but also laying the bulk of the track for the ghost train, which would begin its departure from the newly constructed Depot of the Dead within the week.

"She's looking good, Tommy. I'd keep going, but I could stand to get a little dinner in me. Besides, the wife hasn't been back out, which means she's been in there stewing. I'm going to have to face the music at some point. Might as well do it now before she gets worse."

"Okay, Mr. Bennett. Is there anything else you want me to do while you're getting yelled at?"

Lyle laughed. "No, you can go on home. We're ahead of schedule. Getting the rest of the stuff up by next weekend should be a cinch."

"Okay," Tommy replied. He shoved his hands in his jeans pockets and sighed. "Goodnight, Mr. Bennett. I hope you aren't in too much trouble."

Lyle detected a trace of sadness in the boy's eyes. "Hold up now. Is your mom home yet?"

"No," Tommy replied. "She won't be back until after nine."

"I see. Well, tell you what. How about you come back after dinner. It'll be too dark to do much outside, but I've got something in the house that I'd like to get your opinion on."

Tommy was all smiles. "Really?"

"Yes, sir. I want this to be the biggest and best Halloween ever; one that nobody will ever forget. To do that, I'll need all the help you can give me."

"Sounds like a plan. I'll see you soon, Mr. Bennett." The boy scampered across the street, turning once to wave.

Lyle smiled and returned the gesture. Before going inside, he glanced up and marveled at an October sky which was pink and innocent of clouds. Looking further to the east, the fiery hues dissipated, changing from warm reds to deep blues before eventually being swallowed up by the invading darkness. Night was coming, and with it, a full moon.

"Could make for an interesting evening," Lyle mused. He rubbed at his arms as he crossed the drive, fending off the slight chill in the air which had begun to nip at his skin. Moments later, he entered the confines of his more temperate home, closing the door soundly behind him.

It would be the last anyone saw of Lyle Bennett.

5

It was all rather peculiar, come to think of it. He and the boy had worked outside for a good three hours after hiding from Marjorie, and in all that time, she hadn't made another appearance. Not that that was a bad thing, mind you, it was just a little surprising. Lyle had expected a small reprieve of an hour or so before his wife came looking for him again, but three was a new record.

Even now, as Lyle moved past the stairs in the entryway and made his way through the living room, there was no sign of the woman

"Marge, dear," the man called out, thinking she might be in the kitchen preparing dinner. Though there were no aromas of food cooking, that didn't mean she wasn't busy prepping something which would soon hit the oven or a frying pan.

Marjorie wasn't in the kitchen, either. A mug wearing the *Mabel's Morning Glory* logo sat on the counter near the sink. It was the same one Lyle had used for coffee that morning and the only indication of anyone having been in the room all day.

Well, my goodness. Wherever could she be? Maybe upstairs napping? Or still upset with me and on strike? The latter was likely the correct choice.

The thought occurred to Lyle that no dinner in progress might work in his favor, as he could offer to take Marjorie to Buonasera for dinner. The place was regarded as *the* spot in Shadow Lake if you were looking for authentic Italian cuisine and fine wine. While his wife wasn't big on wine per se, she absolutely adored the chicken Pomodoro served at Buonasera. Lyle reasoned that such a gesture could go far in getting him out of hot water (or, at the very least, make the waters a bit more temperate).

The man was making his way through the dining room, still rubbing his hands together with self-congratulatory delight, when the sounds of music drifted down from one of the upstairs rooms. The unexpectedness of it momentarily stopped Lyle in his tracks and he cocked his head to listen.

Frank Sinatra. The track playing was one of his favorites: *I've Got You Under My Skin*.

Hearing the crooner do what he always did best wasn't odd in the least. Marjorie playing the song, however, was practically unheard of. To his knowledge, she didn't even know how to work the compact disc player in the bedroom. In those rare instances when Marjorie had listened to a cd, it was always Lyle who'd worked the equipment, due to the woman's self-described impairment of anything technology related.

Lyle was in motion again, moving into the entryway and starting up the stairs at a brisk pace. Halfway up, he stopped. The music was loud—too loud—playing at a volume which Marjorie would never tolerate, much less listen at. There had been another sound as well, a faint one, buried beneath the brass instruments and the smooth baritone of Mr. Sinatra. It had been a cry of sorts—high and unnatural; sounding not quite human.

Lyle craned his neck and listened, hearing nothing now other than music. Still, there was a sudden queasiness in his gut telling him something was off. To an extent, the sensation had been with him ever since he'd stepped back inside the house, but he had ignored it, brushing it aside as if it were nothing more than a bothersome insect. Yet now, as he trudged carefully up the remaining steps, he could no longer disregard the solicitous feeling crawling over him. The fly had become a swarm.

Straight ahead, at the end of the dark hallway, a thin strip of light spilled out from beneath the bedroom door on the right. Lyle moved towards it with trepidation, a heavy weight settling into his bones. "Marge, honey," he called out again, only this time the words were strained and broken.

There was no reply, save for Sinatra snapping to the beat of the song. Shortly thereafter, a trombone began to bellow, the sweeping intensity of its register filling the dim hall. With each quick, powerful bleat, Lyle could feel his eardrums pulse. At the same time, small tremors raced up his legs, as if he were standing in the middle of a bridge while a convoy of eighteen-wheelers raced by.

The old man felt a cold terror in his heart as he neared the bedroom, though he could not pinpoint the exact reason why. Yes, his wife was acting a little out of character tonight, but that on its own shouldn't have been cause for alarm. At least, not of the magnitude he was experiencing at present.

Yet, there was . . . something. He couldn't touch it, couldn't see it, but it *was* there. If he didn't know better, Lyle would have thought the very air around him had become a living, breathing, and wholly malevolent entity.

The bedroom door was pulled to, leaving a small crack between the door and the frame; just enough for a sliver of yellow light to escape. The uneasy feeling in Lyle's gut intensified. He could see his hand shaking as he reached for the knob.

Go on in, the invisible entity seemed to say, its imperceptible fingers pressing in on his back.

Lyle didn't want to. *Why? What are you afraid of?*

Some small part of his mind tried to reason, telling him it was nothing; that his wife was fine. That he would enter the room and, after some doing, make up with her and off they would go in the Caddy for chicken Pomodoro and tiramisu.

Yet, in a larger sense, he believed otherwise, for the terror within him continued to mount. He feared whatever awaited him on the other side of that door, thinking it to be more awful than anything he could ever imagine.

Lyle gripped the knob tight and closed his eyes. His heart beat heavy against his ribcage, while perspiration cascaded down his forehead, the salt of it stinging his eyes. He licked his lips, took a deep breath, and swung the door open in the same manner as one might rip off a bandage.

"Marjorie?" Lyle's voice cracked. His blood turned to ice and the inside of his mouth became like fine grit sandpaper.

His wife was dead.

Her body hung on the wall over the bed like a scarecrow, arms outstretched and head lopped to one side. The woman's jaw had gone slack and her wide-open mouth appeared bloodied and swollen, her tongue having been cut away. Above her head, scrawled in blood, was the message:

U SEE, WISHES DO COME TRUE

Lyle's eyes darted back and forth, playing over the other atrocities in the room: the trick-or-treat candy intermingled with double-edged razor blades and strewn about the bed, the lacerations up and down his wife's arms where more of those same blades had been inserted beneath her skin, and the ceramic figurine of a cat on the nightstand—a calico lying on its back juggling a ball of yarn—over which Marjorie's tongue had been placed just so.

There was a dark irony in both the placement of the organ and the song currently spinning on the cd player, yet both were lost on Lyle, for he was too terror-stricken to notice such things.

"Yes, I've got you . . . under my skin."

Mr. Sinatra crooned the words one final time in his smooth, upbeat rhythm before the disc in the player ground to a stop and the room fell quiet.

"My God," Lyle whispered through trembling lips. His eyes were slicked with hot tears and his chest heaved, causing the breath to exit his body in shuddered bursts. The room was pressing in on him, as if the entity he'd sensed prior had coiled itself around his torso and begun to squeeze. At the same time, the ground appeared to shift beneath his already unsteady legs, causing him to stumble backwards and knock into a dresser.

On the wall above the dresser was yet another message scrawled in blood. This one read:

SOMEONE'Z IN THE HOUSE

Had Lyle turned after colliding with the piece of furniture, he'd have seen the message. He would have also seen the thing which now stirred in the shadows behind him, its ashen face emerging from beyond the darkness. But he didn't turn. He could only stare in stilted shock at the lifeless form hanging above the bed.

"Marjorie," Lyle cried out, crumpling to his knees. "Who? Who did this to you?"

The answer came to him straightaway, not by way of voice, but in the form of a dozen tiny bells jingling all at once.

6

Barely an hour had passed since Tommy returned home from the Bennett residence and already he was restless. Having finished a dinner of nuked hot dogs and macaroni and cheese (there was better food in the pantry, he just hadn't been interested in taking the time to prepare a proper meal), there was nothing more to do but wait. A difficult task when all he could think about was getting back to Lyle and seeing what kind of gruesome new surprises his friend had up his sleeve.

Another glance at the clock revealed the time to be just after seven. Was it too soon to return? Tommy thought perhaps it was. The last thing he wanted to do was show up before the couple had finished eating, as that would only give Mrs. Bennett something else to holler about. Another thirty minutes should suffice. But what to do for half an hour?

He tried reading the comic book the old man had given him, but found himself retracing the words over and over. While he normally loved books, especially of the comic variety, his excitement level was ratcheted too high, thus impeding his brain's ability to attain the level of focus required for reading.

So, now what?

Tommy sat the comic book aside and picked up the television remote. Clicking through the channels, he was delighted to discover a horror movie marathon running on one of the cable stations. The movie playing now was unfamiliar to the boy. The premise had to do with an addictive dairy-like dessert called, *The Stuff*, an extraterrestrial substance that turned people into mindless puppets while devouring them from the inside. It was the type of flick Mr. Bennett referred to as a Friday night pizza movie, which is to say it was B-grade schlock that was jam packed with silly special effects and bad acting, but also wildly entertaining. It was the sort of thing a nine-year old boy like Tommy would go nuts over. And he did. By the time he tore his eyes away from the television, and the killer *Cool-Whip* doing its nasty business, forty minutes had elapsed.

"Damn," the boy muttered, happy his mother wasn't around to hear his blatant use of a red word. He clicked off the television and threw a hoodie over his white T-shirt before running outside and scrambling across the street.

Reaching the Bennett residence moments later, he raised a hand to knock, but found the front door standing ajar. Tommy pushed the door open just wide enough that he could poke his head inside. The front entry was dark with no one in sight.

"Hello? It's me, Mr. Bennett."

The boy waited, hearing nothing.

"Mr. Bennett?" He raised his voice in a full-on shout.

Somewhere upstairs a floorboard creaked, yet no one answered.

Tommy opened the door wider and stepped inside. He wasn't sure why the front door was open to begin with, unless Lyle had left it that way and gone down to his workshop. If Mrs. Bennett had turned in early, he may have wanted to make sure his little apprentice didn't ring the doorbell upon arrival and disturb her.

The boy closed the door gingerly behind him and tip-toed across the entry at a judicious pace. Several steps in, his foot came down on something solid. He stepped back and knelt to inspect the item. Turning the object over in his hand revealed it to be the pendant which Lyle had shown him that morning; the one belonging to the lost lady of the lake. Mr. Bennett must have had a hole in his jeans pocket, as Tommy couldn't imagine him being so careless as to leave the item on the floor. He knew how upset the old guy would be if he were to lose such a treasure, so he dropped the stone in his own pocket for safekeeping and continued forward.

An impromptu scream pierced the silence, causing the boy to freeze in his tracks. A second bloodcurdling screech followed on the heels of the first, echoing from the rear of the house.

The cries weren't Marjorie Bennett's. Not that Tommy had ever heard her scream—not in terror, anyway—but the shrieks were too high to have come from the old woman. She would have sounded deeper, hoarser. Not to mention, these screams had another quality to them which was a bit suspect. He couldn't think of how to describe the sound other than thin and artificial. No, artificial wasn't quite right. He knew they'd originated from a real person, but they lacked presence, as if they'd been . . . recorded. *Yes, that was it!*

Emboldened by this realization, Tommy pressed on, going past the dining room to the kitchen, where a single light burned above the sink. This room, like the others, was unoccupied, but a door off the side of the kitchen stood open. Beyond this door, were the stairs leading down to the basement. It was there the screams had originated. Even now, as Tommy stood upon the top step, peering into the dimly lit confines of the room below, he could make out the sounds of people talking on a television, their conversation bookended with eerie music.

"Mr. Bennett. It's Tommy. You down there?"

There was no answer, but this didn't faze the boy in the least. Between the movie's volume and Lyle's less than perfect hearing, he doubted his presence would become known until he was right on top of the man.

Tommy trotted down the steps at a brisk pace, bounding over the last two altogether. At the base of the stairs, against the far wall, sat the washer and dryer, next to which was a folding table and a small hanging rack. Just to the left of the table stood the barrel with ZIMBO THE AMAZING CLOWN painted across the front. The barrel's namesake, however, was no longer propped up against his trusty cask. Lyle must have already moved the clown to the shed, making it possible for his wife to once again do her laundry in peace.

Tommy veered to his left—the only direction one could go—and gazed across the dark space. He'd expected the room to be well lit, with Lyle hard at work on a new monster, but instead found mostly darkness. The only source of light within the dank and sullied space came from the television at the far opposite end of the basement. He allowed his eyes time to adjust to the dim surroundings before inching his way across the room, being careful to skirt Lyle's wooden work table which was obscured within the blackness.

Beyond the shop space was the old man's personal retreat, a finished area resembling a small family room. The area held a television, a well-stocked bookshelf, a microwave, and a mini-fridge. There was a worn leather couch the color of whiskey positioned across from the TV, and a rather shoddy looking recliner near the bookshelf which served as a reading chair. The room wasn't much to look at, but it contained all the things Lyle needed for relaxing.

As he approached, Tommy realized the movie playing on the television was the same one he had been watching back at his house: *The Stuff.* And boy, was the maniacal whipped cream ever wreaking havoc. While this explained the screaming he'd heard while upstairs, there was something else which stopped him short: a headless human form sat on the couch.

Its feet were planted firmly on the ground, the fingers of its right hand curled around a mound of yellow kernels from a bucket of popcorn positioned between denim clad thighs. The flickering light of the television illuminated the empty space between the collar where, instead of a gory display of torn muscle and sinew, a long row of neat little stitches ran in a straight-line parallel with the shoulders.

Tommy presumed the figure to be a man. He came to this conclusion based solely upon the clothing, which consisted of dark jeans and a pale-yellow polo shirt. They looked to be the same ones his elder friend had been wearing that afternoon, however, this couldn't have been Lyle, because Lyle had a face and a head, something the form on the couch was missing.

Who . . . WHAT . . . is this?

Tommy stood, unblinking. A nervous energy filled him. It wasn't fear—not yet—so much as it was a form of anxiety; the same jittery feeling he'd get whenever he'd have to stand up in front of his class and give a speech, or anytime Brooklyn Emerson, the prettiest girl at Pine Ridge Elementary, would speak to him. The sensation was akin to consuming a gallon of popping candy and having it explode in his gut all at once.

Was this what Mr. Bennett had wanted to show him? It certainly made sense, given the man's apparent fascination with the headless horseman. And it would have been just like the old guy to leave the front door open and then steal away, waiting until his guest happened upon the meticulously staged scene to see what kind of reaction his new creation would garner.

"Nice try, Mr. Bennett!"

Then again, the boy conceded, were he to have seen this in his own house, he would have screamed bloody murder just before shitting his pants.

Another red word. Did it even count if you didn't speak it? Who the hell knew?

With a shrug, he moved closer to the being on the couch, admiring the macabre sight. Although the thing was motionless, it seemed as if it might somehow be alive and aware . . . still knowing, still seeing, still plotting. The thought sent goose shivers over Tommy. He knew the thing in front of him to be nothing more than an elaborate fake, but even so, it was a damn good fake.

"I like it, Mr. Bennett," Tommy yelled. "But you need to dress it in something else. Maybe a dark suit and cape, like the horseman in the comic you gave me. Because your clothes aren't very scary."

The fact that Lyle did not respond then should have given the boy pause and been the first indication that something was very wrong. Were Tommy not still captivated by the headless form, it may have. But, as it were, he marveled at the texture and color of the skin on the hand in the popcorn bucket; the way the tendons and veins stuck out, the intricate, fine hairs just below the knuckles, and the hardened callouses along the sides of the thumb and forefinger.

"It all looks so . . . real."

Tommy reached for the headless figure, but before he could make contact, the television went out, leaving him in total darkness.

"Mr. Bennett?"

When there was no answer—no sound of any movement in the house—the first real pin pricks of fear began to jab at the boy.

"Mr. Bennett? You win. I'm scared, okay? Now, please turn the lights back on."

The lights came on, but they weren't the ones Tommy had been expecting. On the back wall, tucked into the corner adjacent to the television, a series of colorful bulbs flashed in a chase pattern along the top of an arcade machine. It was one of those games of skill where you maneuvered a metal claw via a joystick in a one-shot effort to grab a prize out of a bin. The game was more luck than skill, but Tommy had played the one at the Save-a-lot where his mom worked. On several occasions, he'd even managed a win.

Cool! When had Mr. Bennett scored one of these? The man was full of surprises tonight.

Whimsical calliope music rang out, and a cartoonish voice prompted: *Step right up and win yourself a prize. Come one, come all, have yourselves a ball!*

Tommy went to the machine and peered at the contents of the prize bin.

"Huh?" He scrunched up his face, bewildered by what he saw. Where were the stuffed animals? The rubber balls? The keychains? The Rubik's cubes? There was only a singular prize to be had in this machine: a clown. There were scores of the jointed action figures in the bin and all were identical—painted to resemble the life-sized circus statue that Mr. Bennett had brought home with him from the flea market.

Tommy thought it a weird happenstance. After all, he'd never even heard of Zimbo before today. It wasn't like the clown was an icon of pop culture like the Joker or Pennywise. Who would be cranking out his likeness on a mass scale? And why would Mr. Bennett want so many of them? More questions for which the boy had no answer, at least not until he could ask the man himself.

Right now, it was of little consequence. The game was set to free play and Tommy was more than willing to test his skill. He gripped the joystick and positioned the claw over a single figure near the back of the bin. This one stuck up higher than the rest, its right arm bent at the elbow and forming a nice gap for one of the metal fingers to slip through.

He overshot the figure on the first attempt. On his second, the tip of the claw grazed along the forearm, missing the gap by only millimeters. The boy came close to spouting another red word, but refrained. Why get upset when he had nothing to lose? He could play until he won without it costing a single dime. And that's what he intended to do. It took three more attempts, but on the fifth try, the metal finger looped through the gap in the arm with perfect precision, hooking the figure and pulling it up into the air.

A short victory dance ensued, stopping once the claw had dropped the toy into the prize receptacle. Without hesitation, Tommy thrust his hand through the hinged access door to collect his bounty. Something inside the machine seized him by the wrist.

The boy yelped and pulled away. The thing released its grip, causing the young man to tumble backwards and fall on his ass. He stayed there, propped up on elbows, wondering what had just happened. Was this another one of Mr. Bennett's tricks? Had he rigged the machine with some device to scare people?

The prize door opened, hinging outward as an arm emerged. A gloved hand waved, its fingers wiggling in animated fashion. Tommy's eyes widened and he scrambled to his feet, watching with a mixture of fascination and horror as the machine birthed a living thing.

There were two hands now. They gripped the sides of the small opening, providing leverage for a pale white head which slowly came into view. It twisted back and forth within the opening, while three tufts of orange hair sprouted along the scalp like new spring vines trailing over a lattice. The head reared back and the face of Zimbo stared at the boy.

"Hi-ya, kid," the clown cracked.

Tommy didn't budge. He could only stare in disbelief.

Zimbo brought his hands together and cracked his knuckles. With another wriggle of his fingers, he thrust his arms outward. They were thin and gangly at first, looking like the gaunt appendages of the sci-fi alien figures in Lyle's yard. Once the clown had its hands planted on the floor, the tissue around the arms plumped up, just before the bright polka-dotted sleeves moved down over the pale skin like motorized curtains.

The shoulders and upper torso came next, twisting and bending through the access door in ways which were not humanly possible. With a sudden lunge and a sound like that of a toy pop gun, Zimbo shot forth, breaking free from the machine. He somersaulted across the basement floor before springing into a standing position a few feet from the young boy. He wobbled on legs which were bony and disproportionate to the rest of his body, but like the arms before them, the calves and thighs began to change right before Tommy's eyes, filling out as if they were rubber balloons being pumped with air.

Pff-wump! . . . Pff-wump! The bright red shoes followed, inflating to four times their original size, going from a pair of tens to whatever the norm was for clown attire.

"That's more like it," Zimbo said, lifting one foot and rolling it in circles. He looked over at the boy and grinned. "Now, are you ready to have your mind blown?"

Tommy's mind was *already* blown, but rather than say anything, he took a cautious step backward. If this was part of Mr. Bennet's game, it was no longer amusing.

"What's the matter, kid. Cat got your tongue?" Zimbo frowned. He cradled his chin in the palm of one hand, tapping an index finger against his cheek. "No, that can't be, can it? The cat already has Marjorie's tongue. Must just be that you're a shy boy. Is that it?"

"Where's Mr. Bennett?" Tommy asked, his voice quivering.

"The evening was too much for him. He got *everything* he wished for, but it was more than he could take. I'm afraid the poor man lost his head." The clown shifted his eyes to the headless figure on the couch and made a long, sad face.

Tommy's heart began to race. *That's not Lyle. That can't be Lyle.*

"I . . . I've gotta go home."

"Say it isn't so," Zimbo replied, pressing his hands to his chest as if he'd been pierced with a dagger. "We haven't started having fun yet. Surely you can stick around for just one game." He lifted a finger in the air and stood at attention. "I know! How's about I show you my magic flower? It's a real gas. All the kids love it."

The boy's palms were slicked with a cold sweat and his heart thundered, the beating of it merciless against his chest. The cords in his throat began to tighten as the darkness in the room crept in on him, drawing closer until it was almost suffocating.

Zimbo leaned over and tugged at the plastic daisy stuck to his lapel, causing a burst of liquid to spray from the yellow domed center of the flower. The stream shot across the room, the crimson colored substance splashing across the arm of the couch and staining the whiskey colored fabric a deep red.

Blood. The liquid in the flower is blood.

Zimbo's lips parted and he howled with demented laughter.

Tommy retreated across the room in a hurry, not daring to turn around for even a single glance lest he find himself nose to nose with the monstrous clown. Hot tears streamed down his cheeks as he mounted the steps, leaping over them two at a time. As he ascended, he pleaded with a God he otherwise never spoke to, begging Him to spare his life, all the while fearing there would be no clemency.

Bounding through the door at the top of the stairs, Tommy skidded to a halt. A man dressed in a surgical gown and face mask stood at the kitchen sink with his back to the boy. If he'd heard the young man enter the room, he didn't let on. He just stood there, humming, while continuing to work at whatever it was he was doing.

A few feet away, the refrigerator stood open, and a bare shoulder could be seen jutting out beyond the lip of the stainless-steel door. Laid out across the linoleum tile, partly wedged between the inner part of the door, was a body. Dressed in pink Converse shoes and cream-colored cutoff shorts that appeared almost tan next to pallid blue-tinged skin, the corpse was that of a young woman. The sight of the cadaver, gruesome as it was, could have been any one of Mr. Bennet's many props (most of which were in much heavier stages of decomposition), but there was one thing—one small detail—which caused the boy to grow cold: adorning the listless wrist of the left arm was a pink and blue friendship bracelet with the letter ***R*** woven in white.

(You know, don't you? You know who it is.)

No. It's not her. It's not . . .

Tommy's gaze remained locked on the bracelet. He knew it to be Robin's the moment he saw it. His sister had worn it faithfully ever since her best friend, Jennifer, had gifted her with it. She'd had it on the night she died. And she'd been buried with it.

The cadaver's ashen fingers, which covered her palm like the shriveled legs of a dead spider, began to twitch, sending a stab of fright deep into the heart of the boy. With a gasp, he shrunk back as the girl's head rolled to the side in a slow and steady motion.

Tommy was scared—really scared. His armpits were sweating, sending multitudes of damp tracks racing down the sides of his ribcage, while beads of perspiration dotted his trembling upper lip.

(Do you see now?)

It can't be . . . it can't be her!

But it was Robin, and she was looking at him now, her crescent moons of eyes sunk deep within their sockets. She stretched a hand towards Tommy, the fingers gnarled and hooked into claws. Her dry, cracked lips parted, and with a strangled rasp, she called out her brother's name.

"Well, look who finally came home." It was the man at the sink. He was facing the boy now, holding in his right hand a syringe with a needle several inches long. Inside the tube, a neon green solution swirled about in an ominous manner, promising death to whoever's veins it should kiss.

The man ripped away his surgical mask, revealing a face which Tommy had hoped he'd never see again. Gus hadn't been sighted since fleeing town after Robin's death, yet the man appeared unchanged, his expression hard and cruel; his gaze still burning with tempestuous rage. He sneered, depressing the plunger on the syringe and sending a gush of the green liquid into the air. "Come here, boy, and take your medicine."

Another surge of terror swept over Tommy and he bolted for the exit. Running through the dining room and arriving at the front door, he was slowed only by the weight of his body slamming into it. He pawed at the knob, finding that the thing did not want to turn. He fumbled back and forth with the lock, suddenly all thumbs.

A voice called from behind. "Tommy. Oh, Tommy boy."

Zimbo stood at the foot of the stairs holding a bouquet of red balloons. Within each floating ball bobbed a human head. There were men and women alike, their features muddied and distorted by the curvature of the helium filled rubber. Still, Tommy could make out the eyes which were rolled back in the skull and the mouths that were frozen in screams of agony.

The clown's lips pulled back over a mouthful of yellow teeth; teeth which had become long and sharp like the serrated edge of a knife. When he spoke, his voice was low and dangerous. "Come upstairs with me, Tommy. I've got such wonderful sights to show you."

With a click that sounded of salvation, Tommy threw the front door open and ran breathlessly out into the night. He beat a path through the yard, not stopping until he was back in his own home, with his own front door latched securely behind him. He rocketed up the stairs to his bedroom and collapsed on the bed, feeling his drumming heart rising into his throat. He lay there for some time, swallowing hard while attempting to catch his breath. When he could no longer hear the blood rushing between his ears, he stood up and made his way to the window, where he peeled back the mini blinds and peered across the street.

A light was on in Mr. Bennet's bedroom. Moving left to right behind the drawn curtains was a human shape. The form stopped for a brief interval, seemingly aware it was being watched, and then moved out of sight.

The boy tried to determine who it was he'd seen, but the shape had been too vague and undefined to say with any real certainty. He fished his cellphone out of his pocket and dialed Lyle's number. After four rings, the line went to voicemail. Tommy ended the call and hit redial. Three times he did this, each attempt ending in the same result. If this had been an elaborate hoax, wouldn't the old man pick up his phone and have a good laugh over scaring the shit out of his young charge?

He stole another look out the window. The bedroom lights were extinguished now, making the house appear as nothing more than an empty shell beneath a dark and cloudless sky.

Tommy wanted to believe—needed to believe—that the silhouette behind the curtain had been Mr. Bennett. He struggled to make sense of things, unsure how much—if any—of what he'd witnessed had been real. Perhaps his old friend had found a way to make the impossible appear possible, and had used him as his first test subject. The theory sounded like a stretch, even to a young mind such as his, but it seemed a hell of a lot more plausible than a toy clown coming to life, or his dead and buried sister being reanimated in the Bennett's kitchen.

Tommy fell back on his bed again, mind spinning. He considered calling the police, but what could he say that wouldn't sound like some sort of a prank? Still, a part of him wanted to do just that, no matter how much of a raving lunatic he came across as. To do so, however, meant that he had to acknowledge the existence of ghosts and monsters (he loved the idea of them, just not their manifestation in the physical realm). Moreover, it meant the Bennett's were dead, something his mind couldn't yet accept. Instead, he kept telling himself that there had to be an explanation for everything; that tomorrow morning he'd find Mr. Bennett hard at work in his yard. And when he did, the man would look up at him with that familiar twinkle in his eye, grin his ornery grin, and say, "Gotcha!"

Washed out and exhausted, Tommy closed his eyes and tried to push away the horrifying images which had been etched into his memory. Time and again he reassured himself that none of what he'd seen had been real; that it was as fictitious as *The Stuff*, albeit with better acting and much more convincing effects.

Gotcha, he kept hearing Lyle say. *I got you good, didn't I?*

Those words were still on the boy's lips when, in due course, he began to slip into the realm of dreams—something there would be no shortage of on this night.

"Gotcha," he mumbled one last time. "Gotcha g—"
Tommy slept.

7

When Landon Stephens noticed his boss, Frank Andrews, coming up the Bennett walk without coffee in hand, he winced a little. Sheriff Andrews was a bearish man on the best of mornings, but in those instances where duty preempted the customary coffee and donut pit stop, he could be downright contentious. With his push broom mustache, considerable paunch, Aviator sunglasses, and standard issue campaign hat perched atop his head, Frank could have passed for the second coming of Buford T. Justice. But, whereas Sheriff Justice's biggest headache was a '70's sex symbol in a Firebird, Franklin Andrews chased things which were darker, more mysterious, and yet every bit as elusive as Buford's bandit.

"What do you got, Stephens?" the sheriff asked, dispensing with the triteness of formal greetings.

"It's an ugly one, sir. I'd go as far as to say, the worst yet," the deputy replied.

"Worse than the Adams case?"

Frank was referring to Gillian Adams, who had hacked up her father with an axe upon his return home from visiting an out of town relative. Dubbed the Lizzie Borden of Shadow Lake by the local papers, Gillian was now a ward of the state and would be living out the remainder of her days at the Elmhurst Asylum on the eastern edge of town.

"Much worse," Landon replied. "That case was gruesome, no doubt about it. Her attack was savage and messy, but this, well, this is on another level. These murders were calculated, sadistic, possibly even ritualistic in their execution."

“More crazy sons of bitches,” the sheriff muttered. "Getting awful tired of it, Stephens. I’m too old to be dealing with this shit.”

“I don’t know how you’ve done it this long. Me, I’ve only been here two years and it’s already getting under my skin. I’ll tell you one thing, sir. Nothing, and I mean nothing, could have prepared me for what I saw today."

“What do you know so far?” Frank kept one ear on his deputy while surveying the horror show that was the front yard.

“Victims are Lyle and Marjorie Bennett. We found Marjorie hanging on the wall of her bedroom, razor blades jammed under her skin and her tongue on the nightstand. Lyle, at least we think it’s Lyle, was propped upright on a couch in the basement with a bucket of popcorn in his lap. He’d been placed there as if he were watching television.”

“You say you think the male vic is Lyle? Why the uncertainty?”

“That’s the thing, sir,” the deputy replied, a pained expression on his face. “There’s no head on the male victim. Hard to say where the decapitation occurred because there is no mess that we can see. Although, given that the killer took the time to sew up the neck, it’s possible they cleaned up.”

Frank stared at the deputy as if the man might be pulling his leg, but he knew better. For starters, the grisliness of any murder scene could be measured by how pale and clammy the deputy’s skin appeared, and right now he looked like an albino getting out of the shower. Secondly, this was just the kind of bizarro homicide that would only occur in his little burg. Why couldn’t people here just get shot or strangled? Instead, it seemed as if every death was scripted for a

Hollywood screamer. "Do we know the whereabouts of the head?"

"Hasn't turned up so far, no."

The sheriff plucked the hat from his head and wiped his brow with the back of his arm. "If it's not in the house, I'd start sorting through all this." He gestured towards the various crypts, coffins, and other monstrosities inhabiting the yard.

"Deputy Arwood is already on it, sir. He started here in front and has moved around back. Forensics is inside right now. So far, they haven't turned up any smoking guns."

"No, of course they haven't," Frank exhaled. "We both know how that always goes. The Adams case was one of those rare ones where we actually lucked out and caught the perp red handed."

Landon smirked. "Was that a joke, boss?"

The sheriff frowned impatiently. "You ever known me to be a jokester, Stephens?"

"No, sir. That's why I was checking. If you had been, that would have been another shock to my system today and I might have needed a furlough to maintain my mental health."

"Never takes long for that spark of yours to show, does it?"

Landon opened his mouth to respond, but the sheriff cut him off. "Who called this in, anyway?"

"Tommy Prescott, the young boy who lives across the street. Seems he witnessed some strange activity here last night and became concerned when he couldn't raise anyone this morning."

"Last night?" Frank barked. "And he's just now calling it in?"

"It would seem so."

"Did you get his statement? What exactly did he see?"

"I did," the deputy replied. "The boy claims he saw Gus Larson inside the residence."

"Gus Larson?" Frank hollered. "That waste of breath who drugged and killed Robin Prescott? We need roadblocks set up right now, Stephens. If that piece of garbage is back in this town, I want to hang his ass. My God, how much time have we already lost?"

"I can call in those roadblocks, but there's more," Landon replied. "Something you might want to consider before making that decision."

"What is it? Do I even want to know?"

"Maybe not," the deputy grimaced. "The boy also said he saw his sister in the house."

The sheriff's countenance fell. He looked like someone who had just inherited a large sum of money, only to be told in the next instant that he had two weeks left to live. "His sister? Robin Prescott? In the house? And she was alive?"

"Uh . . . in a manner of speaking." The deputy cleared his throat before continuing. "She was more like a zombie."

"Are you shitting me right now?"

"I wish I were, but that's what he said. Oh, and there was a clown also . . . sir. He believes the clown might have killed the Bennett's. Claims the thing had a bunch of helium balloons filled with human heads."

Frank's face turned the color of lava. "That's rich, isn't it? Did you tell that little shit that this isn't a game? That people are dead here? I should haul his ass in for obstruction. I don't care if he is just out of diapers."

"He's nine," the deputy replied, but the sheriff went on with his tirade, not hearing.

"So, we are to believe that a *clown* pinned Marjorie Bennett to the wall and carved out her tongue, after which, he proceeded to lop off Lyle Bennett's head, taking the time to sew up the wound and clean up the scene before stuffing the old man's head inside a helium balloon? Then what? I can only guess that he floated off to Happy Town! Oh, and somewhere in there, Gus and the kid's dead sister showed up to watch this circus?"

"That's good, sir. Should I put that in my report?"

"You'll do no such thing, deputy," the sheriff fumed. There was a time he'd have threatened his subordinate with disciplinary action for such a remark, but he'd come to respect officer Stephens early on, even if the guy did enjoy poking at him. Landon was a good man, with high morals and an exemplary work ethic, so he could forgive him for being a bit of a smart ass. "We have nothing, Stephens. Not a damn thing. We can't use that boy's testimony. I can't for the life of me imagine why he would make up such things, tarnishing the memory of his sister in the process."

"I know. I don't think he's trying to be funny, though," Landon replied. "He's scared; terrified to be more accurate. I think he truly believes what he told me. Now I know it's crazy, as he couldn't possibly have seen the things he claims, but I do believe he saw something bad. And with this house looking the way it does inside and out, like some sort of Halloween theme park, it's possible his young mind was so overloaded by the experience that he's not even sure what he saw. The fragments of what's real and what's not have meshed together into a kind of nightmare that he thinks is reality."

"It's good logic, I suppose," Frank nodded. "As much as I'd like to argue, it would be hard for me to do so."

Landon grinned like a bashful school kid.

"And you seem to be getting much better with these cases," the sheriff added.

"Oh, I don't know. I just always liked psychology."

"I'm not talking about that, Stephens," Frank said. "I meant you've come a long way since seeing your first stiff. You're handling these crime scenes like a champ now."

My first stiff, Landon mused to himself. Certainly no one had ever accused the sheriff of being an overly tactful man.

"If, by that, you mean I'm able to keep my food down, then yes, I suppose I have improved. But handling it well? That's debatable. It's always hard to stomach."

"That it is, son. If it didn't bother you on some level, I'd be worried."

The deputy looked up at the house, staring at the bedroom where Mrs. Bennett was still hanging on a wall. "Yeah, but who does this, boss? I've never seen anything this bad. Ever. It's inhuman."

"Perhaps. But when a town this size can keep an insane asylum stocked, you have to assume there's a fair amount of crazy going around."

"I've met an oddball or two, but most in this town are good people, sheriff. I think there's more to it. There has to be."

Frank rolled his eyes. "You're not going there again, are you? How many times have we had this discussion."

"I know," Landon replied. "It's just that, between all the missing persons and the unsolved cases we work, there's a weirdness to it all which is undeniable. Like that Turner fellow a couple months back; the one whose daughter had been missing. I got the call from him saying his girl had shown up at the back door in the middle of the night. He'd said he was ecstatic at first; about to let her in, when he noticed the blood on her pajamas. After a closer look, he could see she'd been split wide open and gutted. Yet, there she stood, rapping on the glass and staring at him with a smile on her face. You remember that one?"

"Of course I remember," the sheriff bristled. "We found no trace of her, nor was there any evidence she'd ever been there, not even a single drop of blood. Just another story made up to keep this damned notion of the witch and her curse on the town alive and well."

"He was a distraught father. Why would he make up such a tale? The man was in tears when we interviewed him that night."

"Might follow the same psychological pattern you just pointed out with Tommy Prescott."

Landon sighed. "Not the same thing. Regardless, you have to admit that there's an exceedingly high number of unusual occurrences around here."

"Never said there wasn't. In fact, I believe I told you as much back when you started this job."

"You did. I suppose I just keep circling back to the weirdness of these cases. Even with the Gillian Adams incident, didn't you think it strange that she had no history of mental illness until the day of the murder; the very day that she also claims her dead husband started popping up?"

"Hell, I don't know, kid," the sheriff groaned. "Why do you keep hassling me? Would it make you feel better if I said I believed there was a century old witch running around the woods causing all of this?"

Landon shrugged. This was one argument he knew he was never going to win. Probably best to leave it be. "I don't know. Not really, I suppose."

"Then lighten up, son." Frank returned the hat to his head and sighed. "You know what I could use right now?"

"A donut from Mabel's?" Landon grinned.

The sheriff shot the deputy a hard glance. "A drink, Stephens. A good stiff drink."

"It's just after eight in the morning, sir. Do you think that would be acceptable?"

"Don't patronize me, son." Frank replied, starting to walk in the direction of the front door. "I'm going inside this spook house to do my part, and when I come out, I'm having a drink."

"Well, no." Landon laughed. "I was only asking because I was thinking I might join you."

The sheriff halted. He turned, slipped the Aviators down along the bridge of his nose, and peered over the dark lenses in disbelief. "You know what I hate about you? That I can never tell if you're serious or shoveling bullshit."

Landon's grin widened. "Serious, sir. This time, anyway."

Frank chuckled. "The boy scout wants a drink? By God, now I have seen it all. Stephens at the bar. I wouldn't miss that for the world." Turning to go inside, he stopped at the doorway and shouted back: "Hang tight, son. We'll go together. First shot is on me."

Once the sheriff was out of sight, Landon's smile faded. He wasn't much of a drinker, obviously, but if he kept walking into gorefests like this, that could change. The grim sight of the Bennett couple wasn't the main reason he had agreed to accompany Frank to the bar, however. No, the real reason he needed a drink was because he planned to tender his resignation. Before this morning, he had still been struggling with that decision, but after arriving on this call and subsequently interviewing a terrified nine-year-old boy, it became clear that it was the only decision.

Standing and looking out across the faux cemetery in Lyle Bennett's front yard, Landon recalled what his then newlywed wife had said to him after he'd finished training at the police academy in Los Angeles: *Move somewhere safer.* That's what she'd said, and that's what Landon thought they had done after packing up and relocating to Shadow Lake.

When he'd first learned of the alleged curse and the witch, Landon had given it no more than a cursory thought, thinking it to be nothing but a scary story suitable for telling around a campfire. Then, as the cases rolled in, his opinion shifted over time. He was more open minded than Frank Andrews, and couldn't rule out the possibility that there was some underlying evil in this town which was the driving force behind the gruesome deaths and the mysterious disappearances.

Even so, Landon hadn't considered leaving until three weeks ago, when his wife came to him and said they were expecting. Once the thrilling high of the news had tempered, the thought occurred that this might not be the best place for raising a child. He recalled the busload of school kids that had gone missing back in '78, the Turner girl, whose father claimed had paid him a visit in her bloodied pajamas, the little Adams kid, now motherless, and most recently, a terrified Tommy Prescott. He couldn't bear the thought of his own son or daughter ending up in such dire straits. Not to mention, the odds were better that a child birthed in this town could end up being the Antichrist.

Move somewhere safer, he heard his wife say again.

"Well, sweetheart, that's just what we're going to do," Landon muttered aloud. "Only this time, it will be for real."

8

ONE WEEK LATER . . . HALLOWEEN

Tommy's eyes lingered over the final frame of *The Legend of Sleepy Hollow* comic book. He lay in his bed, pondering the story for a long moment, then gently tossed the book aside. The comic landed on the edge of the mattress, where it hung at a precarious angle for several moments before succumbing to the pull of gravity and sliding onto a floor littered with candy wrappers.

A plastic jack-o-lantern pail sat to the right of the boy and he pulled it to him, rummaging through the contents and fishing out a Choco-Whirl. He popped the candy into his mouth and began to chew. Why was he even still eating? He wasn't at all hungry. Besides, none of the candy tasted right. It wasn't that there was anything wrong with the stash he'd collected during his trick-or-treat outing, but his mood over the past week had somehow affected his taste buds. Everything he ate either tasted bland and flavorless, or produced an unusual aftertaste which remained on his tongue long after the food was gone.

With a scowl of disappointment, he pushed the pail away. The wrapper he chucked into the air, where it spiraled downward in an acrobatic tumble, adding yet another colorful addition to the discard pile on the bedroom floor.

Once again, Tommy's thoughts returned to the story he'd just read. He liked it just fine, but was left feeling melancholy. After all, the tale of Sleepy Hollow had been one of Lyle's favorites. Now his old friend was gone. It didn't seem fair. Why would anyone want to hurt Mr. Bennett?

Tommy still didn't know the details of what had happened on that dreadful night. As much as he hoped the man on the couch hadn't been Lyle, he doubted he'd ever know, as the specifics of how the man and his wife had been killed were never released to the public. All he knew for certain was that there were still no leads and no suspects.

He recalled the account of events which he'd given that policeman, feeling his cheeks grow hot. The story had been the truth as he knew it, but to anyone else, he was aware of how ridiculous it must have sounded. Tommy was sure the guy thought he was lying. He probably went back to the station, gathered the other men in blue around, and recounted the whole story. Afterwards, they would have shared a good laugh. *Kid should be a writer with an imagination like that*, one of them might have said. Others may have suggested he be taken to Elmhurst so he could look at ink blots and tell the doctors what it was he saw in them. *Clowns and headless old men, you say? Guess you are missing some screws. Take his chocolate milk, stat! Lock him in a padded cell.*

Tommy sighed. He hated the way he felt. It was a constant shift between grief and anger. At times, that anger was directed at Lyle. He hated the man for leaving him, even though he knew it hadn't been done by choice. Of course, soon after, when reason had returned, the boy would feel bad for having such thoughts and would burst into tears. Even worse, there were moments when it seemed as if someone had flipped a switch in his brain, turning on every single emotion at the exact same time. It was overwhelming, especially for a boy his age.

By days' end, Tommy was exhausted. The evenings, however, brought with them a whole other set of issues. He would lie awake for hours, terrorized by the face of Zimbo. When he did manage to find sleep, it was often fitful and wrought with nightmares. Several times over the course of a single night he'd awake in a cold sweat, always expecting to find the murderous clown hovering over his bed; no doubt come to add the head of a boy to his balloon collection.

Figuring tonight wouldn't be any different, Tommy climbed out of bed and made his way to his mother's medicine cabinet. He filled a paper Dixie cup with some water from the sink, popped the cap on a bottle of sleeping pills, and downed two of the small white pills. That ought to do it. If those things could chase away his mom's demons long enough to allow her sleep, then they should certainly do the same for him.

Before crawling back in bed, Tommy went to his window and looked down on Mr. Bennett's yard. Yellow police tape was still strung around the perimeter. Instead of being full of life, as it should be on Halloween night, the place was dark and still. There were no trains departing from the Depot of the Dead, no bats flitting about, no monsters moaning, wolves howling, or witches cackling. Every creature was in its respective place around the yard, yet all were as lifeless as the man who had put them there. Tommy wondered how long it would be before someone came to dismantle the displays. And when they did, where would it all go? Where would any of Lyle's things go?

With another defeated sigh, the boy returned to his bed and pulled back the sheets to climb in. He stopped, a sudden realization coming over him. With a zealous, almost wild look in his eye, he yanked open the top drawer of his nightstand and looked inside.

There it was. Right where he had left it.

With a quick and purposeful motion, Tommy retrieved the pendant from inside. He sat back on the bed, rubbing his thumb over the smooth stone. Hadn't Mr. Bennett said the thing was like a genie; able to grant wishes to whomever possessed it? Without haste, the boy blurted out: "I wish you could come back, Mr. Bennett. I wish I could see you, even if it was just one more time."

Tommy stopped rubbing the pendant and waited.

Nothing.

He waited a little longer, thinking the thing might light up, or twitch, or something. But it only sat there like the worthless stone it was.

"Don't be stupid," he told himself. "You're too old to believe in magic. This thing isn't going to grant your wish. It probably never even belonged to the witch in the first place."

Disheartened, Tommy dropped the stone back into the drawer and crawled into bed. After staring up at the ceiling for a while, trying to clear his mind, he moved his pail of trick-or-treat candy from the mattress over to the nightstand and clicked off the lamp.

"Just a stupid old rock," he lamented, rolling onto his side and pulling the blanket up to his chin. What Tommy didn't realize as he closed his eyes and drifted off to sleep, was threefold:

First . . .

His wish had been heard.

Second . . .

At that very moment, in a cemetery only a few miles away, the loose earth covering a fresh grave had already begun to turn.

And third . . .

Before the night was over, an old friend would come calling.

www.ingramcontent.com/pod-product-compliance
Lightning Source LLC
Chambersburg PA
CBHW030810310726
48980CB00006B/444/J

* 9 7 8 0 6 9 2 8 7 9 6 0 3 *